Matthew Condon has published many works of fiction, including his critically acclaimed and best-selling *The Trout Opera*, and non-fiction, including *Brisbane*. He is a journalist based in Brisbane.

The TOE TAG QUINTET

MATTHEW CONDON

VINTAGE BOOKS

Australia

A Vintage book
Published by Random House Australia Pty Ltd
Level 3, 100 Pacific Highway, North Sydney NSW 2060
www.randomhouse.com.au

First published by Vintage in 2012

Addresses for companies within the Random House
Group can be found at www.randomhouse.com.au/offices

National Library of Australia
Cataloguing-in-Publication Entry

Condon, Matthew (Matthew Steven), 1962–
The toe tag quintet / Matthew Condon

ISBN 978 1 74275 669 1 (pbk)

A823.3

Cover photographs by Corbis; iStock
Cover design by Luke Causby
Typeset in Bembo 12 on 15 pt by Midland Typesetters,
Australia
Printed in Australia by Griffin Press, an accredited ISO
AS/NZS 14001:2004 Environmental Management
System printer

Random House Australia uses papers that are natural,
renewable and recyclable products and made from
wood grown in sustainable forests. The logging and
manufacturing processes are expected to conform to the
environmental regulations of the country of origin.

For Katie Kate, Finn and Bridie Rose – again

THE TOE TAG QUINTET: FIVE NOVELLAS OF
MURDER AND MAYHEM

Murder Most Abstract
The Murder Tree
Murder on the Vine
Murder, She Tweeted
The Good Murder Guide

ONE

MURDER MOST ABSTRACT

1

'I LOVED THAT shirt, Reginald.'

I was gazing out of the window, beyond the tangle of clear tubes, at the flowerless jacaranda tree outside.

'And which shirt might that have been?' asked Reginald, not very enthusiastically – not in an *interested* way, but as if to say if it pacified me to send out some noise with his exhalation, he'd send out some noise.

Reginald was my nurse, and there was an aura about Reginald that said his job of dressing bullet wounds and other sundry abrasions that came into his care was a temporary step to grander things. It was so complete about Reginald, this aura, that I sensed his entire life was a stepping stone to some nirvana. If Reginald's flat life had a scent, it would be the human breath contained in a week-old balloon. Somebody else's breath, at that.

'The Hawaiian,' I said, to the tree.

I shouldn't be here. In a hospital bed. With a bullet in my thigh. And a hole punched clean through my side. It had taken the surgeons hours just to pick out the fibres of my new retirement shirt from the wound. All those threads that used to be pretty coconut trees and hibiscus and a little grass hut. I loved that shirt.

Why shouldn't I be here? I'm happy-go-lucky. I'm that guy who stands by the piano near the end of a party and belts out 'My Way', pâté on my breath and a fragment of maraschino cherry caught in my front teeth. At Christmas I like to pop those festive crackers and slip on a little paper hat. And I'll wear the hat all day – or at least until it tears and ends up in the kitchen tidy all stained with oily finger-prints from the chicken and turkey legs. I have an apron I wear when I barbecue, which shows the torso of a woman in bra and briefs and fishnet stockings. Ha, ha. I could be a grandfather, for crying out loud.

That's why I shouldn't be here. Thirty-seven years in the New South Wales police force, a number of those commanding the meanest, toughest, bloodiest precinct in Sydney, and I never took a bullet. Someone once cracked my head with a hammer. I've been glassed in a pub. Put in a chokehold. Pinned in a totalled patrol car. Kicked in the guts, accidentally, by a police horse. Had a glass of expensive wine thrown in my face by a woman con artist with expensive taste in wines. And felt the muzzle of a .38 pressed against my temple. But that was all a long time ago.

Yet I retire to Queensland and I get shot – not once, but twice. You can understand why I'm not happy.

If you'd said to me two weeks ago that instead of taking out my new silver dinghy, *Pig Pen*, on the Broadwater at the Gold Coast and throwing in a lazy line, or sitting on the balcony of the Main Beach Surf Club with a cold one at hand and watching the setting sun stain the whitewashed waves a fluorescent pink, I'd be banged up in this little white room, I may have laughed.

Get me laughing now and the bags, tubes and wires that hang off me will gurgle and sway, and make their own music, and become a tune that will forever haunt me, much like 'A Horse with No Name', or 'Knights in White Satin'.

I can hardly move. All day I look at a little square of sky and a tree they tell me was heavy with purple flowers just a couple of months ago. Purple as a fresh bruise. Maybe it's the morphine, but I feel connected, somehow, to that tree.

Reginald tells me I'm lucky to have a room at all and that I should be grateful. Look out the window to the carriage-way at the front of the hospital, he says. Bumper to bumper with ambulances, and in the back of them people that can't get a swish hospital bed like me. (Reginald says 'swish' a lot. I have not heard the word 'swish' since I was a boy visiting my feisty old Irish grandmother in her flat in Five Dock. Fancy English crockery, for example, was very 'swish'.)

'Did you just say "swish"?' I ask him, but he ignores me.

He says my picture has been in the newspapers and I look a lot older in real life. Thank you, Reginald. I want to tell him, facetiously, that I don't like the view and that now I'm a celebrity I should be afforded something more splendid. But in the orbit of old balloon breath I too have become flat and tired. Dullness can be infectious.

'Is it grape season, Reginald?' I ask him.

It is another thing – as an observant former detective – I know about Reginald. He carries the ever-so-slight wince on one side of his face of the mercilessly teased. It is a flinch in advance of the insult.

So I ask him inane questions about grapes and watch the wrinkles deepen around his left eye.

On occasion I feel like giving him one of my famous verbal blasts. But I don't. I'm not in a position to savage the man who removes my bedpan.

'Don't listen to me,' I say diplomatically. It is a saying I have always used a lot. It means, you must listen to me very attentively. The officers under me knew that. So did not-an-inconsiderable few of the junkies, carjackers, dope dealers, hustlers and street grubs I used to come up against. I used to talk with my fists, as they say. Or used to say. Who uses fists now, in the bang-bang age?

I feel sorry for modern coppers, facing multi-million-dollar lawsuits for bruising with handcuffs the delicate wrists of their prissy offenders, or twelve months of counselling and possibly suspended pay if they don't refer to the drunken, writhing deadbeats they have apprehended as sir or madam. Don't get me started.

What exactly does Reginald think when he's polishing my silver kidney-shaped ablution bowl?

'Don't listen to me, Reginald,' I say, meaning, this time, go away.

Over time I suspect my nurse has developed a little touché strategy of his own.

I will say, 'Is there a furnace in the hospital basement, Reginald, for getting rid of unwanted human bits?'

And he will reply, 'You can see forever from the helicopter pad on the roof. On a clear day, all the way to Moreton Bay.'

But Moreton Bay is the last place on earth I want to see, let alone entertain at length in my weary, gnarled, nicked and scarred fifty-nine-year-old melon. I would be happy never to see again the glittering diamante surface of the bay. The islands. The islets.

Me and Moreton Bay? It's a complicated relationship.

At night I want to close my eyes, just to remove myself from Reginald and his increasingly prolific bons mots. He has moved on to ward grotesqueries, just to pee me off. Guess what I saw on the seventh floor? I've had it up to the gills with his florid descriptions of wounded, hacked, sliced, bruised, distended, fried and vanished human body parts. At his ceaseless monologue of the things that can happen, out there in the big world, to the human body.

'It's tough as nuts, the body,' says Nurse Reginald, 'but at the same time, well, it's as weak as water. It's truly amazing how we get through the day, how we survive, don't you think?'

I get the sense I'm being used as a human whetstone to sharpen this clown's social skills.

He reminds me of an article I read about the dreaded fire ant, now surrounding much of Brisbane like a terribly patient Roman army. They grab on to the skin with their pincers, and then sting not once but in a neat, complete circle, pivoting from the central axis of where they've taken hold of your flesh. The perfection of nature. Reginald has made me come out in a rash.

But if I did close my eyes against his presence, I'd be back in the bay at night, fighting for breath, and I'd be on that island, staring down the muzzle flash of that gun, and I'd be entangled in a mystery about an artist I'd never even heard of before I came up north to enjoy my twilight years.

Before I passed – by chance – an old acquaintance from the underworld of Sydney's Kings Cross and I was innocently enjoying the sun and minding my own business down at Main Beach.

So I couldn't close my eyes. I was stuck with Reginald.

'Could I possibly have more water?' I ask.

And he begrudgingly pours it.

'We're on level four, you know,' he says.

I'm confused. I have heard Reginald trying to discuss cryptic crosswords with the constable stationed on guard outside my hospital room. 'I thought this was the fifth floor,' I say.

'No, ninny.' First 'swish', and now 'ninny'. I begin to contemplate that Nurse Reginald is in fact the reincarnation of my grandmother. 'Level-four water restrictions.'

Is he serious? Queensland is paradise on earth, isn't it? Bountiful. An embarrassment of riches.

'Just make it half a glass, then,' I say.

He doesn't find this funny. 'Level four is not funny.' He grumpily leaves the room. He's done this walk-out before, when I quizzed him on what it meant to say that Brisbane is 'the new black'. I've seen these advertisement signs everywhere. What is the new black? What was the old black? He turned his nose up at me, swivelled on his heels and left. For what it's worth, I've seen more black in Brisbane in the last fortnight than at any point in my life.

I shouldn't be here. There I was, minding my own business on the coast. Enjoying a brief stay in the Main Beach Caravan Park while my wife finalised the sale of our house in Sydney and I hunted for our luxury retirement villa in Paradise.

There I was one fine morning, strolling down Tedder Avenue just after seven to pick up the daily newspaper, when I passed him and caught his eye. Dapper Daniel the Antiques Man, a.k.a. the Boltcutter, a.k.a. the scumbag who, on a cold night a long time ago in the dunes of Wanda Beach, put a pistol to my young, naïve, fresh-out-of-the-police-academy head, and threatened to blow me and my brains into infinity.

The very same Boltcutter, padding past me like any other retired southern gent in his leather loafers, yachting shorts and fruity Hawaiian shirt. Just like mine.

Our eyes met for a millisecond. And the hair on my neck bristled.

2

I FIRST MET my wife Peg on a TAA flight from Sydney to Brisbane in 1971. Peg was a hostess, as they used to call them, before the word was deemed politically incorrect. Now they're flight attendants. This doesn't make sense to me. Waiters aren't 'food attendants'. Now that I think of it, is 'politically incorrect' a logical or correct term? I have my doubts.

I'm getting off the track. I'll blame the morphine. (Reginald takes no offence in being called the traditionally female-gendered word 'nurse'. He does not find it politically incorrect at all. One day, he says, he would *love* to be called 'matron'. I'm growing suspicious of Reginald.)

Anyway, that flight in 1971 proved to be some sort of trip. It was my first to the Sunshine State. And en route, I met my wife. Not bad.

I had heard a lot about Queensland, even as a young officer wet behind the ears. And not all of it was good.

I had been seconded, early on, to 21 Division, the notorious vice squad, having spent some uneventful early months at Rose Bay police station in Sydney. I'd had my share of the odd harbour body or two, petty burglars, car crashes, noise complaints and the occasional domestic dispute. You have a domestic dispute in some of those streets jam-packed with blocks of flats and, let me tell you, half the suburb can hear it.

Prior to my graduation from the academy I had toyed with studying the human mind. I was intrigued by psycho-analysis. Peg says it was a 'cry for help' – that I was trying to understand myself a little better. Smart woman, Peg.

So I dipped into it by correspondence, and when my superiors heard about this I was suddenly the egghead of my police year. They called me, however briefly, 'the Professor'. (That nickname was replaced, permanently, not long after with 'Dusty', after dustbin, and my propensity to attract dust, flies, and other unspeakable societal detritus. The Boltcutter, however, was one piece of muck I thought I had wiped from my shoes many years before. Such is life.) It didn't take much to be academically head and shoulders above the crowd in the New South Wales police service in the late sixties.

Anyway, my cursory look into Freud somehow fast-tracked my career, and I was thrown head-first into 21 Division. We were a mobile unit, charged with sniffing out illegal gambling dens and other lowlife hellholes of disreputable behaviour. There were things I saw that I had never previously contemplated could be performed by human beings. I'll spare you the tasty details. Suffice to say, it made my tenure at lovely Rose Bay look like Nurse Reginald's elusive nirvana.

I had been chosen, I later heard, by the commissioner himself – Norman 'the Foreman' Allan – who had an almost obsessive desire to see educated officers in his ranks. Apparently a few months of dipping into Freud's Wolf Man theories and his bizarre sexual hypotheses qualified me as a learned gent in Norm's eyes.

I'd only been in 21 Division a month when I was called into the office – the relatively new Bourbon & Beefsteak Bar – and told I was to be part of a 'very special mission' to Queensland. All hush-hush. The press grubs were not to know.

'You heard of a sheila called Wendy "Legs" Lockett from Atherton?' my superior asked, scanning the room.

'I've never even heard of Atherton.'

'All right, smart chops. She's a prostitute. Was a prostitute. Was causing all sorts of problems for us in Brisbane. Statutory declarations. Corruption. Fingering blokes left, right and centre.'

'You want me to talk to her?'

'You could try. But she's dead.'

'Oh.'

'The good old-fashioned drug overdose, just before a little court appearance where her testimony could have proved ... er ... rather difficult for one of our boys in Brisbane. I want you to go up there, keep your ears open, find out what the talk is on her. Rumours. Theories. That sort of stuff. Even you could manage that, couldn't you, Dusty?'

Funny how life works. I was flying up to Queensland to spy on a dead prostitute and I met my future wife, who spilled coffee on my nice white 21 Division shirt and skinny tie. I was smooth in those days. I told her, as I disembarked, that I needed her home address so I could send her the cleaning bill. Not original in the modern history of courting, but it worked – she gave me her phone number.

'Don't ring too early,' she said. 'My husband likes to sleep in.'

I stood, embarrassed and confused at the door to the plane. Then she winked. 'It's my mother, actually. She enjoys a good lie-in. Goodbye.'

As I walked across the boiling Brisbane tarmac I looked back at the plane and couldn't see her. I had never experienced such humidity. Just walking through it was like trying to swim in your clothes.

I checked into my room at Lennon's – no expense spared for the 21 Division – and took a quick walk around town, just to familiarise myself. I was looking forward to riding on a tram but was told they'd stopped running two years before. I went up into the clocktower of the City Hall to further orientate myself. Nice. I liked Brisbane, and its brown snake of a river. In a city with a river like that, you're going to get a lot of deception, crooks and conmen. And corrupt police. These were thoughts left over from my meagre days as a student of psychology and its multitudinous and infuriating subtexts.

I didn't learn too much about poor Legs. She'd been murdered for certain. The local cops were keeping things pretty close to their chests. But they were just a little too jumpy and tight-lipped for the supposed overdose of a known madam. It was the *way* they didn't care about her run-of-the-mill death that made me think they cared very much about it.

I had a sandwich at the Cubana Café with a young local officer I befriended.

'You're pretty famous up here, you know, you boys of the 21 Division,' he said.

'Is that so?'

'Got a bit of a reputation, you have. We got some tough guys up here too, but they don't go and give themselves a name, like the 21 Division.'

'Fair enough.'

'Don't know why you're asking questions about Legs. She was done out of Sydney, is what I've heard. You probably share a desk with the killer, right?'

This was humour, Queensland-style. The punchlines to jokes also had something a little peculiar about them, a little creepy. I could have told him that I shared a desk with a man called Greaves. Straight. Honest. With horn-rimmed spectacles and ears like tiny pieces of shell pasta. And with one of the keenest, most humourless minds in the business. But why bother?

The young officer laughed. I laughed just to be polite. I had no idea what he was talking about. Had I been sent here on some wild-goose chase? Was I being set up for something?

I telephoned my inspector and told him what I'd learned, which wasn't much. He told me to relax, take a day off, go ride around town on a tram. They don't have trams here any more, I said. I couldn't care less, Dusty, he said.

On the morning I flew back to Sydney, I sat in the crappy little airport terminal and thought of Peg. Would she be on the flight? Would I be lucky enough to have her spill an entire meal down my shirt front? Then I'd have to ring her twice.

It turned out Legs might have been murdered by a Sydney police officer who was so vile, so feared, so terrifying that just to mention his name was dangerous and possible grounds for extinction. Legs had known a lot. Now the girl from Atherton had been returned to anonymity.

I read the local paper while I waited for my plane. There was a small item on page seven about a body being pulled from the Brisbane River over near some place called the New Farm Powerhouse. The body was suspected to be that of a missing art dealer from West End. He was missing two toes and a finger, as well as his life.

Peg wasn't on the plane. As a result, I resented the other hostesses and landed in Sydney without a single stain on my apparel.

As we disembarked, I noticed a very well-dressed gentleman strolling towards the terminal. I noticed him because he had the head of a criminal but was wearing a suit befitting professional gentlemen you might find at the Stock Exchange, or before the Bar.

I noticed him because I had seen him before, in Kings Cross. He ran a small antiques store in Macleay Street, an establishment suspected of nurturing a little casino upstairs.

He would become known to me, in a very short period of time, as the Boltcutter.

3

So when I saw the foul Boltcutter again on my morning stroll in Main Beach, things remembered, and quite a significant few that I would have preferred to forget, rained in on my splendour. I knew it was him immediately, despite his tremendous increase in physical volume, the disappearance of anything resembling a neck, the great laval descent of flesh about his head and shoulders. He looked like someone had filled him with air and slowly melted him.

I picked up my newspaper that day and returned directly to my rented caravan not far from the surf club. I checked over my shoulder repeatedly during the short walk. I took mental notes of vehicle numberplates. I surreptitiously observed high-rise car-park entranceways, building enclaves and any other potential nooks and roosts for a possible assassin. On that single walk, which I'd taken many times in the past few weeks, I noticed at least six general security cameras. I had not had to look for them before.

My van, too, suddenly felt exposed. Not just to the weather. On a couple of nights I had been woken by a vicious onshore breeze shaking and rattling my little temporary aluminium home. There was a line of pine trees at the back of the park, and a handful of unidentified flora on the southern boundary, but nothing I would consider good cover. I guess families on holidays on the Gold Coast don't have much of a need for good cover against gunmen from their past. I began to feel very alone.

I telephoned Peg from the caravan park.

'You won't believe who I saw in the street today,' I said to Peg.

'Elvis.'

'It's going to take you a while to settle in here I'm afraid, Peg.'

'Why do you say that?'

'If you knew the Gold Coast half as well as I'm coming to – and I'm way ahead of you already – there are more Elvis impersonators here than Las Vegas. So any joke you care to offer about Elvis on the Gold Coast is almost guaranteed not to produce a laugh.'

'I liked you better when you were a cop. You spoke more economically. The offender decamped ... the person of interest is helping police with inquiries ... that sort of stuff. Now you have, as our son would say, a little too much air in the mattress.'

'That used to be the standard criticism of my physique.'

'Your big belly.'

'If you want to put it that way, yes, my big belly. I think I might join a gym.'

'What were you saying?'

'Thank you for your interest. Today I ran into a ghost from the past.'

'I'm glad you're making friends.'

'A gangster, Peg. One of the more ruthless sadists from the old days up at the Cross.' I didn't even want to mention his name.

'He must be an old retired gent now, like you.'

'More than thirty years later, and a thousand kilometres from his old turf, and I happen to walk past him – hardly a foot between us – in my retirement.'

'Gangsters have to retire too, don't they?'

'Gangsters don't retire, Peg. It's not a job, it's a lifestyle.'

'Packing heat, was he?'

'Packing heat? Not even old coppers say 'packing heat', Peg. I get the feeling you're not showing the same level of concern as I am.'

'So these things happen. You're moving to the coast. A face you know passes by. Who cares? Maybe he was on holiday. Maybe he plays bowls and eats out on his pensioner's card. How's the house-hunting going, by the way?'

I slept poorly that night. A huge, rolling, boiling thunderstorm had swept over the hinterland in the west and headed out to sea. I had never seen storms like the ones I saw in Queensland. Vicious. Without a hint of humanity. Like some people I knew.

My little van shivered on its concrete apron, and as the thunder rumbled around me and the rain pounded the aluminium skin of the Viscount, I recalled the visit I had paid to the Boltcutter back in the Cross of the early seventies, when he was known as the rather ostentatious Dapper Dan the Antiques Man. He got away with the name. Things were different in the seventies.

Every now and then the underlings of 21 Division were sent out to check on the illegal casinos – not that we knew they were there, of course – as part of 'operational procedures'. In short, we let them know we were watching them. I was young, stupid, and eager to get ahead, and during these 'sweeps' I would return with bottles of booze, bowls of fresh pasta, and even little brown envelopes as gifts to 21 Division.

'That's a bribe right there,' I'd say to a senior officer, pointing to the gnocchi. 'Should we proceed with the charge?' I'd be laughed out of the office. The booze, food, and especially the cash, would always magically disappear.

Dapper Dan's antique store had its entrance next to a French patisserie, its window shelves filled with strange, golden breads and exotic desserts and elaborate pyramids of biscuits dipped in chocolate. You could smell it on the street. To pass through that and into Dapper's was like passing from life to death.

As I opened the door, a bell rang. The showroom was dim, reeked of mildew, and was packed floor to ceiling with old bureaux, mirrored wardrobes, suits of armour, hat stands heavy with felt and feather, dolls in clear perspex tombs, shop dummies dressed as ship captains and saloon madams, and whole shelves of stuffed rodents, dogs, birds.

'Hello?' I said loudly, and proceeded into the room. 'Anybody here?' My left ear was brushed by something and I jumped, startled, and lost my porkpie hat to the ground. It was the giant wing of a preserved American eagle, its talons fastened firmly around a motheaten mouse, its teeth bared in agony.

It took a while for my eyes to adjust, then the Dapper seemed to materialise in a rear doorway. He was a shadowed outline wearing a canary yellow suit complete with spats and a fob watch. He also wore white leather gloves.

'May I help you?' He did not move in the doorway. He had one of those voices that was so common in Australia in the forties and fifties. You could hear the English plum rolling around behind a still developing nasally and flat Australian vernacular.

'Good morning,' I said.

I shook his hand, and the glove felt fleshy and cold.

He did not ask me to sit. He did not offer me anything. I could barely see his face in the poor light, and the sunshine trying to pour into the shop front was blocked, diffused, slashed and hacked at by samurai swords, furniture, old clothes, photographs of forgotten faces and dust-coated chandeliers.

'You live upstairs?' I asked.

'How is that any of your business?'

I could see behind him a narrow staircase leading up into complete darkness. Dapper wasn't moving.

'Is that all, constable?'

'It's senior constable.'

'Oh. Pardon *me*. Will that be all?'

'Yes.'

I left slowly and could feel him watching me. There are men in the world who pretend they are something else, and their personas slip and slide and chafe against each other. It makes them easy to spot, with all that chafing. And there are men who show one thing completely, imperviously, and are the absolute opposite underneath. What lies beneath is similarly diamond-hard and immovable. That was Dapper. And that's what made him so frightening.

I knew he could handle a Fabergé egg with the utmost delicacy with those soft white gloves of his. And I knew, too, he'd break your neck without compunction.

'Good day,' he said.

I ducked beneath the eagle's wing and held my hat as I did so. I kept thinking of the tiny little green feather in my hatband. I entered the street and the perfume of freshly baked baguettes.

The next morning when I stepped out of the van, the

world felt reborn, as it so often seems in Queensland after one of their end-of-the-world storms. The grass near my annexe felt cool beneath my feet. Peg was right. I was being a silly youngish-old man still treading suspiciously into the landscape that is retirement. Then I found a card had been slipped beneath the door of my tin home. It was one of those postcards you buy at art galleries, which depicts the works of artists housed by the gallery. This one was from the Queensland Art Gallery. It showed a painting by Ian Fairweather.

Written on the back was: 'Time to visit your Fair Weather Friends'.

Attached to the card with a pretty piece of red ribbon was a shiny bullet.

Who said the Gold Coast wasn't cultured?

4

IT WAS TIME to pay Dapper Dan the Antiques Man, a.k.a. the Boltcutter, a.k.a. one of my Fair Weather Friends, a visit. At least I assumed the Boltcutter was the author of the note. I didn't have many pals in paradise yet, just Verne and Abigail in the van park, Maisy and Bert in the van next to mine, Bob and Patsy behind the bar at the surf club, Geraldo the real-estate agent, and Pep the South American exchange student at the local bottlo.

I didn't tell Peg about the bullet. And I knew I should not have acted on an assumption. But I was bored looking at houses. I was bored heading out in the tinny and bobbing about in the Broadwater with my own thoughts. I missed my old mates and my family. This retirement thing was not all it was cracked up to be. I needed to keep busy. I needed to stickybeak around a little, like I'd always done. I watch those big, dumb, dirty ibis poking their long beaks into rubbish bins and I think – yeah, we've got a bit in common.

One call to an old mate at the Sydney regional police headquarters and I was standing outside the door to a high-rise apartment in Paradise Waters.

The door was painted a shiny, understated black. No

turquoise or peach, and no little conch-shell unit numbers for our Dan.

My only problem was that the elderly gentleman who lived in the apartment was not Dapper Dan the Antiques Man, but a tall, thin, black-robed geezer straight out of a Lon Chaney film. If that wasn't bad enough, he called himself the Priest.

His carer, a small Malaysian man called Robert, led me through the flat to a sitting room full of exquisite, heavy oak antique chairs and table nests. Tea was waiting, a tail of steam issuing from a small, gilt-edged pot. The walls were floor to ceiling with paintings and religious icons. It was all crucifixion, self-flagellation, murder, betrayal, blood and misery. It was the sort of apartment that might be enjoyed by a sadist monk from the Middle Ages, if indeed the sadist monk could get past the wonder of fresh tap water, electric toasters, television, and all the other glorious junk that gluts our modern world.

'Wait, please,' Robert said. He dramatically rolled his hand towards one of the chairs. His permanent smile was unnerving. He wore a tight-fitting satin vest, black waiter's trousers and shoes so polished they seemed to contain their own source of light.

I sat, as Robert had requested, and looked out at the reach of Narrowneck and the ocean. A small red biplane eased past. I could see two container ships on the horizon. I noticed the tips of the pines at the back of my caravan park.

All this crazy summer life going on at ground level – kids on boogie boards being dumped in the surf, old men throwing their pensions into a poker machine, hoons blowing rubber in the Broadbeach car park – and here I was sitting in a silent room that could have belonged to the cellar of an Italian monastery.

When the Priest entered, I automatically stood. He was clearly mentally unhinged, and something about bona fide craziness – so tailored and complete and a world unto itself – commands a triggered respect in human beings. It is, partly, the 'there but for the grace of God go I' factor. I had encountered much of it in 21 Division in the Cross.

He towered over me, and I was six feet in my socks. He had long, thin grey hair that almost reached his shoulders and was parted with frightening exactitude down the middle of his scalp. His face sported a fanatically trimmed white beard. His black cassock was floor-length.

He sat in the chair opposite mine, and with a motion of his finger ordered Robert to pour the tea. Robert left and we faced each other for a few uncomfortable moments.

'And you are?' the Priest finally said.

'Let's just say I'm an old friend of the Dapper's.'

His stare was cold and peculiar. He had long white fingers that were curled over two wood-carved balls at the end of the chair arms.

'I beg your pardon?'

'Dapper Dan. Your flatmate. At least, that was one of the names he went by the last I knew him.'

'I have absolutely no idea who you may be referring to.' He had lowered his head a little and was now studying me as an entomologist might examine a mutated specimen of Sorghum Head moth.

'You don't know anyone by the name of Dapper Dan? A ... well, dapper gentleman?'

'Is this some sort of practical joke?'

'I'm afraid not.'

'Then state your business.'

'I'm just an old acquaintance. New to the area. Wanted to pay my respects. To my Fair Weather Friends. He left me a note.'

I had missed the moment, but at some point the effeminate Robert had turned from tea boy into a miniature parody of a menacing sidekick and bodyguard, the type you might expect to pop up in a bad James Bond film. But one acted by children, for children. A 003 and a half film.

'Fair weather?'

'Correct. Fair weather.'

'Are you some sort of newspaper-crossword cryptologist?'

'I don't even like chess.'

The Priest wriggled in his chair, put a forefinger to his lips, then issued a malevolent smile. 'I'm sorry,' he said quietly. 'We don't seem to be having the same conversation. I am a dealer and collector of fine arts. My particular passion is the work of sculptor Etienne Bobillet. I thought you were a client of my business partner, Mr Seelenleben, who handles more contemporary works and in particular Australian art – if that is not an oxymoron – and as he is on business interstate, I agreed to see you out of courtesy to him. This note you received about Fair Weather Friends. I can only assume it pertains to the work of the artist Ian Fairweather, of which Mr Seelenleben is a specialist. Does this make any sense to you?'

'Not the foggiest.'

'You are not seeking assistance in the purchase or sale of a Fairweather?'

'Nope.'

'Then we are wasting each other's time.'

He stood again and for a moment I was reminded of my early psychology textbooks and Nietzsche's famous paper on the 'pale criminal', the great disrupters of humanity, always running away from their darker selves.

Robert came to my side and made to lead me out of the dungeon.

'Is there any way I could contact Mr Seelenleben?'

'I'm afraid not,' the Priest said.

'Can I leave a message?'

'No.'

As Robert steered me by the arm towards the door I noticed, on a small wooden hutch, a framed photograph of a woman and three children – one of those terribly formal 1960s pictures that fathers often had on their desks at work. The colours were all bleached-out pastels.

I stopped and picked up the frame and studied it.

'Your children?' I asked the Priest.

'Yes.'

'You come now,' Robert protested.

'Wife, too?'

'Yes. In a former life.'

I saw a crucifix on the wall behind the happy mother and children. I believed, too, the picture was a portal in this apartment of death. A small window into a part of the Priest that he could not, despite everything, keep sealed. I took a punt on the cross and feeling the picture gave me.

'You had holy orders?'

'Anglican minister.'

'Since retired,' I said.

'Since retired.'

I put the picture down. Robert was virtually pushing me towards the black door.

'Gave up the Good Lord for art. There are lesser things to abandon Him for.'

I was poking and prodding the underbelly of the Priest. I wanted to break through to something, anything. 'To leave your wife and children for as well, I suppose. Though my experience tells me that moral abandonment is usually enacted for another person, not a room full of objects. Nietzsche got it right, you know.'

It did the trick. He came to the open doorway and stood in the black frame.

'You are a private detective?' he asked.

I turned and stood facing him in the hallway.

'I'm a private citizen.'

'A first-year psychology student, then.'

'Second year. Before that, I spent almost forty years chasing pale criminals.'

'Mr Seelenleben will be back on Thursday, if you'd prefer to call in then.'

I pressed the button to the elevator.

'Seelenleben,' I said as I waited. 'It was a word Freud used. It refers to the inner life of the child. Tell your boy-friend I'll call Thursday.'

'My goodness,' the Priest said malevolently as I entered the lift. 'You could almost pass for third year.'

'And up yours too, Jack,' I said, as the lift doors closed. 'Or is that Pastor Jack?'

5

THE THING I always found about real–estate agents was they were fonts of information about people's private lives. They had their turf and they eventually knew, over time, which client used what type of shampoo, who ate fresh food and who preferred packaged, personal habits and fetishes, who was clean and who was slovenly, who had real money and who pretended to have money. They saw signs of domestic violence, loneliness, anxiety, contentment. There was very little that went on in human life and interaction on their watch that they didn't know about.

Of course my agent, Geraldo, had a few tales to tell about the Priest and the Boltcutter.

'Odd to you, my friend,' he said during one of our morning house inspections. 'But let me tell you, quite mild for the Gold Coast.'

'That's mild? The painted men with their guts hanging out? The murderous monks?'

'In that building alone there are more fruit-loops than a cereal factory.' He looked at me, expecting a laugh. It was obviously one of his well-used lines. I dutifully guffawed. It pleased Geraldo.

'There is an old woman in the penthouse there who has

not stepped outside since 1987,' he said, his eyebrows raised. 'She owns half of Pitt Street in Sydney. The rental cheques – millions, may I say – keep coming in. I know the janitor. The cheques are all over the place, like litter. Millions, I say. She just sits by the window all day staring out at the ocean. You want tragedies, you've come to the right place.'

'But the gentlemen in the medieval grotto?'

'Wheeler-dealers,' he continued, 'but who isn't, up here? They're a little Steptoe and Son operation though. Could be a front. A fraud. A cover. You getting my drift?'

'I know what a cover is, yes.'

'Who knows. Drugs. Prostitutes. A friend of a friend knows of one southern gentleman who came up here to retire, so to speak, and wanted to start a strip club.'

'So? Sounds like a good way to pass your twilight years. Better than philately.'

'Or collecting stamps.'

'Precisely, Geraldo.'

'The thing is, he wanted to open a club for people who liked watching other people dressed up as zebras.'

'Just zebras?'

'Just zebras.'

'I thought I'd heard of them all,' I said wearily.

'Your Priest and his antiques? Dead people's rubbish, as far as I'm concerned. I'm a modern guy, on the other hand. I'm a clean lines, glass and pale timber sort of guy.'

He was also – after more than an hour – an annoying, pain in the backside sort of guy. We inspected several canal-side villas that were like those I imagined Australian second-rate former television celebrities might have fawned over in the seventies. They already looked old and something out of early California porno films. They were seedy and decaying.

I missed the history of Sydney architecture. The rows of terraces. The semis. The art-deco apartment blocks. I told Geraldo this.

'You want history, you better retire somewhere else,' he snorted. 'We have buildings here torn down after twenty years and rebuilt. Nineteen seventies is ancient, my friend. This is a place of renewal. Rebirth. We turn the sod here pretty regularly.'

'No heritage-listed buildings on the Gold Coast?'

He pulled pensively at his earlobe. 'I think there's an old toilet block on the highway near Labrador from the fifties.'

Back in my van that afternoon I did my old system-card trick – something I picked up from a colleague in 21 Division. Using those little five- by three-inch ruled cards, once the mainstay of library index systems and public-service filing cabinets, I wrote a name, location or event on a single card and then laid them out on the table in front of me. It was always a puzzle. A confusing jumble of facts and faces. Eventually, if I worked at it hard enough, I could see the pattern that lurked behind the cards.

'Do you think you may have lost your footing?' asked Peg that night, which was her way of saying I could not let go of my work, my old life.

I didn't tell her that I had, resting next to the sugar canister on my little table in the caravan, a shiny bullet. Sometimes I picked it up and turned it over and squeezed it. It was real, all right. It was the footing I needed.

The cards told me I had seen an old colleague from my past – the Boltcutter. I had met his possible partner, the Priest. I knew the Boltcutter, a.k.a. Dapper Dan, was travel-ling nicely under another pseudonym, albeit a strange one. And I had received a hand-delivered bullet with a calling card attached. I knew, too, thanks to the Priest, that Fair

Weather was a pun on words, and referred to some artist bloke called Ian Fairweather. What I didn't know was who wrote the note on the bullet. And why had it been delivered to me?

I was at the doors of the Southport Public Library when they opened the next morning. There were several octogenarians there, itching to get inside and continue their research into their family trees. I could understand their addiction. I was only a year or so off the family tree obsession myself.

I found a book on Fairweather and took notes on my little system cards.

When it comes to art, I'm the sort of guy who likes to see what he's looking at. Comes from being a cop for so long, I suppose. None of this symbolism and deeper meaning. Whistler's mother? You know right there it's Whistler's mother. And God save poor old Whistler, I say, after one look at her sourpuss.

Take Picasso. Marvellous stuff, the early pictures, before he started putting people's noses on their foreheads and eyes on their cheeks. Those faces look like a plate full of offal to me. Makes me bilious just to look at them. I've never liked Picasso. And I've never liked tripe.

As for this Fairweather. He was a bit of an offal style of guy to my eyes, but he had something else that instantly appealed to me. What was it? A sort of delicate, childish touch that was impossible not to like. Through all the tangled limbs and thickets of humanity the guy had a big heart. And through the crazy patterns and trees there was something beautiful he was reaching out for and never quite getting. He was like Nurse Reginald, but with talent.

I was shocked to learn he had spent much of his life in a handmade hut on Bribie Island. That he'd embarked on insane adventures and was lucky to have lived as long as

he did. That he painted on sheets of newspaper and cardboard and that now his work was held in galleries all over
the world, from the Tate in London to the Queensland Art
Gallery which, I also learned from a friendly librarian, had
just reopened after an extensive makeover with a substantial
Fairweather collection.

I was going to have to go up to Brisbane and take a good
close look at our Mr Fairweather.

I had a decent steak at the Southport RSL and phoned
my old mate Freddy Tingle in Sydney. We'd used him
for years on fraud cases and he'd been a bonanza for us,
especially when it came to the art world. He'd have to
be seventy years old by now. He still ran a little gallery in
Darlinghurst, in a back lane next to an S&M boutique.

Freddy had a standard joke. Sometimes, he'd say, the
S&M customers came into his gallery by mistake, and when
reminded of their error, they asked, 'Well, while I'm here,
do you mind hanging me?' Boom, boom.

'Fairweather?' Freddy said on the phone. 'You want to
buy or sell?'

'Neither. Is he a big name these days? What's he getting
on the market?'

'Let's put it this way – if you've got a Fairweather, I'd
hang on to it. One of his abstract soliloquies sold at auction
for $80,000, which I think was a steal. For a smallish picture
painted on a page of *The Courier-Mail* newspaper. That
was in the seventies. Recently? A major work topped one
million dollars.'

'Who's the best person to see in Brisbane about
Fairweather?'

'I always used James Fenton Browne. A terrific appraiser
of Fairweather. He could sniff a Fairweather fake a mile off.'

'Used?'

'They found him eaten out by crabs in Moreton Bay about a month ago.'

'Are you serious?' I suddenly remembered a story about the mystery of the Crab Pot Hand in the local newspaper.

'Some place called Peel Island. They almost didn't find him in the mangroves. Until a local fisherman pulled up his crab pot and found nothing in it. Just poor old James Fenton Browne's left hand.'

I felt squeamish. I saw the dead art appraiser with eyes on his forehead and a nose coming out of his neck.

Picasso had a lot to answer for.

6

I ALWAYS KNOW when I'm being followed. That's not intuition or street smarts or an irregularly well-honed radar. I thank the French for this quality in my life.

I drive a Peugeot 504, white, with light-brown upholstery still as good as the day the car rolled off its factory floor, except where the stuffing is blooming like old yellow carnations out of rips and tears. I love that car. I bought it shortly after Peg and I got married and, despite her protestations, I have refused to get rid of it. Bury me at wounded Peugeot, I tell her.

If it was good enough for De Gaulle, it'll do me.

The one thing I know is that I can't go over 80 km an hour in the old warhorse. Well, I can. It can physically go faster. But if I bust 80, the steering wheel starts to shake and a thin branch of smoke, as blue-grey as from the tip of a Gauloise, issues from the steering column. Pffft, I have been known to exhort. So what? It is French, after all. Of course it smokes.

So on the day I headed up to Brisbane in my Gallic rattler, I never exceeded the car's known limit, which, on the Gold Coast to Brisbane superhighway is not even a canter, and I noticed in my trembling rear-vision mirror a large black sedan creeping along at the same pace about 200 metres behind me.

As I said, it didn't take a Mensa membership to deduce the obvious.

The black car was still keeping pace with me when I pulled into Little Stanley Street and disappeared into an underground car park. I cruised around for a while and waited for my pursuers to follow suit. They didn't.

When I parked and climbed the stairs to South Bank, it only took a few minutes for two goons to suddenly appear in my peripheral vision. They were wearing black suits and black shades. Nobody wore black suits and black shades in Queensland, unless they were undertakers with light-sensitive eye conditions. Or first years in Gangster 101. Or members of Johnny Cash's extended family.

They followed me into the newly refurbished Queensland Art Gallery. Didn't even remove their sunglasses. I went straight to the Fairweather room. I harboured a humorous fantasy that one of the guards might recommend the goons remove their shades to best appreciate Fairweather's subtle colourations. I might even suggest it myself.

Besides, they weren't going to inflict grievous bodily harm on me in an art gallery. This wasn't *The Da Vinci Code*, though I think I was one of the few people on earth who had not read the book. In the film I'd only made it to the part where they find the old man naked in the Louvre. I did not like to think of old men dead and naked. It turned my stomach like the offal Picassos.

When it transpired the dead Da Vinci pensioner had scrawled clues to his killers in his own blood, I turned off the DVD. I had experienced enough death to know that victims of fatal shootings don't present intellectual riddles in blood before expiration. They are too busy calling for their mother, or holding their innards in, or trying to locate a missing part of their skull, or not.

I wasn't exactly sure what I was looking for. Was I seeking the crab-nibbled James Fenton Browne amidst all this beauty? For the Fairweathers, face to face, were extremely beautiful. A book could not reproduce their ethereal quality, the life of them that seemed to hover above ordinary sheets of paper and cardboard and fragments of masonite.

I had come to art late in life. You don't get much time to ponder Courbet's line work or Rockwell's romanticism when you're banging villains' heads against cobblestones in Surry Hills or saving some junkie from drowning in Rushcutters Bay. I'm the sort of guy who, when I was young and didn't know any better, bought poster prints of famous art works like Van Gogh's sunflowers or Monet's lilies with VAN GOGH and MONET in big letters along the bottom and got them framed. We once had a little tile hanging on a nail on the lavatory door which read: 'Here 'Tis, Hers or His, So in You Whiz, on Private Biz'. Not one of the great works of art, but direct.

No. I had to meet Mr Freud before I knew what to look for in a picture.

The goons were pretending to be viewing works in the adjoining room and kept poking their heads into the Fairweather space to see if I was still there. I took out my little system cards and jotted a few notes about the Bribie Island artist. I had never heard of Bribie Island. Seeing how he painted, I assumed it was in Indonesia or Tahiti.

I was very taken by the Fairweathers' renditions of mother and child. I felt a lot of love in Fairweather. I thought for a moment I might pop into the gallery shop on the way out and see if they had some posters of his paintings with FAIRWEATHER written across the bottom.

Turning my back on the goons, I made some more notes about a wonderful picture of women bathing and heard someone cough lightly behind me.

'May I help you?' a voice said.

'Not really,' I said, finishing my jottings on Fairweather's failed raft expedition from Darwin to Bali. Just as the cough was delivered I had a strange sense of déjà vu. There had been a case, many years ago in Sydney, involving the corrupt magistrate Murray Farquhar and a number of famous artworks. I was starting to think one of them might have been a Fairweather. I was hastily writing this down, when another cough cut through my thoughts.

'Are you quite sure you don't need any assistance?'

I turned, annoyed. It was a well-presented gentleman, also in a suit – this one a fitted three-button number, dark blue, with the finest pinstripe through it, as delicate as trails of spider web.

The gentleman inside the suit had the facial bone structure of a flyweight boxer – striking cheekbones, heavy around the eye sockets, small of ear – and the sartorial splendour of an old-fashioned dandy. Like the Dapper, too, he had a physique that juxtaposed rudely with such delicate cloth.

The goons were nowhere to be seen.

I studied him for several uncomfortable moments. It was one of my old tricks of the trade. I had patience. I was, more often than not, impervious to embarrassment. I could stare and stare with impunity. This talent had elicited many confessions in my career with 21 Division.

I barely blinked at the pretty, gift-wrapped boxer standing a foot from me in the Fairweather room.

'Tell me one thing,' I finally said. 'Is it Suit Day in Brisbane? I didn't think anyone wore them up here.'

'What did you think we wore? Pith helmets and linen?'

'It takes a lot of guts to wear a pith helmet, you know.'

'Oh, I know.'

'Good, just as long as you know.' I smiled.

'You're positive there's nothing I can help you with.'

'A gin and tonic would be nice, actually.'

His mouth, as small and neat and lipless and clean as if it had been quickly made by the slash of a Stanley knife, did not move.

'I am Dexter Dupont. The gallery director. And you're looking for the tradesman's entrance?'

'Now, Dexter, don't be rude. I want nothing to do with your tradesmen's entrance. And remember, I too have a capacity for cruelty, particularly with words.'

'Is that so?'

'That is so.'

'Give me an example.'

'I would, if only you could get to Dupont. Do you get it?'

'Congratulations. I have a small gift for you. You are the one millionth person to make that joke.'

I tucked my notes into my shirt pocket. 'Why don't you give me an early birthday present and get out of my personal space? I am a private citizen. A Fairweather fan, you might say. And I'd like to be left to contemplate his works, in particular his religious period, in peace. Thank you, Dexter.'

He didn't move.

'We have a mutual friend who is very distressed.'

'I am a retiree soaking up some culture. I am submerged in art, Dexter. Go away.'

'A gentleman friend of yours on the Gold Coast. You have made him most agitated. Most aggrieved.'

'Big country town up here, isn't it? Can't break wind

without it turning up in the newspaper. Our mutual friend should know to keep his trap shut. Loose lips and all that. Words sometimes have a way of biting their owners, turning up in court, magically transforming into evidence. Your worship.'

'I am aware of that. It is why I was waiting for you.'

'Popular, ain't I?'

'And it is why I'd like you to come up to my office.'

'Is that so?'

'It is.'

'What for? You want me to explain Fairweather's mystic symbolism to you?'

'I need your help.'

'With regard to?'

'With regard to murder.'

7

THE PEUGEOT STARTED to smoke by the time I got over the bridge to Bribie Island. As I puttered above Pumicestone Passage I was half-hanging out of the driver's side window, it was so bad in the cabin. It did not smell like French tobacco. It smelled like burning human hair and dust.

I was tired and emotional and so was the car. We repaired to a patch of shade just off the bridge. Looking out at the grey water and gun-metal clouds, I had an existential moment. What was I doing here? I asked myself. I imagine the car asked it also.

It had been a long, restless night in Brisbane. I had stayed at a cheap motel not far from the Gallery of Modern Art, near the spritely little spans of the William Jolly Bridge. In my head I went over and over my meeting with Dexter Dupont, the gallery director. I awoke at six in the morning. I had been haunted, some time in the night, by an image of the departed art appraiser James Fenton Browne lying on his back, crucifix-style, with spears of mangrove growing through his corpse. Small crabs ferried in and out of his eye sockets, and bluebottles were tangled in his hair.

I had always thought this part of the country a happy-go-lucky place. Bridges were called Jolly. There were suburbs called Sunshine. Yet the brighter the light, the darker the shadow, and I had somehow fallen into south-east Queensland's malevolent alter ego. And this wasn't the drug world. This was the art world, for crying out loud.

A friend of a friend at the Homicide Squad had agreed to see me at the Roma Street headquarters and share a few scant facts about Fenton Browne's demise. He was one of those slick young coppers, highly educated, with an ironed crease down the sleeves of his shirt. I was shambolic, weary, and wearing stained leather scuffs. He gave me a cursory five minutes.

'And your interest in this case?' he said, leading me out, almost by the arm.

'Curiosity,' I said.

'And we all know what curiosity did, don't we?' he said, smiling patronisingly. I had become, in his eyes, some ex-cop who could not let go of his police pedigree, and now bumbled about bothering working officers with this hobby, much as older men may take up orchid-growing or whit-tling. It mattered nought that I had taken down some of the most notorious men in Australian criminal history. Smelled their breaths, quite literally, in a couple of situations.

This perfumed, crew-cut desk jockey steered me through the foyer and on to the street.

'Well,' he said, in the sing-song voice of a kindergarten teacher. 'Good luck with it.'

'Up yours,' I mumbled to myself.

The day remained gloomy and overcast, much like my internal demeanour. I struck out for Bribie Island. It was further from Brisbane than I expected. Like most men, I like a good drive. Indeed, I'd solved many problems on the highway. I find, when I'm in motion, the rushing Australian bush − its endless mundane walls of gum and wattle, its

sheer excruciating drabness — is extremely conducive to
concentrated thought. I imagine our early explorers experienced the same thing atop horses and camels. The bush,
in its monotony, throws the consciousness back on itself.
Makes an external journey an internal one. This can be illu-
minating, or dangerous. Ask Burke and Wills.

On my expedition to Bribie I tried to hover above the
information I had, as an early mapmaker might have done. I
have been fascinated by maps since I was a boy, and remain
in awe of the first cartographers' art — how they layered
gossamer lines, coordinates, geology one on the other and
eventually came up with a picture of the whole.

It was a practice applicable to Fairweather's paintings.
What Dexter Dupont did not know the day he conversed
with me in the gallery, and then spun me a cock and bull
story about the departed James Fenton Browne, was that I
had seen something in Fairweather's *Epiphany*, and again in
his *Glasshouse Mountains*, that had given my slowly emerging
picture of this case a defining contour.

Fairweather had shown me the heart of darkness here, in
this geography. And that warning had, I felt, given me some
sort of advantage.

But my reading of the Fairweather story did not prepare
me for Bribie Island. I had expected a little fishing village
with a clutch of casuarinas tickling the shoreline, but it was a
hive of big development, like most of the Queensland coast.

Fairweather had complained of urban encroachment
way back in the sixties, when he used to wander about the
island in soiled pyjama trousers. He even painted about
the invasion of his Shangri-la. The building of the bridge
over Pumicestone Passage had rightly caused him alarm. In
the outside world his prodigious talents were finally being
recognised. Now the world had access to him. And come

they did, from local journalists to art critic Robert Hughes to Nobel Laureate Patrick White.

Fairweather had become the very cliché of the artist who lives for only his art. The poet in the garret was in his case the master painter in a Balinese-style hut of his own making. No running water. No refrigeration. No stove.

But the Fairweather story was more than that. In that dim hut on Bribie he wrestled with the great questions, and created a record of his metaphysical struggles with house paint on cheap canvas, cardboard and even sheets of newspaper. In a rat-infested hovel he laid out map after map of his consciousness. He ate kippers, drank rotgut and painted and painted, as the world crept closer.

When the Peugeot had cooled down, I secured a map from the visitors' centre and drove the short distance to the park that had been consecrated in Fairweather's honour. It was here his huts had once stood, where he did his major works that now hang in temperature-controlled galleries around the world.

I drove past rows and rows of muffler repair shops and takeaway joints and newish housing estates. It didn't feel right. I had read reports of Fairweather's hideaway being almost impossible to find, deep in the bush. But where was the bush?

I was not thinking of the fifties and sixties. It had been more than thirty years since his death. And as I came upon the little straggly pine grove that was Fairweather Park, I felt a pang of sadness for the artist. It was surrounded by bitumen roads, a bus stop, and a regulation Australian suburb.

The huts were gone. The solitude was gone. His cairn of kipper tins – all gone.

I eventually parked off the main road and wandered through the pine grove. The sandy floor of the park shifted underfoot. There was rubbish littered over the pine needles and leaves. In the centre of an amphitheatre of sunken earth, sporadically decorated with flaking timber bench seats, were a huge, misshaped boulder and a plaque to Fairweather. On the concrete apron at the base of the memorial some kids had scrawled graffiti.

I sat for a long time in Fairweather's grove. I strained to hear the birds he so loved, but only heard the distant gear change of trucks and the staccato thud of heavy machinery. Somewhere, in a nearby house, Willie Nelson was singing about being on the road again.

Tom Wolfe was right. You can't go home again.

It was dark inside that sorrowful glade. It was late afternoon but the park seemed to have its own light, irrespective of time, and it was as gloomy as twilight. I could just make out the spectral shape of my white Peugeot through the trees. It seemed to me as blurry-edged and mysterious as the weird, haunting blotches of white in Fairweather's *The Bathers*.

I connected a couple of dots that afternoon in the glade. In my thoughts I travelled all the way back to the death of Legs, the madam from Atherton, and to a young Boltcutter in his antique store at the Cross. Then there was a newspaper brief from a long time ago about a murdered Brisbane art dealer. It nibbled at me like a Bribie sandfly. I'd have to hit the archives.

When I headed for my car it was almost pitch black in the forest. I stumbled through the sand and undergrowth. I saw the figure of the man at the last moment. A silhouette, blacker than black.

I even remember the crack across the back of my head.

Then nothing.

8

WHEN I FINALLY opened my eyes again I understood two things.

Firstly, gentlemen of a certain age shouldn't put themselves too often in a position of being bludgeoned on the back of the head with a blunt object. There are less painful ways to see stars, and more pleasurable paths to a massive headache.

Secondly, I was convinced I was dead. I was in a room with a single light glowing feebly in the distance, and crouched over me were an old man and woman.

They pulled me up to a sitting position. I was on an old imitation leather couch. 'You're okay,' the woman said, pressing a cold, damp flannel to my forehead. The flannel had little African violets stitched around its perimeter.

The room started coming into focus. A recliner rocker with a flip-out footstool. A nest of coffee tables. Cream carpet so old it bore grey tracks of human traffic. A huge, old-fashioned imitation mahogany cabinet television set with a curly copper antenna on the top at one end, and a small white bust of Lenin at the other. There were nondescript pictures on the wall, the type of Hawaiian beach scenes that you could, once upon a time, buy by the metre from somewhere.

'You want drink?' the old man said. 'Here, drink.'

He pressed a big glass tumbler into my hand. It was warm orange-crush cordial. It smelled like a neglected fish pond.

'You'll stay for tea,' the woman said, wiping her hands on her apron and shuffling over to the open kitchen behind the recliner rocker. I could see through the window a sole street light and the scissor shadows of palm trees.

The old man hobbled over to the rocker, rested his cane against one of the arms, and eased into the chair. It squeaked loudly under his weight.

I had no idea where I was or who these people were. If this was heaven, it could've done with a good scrub, some new furniture and a squirt of room deodoriser.

'Am sorry,' the old man said.

'He's SORRY,' the old woman shouted from behind the kitchen bench. I had witnessed this dynamic with older people. The deaf husband. The wife, in compensation, turning up her own volume, then forgetting lots of other people in the world weren't deaf. Her voice went into my tender eardrum like someone knocking a knitting needle into my brain with a rubber mallet.

'Was mistaken identity,' he said.

'MISTAKEN IDENTITY,' said his wife. I winced.

'Where am I?' I asked.

'I'm Igor. This my wife, Manya. You at Bribie.'

Bribie. The Fairweather forest. Yes. Heading for my car. Lights out.

'Who are you?'

'I told you. Igor.'

'He's IGOR.'

'Igor, why did you knock me unconscious?'

'Was mistake. I thought you were the man coming with the shovel.'

'I don't understand.'

'For a month, a man come with the shovel. Always at night he come. We keep a watch over the park. He was our good friend, EE-arn Farr-weather. We keep a watch for the last thirty years, you know, make sure is nice for him, his last resting place and things like that.'

'His last resting place?'

'His ashes spread there.'

'HIS ASHES.'

'So in the past few weeks, the neighbours and other peoples, they see the man come at night with the shovel. I never seen him, until tonight. And bop, I hit you on head, thinking is you. Is it you?'

'No, it's not.'

'That's what my friend Bruce say. He here before, take a good look at you, and says – no, Igor, is not the man with the shovel.'

With the shouting from Manya and a lump the size of half a cricket ball on the back of my head and Igor's lurching Russo-English, I was completely disoriented.

'You're telling me that for the last month a man has been coming to Fairweather's park late at night with a shovel, digging around for something, and he's been observed by neighbours and passers-by. You thought I was that man. So you tried to kill me with your walking stick.'

'It was small spade actually.'

'SMALL SPADE,' Manya shouted to the imitation walnut kitchen cabinets as she chopped vegetables. She chopped loudly as well. Every blade-strike into the bread board tapped at my bruised cranium.

'He was my good friend, EE-arn. I had only taxi on the island for a long time and he have no car, so I drove him everywhere he want to go. Not many places to go on Bribie, you understand. But I run him around and do errands for him, and he was very good to me. I take some of Manya's cooking to his huts sometime, just so he have a hot meal in him. Sometimes he ate and sometimes no. He was strange man, but good man, EE-arn.'

From my seat on the crinkly vinyl couch I could not see the old man's face across the room, just the occasional reflection of the overhead light in his enormous, black-rimmed spectacles.

'This man, the one with the shovel, what would he be looking for?'

The old man retrieved his cane and toyed with what looked like a cast-iron wolf's head handle. He shrugged his shoulders.

'What all the others been looking for.'

'And what's that.'

'Money. Paintings. Ever since he die – 1974 – the strangers coming to pick over poor EE-arn. They think he rich, you see. That he bury the treasure. They think, how can such a great man, famous man, live like pauper? You know pauper?'

'PAUPER.'

'Paw-paw?'

'PAUPER!'

'They think, his name in paper and his pictures so they get a lot of money, so where the money? Is the way they think in capitalist society. They always seek the money. If is not visible to the eye, is buried. Money, money, money. But EE-arn, he don't care about the money. He a rich man inside, not on outside, you understand?'

'I think so.'

'For year after year they come to me, the bigwigs from the city. You got EE-arn's money? Where the money?

How about the pictures, you must have the pictures? When he die – the pictures, they just disappear, whoof. Like that. Whoof. His place picked clean overnight. Whoof. All gone.'

Manya startled sizzling onions in a pan. The smell filled the small house. I felt nauseous.

'You think the man with the shovel was looking for some lost Fairweathers?'

'Maybe. But what's lost to some people is not lost to others. You see?'

'I'm not sure I do.'

'Sometime EE-arn, he drunk, you know. We sit around the fire at the huts. He say, Igor, here, you have this picture, I know you like. Igor, take this one for Manya, she like. When he get drunk he don't care, he like good communist, everything that his belong to everyone. He would be national treasure in Russia, but not in Australia, with the mosquitoes and toad fishes. He would have been a great man.'

He thumped the cane on the floor. The statue of Lenin stared in on us. I gently touched the new foothill on the back of my head.

He continued. 'Before the man with the spade, there was other man. At least he not come in the night time, like a thief.'

'The other man?'

'I tell him, there nothing. But he insist. He say I must have seen them, I must have seen them.'

'Seen what, exactly?'

'The great pictures of the lepers.'

'The lepers?'

'The lepers.'

'THE LEPERS.'

I was about to be sick. The onion aroma swirled around the room. Something else joined them in the pan. I recognised it from my childhood. Liver.

Then the old man rose and went to a small cane basket on the kitchen bench. He retrieved a business card and came back and handed it to me.

'Here,' he said. 'The man who wanted the lepers.'

It was a business card, all right. For James Fenton Browne.

9

I WOKE THE next morning with a headache that could drop a
herd of wildebeest. I felt it before I'd even opened my eyes.
When I did, my problems were only compounded.

I had slept on a small fold-out mattress with its net
of lumpy, rusted springs imprinted across my back and
buttocks, despite a wafer-thin mattress and sheets thick with
patterns of African violets provided by my hosts, Igor and
Manya. On the wall opposite me was a photograph from
what looked like the fifties of Russian peasants stacking
sheaves of wheat.

And standing at the door, with his Lenin-esque shaved
head, ratty grey goatee and wolf's head cane was Igor.

'You sleep good?'

'Good,' I said. I was too weary to debate.

'Good. Come eat.'

The house still smelled of the liver and onions, and when
I stumbled out to the kitchenette there was a huge plate
of it waiting for me.

'Excuse me,' I said. I found the bathroom at the end of
the hall and threw up.

I returned to the kitchen. The offensive plate had been
removed.

'CUP OF TEA?' Manya asked.

'Yes, thank you.'

I took the chipped enamel mug full of sweet, steaming tea and nursed it in my hands. I wondered how Peg was going with the packing in Sydney. I wondered if, in her wildest dreams, she would have believed I was sipping tea in a fibro bungalow with two Bribie Island pensioners, with a bruise on the back of my head the size of a halved breakfast grapefruit, and being stared at by an effigy of the leader of the Russian Revolution, dust caught in the lines of his face and the folds of his suit collar.

'You come,' Igor said, and I followed him out to the front of the house, down the side to a bleached timber garage with a corrugated iron roof the colour of faded ox blood.

There was an ancient Humber parked inside the shed. It was partially covered in a grey tarpaulin. Past a bench covered in curlings of wood and a lathe and a wall of haphazardly arranged tools hanging on nails, we entered a separate room at the back.

'You look,' said Igor. He was panting a little from the effort of the walk from the house. He pulled back a curtain of cloth and revealed several shelves of junk.

'This,' he said, almost ceremonially, 'is all I have left of EE-arn.'

There, stacked loosely on the shelves, were billy cans and old flame-scarred kettles, a handful of small, hardened paint brushes, some rust-edged tins of house paint with the labels obscured by veils of drip, a couple of stone wine bottles wrapped in rotting wicker, candles down to the stub sitting in pitted kipper cans, some coils of rope, a single leather sandal that look like it was dated from the time of Christ, a few empty glass jars, a ball-headed hammer and a cardboard box full of old magazines, curled paperbacks and sheaves of yellowed paper.

I delicately touched one of the covers of the paperbacks. Ellery Queen.

'Poor EE-arn,' the old man said. His eyes were moist through the thick and enormous lenses of his spectacles.

Later, we sat together on two garden chairs beneath the canopy of a spectacular frangipani tree.

'Igor,' I said, 'what do you remember of James Fenton Browne?'

He blew his nose and tucked the checked handkerchief into his trouser pocket.

'I told you already,' he said. 'This man Browne, he want what all the other want. The pictures of EE-arn. I say I no have pictures. He say that's okay, what you got of EE-arns? I say I got some stuff from the camp after he die. Just the pots and pans. He say, Igor, let me have a look. Maybe we buy for a museum.'

'A museum?'

'A museum of EE-arn. He famous artist now. He have own museum. I say it all I got left of my good friend EE-arn.' He removed the handkerchief again, took off his glasses, and dabbed at his eyes. I knew Fairweather had not just been Igor's good friend. He had perhaps been his last friend.

'Did you show him?'

'Yes, I show him. Just like I show you now. I say I don't want to sell. EE-arn not for sale. He say just let me look through in private. He say he a big art dealer. He look at picture and can tell you how much money is worth picture. He say let me look in private. That he a big EE-arn friend too. I let him, in private. When I come back he looking through the papers in the box. He did what you did, touch the books. Then he say thank you and go away.'

'Did he take anything with him?'

'What there to take? Just junk. But special because it belong to my friend EE–arn.'

'Did you ever take a close look at the papers in the box?'

'Is just papers, you understand? This EE–arn, he a strange man. He like to write things down all the time. He write on anything he can find. He write on leaves and jam tins. He write on backs of envelopes and bus tickets. He write over the prescriptions he get from the doctor, for his sickness, you know?'

'Did he keep a journal? A diary?'

Igor raised his hand and pointed at me with an index finger. A smile had appeared on his face. 'He say – Igor, everything a diary. The whole *world* a diary. That I never forget.'

I was beginning to suspect that James Fenton Browne had found something more interesting than an old Ellery Queen novel in Igor's dusty shed. I was beginning to feel I was *in* an Ellery Queen novel.

'How did he seem, this Mr Browne, when he left you?'

'How he seem? Very happy. He give Manya a kiss. He try to give me one too but I know his type, this Mr Browne. I was in Russian navy.'

'Have you seen him since?'

'I no see Mr Browne since then. Whoof, he vanish.'

Whoof, indeed. More like bang, bang. A little birdy had told me our kissy kissy art appraiser had gone bye bye with one bullet to the back of the head. The Moreton Bay crabs did the rest of the damage.

I didn't want to tell Igor. I didn't think he could handle, let alone comprehend, the dark machinery of the criminal world. That quite possibly a piece of forgotten paper, some jottings on an envelope, a few scrawled notes on a bus ticket that had sat innocuously in his back shed for three decades had spread their tentacles and led to the delicate Mr Browne's brains rendered fish food in the bay. Russian navy or not, he was still an old man.

'Last night, you mentioned lepers.'

'Leopards?'

'LEPERS.'

I could see Manya in the kitchen window. 'WHAT?' she shouted.

'NOTHING.' I said, waving to her.

'Lepers,' Igor said.

'Yes.'

'Mr Browne was looking for the pictures of the lepers.'

'That's right. That's what you said.'

'The man with the shovel, who I thought was you, he too I think looks for the pictures of the lepers.'

'Igor, what did you mean by the lepers?'

'They the ones at Peel Island.'

'Peel Island?'

'They had the lepers on that island. EE-arn, he was fascinated with the lepers. For EE-arn, he was like the leper. And those other lepers on the island, they were like the brothers and sisters of EE-arn. He say that. Igor, he say, the lepers is my family. They my only family, Igor, except you and Manya.'

'When was this, Igor?'

'Not long after he come here, you know. In fifties. He learn about the lepers. He build a raft from drums and wood on the beach. Manya give him sheet for the sail. I say, EE-arn, that raft, she won't make out of the passage. He say, Igor, I sail to the lepers, my brothers and sisters. He go make pictures of them. He say God is with the lepers, and he want to go paint God. Ha! Poor EE-arn.'

I had never read of any paintings of the lepers of Peel Island by Ian Fairweather. I had never seen any. I had never come across any type of reference to them whatsoever. My cunning little mind told me that an unknown and unseen series of paintings of God and his children by Fairweather might be very valuable indeed.

'He say, no use to stop me, EE–arn, I go,' Igor said. He had dabbed his eyes with the handkerchief again. I didn't know if he was laughing or crying. 'Then he vanish, whoof, for two week, and when he come back I say, where you been, EE–arn, you find God? And he say even better, he find a girlfriend on Peel Island.'

'A girlfriend?'

'I say, good on you EE–arn, but I know it not true. I know EE–arn was like the Mr Browne. He the type I saw in the Russian navy. He never tell me. I just know, you know?'

'I know.'

'But I see her picture. He did picture of his girlfriend. Her name Rosemary. I seen it. Then he never talk about her again.'

It was getting hot under the frangipani tree. Igor stared silently into a mass of rotting white and yellow flowers.

I swallowed with a dry throat. My head throbbed.

It looked like I was heading to Peel Island in search of God.

10

'You got a bit of mail.'

I returned to the van park at Main Beach with, I might say, a measure of relief. Verne the proprietor had displayed two substantial bundles of letters and packages on the front counter.

'What did you say you did again, before you retired?'

'Alpaca breeder.'

'Fair enough.' Verne nudged the mail in my direction.

If ever I wanted to effectively disappear from the world, I'd head straight for a caravan park. They're deliciously anonymous, egalitarian, private. Everybody wants to know your business but no one would be rude enough not to take you on your word. They're remote islands unto themselves. Refuges. Little Petri dishes of lives, lost dreams, spoiled marriages, family conflicts, flight and homecoming. They are places open to the world, exposed to the elements, vulnerable, yet they discourage prying and invasion of personal space.

You are a sheet of canvas or a slice of aluminium away from the elements, from the great unpredictable force of nature and – permit me to be dramatic – a skein stands between life and death; between you and a deadly storm, or a predator. Yet you feel safe. We are like members of an exclusive club with a secret handshake, we van-park dwellers. We are all accidental families.

Peg had puzzled about why I had not taken a motel during my solo sabbatical on the Gold Coast. But how could I explain to her the peccadilloes of men of a certain age? Would she understand the yearning for simplicity? The desire to replicate an unbridled happiness that the busyness of life had somehow buried under layers of responsibility, menial tasks, useless diversions, triviality and the junkyard of material possessions, ambitions, one-upmanship, fake friendships and webs of behaviour so foreign to our actual selves that even the smallest critical distance would induce horror at what we'd become?

Would you get it, Peg? A lifetime of thinking you're important, only to be dropped into a civilian life where your epaulettes, literally and figuratively, no longer matter, are even a source of amusement? To one day be young and strong of limb and doing something that matters, and the next, emerge into some strange, uncharted place where your back permanently aches, hair grows from your ears, your belly keeps getting bigger but your legs become thin, your arms have no strength, and it takes an hour a day after rising for the twinges to disappear? To see a thick shock of black hair in the mirror, only to wipe away the steam on the glass and see a stranger with grey tufts and an ashen pallor looking back at you?

Oh, it hits us men hard, dear Peg. It's a low blow. It explained, at least to me, why I had become involved in this crazy case.

A young constable once asked me what it was like to spend your days head to head with heartless killers and standover men and street toughs who would extinguish a life as unthinkingly as cracking their morning egg with a teaspoon. I told him not to be hypnotised by the myth of death. Death is not always delivered at the end of a gun or the blade of a knife or at the hands of a giant. I told him a story an old copper told me when I was a young constable. The lion can always chase down and slaughter the nimble-footed impala. But never forget that an impala can accidentally break one of its delicate legs, and be killed by ants. Death can come in many ways, I told him. And often in the most benign fashion.

He was dead himself seven months later, impaled on a cast-iron fence in pursuit, while off-duty, of a smack-addicted bag-snatcher in one of Sydney's most salubrious suburbs. I have often thought of that fresh-faced officer and, strangely, the fence, waiting there for more than a century, painted and repainted over time, almost made for its unforeseen victim from the future. Watch for the lion, I've always said, but also keep an eye out for the ants.

I went straight across to the surf club with my mail. I had come to view the club, with its lovely vista of the Pacific Ocean out front and the sounds of squealing children and the crash of surf and the sad music of the poker machines out the back, as my own proxy office. It beat my old HQ in Parramatta.

There, at a table buffeted by sea gusts, I could peruse my mail, inspect my little system cards and puzzle over the case. I could do this nibbling on salt-and-pepper calamari and a bitterly cold bitter.

On this day, though, I was beginning to feel a familiar malaise. It had happened many times before, but not for a long while. It was a cloying feeling, a palpable discomfort when I found myself deep inside something I didn't fully understand.

I used to believe that you could learn a lot about a place by the types of murders it had hosted. I have never been fond of Adelaide, for example, with all its church spires and pretty boulevards, because I know from its history of deeply perverse killings that the city has a disturbing undercurrent, another dark Adelaide that operates concurrently with the pious, floral, prettily dressed one.

Melbourne. European in architecture and attitude, and European in its way of murder. Trench coats. Hand guns in alleys. Mafioso. And Sydney. All rude and loud and bluff and bluster. Impatient and cruel. A magnet for glamour, which also made it a magnet for grit.

Then there was Queensland. The Gold Coast was to my eyes Las Vegas on trainer wheels. A single, glowing strip of cash and bad perfume. Of vice and teenage angst. Of ceaseless deals on and under the table. The Gold Coast was a twenty-four-hour crap shoot, and its deaths reflected that too.

But what of Brisbane? It was fresh. In transition. On the make. The shadows it cast were hardly black. They were grey. Opaque. They were the type of shadows caught at twilight. This was a twilight city. A part of it held on to the past, and another moved inexorably into a future. Brisbane was a flux metropolis.

From the little I had learned, it seemed too, to me now, a city of deep allegiances. And the by-product of entrenched loyalty was the grudge. I could feel the thick reeds of grudge tangling at my ankles when I was in Brisbane. People were patient here, in the sun. They knew how to bide their time.

For time was different in the river city. Time was different things to different people up here. And when you have a malleable clock, you have protons and neutrons firing in all sorts of directions. It gave the city a slovenly, haphazard appearance. Oh, it's the humidity. It's the sunshine, people would tell you. But there was genuine design beneath this, the country's most laissez-faire and 'liveable' city.

It was this surface unpredictability, this carefree relaxedness, which made Brisbane impossible to read. And also very dangerous when it wanted to be. Murders there had a purpose, a point to make, and a lot of them sank a deep bore into the past.

I pondered this at the surf club, still nursing a tender head courtesy of Igor the Russian. I couldn't get poor James Fenton Browne out of my aforementioned wounded head. I had a feeling Dexter Dupont was trying to tell me something but couldn't, for reasons of his own survival.

And an old Brisbane murder had left a welt in my pale ankle. On my way back from Bribie I'd stopped in at the offices of *The Courier-Mail*, and there, in front of a microfiche machine in the newspaper's small, crypt-like library, after an eternity of spooling brittle rolls of film, I had added yet another befuddling piece to the jigsaw of this case. An old newspaper story, a copy of which I held on the deck of the surf club in the face of a stiff, briny onshore breeze.

His name was Anton Johns, 37, an art appraiser formerly of Hamilton, Brisbane. He'd had a nice house on the river, the walls groaning with the pop art of minor Warhols and his namesake, Jasper Johns. Anton entertained all types at all hours, according to neighbours. He was a 'bohemian', with an Errol Flynn moustache, shoulder-length hair, and a penchant for wearing a cape − garb more commonly found in Viennese opera houses in the nineteenth century.

Mr Johns had been found dead in the Brisbane River not far from the William Jolly Bridge late one afternoon in 1971. Two fingers had been cut clean from his left hand.

All this had happened just days after the prostitute Legs was found dead of a drug overdose.

And it had happened within a few hundred metres of the hotel room of a young police officer from Sydney's 21 Division who, as the body was hooked out of the river, was packing his overnight bag and heading for the airport and home and possibly into the arms of his future wife.

Anton Johns, the article revealed, was known around town and in art circles as the Priest.

How, then, could he be living in an apartment building that I could see from my caravan park a full thirty-five years later?

11

UP HERE, PEOPLE wait for more than ten minutes in traffic and they call it gridlock. They can have fresh seafood, steaks as big as hubcaps and delicious produce prepared by master chefs for a pittance, and they question the size of their bills. They can park in the CBD without having to put a second mortgage on the house, can enjoy some of the great natural beaches on earth and winter lasts for half an hour. It is one of the great mysteries to me, as a freshly-minted retiree to this part of the world, why Queenslanders quite simply take for granted the riches at their disposal.

It's staggering to have great, primordial rainforests reachable by car in the time it used to take me to travel the nine kilometres from my house in inner Sydney to the Parramatta office of regional police headquarters. And still they grizzle.

After I'd gone through my case notes at the Main Beach Surf Club, I took *Pig Pen* out on to the Broadwater. I needed to clear my head. Not far past the Spit seaway I beached on South Stradbroke and threw in a lazy line. Looking south, I could see the Gold Coast metropolis, so close you could almost touch it, yet here I was with my bare feet in the sand waiting for the scream of my Alvey.

If I had a spare hand, I would have pinched myself.

Later, I pulled up some shade under a casuarina and read through the information my son, Jack, had sent me on Peel Island. I am a complete computer Luddite. My generation missed computers. Our brains don't work that way. This is a source of great disappointment to my son. When I need something, I telephone him, then he goes on to the internet, retrieves it, prints it out and posts it to me.

He calls mine a medieval way of retrieving information. I tell him – up yours. I enlighten him that it didn't hurt the younger generation to know how to lick a stamp. He says, Dad, they're self-adhesive these days. I tell him not to speak to his father like that.

What was the connection between all these deaths in the art world going back to the seventies, Ian Fairweather, Peel Island and the creeping feeling that my presence in southeast Queensland was not particularly appreciated?

Verne, the van park manager, informed me, on the quiet, that a stranger had been seen loitering about my annexe during my sojourn in Brisbane as houseguest of Igor the Terrible. Verne winked repeatedly when he told me this, indicating that whatever I was mixed up in was not his concern, though it was best I knew of these developments. It was a knowing wink between two old guys, without the nudge.

'Just giving you the heads up,' Verne said, with his annoying click of the tongue. I had heard Jack use this catchphrase – heads up – and wondered from whom Verne might have absorbed it. It sounded very odd coming out of this leathery, canvas-hatted Queenslander.

Two of my semi-permanent neighbours at Main Beach had also spotted the mysterious shadow-play of an intruder on the candy-striped annexe that extended off my caravan. There had been 'a little jiggle' at my front door. And then the stranger was gone.

My immediate suspect was the Boltcutter, coming to finish the job he had started all those years ago in the dunes of Wanda Beach when I'd felt the cold muzzle of his gun at my left temple. My thoughts, that night amongst the seagrass, had not, curiously enough, been of my wife Peg tucked up at home. Nor did my life spool before my eyes. They were concerned with the frosty touch of the gun at my head, and my conviction that the doorway to oblivion was round, black and infinite.

It was too hot and glary to read on Straddy. I stretched out in the lattice shade of the casuarina and fell asleep. Two and a half hours later I woke, not knowing where I was. It can be very discombobulating when the first thing you see after a deep nap is a large motorised fibreglass banana gliding past in the boat channel.

I was as red as a rash on a baby's backside. It hurt to move. I didn't need to be reminded in this way that I was still a novice Queenslander.

Back at the caravan my sunburn deepened and by late afternoon I was as hot as a sliver of radioactive waste. Verne, hearing my whimpering, poked his big, sun-spotted melon through the flap of my annexe and asked if he could help.

'Yeah,' I told him. 'Cover me head to foot in cold T-bones. Dunk me in chilled yak's milk. Anything.'

I ended up being nursed that evening by Verne's wife, Abigail, who permitted me use of their tiny bathtub, which she filled with tepid water and pungent smatterings of tea-tree oil. Whilst Verne did the van park's rubbish run, she popped her head into the bathroom several times to check on my welfare. She was, in fact, a little *too* interested in my welfare. She lingered at the door and shook her head in pity. She looked like a chef waiting impatiently to remove a lobster from the pot.

Back in the van Verne had left me several messages from my estate agent telling me he had many 'delicious' prospects for me to view in the morning. There was another from Peg, who said the packing up in Sydney was almost done and she'd be on the road in a couple of days. And what did I want to do with the broken karaoke machine in the garage?

I ignored the messages, and instead rang Jack to ask him to saddle up on the internet and find me even remote references to a woman, first name 'Rosemary', who might have been a nurse on Peel Island in the fifties.

Within the hour Verne slipped a sheaf of faxes beneath my van door. Jack had tracked down three Rosemary's on the internet, who may or may not have been my Peel Island nurse. He had found two Brisbane area phone numbers for two of the Rosemary's who may or may not have been stationed on Peel Island when Ian Fairweather may or may not have made his pilgrimage to Peel Island, that outpost of suffering and misery and loneliness, where poor James Fenton Browne took his last breath.

I was hesitant to ring the numbers. I was battered and bruised. It was a hall of mirrors. Alice's wonderland. Every known cliché for a confusing passage to hell. I'd had enough warnings to bolt the van door shut and pull the sheet over my head. Would one of these calls simply trigger another train of events? A train that could end, quite frankly, in disaster?

The first phone number for the woman who may or may not be Rosemary, the Peel Island nurse, rang out.

The second was answered on the fifth ring.

'Is this Rosemary?' I asked.

'Yes,' the woman said. She sounded old but spritely.

I explained who I was, though it may have sounded ludicrous to her. Then I asked, 'Were you ever a nurse at the leprosarium on Peel Island in the nineteen fifties?'

'Why, yes,' she said.

Before I'd realised it, I'd turned into the eager young constable of the sixties.

'Rosemary, did you or did you not ever meet a painter by the name of Ian Fairweather on Peel Island in the nineteen fifties?'

There was a long silence.

'Perhaps you'd like to meet for morning tea?' she said sweetly.

12

IT WAS THE novelist William Faulkner who said, 'The past is not dead. In fact, it's not even past.' And it's a quote that tumbled into my sunburned head as I read about the notorious Peel Island before my meeting with Rosemary, who quite possibly held a secret about the painter Ian Fairweather and indeed the clues to a string of murders dating back more than thirty years.

Life's strange, isn't it, when a gentle elderly lady living quietly in an old Queenslander in bayside Manly could unwittingly possess information from the past that may solve a bloody puzzle in the present.

Dear old Rosemary Pentimento, taking her morning walk on the path above the rust-red shoreline of Moreton Bay, the rubber nib of her cane gripping the concrete pathway, the salted gusts riffling her dress, while out in the bay, ancient Peel Island sees the sunsets and dawns come and go, century after century. And a ragged, overweight old ex-cop in the middle of this mess tries to draw longitude and latitude and invisible isobars together, grasping at earth and sky, to form a picture of the past that will solve a riddle of the moment.

Faulkner and Peel and the Boltcutter and the missing

eyes of James Fenton Browne. It was all getting too much for me.

I needed a beer. I repaired to my usual table at the surf club for the comfort of the singing poker machines, the voices of excited children drifting in and out, the mutter of gulls. I needed to be tethered to real life to face the historical horrors of Peel Island.

You would have heard of it, Peel Island – an idyllic little 400-hectare jewel of an island in Moreton Bay that, if you study a map of it as closely as I have, resembles a strange, upside down marine creature of mythic quality or, if you want to be more pedestrian about it, a side of beef hanging off a hook in a butcher's cold room.

It sits off Dunwich on North Stradbroke Island, a forgotten fragment, still with the mantle of death about it, even though the leprosarium and quarantine stations have been shut down for almost half a century.

Studying local historian Peter Ludlow's extensive writings on the island, the whole place and its history disturbed me. If Queensland was fresh and positive and physically beautiful – which it was – here was its black spot, its own backyard heart of darkness.

I'll spare you the most harrowing details, though Peel Island and human suffering are indivisible. In the late eighteen hundreds it became a quarantine station when diseases like typhoid and cholera arrived by ship along with their European hosts. The infected, within sight of the Australian mainland, were lodged in draughty houses, huts and even tents. Their chest-loads of possessions were aired on the beach or on the grass in front of their rustic huts. Clothes and blankets were scoured.

It would later become the Inebriate Asylum. A postage stamp of earth, surrounded by shark-infested waters, where alcoholics dried out. I couldn't imagine the daily horror, the scything duties and work in the mattress factory amidst the tremors and delirium and nightmares of withdrawing from an addiction. According to Ludlow's history, one patient wrote that Peel Island was 'this most awful degraded Hell I can imagine darkening God's earth'.

(In another time, would Peg have sent me to this place? At one stage in my life, after I was transferred from 21 Division citing 'mental exhaustion', it may not have been out of the realms of possibility.)

As is the way of human nature, it too became a place where those souls amongst us who did not fit in to what we like to call 'polite society' were dumped by their families and forgotten. A place just a quick tinny ride from Cleveland, which may as well have been the edge of the world. A place from which you didn't return.

Then came the lepers at the beginning of the twentieth century. Another chapter of horror.

I began to understand what had been so attractive about Peel to Fairweather, the hermit genius. Here was a community that exactly mirrored his inner isolation and turmoil. The feelings of abandonment he'd suffered since early childhood, when he was loaned out to ageing aunts and other relatives while his parents continued their gala lives in India, before reuniting with him when he was ten. His knowledge that he did not fit into the strictures and structures of functioning society. Peel Island was his inner psyche. He *was* Peel Island.

It took me a couple of days to ingest the material. Then I hauled the old Peugeot up to Manly, and took tea with Mrs Rosemary Pentimento.

She was exactly as I imagined. A small-framed woman with a wistful little blue-grey cloud of loosely curled hair, and eyes to match. I shook her hand at the front door to her immaculately neat timber cottage and her skin felt as soft and fragile as rice paper.

'It's nice to have company,' she said, ushering me towards a chair on her sunny front balcony. It was completely enclosed on two sides by glass louvers, and for a moment I felt I was floating underwater.

On a small table sat a teapot and two cups and saucers, all with matching red roses embossed in the glaze, and a plate of golden-topped scones. I felt I had entered another decade.

She sat in the chair opposite me and folded her hands.

'Thank you for seeing me.'

'Oh, it's nice to see a face other than my doctor's,' she said, smiling.

'I may be wasting your time, Mrs Pentimento. I am acting only on hunches.'

'You wanted to know about Fairweather?'

'That's right.'

'I am amazed at the sudden interest in him.'

'Sudden?'

'In the past few months you are the fourth person who has sat in that chair wanting to know about Fairweather.'

'I am?'

'One was someone who, once upon a time, we might have referred to as a "spiv". Are you familiar with the term?'

'I am.'

'An objectionable man, he was. I have for many years been involved with the local school of arts, and he was – how may I put it? Not the sort of gentleman I would have expected to be interested in the finer arts.'

She seemed to blush at this.

'And the other person?'

'A young man. Agitated, as the young tend to be these

days. But most knowledgeable not so much about Fairweather but about Peel Island and its inmates over the years.'

'And the third?'

'You may have seen him in the paper. The director of
the gallery.'

'Dexter Dupont.'

'Yes. Mr Dupont. He was most surprised at my knowledge of French. Not what he expected from a little old
biddy by the bay.'

I couldn't help thinking there was a song in that – 'The
Little Old Biddy by the Bay'.

She told me of her extraordinary life, writing for many
years for local newspapers under a male pseudonym;
drawing the inmates at the hospital on Peel Island where
she worked as a nurse; travels throughout Europe and the
United States.

But I needed to know about Fairweather.

'I met him, yes,' she said, smiling and looking down at
her hands. 'There was talk for years that we had become
... Well, romantically attached. But we all know Mr
Fairweather was not inclined towards the fairer sex. Nor
the other, in fact. It is my belief he was the only completely
sexless man I have ever met. Excuse my language.'

He had stayed in one of the abandoned shacks for eleven
days. He ate little. He sat quietly with several of the patients
of Peel Island. Then he went away.

'And the paintings?' I asked, almost impatiently.

'Ah, the paintings.'

'Were there any?'

'You may not believe this, but when he left the island
I went to his shack. Out of curiosity, I suppose. A bit of a
stickybeak I was. They were draughty, the huts. Shocking
in winter, and in a storm. And he did what he had always

done, or so I read. He had stuffed every crack in that place with canvasses.'

I had indeed been told about this habit of Fairweather's by Igor the Russian taxi driver. Once a painting was done it meant little to the master. It was the act of creation that was important. The finished work was the detritus of that process.

'Do you remember how many there were? What they were of? Can you ...'

'I retrieved them, of course. Some were not salvageable. There were twenty-two that I recovered.'

I swallowed loudly. 'And ... you ... where are they now?'

'I stored them in the hospital. I tried to get in touch with Ian but he seemed to have vanished. He had an assistant, a foreign gentleman. He told me he looked after all of Mr Fairweather's business.'

'An assistant?'

'A large gentleman with a shaved head. I didn't think much of him. He wore thongs and smelled of diesel. Then my work on the island ended. I went back to the mainland, got married and had children. I returned to civilian life, as they say.'

'And that was it?'

'That was it.'

'Oh.'

'They were horrible pictures. Beautiful, but horrible. I never saw them again. I never wanted to.'

I studied her across the table. Was I being conned? Did she know more than she was telling me? Did she have the Fairweathers stashed in an air-conditioned vault?

And who was the agitated young man who had come to visit? Was it the doomed James Fenton Browne? As for the thonged assistant, it appeared I had more to discuss with Igor the Terrible.

'I hope that helps you,' she said.

'Yes, thank you.' I sipped the dregs of my tea, which had gone stone cold.

13

IT WAS TIME to go sailing.

But first I had to see my old friend Igor once more. He was holding back on me like the good retired KGB agent that he probably was. I planned to hold him down in his recliner rocker armed with his dusty bust of Lenin until he talked. Once upon a time I had ways of making people talk. Brandishing a plaster revolutionary had not been one of them.

I towed *Pig Pen* all the way up the highway, over the Gateway Bridge and on to Bribie Island. I could feel my little tin dinghy pulling at the tail of the Peugeot. I fully expected the steering column to smoke.

En route to Bribie I thought of Rosemary Pentimento, the Little Old Biddy by the Bay, and how there were so many people in every city in the world, sitting quietly in their homes, whiling away the years, with so much of the past in their heads. So many stories of life and loves, of great encounters and historical moments. All of this history, enough to fill countless volumes, but ebbing towards oblivion. Stories that were the invisible connecting tissue to recorded history. And who was collecting it? Nobody. It seemed to me we no longer cared about our stories.

Our own heritage. Even our own antecedents. People had enough personal data in their own backyards to occupy and entertain them for a lifetime. And nobody seemed to care any more.

My son is an IT boffin. You can't tell him anything because he always has those iPod earphones in his ears. You can't show him anything because he's already seen it on the internet. How quickly things have changed. I filled the cabin of the Peugeot with the gloomy clouds of my introspection all the way to Igor the Terrible's house.

I pulled into the old man's driveway. It was eerily quiet. As quiet as Red Square in the dead of winter. (Not that I'd been there, but a quick call to Jack and no doubt he could produce reams of paperwork on the subject.)

From the veranda I could hear someone sobbing. It was Manya — I could see her in the kitchen, her head in her hands. I tapped on the flyscreen door.

'Manya?' I said timidly. I tapped again. She looked up, startled.

'Manya, it's me.'

She put on her glasses and craned towards the door.

'OHHH,' she said, waving me in.

'Manya. What's happened?'

'It's IGOR,' she said, her face red, her eyes puffy and tear-filled. 'He have a HEART ATTACK.' I walked her from the kitchen and into the lounge. I was about to lower her into the big brown rocker, then thought better of it, and steered her towards the couch.

'POOR IGOR,' she said.

'Manya. Tell me what happened.'

It had been a heart attack all right, early that morning, but not your usual act of God. It took me an hour to extract the truth.

'They come in here with GUN,' she howled. 'They put to IGOR'S HEAD and say, "TELL US, TELL US, or we PUT YOUR BRAINS ALL OVER WALL."'

'Calm down, Manya, it's all right. Who was it?'

'How do I know? MEN WITH GUN. They make him draw on piece of paper. Write down. I was in shock. I couldn't SPEAK. They say, "Don't move or we BLOW YOUR BRAINS OUT TOO." I see Igor go pale, and sweating, then when he finished drawing of island he GRAB HIS CHEST and the men go. I never forget their faces. NEVER. Ohhhhh, POOR IGOR.'

'The island? He drew an island?'

'WHAT?'

'IGOR DREW AN ISLAND?' I shouted back at her. I was getting a headache with all the shouting. Every time I was around these people I seemed to get a headache.

'Yes, EE-arn's island. He dead thirty year, EE-arn, and still he haunt us. I must get back to HOSP-EE-TAL.'

'Manya, Manya, slow down. Have you called the police?'

'I no call police.'

'Why not?'

'Igor don't like no police. Every little tap on the door, Igor, he worried. He been worried about the tap on the door half his life. First in RUSSIA and now BRIBIE ISLAND. It all EE-ARN'S FAULT.'

'Tell me about the men.'

'How they do this to AN OLD MAN? One he dresses in a suit the colour of the banana. YELLOW LIKE BANANA. He have the gun. The other a hood, like a street kid. I never seen him. But I know the YELLOW MAN. I seen him before a long time ago. I could NEVER FORGET such a man.'

It had to be the Boltcutter, Dapper Dan himself, with one of his disposable, drugged-up street urchins as sidekick.

Igor was lucky to be alive and with all his fingers and toes intact, let alone his brains. As was Manya.

'What do you mean, you'd met him before? Manya? MANYA. Think clearly for me.'

'Long time ago. We sell him EE-arn pictures. One every now and then. When we need the money.'

'You did? When?'

'Before EE-arn die.'

'Before?'

'BEFORE. Then after EE-arn die, too. Igor say NEVER TELL ANYONE. But now I tell. Igor not want to go to jail. He say EE-arn gave him pictures, but there were SO MANY. Ohhhh, IGOR. Then we go to island for the other pictures. The SECRET pictures of the LEPERS. And Igor, he think he get smart. He bring back one but the rest he bury on island. For the FUTURE Manya, he say. This EE-arn, he be BIG one day. We finally sell the one LEPER picture not long ago, see, to this man in the yellow suit. He pay us cash. Then I see this PICTURE, it go for ONE MILLION DOLLARS. They say this EE-arn's MASTERPIECE. Can you believe? And Igor, he FURIOUS. He say we got ripped OFF by this man. So they talk on the phone and Igor say he got plenty more where that came from and he going to SELL TO SOMEONE ELSE, goodbye. Then we get tap on the door. Now Igor DYING.'

'Manya, do you have relatives you could stay with for a while?'

'Yes. In D'yakovskoye.'

'In Russia.'

'OF COURSE IN BLOODY RUSSIA.'

'Listen, Manya. Listen to me carefully. This is what we're going to do.'

Which is how I found myself casting off from Cleveland

in *Pig Pen* with an agitated, at times hysterical seventy-seven-year-old Russian immigrant with a shouting problem, and heading for Peel Island.

She had protested LOUDLY when I failed to take the off-ramp to the hospital where poor Igor lay, tubed up and semi-comatose. She'd threatened to jump from the car and we'd had a minor wrestling match in the front seat of the Peugeot for a few anxious moments, sending it drunkenly across three lanes of highway at the car's top speed, with *Pig Pen* swaying and bobbing dangerously behind.

But eventually I calmed her down with direct threats of calls to the police and immigration officials – even to the estate of EE-arn.

I would find out later that for a long time the lives of these Russians of Bribie Island had been unwittingly intersecting with major Sydney, London and Paris gangsters and even a profoundly corrupt former New South Wales magistrate, and they had been, on more than one occasion, within a whisker of being deprived of their breezy Bribie idyll on Red Emperor Drive (where else would a former communist sympathiser live on Bribie Island?).

An industry had also grown around people like Igor and Manya – a shadow-cabinet world of price-jacking contemporary art, fake bidders, press manipulation, forgeries, bogus auctions and corrupt appraisers. I had no doubt James Fenton Browne and Anton Johns had been guilty of the same crime in the art world. They were both genuinely interested in the art itself. Silly, deluded souls.

I had very little experience with boats, both on the trailer and in the water. Especially in the water. What do you expect from a cop whose beat was the most heavily populated urbanised postcode in Australia? My job did not include membership of the CYC.

I ordered Manya into the bow and with great exertion pushed the dinghy from the ramp and struggled into the back of the boat. The motor started first go, thank goodness, filling me with the false music of hope, along with a generous burst of outboard fumes.

It was mid-afternoon. I knew nothing of the nautical logistics of Moreton Bay. And there were dark clouds on the horizon.

What could possibly go wrong?

14

Do you know what it feels like when a bullet passes through your hair? Well, let me tell you, you don't want to know. Especially if you sport a short-back-and-sides.

I had thrown out the anchor of *Pig Pen* just offshore at Peel Island. Manya was sobbing quietly at the front of the boat. We were bobbing in just a metre or so of water. It was twilight, my most loathed time of day.

'You wait here,' I said to her, making a pronounced 'stop' sign with my right palm. 'Poor IGOR,' she blubbered. I stepped into cold, slimy mud.

On the perilous trip from Cleveland she had told me where Igor had stashed his cache of Fairweather canvasses. Buried in an old meat safe Igor had lined himself with fibro sheeting and canvas. Behind the last hut in the row of female quarters.

I squelched through the mud with great difficulty and a measure of fear. Queenslanders may be used to wandering around barefooted and wading into wild water with nothing to protect their hooves, but not so a kid from South Sydney.

I wished Peg could see me. What am I doing? Well, darling, I'm retrieving millions of dollars' worth of lost art

from a former leper colony on an island in the gathering
dark with nothing on my feet, no shovel to help recover
the buried treasure, and with an old killer of my acquaintance brandishing a loaded weapon, and likely to pop out
from behind a groundsel bush at any second. Oh yes, and
it's possible I'm being pursued by a French gallery director;
a tall, Albino former Anglican priest impersonating a long-
deceased art dealer; and our real-estate agent Geraldo for
not returning his calls about a spectacular canal-front home
with lap pool and jukebox.

Instead, someone shouted at me from the island's shore.
'You – stop!' It was the voice of a jockey. Or an adolescent
boy. 'You – stop, now!'

'What?' I asked. I was pretty sure I didn't know anyone
on Peel Island. Then I saw the muzzle flash and felt the heat
of a bullet singe the hairs on my right ear.

Before I even realised what was happening, I let out a
feeble 'Who?' – like some stunned, ageing owl caught in
unfamiliar surrounds. And that's when another bullet went
clean through the left side of my torso.

I stood in shock. I suddenly felt very heavy. The mud was
rising up to my ankles. My mouth was open in a perfect black
'O', or at least that's how I saw myself, for as the ferocious
heat from the wound began slamming through my body, I did
have what could only have been a nanosecond-long out-of-
body experience. And the 'O' of my mouth was like a giant
full stop. Perhaps that's how life ended. With punctuation.

Then my assassin stepped forward onto the grey sand and
for a moment I thought I recognised his outline. Where had
I seen it? I knew that shape. At that second, the tall, ghostly
figure of Anton Johns appeared from the row of old Lazaret
buildings that were now just black geometric objects in
the gloom.

Keep moving, I told myself. Keep stepping forward. I stopped just a few metres from land, for the whole area was suddenly lit up with gun flashes that were not directed at me. The bones of trees and the pale timbers of ancient buildings were X-rayed by the weapon flashes. Then everything turned black again.

At that point I did not feel any pain. Adrenalin lifted me out of the mud and onto dry land. Dead in the foliage – for a second time in his life – was the long, insect-like Anton Johns, his white hair askew and decorated with spots of his own blood. Not far away was the prostrate body of his little bodyguard, Robert, who was responsible for the hole through my person. I would have kicked him, hard, if it hadn't disrespected the dear departed.

My legs crumpled and I dropped to the sand and spinifex. I could hear Manya's ghostly wail from the dinghy.

I was trying to work out an exit strategy when I heard the gun click at my right ear. I was burning up, and when the muzzle touched my neck it was so cold it felt the opposite, like the branding iron from hell.

'Daniel?' I said.

'How nice that we could meet again. I am having a profound feeling of déjà vu.'

'Wanda Beach. 1969.'

'Oh yes. When we were in our prime. Now look at us. Two old men at twilight.'

I could smell his expensive aftershave behind the mud and the brine of the bay. He had taste, I'll give him that.

'Your boyfriend, Anton. That's no way to treat the ones you love, Daniel.'

'He was just a fair-weather friend.'

'Is that a joke?'

'You like it? He served his purpose. I'd been planning

this little project for thirty years. I've always had patience, you know.'

'They call it delayed gratification.'

'Do they? Delayed or not, Mr Fairweather will now underwrite my retirement.'

'And poor James Fenton Browne? Fenton's from Shakespeare, you know.'

'Of course I know. What do you take me for, a philistine? *The Merry Wives of Windsor*. And you, my dear fellow, have become Falstaff since our days cavorting at Wanda Beach.'

'Fenton could not resist the high life, could he?'

'No, he couldn't. And Fairweather is all the merry wives I could dream of. Are we finished with the gratuitous literary references? I told you I was patient. It's now time to finish the Wanda job, albeit almost forty years later ...'

What had I expected to happen? In the movies, Manya may have quietly snuck out of the dinghy and clubbed the Boltcutter with the anchor. She may have been an ex-KGB agent and killed him with a sudden blow to the neck. But this was not a Hollywood flick.

I could feel the muzzle on my neck, then pressed against my forehead. I could hear crickets and the faint slap of water and the shift of crab claws in the primordial mud, or so I thought.

When the world went white it did not register to me that I was dead at all. This isn't so bad, I remember thinking. White is nicer than black, isn't it?

When I opened my eyes I was lying on my side, holding my thigh. The world was tilted sideways. Lying next to me was the inimitable head of Dapper Dan the Antiques Man, a.k.a. the Boltcutter, his eyes wide open, his mouth agape. How small he looked with the top of his head blown off above the eyebrows.

I recall a lamp being lit and placed amongst the strands of sea grass. And seeing the youngish man sit on the sand, grasp his knees, and drop his revolver.

He didn't even look at me. He was staring, bemused I supposed, at the old woman howling in the dinghy anchored in the shallows. 'EEEE-GORRRR,' she wailed to the gathering storm clouds, her arms raised in the air.

Three days after I was admitted to hospital, a gentleman matching the description of that young man, my saviour of Peel Island, visited my bedside. Turns out this kid had as much patience as the dead Dapper, and for more than two decades – or from a specific day when he was just twelve years old – he had been hunting a very special person, namely his mother's murderer. And all that research and observation and playing private detective had come to its explosive conclusion on Peel Island. I just happened to be a piece of collateral damage.

He gently placed a small piece of rolled parchment, tied with a red piece of ribbon, on my food table. The ribbon looked familiar. I had received a gift from this stranger before – a polished bullet.

He stood until I unwrapped the roll of mildewed canvas. It was a soiled painting. A head. The mouth wide and forming an 'O'. The skin scabrous. The eyes dull and dead. It was signed 'Fairweather, 1959'.

'A memento,' the man said. 'Of our adventure.'

'How very kind of you.'

'You're welcome.'

'So I meet my doppelganger, at last. The man who has been my shadow for the past few weeks. The man who ruined my retirement.'

'I needed you,' he said. 'To bring me in. You completed the puzzle. You led me to ...'

'The Boltcutter.'

'Correct.'

'The retired gangster and art lover.'

'The one and only.'

'And why would that piece of human ebola virus interest a young man such as you?'

'He killed my mother.'

'He did, did he? And who was your mother?'

'They called her Legs. But to me, she was just Mum.'

Later in the week I read in *The Courier-Mail* that the Queensland Art Gallery had been left an anonymous bequest of several previously unknown masterpieces by the late, great painter Ian Fairweather. There was a photograph of my friend Dexter Dupont smiling beside one of the pictures. He had teeth after all, did Dexter.

I stayed in hospital for a month. In that time Peg arrived on the Gold Coast, found us a house, moved the furniture in and redecorated the place. She even took a few tips from Nurse Reginald, apparently an interior decorator in his spare time.

That first night in my new home, having pushed myself around the house (and almost into the canal out the back) in my wheelchair and inspected the walls heavy with effigies of plaster seahorses and starfish and paintings of pelicans sleeping on wharf pylons and schools of dolphins passing through sun-dappled water, I asked, 'And my retirement painting? From the hospital?'

'That ratty old thing?' she said. 'Turfed it, my love. It was so *not* the Gold Coast.'

After dinner I sat alone on the back balcony looking down at *Pig Pen*, lashed to a jetty big enough to accommodate a cruise ship.

Peg put a VB in my hand. 'Why don't you take the boat out tomorrow? Throw in a line? You're retired, for goodness sake. How's the weather looking?'

'The weather?' I said, after a long time. 'Fair.'

TWO

THE MURDER TREE

1

IT HAS OFTEN been said that prior to the moment of death, your life flashes before your eyes.

By flash, do they mean a condensed nanosecond of all you've experienced from the crib? Or a spool of film, projected at incredible speed, all blurred and making no sense? I prefer a good old-fashioned slide show, with motes of dust tumbling in the heat and light from the clunky projector, and the screen askew on a rust-pitted stand. But a flash? I've staged slide nights that made *Lawrence of Arabia* look like an advertisement for ChapStick.

And when it comes to this final look back, who would know if it happens or not? The person experiencing it, the only punter in the house, is dead anyway. Aren't they? I'm as sceptical of this as the tunnel-of-white-light loonies. If death is like driving through the sooty tube under Sydney Harbour, I'll be buggered if I'm paying a toll for the privilege. As my Uncle Felix said on his own deathbed – fiddlesticks.

It was precisely this time last year that my brick-like, stoic mug made it into the newspapers because of all that hullabaloo about Ian Fairweather and Bribie Island, the gangster known as the Boltcutter and the mad race across

Moreton Bay to Peel Island where all the fun and games turned fatal.

After that little adventure, for six months, when I should have been taking out the tinny on the Broadwater and giving the Alvey a workout, I convalesced at home on a plastic banana lounge overlooking the canal. I read cheap detective novels and monitored the curious life of man-made canals with a pair of horse-racing binoculars. It's more interesting than you think. I kept a little logbook by my side, and if I leaf through it now I could tell you that from my sagging fold-out bed I saw several shark fins scissor past, the usual charter boats groaning with tourists, a gondola featuring a genuine gondolier complete with straw hat, tight trousers and striped shirt (I'm uncertain, to this day, whether he was real, or the colourful by-product of my extensive medications) and a naked young lady who zipped by on a jetski, though even she could have been a blurred dream from my youth.

In short, I inched towards my normal self, albeit with a couple of plugged holes in my leg and midriff, and the nightmares of the Priest and the Boltcutter stopped. That's when I declared to my Peg that it was time I returned to bona fide retirement.

'No more hijinks?' she repeatedly asked. Peg had never really grasped the dangers of my previous employment as a police officer. Nor the accidental adventures of last year. She seemed to think that cleaning the streets of criminal vermin, putting life and limb at risk, and getting shot were things men did to let off a little steam and satisfy something in their primitive natures.

'No more hijinks,' I said.

For several weeks, early in my recovery, Peg had returned to Sydney to stay with friends and I had been assigned police protection. I told them it was a waste of time – that if one of the Boltcutter's associates really wanted to exact revenge on his expired, bullet-riddled behalf, it wouldn't be difficult to steal up on a prostrate ex-copper about to turn sixty dozing off on a banana lounge. When you live on a canal, all manner of murk can inch in with the tide.

So it was I spent interminable hours playing poker on the back deck with my young constable protector, Rory – a wet, fresh-faced kid with an uncertain grasp of his chosen profession. Having said that, he was a whiz on the barbecue and cooked a mean New York cut steak.

'Rory,' I said to him one evening, feeling either heavily philosophical or a tad light-headed from antibiotics washed down with VB. 'Do you really want to end up like me?'

'Waddya mean?' he said.

'Waddya *mean* waddya mean? Look at me, Rory. I should be supping at the table of life's rewards. Visited by loving grandchildren and as full as a Catholic girl's sock with pride at a career spent serving my fellow citizens. Instead, here I lie, fat and foul, sniffing not the roses, Rory, not the roses, but catching a whiff of human sewage off my canal of dreams ...'

I'd lost Rory at that point. I'd lost myself. Write this down as a life lesson from an old warrior – never mix booze with lorazepam.

'Whatever,' Rory said, bored in the way that the youth of today get bored when life fails to seize them by the throat. He put his head in his hands.

'Rory. RORY,' I continued. 'What do you want to DO with your life, son. Inspector? Commissioner?'

'I wanna do schoolies next year,' said Rory.

At my request, Rory went back to his usual roster and I was left alone on the canal, albeit with a little snub-nosed companion tucked inside the small blue esky that sat permanently beside the sagging banana.

Then Peg returned, and steadily I recovered, making little excursions to the monstrous shopping precinct, Pacific Fair, where I nearly got skittled and killed by the kiddies' train that tootles about the complex (the driver alleged he sounded his choo choo whistle, but I'll be damned if I heard it), and back to The Spit, where Peg wheeled my chair beneath a casuarina and I nibbled on crab sandwiches, wondering if I'd ever rejoin society in quite the same way again.

But the human spirit is an amazing thing, and just a few months ago I was walking awkwardly with a cane, and the month after that I was back in my faithful Peugeot 504 running errands and generally introducing myself to the world once more.

It was during this ebullient period that I struck upon a nice, quiet and safe hobby to, as Peg so eloquently put it, keep me out of the hijinks game. I had decided one evening, staring at the wind-ravaged palm tree at the rear of our house, that I would study genealogy and flesh out the leaves on my hitherto bare and undiscovered family tree.

'It's time I traced my roots,' I announced to Peg.

'That's nice,' she said with the same degree of interest she had expressed in prior obsessions of mine, such as tracking every movie appearance of the Peugeot 504 (personal highlight? *The Day of the Jackal*) and my interest in time travel.

'As my first senior-sergeant once told me, you shake a tree hard enough, you never know what nuts might fall out.'

'That's nice,' she said.

'Who knows what I might find, right? Murderers, poets, potters? I'll be facing the ultimate question, Peg. Who am I?

What is it that made me who I am today? Where am I from? And, in turn, what is my purpose? I have stared down death, Peg. It's natural to be asking these things.'

'Okay,' she said, leafing through a magazine.

'And how much trouble can you get into, tracing your family tree?'

That is the question that has come back to haunt me, as I sit here, chained by both wrists and ankles, with an eyeless hood over my head, in a pitch-black room deep inside Queensland's oldest building – the convict windmill on Wickham Terrace.

Who could have known that a few insignificant trips to the refurbished State Library on the banks of the Brisbane River, during which I often daydreamed through the library windows, would lead me up the river's winding course to the great Wivenhoe and Somerset dams, and to a corpse fatefully uncovered by our endless drought, and – thus – to the heart of a mystery that had waited almost two centuries to surface? That just a year after the last fiasco I would be in hijinks up to my cauliflower ears, *again*?

These, and other things in that so-called film of my life, unspooled before me as I waited, in agony, for my fate inside that old windmill, a citadel to Brisbane's brutal founding.

Then I heard a padlock spring open, a chain rattle and footsteps echo towards me.

2

WHEN I WAS a child, growing up in the greasy back lanes of South Sydney, the highlight of my week was quite literally the call of the rabbit-oh, and I experienced both a perverse attraction and a stomach-turning revulsion at the rows of skinned rabbits swinging with the gait of the horse and carriage as it passed the front of our crumbling terrace house. I didn't know it then, but I would later earn my living in a profession in which blood and guts were a common part of the landscape.

Another highlight of my childhoold was learning that in the nineteenth century, a member of our family had been a bushranger. I became obsessed with bushrangers, and of course Ned Kelly. I was punished for cutting a rectangle out of our only bucket. I ambushed innocent passers-by on our street, ordering them to stand and deliver. They rarely stood, and more often than not delivered a cuff across the back of my square head. There was a kid in my class at school whose name was Glen Rowan. I thought he was the luckiest boy in Australia.

Memory is a strange thing. I had never seen a genuine South Sydney rabbit-oh because they petered out around the end of the Great Depression. But my grandfather had

told me of them and must have described them so power-
fully that they became a part of the family's collective
memory, and in turn evolved into an actual experience for
me. If I close my eyes I can still see them, yet in fact I never
witnessed them. How can this happen?

As a grown man, I saw it time and again while taking the
confessions of assorted felons. If you ever want to meet
the most imaginative and creative people in society, forget
the novelists and painters, the poets and filmmakers. A
seasoned hit man or con artist can out-create them hands
down; can invent the most convoluted, plausible and
believable narratives time and again without missing a beat.
To be a great criminal is to be a great artist.

I have listened to murderers who can describe a room or
restaurant or train carriage in which they swear they were
during a killing – the architecture of their alibi – down to
such fine detail that I've later had to verify it, or not, with
my own eyes. The minutiae of their imaginings can be
so great, you can smell the coq au vin drifting out from a
restaurant kitchen, or hear a specific bus rumbling past a
specific house on a specific street at an exact time. They're
so convincing they end up convincing themselves, and all
that comes of this are muddied waters and a lot of wasted
legal fees at trial.

As for the bushranger, I have never been able to prove or
disprove the existence of one in my antecedents, and it has
been a question that has haunted my life. Peg says, get over
it. But I'm a curious fellow, and I hate things left unfinished.

That's how I found myself hitting the highway to
Brisbane in my coughing, trembling Peugeot, to once again
begin a peaceful and measured retirement. I had had a most
violent, unexpected retirement *interruptus*, and I was keen to
get it back on track.

This time Peg had organised my first mobile telephone.

'Now, if you get into any more mischief,' she said in her sing-along voice, reserved, or so I'd thought, for our son, 'you can ring home.'

She had of course seen me staring at it on the kitchen bench as if it was foreign matter dropped from outer space, and nudged me towards it.

'Even *you* can work out how to use it,' she said. 'Green is for go. Red for stop.'

'Get ready for the yellow light. Thanks, Big Ted.'

'You can do it.'

How wrong she was. And how totally incorrect she was to think that some flimsy piece of plastic and computer chip could possibly keep me safe in the advent of 'mischief'. I couldn't see it stopping a speeding bullet.

Yet there it remained, in the glove compartment of the car, and it was still there, chirping merrily, in the cool of the library car park during the hours I spent upstairs, chafing my feet merrily against the floral carpets during those tentative investigations into my family history.

I have a Queensland connection, you see. It was in this fair state that my relatives settled, a long way from the Irish peat bogs of our ancestral home, and scratched out a new life. It was Queensland that proved the perfect Petri dish for the family bushranger. If he had existed, I'd find him here in the State Library records.

What I had not anticipated was the popularity of genealogy. Arriving at the library mid-morning, I was immediately lured by the smell of roasted coffee beans at Tognini's Café, and sat out on the comfortable cream chairs leafing through my newspaper. I thought I had all the time in the world.

When I finally ambled up to the research room I noticed a queue the likes of which you usually only saw at All You

Can Eat food troughs in your local RSL. I stood in the line behind an elderly man with giant ears, and in those ears were lodged a pair of giant hearing aids. Each had several small antennae poking from the device. He looked like Ray Walston in *My Favorite Martian*. I bet he got great reception on SBS.

'How long, do you reckon?' I asked him.

He ignored me. There was a faint whistle about him and his monstrous electronic extrusions. I guessed he couldn't walk fifty metres without a pack of dogs following him.

I could see into the family-history zone and old men and women were hunched over computers and microfiche machines, so I decided to leave it until lunchtime. I had a hunch most of them would clear out around then.

It proved to be the right decision. It gave me time to explore the library. Somehow, I found myself in a red cube of a room with a little terrace of seats that seemed to hang out over the river itself.

I was the only person in this peculiar but deeply satisfying room, and the little slivers of light reflecting off the surface of the river meandered through the room like a school of pilchards. After a while, I forgot about the family bushranger; the dark, leafless limbs of my family tree yet to be explored; the healing bullet wounds in my leg and torso. I was having, as I had read about but never quite understood, a transcendental moment beside the Brisbane River.

In the end I got the nods. But I didn't want to leave the room. I would become a Buddhist. I wanted to be connected to all of nature and its beauty and be kind to animals and fill my person full of peace, tight as a helium balloon.

I watched the CityCats glide past like colourful, buoyant moments from my life as a heathen, carouser and all-round larrikin. I got lost in thoughts of the great Brisbane River itself, forming in the Stanley Ranges, meandering down to the city and pushing out into Moreton Bay, and felt I was hovering over it – a curious passage it has, curling and folding back on itself, as if resistant to dissipate and join the salted bay – and viewing my life in its entirety.

Then a single noise dropped me out of my reverie. A small clink. I turned, and there, sitting on one of the wooden benches near the back of the empty room, was a tiny bonsai tree in a jade-green glazed pot.

It had not been there when I entered. I stood, my wounds suddenly dull with pain, and approached the little tree. I sat beside it. Studied it. I'm no botanist, but it looked like the perfect, miniature facsimile of the grand fig trees you see around Brisbane. Under the pot was a gold envelope.

I retrieved the envelope and opened it, and inside was a single photograph.

It was a mistake, of course. To sit beside that beautiful tree, and to open the gold envelope. I knew it as I slid out the photograph. I could hear the 10 x 15 cm sheet chafe against the envelope as loud as the rumble of thunder in that peaceful room.

In the picture was a corpse, the likes of which I had never before seen. Partially mummified, the skin around the teeth stretched back, the eye sockets black as eternity, the body dressed in some sort of military uniform, the feet still shod in heavy boots, and in the exact centre of the forehead was a hole as big as a fifty-cent piece.

On the back of the picture was a mobile-phone number written in pencil. And one word, in capitals: LOGAN.

The room was a frenzy of reflected light. I thought only one thing – here we go again.

3

A LONG TIME ago, when I was a young firebrand cop in Sydney's notorious 21 Division, I saw a man killed by my partner, Greaves, during an ambush in the basement of a Kings Cross nightclub.

I didn't know, at the time, that Greaves had killed him. The victim was just a dark shape on the other side of his own blue muzzle flash, and I had closed my eyes and fired into the roof while Greaves' gun discharged with more accuracy. In that dank, mouldy space below the street, my partner had put a bullet through a stranger's heart.

Eventually, in the silence that followed, with the cordite burning the backs of our throats, we found a light and cautiously made our way over to the body. He was still breathing (gurgling, to be accurate), and Greaves applied what first aid he knew, but the man died right there before our eyes.

There was no question of taking time off work, just because you'd executed your duty. The deceased's own bullet had grazed my temple and carved a neat divot above my left ear, but I was at the station the next morning. Greaves, too, punched the clock for his regular shift.

We were both ordered to visit someone who was then

new to the force – a police psychologist – and we twiddled our thumbs and grunted a few answers to satisfy the young man on the other side of the desk. He looked barely out of high school. He did, ultimately, become my friend, and years later he offered some analysis of my proclivity for finding trouble. Or mischief, in Peg's words.

'To put it very simply, it's your face and manner,' the psychologist told me. 'You have the sort of demeanour that encourages people to tell you their stories. They don't need to, they're *compelled* to.'

'I have a compelling face,' I said.

'In a manner of speaking, yes.'

'Tell me something I don't already know,' I told him.

This all came back to me as I carried the bonsai tree and the mysterious gold envelope into the family-history area of the State Library. I felt a right goose with the tree, and I attracted some strange looks. But libraries are places where peculiar things happen, for some reason, and where the whole gamut of human eccentricity is on display. If you're at a party and you want to hear some curly stories about human nature, and there's a librarian present, stick to them like glue. They'll entertain you all night.

So my tree was at the low level of strange that day, as I secured a computer terminal and popped the little bonsai at my feet. I was, of course, tempted to telephone the number on the card. It was that old craving, the need to know. But I resisted, for all of a few hours.

I made no headway finding the family bushranger. Genealogy was a complex art, and I had no idea how to enter the labyrinth. I typed names and dates I thought I'd remembered from the tales that had been handed down through generations of my family, but nothing seemed to compute.

A kindly librarian remained patient with me and did all she could to put a little foot ladder at the base of my family tree, but for the life of me I could secure no solid footing.

The elderly Martian next to me with the whistling hearing aids smiled the smile of someone who feels superior in the vicinity of a novice. That smug smirk creased the whole right side of his wrinkly face. He shook his head and winked at me. I noticed that the black hairs on his ears were as long as the antennae poking from his ear pieces.

'You right there?' I finally said, miffed.

'Bit of trouble?'

'You could say that.'

'You got your ships right?'

'Pardon?'

'Got to make sure you get your ships right. The names of your ships. You get the ships wrong and you could be hunting down the wrong trail for years. It's all about the ships.'

I wanted to tell him he was giving me the absolute ships, but I desisted. He was right about one thing. One slip on the genealogical treasure hunt and you're off the track — gone, lost in the thickets of history.

I knew my relatives had come off a ship in Sydney, then made the long overland trek north to Brisbane and on to Gympie and Dalby. It may have been the lure of gold in the former, and of cattle in the latter. These, I guess, were the major currencies in the early to mid-1800s. I simply couldn't remember the name of the ship. I checked birth and death records for Dalby and still nothing.

I had one of those existential moments when I wondered if these relatives had ever lived at all; if the stories on which I'd constructed my life were in fact fairytales. Who knows, maybe there *was* no big, burly bushranger firing guns through my proud heritage, but instead a latrine cleaner or dried-cow-pat merchant flogging his wares and trailing the permanent scent of animal effluent. A true nobody who did nothing and died forgotten. It wasn't something you bragged about at the pub, and Lord knows I'd been crowing about the bushranger for close to fifty years.

I sat facing a blank computer terminal in the library, unsure of where to go next with this project, when I impulsively Googled the name on the back of the envelope. Logan + history + Brisbane.

And there it was, first cab off the rank – Captain Patrick Logan.

I quietly opened the gold envelope and slipped the picture out. The Martian to my left was leaning right in close to his screen and the white light of it smeared his thick spectacles. I had an empty seat to my right. I snatched glances at the corpse in the picture, and the rust-brown jacket in which it was swathed, and the wrap-across flap of the coat secured with a line of elaborate gold buttons, and the clods at each shoulder that once could have been epaulettes.

I went straight to the 'images' search engine, and typed in Logan again, and what I saw sent goosebumps down to the base of my spine. There he was. Captain Logan. Hard as flint. Eyes dark and cold. I had seen many pairs of such eyes. They belonged to men who were not only not afraid to kill at the slightest opportunity, but who enjoyed the act. He had a long, narrow, aquiline nose. Back straight. The evil of the world swirling about him.

I returned to the State Library website's archives page. I couldn't type properly, such was my haste, and I kept having to go back to the search boxes. I finally managed to tap in Logan's name correctly, along with 'death', and I was directed to several items that hinted at a very, very old murder – namely, Logan's.

On the first highlighted line I clicked, the computer froze and a box instantly appeared in the centre of the screen. ACCESS DENIED. SEE STAFF.

I could see the sun lowering itself on to the skyscrapers across the river. I hadn't even noticed that the Martian had packed up and left. I had accidentally tipped over the bonsai fig at my feet and was under the desk, scraping the loose soil off the carpet and back into the pot, when I noticed someone approach the desk.

I re-emerged, red-faced.

'Yes?'

'Could you come with me, please?'

'And you are?'

'Just come with me, please.'

'The tree, it's a gift, for my wife. I accidentally knocked it ...'

'Just follow me, please.'

She was an elderly lady in a floral shift. She wore large spectacles attached to a white plastic chain that dangled down each side of her powdered face. She scared the hell out of me.

So I followed, too terrified to contradict her. She was the stern teacher from primary school we all had – the one who could make your bladder tingle with fear, and who never seemed to stop haunting your dreams.

We entered the elevator, me with my shoulder bag over one arm and a shivering bonsai in one hand, as I trailed behind her and the neat and affirmative clack of her Minnie Mouse-style white shoes. We entered a long, well-lit corridor, then turned left and into a dark corridor, until we finally came to the John Oxley Library.

She opened the door for me and I quietly walked inside. It was empty, except for a man standing in front of the far windows with his hands clasped behind his back. He wore black, and when he turned towards me, I noticed his coat had a familiar wrap-over flap, held by a sequence of brilliantly shiny gold buttons.

And he had a long, narrow, aquiline nose, sharp enough to cut butter.

4

WHAT WAS IT about Queensland that kept tangling me up in the lives of strangers and lunatics? I had a very powerful sense of déjà vu in the chilly air of the John Oxley Library, and the man in the black uniform joined a long line of megalomaniacs I had encountered over the years.

He was short, almost Napoleonic in stature and manner, and he reeked of some deep-seated hatred that would take more than a human lifetime to source. In short (quite literally), he would go to God with the kernel of his psychosis intact and unharmed.

I took my standard line, and attacked first.

'So, you're a Johnny Cash fan, then?' I said.

In the air-conditioned hush of the library, I could almost hear his teeth grind.

I plonked the bonsai down heavily on a nearby desk. I had, en route to meeting Mr Cash, stuffed the golden envelope down the back of my pants. As long as I didn't sit down, all was good.

'You like bonsai?' he said, nodding to the fig.

'Yeah, me like bonsai.'

'A curious art. I imagine it would involve much patience, of which I have short supply.' He had an unusual accent, a gruel perhaps of having lived in other countries, with an old-fashioned Australian boarding-school toffiness behind it. In the darkening library, he could have been twenty years old, or sixty. His hair was cut in an early-sixties-style Beatles bob. It was, quite possibly, the first style he had adopted as a young adult, then maintained all his life: some men's hair remains frozen in the period when they were most vital and exciting and a vibrant part of the world around them. I have always found this extraordinary – how for some, hairstyles are harder to let go than anything else. Mine? It let go on its own.

'I'm new to bonsai,' I said, 'but it does seem to have a cruel appeal to it.'

'Cruel?'

'The dwarfing and managing of nature. The conceit that we can control the world. Play God.'

'Interesting.'

'The human race produces many little kings, you know.'

'Oh yes, I know.'

'I thought you might.'

'There are some bonsai trees that are close to eight hundred years old, did you know that?'

'No, I didn't.'

'Well, now you do.'

'What a little font of trivia you are.'

'Can I make an assumption?'

'Be my guest,' I said.

'Your interest in family trees is possibly linked to your new passion for bonsai. To care for bonsai you must tend the roots very carefully. If I were an amateur psychologist, I would hazard a guess that your search for your family roots, and that little fig of yours, are somehow related.'

'How dare you make an assumption about my little fig,'

I said. 'I would hazard a guess that you would make a terrible psychologist.'

'Fair enough.'

The library lights suddenly flickered on, and he moved away from the window without taking his hands from behind his back. It was truly cold in the room now, yet I felt a bead of sweat trickle towards the gold envelope stuffed down my trousers.

He looked at me with a smirk. I could see now, in the neon light, that he was, in fact, well into his sixties. The dyed bob looked preposterous on his ageing head, like a very bad beret without the cloth sprig in the centre.

'My interest in my family tree, by the way, is none of your goddamn business. Do you make it a habit to monitor the activities of people using the library computers? You're the library detective, are you? Chasing down overdue books?'

'Hardly,' he said.

'Or just a garden-variety busybody without a decent hobby. Am I getting warm?'

The smirk had disappeared and been replaced by a thin, mean line of mouth. His eyes were dark and vicious, as some dogs' eyes are.

'So you have an interest in Captain Patrick Logan ...'

'You have a mad scientist-style office, do you, monitoring peoples' computer activities? A wall of television screens and a big, high-backed chair and a large red button on the desk to destroy the world? I bet you have a big, mean laugh, too, that echoes through the room when you get all girly and giggly with power.'

'What an imagination you have. I seem to remember you from somewhere.'

'I don't think so. Though I was a member of a Beatles

fan club in the sixties. Perhaps we met there. Traded some forty-fives.'

'You were that fellow who made a spectacle of himself last year. Something to do with the illegal sale of some fake Fairweathers.'

'That was my twin brother,' I said. 'He's one of your artsy-fartsy types.'

'Is that so?'

'That is so. So?'

'So Captain Logan, commandant of the great convict colony of Brisbane, Queensland, is part of your own ancestry?'

'I think you must be mistaken,' I said. 'I Googled him by accident, if you must know. I meant to type in Johnny Cash look-alikes, and up he came. Simple slip of the typing fingers. Though it does fascinate me, your Logan fetish. I wouldn't know the bloke if I fell over him, to be honest. May I politely ask something?'

'Go ahead.'

'Who the hell are you and why the hell are you wasting my time with this?'

He sat on the corner of a desk with some difficulty, a short left leg dangling above the carpet, and cradled his square chin with his right hand.

'To understand Brisbane, you must understand Captain Logan,' he said.

'I don't have to understand diddly-squat.'

'I'm afraid you do. Especially people like you.'

'Meaning?'

'You ignore history at your peril. If you'd ever read a book, you might see that.'

'Oh, thank you for that, sir. I apologise. Do I get detention now? I might make life hell for you and come here every day and study your Captain Logan. What do you say to that?'

I was losing patience with this annoying little man. It was dark outside and the peak-hour traffic was at a standstill on the riverside expressway.

'Can I go home now?' I said, turning to leave.

'Patrick Logan was the most notorious sadist of any penal settlement in this country,' he went on. 'The Old Windmill, up on Wickham Terrace. People view that as a quaint reminder of our humble origins. To anyone who knows, it is in fact a citadel to cruelty and murder. What happened there shaped Queensland society. Made us who we are. We owe it all to Logan.'

'Owe it? Murder, rape, pillage? Nice chap.'

'History never ends. You can shape it, prune it, tend to it, like your little fig tree there, but it keeps on flowing through like a subterranean river. Logan's work. It's not done with yet.'

And there it was – the loony factor. I had waited for it, anticipated it, and it had arrived.

'I'm sorry, who are you again? Curator of manuscripts, sadist and fetish section?'

'You could call me a patron of the library.'

'A patron. Aren't patrons people with too much money who want to be a member of clubs that without the moolah wouldn't have them in a pink fit?'

'I am a custodian, of sorts.'

'Now you're a custodian. Of what?'

'Why, history, of course.'

'It's almost six o'clock. Time for you to take your tablets, and for me to get home to dinner.'

'Be careful around Captain Logan,' he said, smirking again. 'History has a habit of repeating itself.'

'For a patron, or custodian, you're fantastically unoriginal.'

He turned his back on me and surveyed the city through the wide glass windows.

I took the bonsai and returned to the Peugeot in the car park under the library. Hopping into the driver's seat, I felt a crinkling in my trousers and retrieved the gold envelope.

In the gloom of the cabin I once again studied the photograph of the corpse. For the first time I noticed a strange, dead tree in the distance, a hundred metres from the body, and around the body itself a patina of cracked and dried mud. It was a riverbed. Or possibly the floor of a country property's dam.

At that instant I heard the shriek of tyres in the underground car park, and just caught the sight of an old Toyota ute heading for the exit. The driver, from the rear, looked to be wearing a large farmer's hat, and there were shovels and rakes poking out the back of the ute tray.

On my new mobile Peg had left me a text message: Stay out of mischief.

How I wish I'd taken her advice.

5

IF YOU'D TOLD me when I first decided to retire to Queensland that just over a year later I might be squatting beside a 177-year-old corpse at Wivenhoe Dam, north-west of Brisbane, I'd have had you committed. Or committed myself. Indeed, if I'd done that when the little voice in my head told me to back away, I wouldn't be in another damn pickle.

But did I listen to the voice of reason? Of course I didn't.

And while I was aware of the severity of south-east Queensland's water crisis, and had watched with mild amusement the political buck-passing, and even taken to using an egg timer in the shower to play my part in solving the wider problem, I could not have imagined in my wildest dreams that the drought would produce not just community angst and a boom in water-tank sales, but a body that just might rewrite the state's history.

For this was not just any corpse photographed half-buried in the cracked surface of one of Wivenhoe's recently exposed flanks as the dam levels dropped, but the earthly remains – I was convinced – of one Captain Patrick Logan. At least that's what my instinct told me.

But let me explain how I got to this point.

Reference books have Logan murdered in 1830 by an

Aboriginal tribe during one of the brutal captain's many explorations in and about the Brisbane valley. Cracked across the back of the head, stripped naked and partially hidden beneath tree branches in the vicinity of the modern-day Wivenhoe. Even his horse was slaughtered. History says Logan's body was then taken back to the settlement and forwarded to Sydney, where he was buried.

My advice to budding scholars? Don't believe everything you read. History can reveal. But it can also conceal.

On the drive back to the Gold Coast the day I got collared by Ringo Starr in the John Oxley Library, something nagged at me. And when I get nagged by something, I can't rest until I've satiated the itch. It made me a good cop. But it has made me a somewhat reckless and unpredictable civilian.

Quite simply, the object of my agitation was Ringo's coat. It was eerily similar to the design of the coat on the unidentified corpse in the photograph that some stranger had left for me in the library's meditation cube. Or had it been left for me? Was it intended for somebody else? Had I accidentally stumbled into a little mystery that might have gone unnoticed if I hadn't decided to awaken my inner Buddhist in the red box by the Brisbane River? Perhaps the bonsai and gold envelope were meant for my friend in the John Oxley upstairs. He'd been waiting for them. I'd inadvertently got in first. Now I had the photograph of a very dead man, though I had only a supposition of who that man might be. (I also had a pretty little bonsai, which I gifted to Peg who, astonished by my generosity, popped it on the kitchen windowsill and looked at me curiously throughout the evening. Can't I buy my wife a dwarfed fig tree if I feel like it? said I, incredulous at her incredulity. Then seeing Logan's portrait on the computer, there was the coat again. Coincidence? I don't think so.

Late that night, I rang the phone number on the back of the photograph.

A man answered. 'Yeah,' he said. He sounded sleepy. Or drunk. Or drugged. Or both.

'Thanks for the bonsai,' I said, after several seconds of silence.

'Yeah.'

'Why don't I come and see you?'

'Yeah.'

He gave me an address and the phone went dead.

Esk, he'd said. What the hell is an esk?

The following morning, under the pretext of once more climbing the family tree, I hit the road for Brisbane and Esk, an hour or so north-west of the city.

It's a delightful drive, if you haven't done it. And it's my belief that everyone should see at least once their city's water supply. Why? It's the source of life. It says a lot about the community it serves. It can tell you things about your past, and your future.

I should have told Peg about my latest bout of mischief. But, I'll be honest – it gave me a thrill to be back on the trail of a mystery. I had not anticipated the stupefying boredom of retirement. I hadn't prepared for it. I hadn't established a little safety net of hobbies and activities for myself. Granted, I didn't expect to be plugged full of holes within months of leaving work. But those many months of rehabilitation brought home the reality of my position.

Peg said my subconscious had sought out danger and adventure during that near-fatal Fairweather farrago last year. I asked her if it was the habit of the subconscious to willingly get its backside shot up. I was being facetious, but I know there was some truth in what she said.

And here I was again, driving to a remote farmhouse

outside Esk to meet a stranger who had a corpse on his property, most likely a gun in the rack beside the front door, and an expansive and lovingly tended Slim Dusty record collection.

I stopped in Esk itself and had a coffee and a sandwich. As I sat there, beside the main drag, I began thinking of Logan and his ill-fated expedition into the valley. He had convicts with him, supplies, horses, and when he set out from the Old Windmill, the soil around it infused with wheat husks and men's blood, he couldn't have known he was soon to meet his death. Or could he? Men like Logan believe they're invincible. Yet history has shown, over and over, that invincible men usually suffer horrible and premature deaths. The frontier. It can be a hell of a dangerous place.

I tried to imagine the valley and the virgin river back in 1830. It must have been extraordinary. The forests untouched. The pristine river beginning its long, winding journey to Moreton Bay. And a hundred years later it was all gone, submerged beneath the Somerset and Wivenhoe dams.

Logan was fearless, I'll give him that. It's no picnic, the Australian bush. It's claimed its share of lives, broken count-less men and women, devoured innocent children. It was and is, as they say, unforgiving.

So Logan came in search of pastures and water, and was delivered into the great void. Had local Aboriginal tribes been responsible? That seemed to be accepted fact. But there would have been hundreds of men with a motive to end his miserable existence. A pack of them who had suffered at the end of his lash and been humiliated as beasts of burden at his beck and call. Logan was a murder waiting to happen.

If the corpse in the photograph was indeed the real Logan, whose body had been brought back to the settlement in 1830, dispatched to Sydney and buried with military honours? Why had the switch been made? And why had the body of the real Logan been buried with such determination that it avoided detection for almost two centuries?

I found the property a further twenty minutes out of town, drove over the cattle grid at the front gate and parked beside a dilapidated farmhouse. I could see a Toyota ute with shovels and mattocks poking out of its tray in a nearby shed.

I knocked on the door and waited. Nothing. The tin roof pinged and groaned in the sunshine.

'Hello?'

Still nothing. I opened the door and peered into a long hallway that ran from the front to the back of the house. There was old, cracked linoleum on the floor.

'Anybody home?' I walked through to the kitchen at the back. I nosed about. There were photographs of the same man with various women and children pinned to the fridge. In each photo his grin was broad enough to reveal two missing front teeth, and in each picture he wore a large, battered straw hat.

Call it an old copper's instinct, but I went down the back steps and climbed through a fence and took a stroll across the dry paddocks. The grass was brittle beneath my boots. Grasshoppers clung to my trouser legs. I could see in the distance the tip of one of the smaller arms of the Wivenhoe Dam. I needed to find that body in the picture. I needed to see it with my own eyes. In this digital age, no photograph can be trusted.

I went down to the edge of the water. You could clearly see the rings, like dirt in a bathtub, where the water level had been, and the layers of caked mud, dry and hard furthest from shore. There were bird, kangaroo and wallaby tracks stitched crazily across the surface. I walked across the hardened mud until I saw a dead tree just like the one in the photograph.

I found the corpse all right.

But it wasn't Captain Logan. There, in a dried-out mud bog and positioned in exactly the same way as our historic corpse, was the body of my toothless friend in the pictures on the fridge in the farmhouse. His straw hat was tilted sideways on his head.

And he had a perfectly neat, ruby-red bullet hole slap-bang in the centre of his forehead.

6

THERE ARE MANY, many people in the world who never leave even the barest trace of a footprint. Nothing – not a scintilla nor skerrick – to mark their time on Earth.

I'm not talking about this carbon-footprint nonsense we hear so much about these days. This great global push to make all of us even smaller, less offensive, less significant. This urgency to turn us into soft-stepping sheep lest we actually show we *exist*. Trust me, when I'm ready to buy the farm, so to speak, I want to leave one big, rude, noticeable divot behind.

Still, as a former homicide detective, I've known the cheapness of life. I've seen the waste. The slaughter of innocents. With each one, it never gets any easier.

This is how the job gets to you. It scratches at the essence of your being, bit by bit. It can throw you into a philosophical cast of mind if you're not careful.

In my early days, as a young cop, I didn't handle it well. I was perfectly ordered and stoic on the outside, but I'd go home at the end of a shift, just as bankers and street cleaners and trawler fishermen clock off, and I'd sit alone in the lounge room into the early hours, leaden with the sights and sounds of the day, strangely uncomforted by the feather snores of my wife coming from the bedroom. We all have our crosses to bear. But I'm not putting down accountants, say, when you compare a day busy with figures and book balancing and one where you come upon a teenager who has decided to end it all by blowing off half her face with Daddy's hunting rifle, or the mummified remains of an elderly lady in an outer suburb, dead of a heart attack for a year without entering the thoughts of anybody living, a plastic shopping bag still gripped in her right hand. Put side by side, the columns don't exactly equate.

Once, during my apprenticeship years, my education on the force, a question presented itself to me — how many people have ever lived on Earth since time began? (These sort of maddening conundrums slip in under the door when you work with violent death.) I read and spoke with people and could never get a satisfactory answer.

Then I discovered a foreword the science-fiction novelist Arthur C. Clarke wrote to his famous novel, *2001: A Space Odyssey*. I wrote it out on one of my five- by three-inch index cards and kept it in my wallet, and when the card got dog-eared and fragile I copied it out again, and again.

Clarke wrote: 'Behind every man now alive stand thirty ghosts, for that is the ratio by which the dead outnumber the living. Since the dawn of time, roughly a hundred billion human beings have walked the planet Earth. Now this is an interesting number, for by a curious coincidence there are approximately a hundred billion stars in our local universe, the Milky Way. So for every man who has ever lived, in this universe, there shines a star.'

For the umpteenth time in my life I thought of these words as I sat beside the body of the straw-hatted farmer by the feeble waters of the Wivenhoe Dam.

The blood around the bullet wound in his head had

crusted and turned rust-brown. His hands were folded in his lap. His head was turned slightly to the side, his eyes were half-open and drowsy-looking, as if he'd been woken from a deep sleep. One eyebrow was lifted a little higher than the other, giving him a visage of dumb surprise. He had not, I reasoned, expected to be turned into a Milky Way star quite so soon.

I tried to close those eyes but they didn't hold. I left him staring into space. As I walked back to his farmhouse I could hear the flies making their ghastly music about him.

I didn't immediately call the police. There was some real work to do before the blue shirts stormed in and turned the place upside down, and decided, considering I'd found the body, that I might make a decent suspect and even contribute to alleviating their murder clear-up statistics as the New Year approached.

My toothless farmer friend in the straw hat, he kept what must have once been a decent spread. His fences were all intact, though the pastures were ankle-high and dry as a bone and hadn't seen cattle in some time. The whole place had the feel of something on the point of collapse. Of desperation. Despite this simple man's incessant labour, fate and nature had conspired against him, and it all felt tired. The drought. It had hollowed him out.

Not far from the old Queenslander he'd called home, I noticed a shed that seemed different from the rest. It had crude, homemade skylights built into the corrugated-iron roof sheeting, and there were new water pumps and a crazy maze of plastic pipes tangled down one side.

I peered through the open doorway. It was hot in there, humid and oven-like. The shed was dominated by two long hand-made trestle tables. A rudimentary watering system had been rigged up above the tables. Right at the end of one of the tables was a cluster of small potted plants. There were boxes and boxes of unopened glazed pots, made in China, and a side-table on which was a selection of small, delicate pruning tools. They were bonsai implements.

I sighed for the poor man. He was starting a new business for himself. Diversifying, in the face of the great drought. At some point he had lit upon the idea of growing and selling bonsai trees. It was doomed from the start. He was a farmer. He worked with living things. It was all he knew. Yet he saw a future in plants, and water. He could not step out of this small, dry square of his. He would have had a better shot at things selling hand-squeezed lemonade out by his front gate, poor man.

I went up into the house and started looking around in the kitchen. In the country, the kitchen is the focal point of business, of family, of life. In one of the drawers of an ancient hutch I found the farmer's paperwork. I tipped it onto the kitchen table. There, near the top of the pile, were more photographs of the corpse I had been abruptly introduced to in the meditation room at the State Library.

I put the kettle on and made a cup of tea, then I sat at the table and carefully studied the pictures for almost an hour.

The dozens of photos, taken from several angles, gave me a greater appreciation of the victim. I had no trained eye for historical apparel, but the jacket that adorned the body looked, to my schoolboy knowledge of Australian history, to be from the 1800s. It was also richly decorated with braid and buttons. Whoever it was had rank of some sort. There were what appeared to be spurs on his rotting boots.

It was the close-up of the skull, though, that fascinated me. There was a huge, shattered entrance wound to the flat forehead. And the photographer, presumably the farmer himself, had rested what could only have been a lead ball nearby, presumably found inside the old skull, rattling about like a marble for an aeon. This was, without hesitation, a most heinous murder. Though I had no concrete evidence, I had no doubt it was Logan.

I pocketed the photographs, washed up my tea cup and put it on the sink rack. As I wiped my hands with a tea towel I stood in front of the fridge and perused the white door, covered in family photos, and little pictures of bonsai trees torn out of gardening magazines, and telephone and power bills fastened with magnets advertising farm machinery and advice on how to spot a terrorist. It was rudimentary stuff, the sort of fridge detritus to be found in kitchens across Australia.

But there was one thing out of place: a white, laminated business card held firmly to the fridge with a John Deere magnet.

In raised black letters it read – Historica. On the flipside were a phone number and a post office box address in Noosa, Sunshine Coast, Queensland.

I wiped my prints off everything I'd touched. If I'd wanted to be fastidious, I could have returned to the corpse on the shores of Wivenhoe and swept out any footprints there too. But in a drought, footprints rarely hold. A single hot breath of wind can send them into eternity. All the way to the Milky Way.

It was midday and hot when I left the property. Time for a dip. Time to savour the sensory delights of Noosa.

I patted the white business card in my pocket, and headed out of the valley.

7

ANSWER ME THIS. In what sort of job could you be standing over the flyblown corpse of a dead Esk farmer one moment, and a few hours later be taking a mint julep on the deck of a mansion overlooking Noosa with a toupée-wearing multi-millionaire?

You see what happens when you begin mucking about inside the dark, secret chambers of the human heart? You don't know where you might end up. As for the complications of the soul, well, don't even start me on that – we could be here for months, years.

But back to the mint julep.

I had left the farmer by the Wivenhoe – he wasn't going anywhere and besides, the police were presumably on their way after my little tip to Crimestoppers – and taken a leisurely drive to Noosa. All my life I had heard of this fabled place. A paradise, they say. The Riviera of Queensland. In my mind it was a fairytale land surrounded by tall walls and moats, and to enter you either had to be extremely wealthy or decked out in white linen from shoe to hat, or preferably both.

So as the Peugeot rolled down from Noosaville to Hastings Street I felt I was entering unfamiliar territory.

At Aroma's café, as children ran amok in the little adjoining square and splashed each other with fountain water, I rang the Historica number on the white business card.

'Yes?' said a voice.

'Historica?'

'Who is this?'

'This is a representative of the Esk Bonsai Corporation.'

'Who?'

'In light of my employer's sudden death, I was wondering if you're still interested in that pallet of Hokidachi or broom-style elms you ordered.'

'Who the hell is this?'

'I could ask the same thing. In fact, I will ask the same thing. Who the hell are you? And what was your lustrous business card doing on a refrigerator door belonging to a fresh corpse?'

Funny, the power of persuasion. Within thirty minutes I had an ice cold mint julep in hand and was sitting opposite a very tall, thin man dressed all in white, from his Italian leather loafers and ankle-tight socks to his eyebrows. On his head was a pitch-black wig. He looked like a burned match.

I sipped the horrid drink – mint, sugar, ice and bourbon whiskey. I was a VB man myself. He hadn't touched his.

'Historica. What is that?' I asked him. 'The name of some fancy new Lexus or Maybach?'

He snorted softly. 'A Maybach is a Maybach. Differentiated by numbers only, I'm afraid.'

'You learn something every day.'

'Historica,' he said, 'is a little group of men and women interested in history. And its proper keeping.'

'So you're all ex-public-school librarians. Am I getting warm?'

'It's a hobby, that's all. For lovers of accurate history.'

We were not alone. He had a substantial phalanx of bodyguards sprinkled throughout the property, and two in the lounge room not far from the deck where we chatted. The bodyguards, like all caricatures, wore black suits. The two in the lounge had blond hair. Of course they did. The *Die Hard* films had a lot to answer for in the world of body-guards. They were the exact opposite to my rich history nut of a new friend.

'Accuracy. Proper keeping. These words and phrases puzzle me,' I said, hiding my disgust at the julep. Mint was for children or people with bad breath.

'We at Historica believe in accountability and correct, documented sources. It's that simple.'

'Like, did Captain Cook's *Endeavour* have four masts or five? That sort of thing.'

'It had three – foremast, mainmast and mizzenmast. Yes, that sort of thing.'

'So you could tell me,' I said, pulling a crumpled photo-graph of the ancient Wivenhoe corpse – not the poor toothless farmer – from my back pocket, 'whether this chap here was some sort of important person from the early days of Brisbane settlement or just a peculiar, history-obsessed git who liked dressing up in old soldier's jackets and ran head-first, literally, into an errant musketball during a mock skirmish with his mates?'

I flicked the picture towards him and it came to rest near his untouched julep. He removed a pair of spectacles from his top pocket and looked down at the picture.

'Interesting.'

'It is, isn't it?'

I could see, in the distance, a fantastic storm building on the horizon. A great bank of black cloud had eclipsed the afternoon sun and birds were wheeling crazily above the white sandy spine of Noosa's beach. Sunbathers continued to lie on their towels, oblivious to the impending apocalypse.

'I could only hazard a guess, but it certainly resembles a colonial military uniform,' he went on.

'You can't be any more accurate than that?'

'No.'

'You've never seen this gentleman before?'

'Under what possible circumstances would I have seen this man before?'

'Didn't your mummy ever tell you never to answer a question with a question?'

I could see his goons become agitated in the lounge room.

He smiled. Not a normal smile. A rich person's smile. No. Let me be more precise. It was the smile of the very, *very* rich, who know that nothing in the mere mortal way of things can touch them. It was a smile both condescending and infantile. The condescension, often, is in their genes. And the childishness stems from never having had to worry about the raft of normal things grown adults have to worry about. Simple things, such as how to exist day to day.

My new white-linen friend also had a coldness, as essential to his make-up as breathing in and out, which probably had its source in the crib in which his mummy had left him, in the care of his nannies and butlers and footmen.

Still, I wasn't here to sympathise with some spoiled adult-infant.

'Listen to me very carefully,' I said to him. 'Tell me why your business card was found on a dead farmer's fridge in the middle of nowhere.'

He paused and glanced up at the coming storm. You could smell the distant rain hitting the hot earth. I knew what he was thinking. He'd have to get inside soon. The winds would come up. And for a man with a very bad toupée, a sudden wind, any wind, was a natural enemy.

'Now you listen to *me* very carefully,' he said, pointing at me with a long forefinger. He showed his teeth for the first time. They were very small and snaggly, like a child's milk teeth. But they were yellow against his obscene whiteness. 'History doesn't repeat itself, you know. Except in the minds of those who do not know history.'

'Confucius?'

'Kahlil Gibran, actually.'

'Let me give you one.'

'Be my guest.'

'Rich plonkers with bad hair and poor dress sense do not tell me what to do.'

I turned away from him to watch the storm. It was going to be a hell of a drive back to the Gold Coast in the leaky Peugeot. And that's what I was thinking about when a suited arm closed like a vice around my neck.

I assume I passed out. For three hours had gone by before I woke to find myself lying on the floor of a dark, industrial-sized freezer with the icy corpse of a nineteenth-century military officer keeping me company.

8

FREEZING TO DEATH is a fascinating process. Hypothermia affects different people in different ways. Men are more prone to death by freezing than women. People have had their limbs turned into popsicles and survived, while others have perished after sustained exposure to winds that have not even reached freezing temperatures.

The metabolism slows. The muscles contract to try to generate heat. In many cases, freezing victims have been known to rip off all their clothes prior to falling into unconsciousness and, ultimately, death, such is the sensation of extreme heat they feel on their skin.

I thought of all these things as I lay next to my dead colonial officer in a giant freezer somewhere, I presumed, in the vicinity of Noosa. As I woke back into the world, the antique corpse wrapped in clear plastic and leaning on my shoulder, I remembered the sickly sweetness of the mint julep, and yellow jagged teeth, and Peg's mobile phone sitting in the glove compartment of the Peugeot when it should have been in my pocket.

It was cold all right, but I wasn't going to panic. Not just yet. I could hear a tremendous booming outside the freezer, which I shared with shelf after shelf of beautiful frozen red emperor and snapper, barramundi and sea perch. I could have been trapped in the belly of a whale.

At least someone had left a small security light on. Where was I? At a fish market? At the back of a restaurant? The rhythmic thundering continued, getting louder and louder. I checked out the freezer. No exits. No interior emergency handles or hatches.

One other thing about freezing to death. If you're carrying a bit of lard, you take longer to die.

Thus I sat on a few boxes of frozen scallops, rubbed my arms and considered my predicament. Grace under pressure, I told myself. Don't panic. Conserve energy.

That's when I grabbed the tail of a nice long flathead and banged it crazily against the freezer wall, shouting my head off for help.

Just a few moments later there was a boom loud enough to shake the entire freezer itself, and the single light, weak and dull as a firefly, went out. Great. Now I was going to freeze to death in the dark. I scrambled back to the scallops on my hands and knees and ended up wrestling with the mud-caked, cling-wrapped corpse. It wasn't one of my finer moments.

Then, blow me down, if it didn't start to feel warmer in that tomb of mine. I thought – here it is, the fire on the skin prior to death. They would find me naked and twisted in agony in a mess of seafood. It would, so it seemed, be an undignified death for me.

But it actually did get warmer, and as time marched on I could hear the fish creak and crack with the thaw and then, suddenly, scaring the living daylights out of both of us, a small goateed man in jeans and a checked shirt opened the door to the freezer and shone a torch straight into my face. I instinctively raised the flathead. Beware the man in fear for his life and armed with a frozen fish.

After our mutual screams had stopped echoing, I said, 'Broken? The freezer?'

And he said, 'Big storm. Lightning. Direct hit on the generator.'

'So,' I said, 'big fish sale now.'

'You bet,' he said.

'Where am I?'

'Seafood storage facility for "Noosa Fresh and Fishy."'

'"Fresh and Fishy?"'

'We distribute seafood to restaurants in Noosa and on the Sunshine Coast. You?'

'Retired detective.'

'On a case?'

'Sort of. Had a drink with your boss. Wears white? A roadkill toupe?'

'Heard of him. Never met him. Only started work for this mob a week ago. Today's me day off, but I came in to check on the generators when the storm hit.'

'You might need a new one.'

'Looks like it,' he said.

'Your boss make it a habit of storing old corpses in here with the fresh seafood?'

'Dunno. I just been told to keep an eye on the fish. Nothin' else. No matter what turns up here.'

'If you no looky, you keep worky.'

'Exactly.'

'At "Noosa Fresh and Fishy."'

'That's it. Hey, you need a jumper or something?'

I could have hugged him.

I also needed to regroup. My mint julep friend could wait. I had a long memory.

★★★

Back on the Gold Coast, I studied the facts I had at hand. I had two bodies, one from another century, the other from a farm in Esk. The local papers were reporting the latter as another 'rural suicide'. I found this curious. My toothless friend had suffered the 'long-term impact of the drought', some senior sergeant was quoted as saying. His family farm had become untenable. They had reduced him to just another statistic. Full stop. Yeah, right. Like the giant full stop in the middle of his sorry forehead.

I had a library patron who had warned me off some innocuous snippet of Brisbane history that was evolving into something not so innocuous after all. I believed, too, that I had accidentally intercepted a bonsai tree and some vital information while sitting innocently in the State Library's meditation room innocently seeking information about my innocent family tree.

Then there was Captain Logan. Dear Patrick. I had never heard of him and all of a sudden he was trying to get me killed. Was the corpse in the freezer that of Logan himself, the Tyrant of Brisbane Town? The very same in the crinkled photograph I had taken from the gold envelope? If so, what of the official reports of his murder by Aboriginal tribes near the site of the ever-dwindling Wivenhoe Dam in 1830? Who was trying to alter history here, and why?

As far as I could ascertain, the Scottish-born Logan, the Moreton Bay penal settlement's third commandant, was notorious for his cruelty in a country that, in its early days of colonisation, had its fair share of British-born tyrants and sadists. He was not averse to ordering 150 lashes for individual convicts. He built cells specifically for solitary confinement, then a flour mill for further mental and physical torture. He also fancied himself as something of

an explorer. He was obsessed with rivers. He charted the
Logan River, named after him.

Then, in October of 1830, with his commission in
Brisbane almost at an end, he made one last journey to
the Brisbane Valley. He was accompanied by his servant,
Private Collison, and five convicts. Near Pine Mountain
they were threatened by Aboriginals, who only let them
pass after Collison discharged his firearm. Heading back to
the settlement a week later on 17 October, Logan noticed
some horse tracks. He had lost a horse in the area on a
previous expedition so he decided to follow them, hoping
to retrieve the animal. He told his party he would meet
them later that day.

When Logan didn't show, his men, unable to locate him,
walked on to Ipswich, where they thought Logan might
be. Further search parties were sent out. According to a
published account, Logan's bloodied waistcoat was discovered, 'as well as some leaves of his notebook'. A day later,
they came upon Logan's horse, 'dead in the bottom of a
shallow creek, covered with boughs'. Then, a few metres
from the horse, 'Logan's body was found ... the back of
the head much beaten with waddies ... in a grave about
two feet deep where the blacks had buried him with his
face downwards. The body was then take[n] up, and put in
blankets and by stages brought to the Limestone Station and
afterwards by water to the settlement.'

His death was not exactly mourned in Brisbane. They
had a song about him, celebrating the 'mortal stroke'
handed out by the local Aboriginals. 'My fellow prisoners,
be exhilarated / that all such monsters such a death may
find.' Hardly a fond remembrance.

Logan's body was then transported to Sydney on a
government schooner.

Or was it? Who on earth had anything to gain from falsifying the details of Logan's death, almost two centuries later? And why, if this indeed was a case of tampered history, had the ruse been perpetrated for so long? It obviously meant a great deal to somebody. Already, an innocent man had been killed, and I had had my own life threatened. For what?

Also, if the corpse that had kept me company in the freezer was actually the legendary Logan himself, he had not been bludgeoned to death with a waddy, that's for sure. He'd been cleanly and efficiently murdered.

There were a thousand convicts in that early penal settlement, and each and every one had a decent motive. But why would anyone care so much all this time later? It didn't make sense.

If I was a detective at the time of Logan's death, there was something I would need to see. The 'leaves of his notebook'. Yes, I would very much have liked to see them.

Still, I had to be content with his jacket, which I'd souvenired off the body in the freezer. I held it, thawed now and limp, and tried to will some truth from it. All I got was the smell of mud and copper. And blood.

9

Peg and I had breakfast on the back deck overlooking the canal at home on the Gold Coast. Just as I began scooping out my grapefruit, a huge tourist boat chugged past. Several people on the top deck took photographs of us. I found it peculiar that a distant shot of me and Peg having breakfast would be archived in someone's holiday album on the other side of the world.

My wife was unusually sullen. She rarely gets sullen. Cruelty to animals and starving children make her that way. And me, of course. Usually me.

'How's the tree going?' she said, looking at me over the rim of her tea cup.

'The tree?'

'Family tree.'

'Oh, the family tree. Very interesting. Fascinating, actually.' I feigned a hearty laugh. 'Oh, the apple didn't fall far from the tree in my family, Peg.'

'You found the bushranger, then?'

'Not exactly.' I avoided eye contact.

'How's that mobile phone I gave you?'

'It's good, Peg. Yes. Very clear reception.'

'Do you have it with you?'

'At all times. See?' By chance and luck, I had slipped it into my shorts pocket that morning. I produced it, as proof.

'Did you get my messages?'

'Messages? It keeps messages?'

'You don't have a clue how to use it, do you?'

'I have never even turned it off since you gave it to me. Look.' The screen was blank. I fumbled with the on/off button. Nothing. 'It's broken,' I said.

'It's out of battery power.'

'It is?'

'How could one of the most intelligent and highly decorated detectives in the history of the New South Wales police force not be able to operate a mobile phone? Once you charge it up, you'll find several messages from me, and another half dozen from your friend, Mr Carpenter.'

'Mr Carpenter?'

'An old friend of yours, he says. Knew you when he worked for the Sydney City Council. Then he migrated north, and worked for the Brisbane City Council. Ring a bell?'

'Water infrastructure.' I toyed with the empty half-bladder of the grapefruit skin.

'Water?'

'I had a case, in the seventies. Extortion. Some lunatic threatened to contaminate the Sydney water supply. Carpenter was a minor public servant, specialised in water.'

'Well, he wants to talk to you.'

'He told me once there were bodies all over the world sealed up in dam walls. A dam wall is quite possibly the most perfect place to conceal a murder victim. He believed there were criminals who licked their lips every time a government proposed a new dam, and through their contacts, or courtesy of a wad of cash, or a gun to the back of a head, bodies, some of them new, some years old and exhumed, were slipped into dam walls. He reckoned you just had to check with the cops, or read the newspapers, to see the statistical rise in killings prior to the concrete pouring of a dam wall. Through the roof.'

'Ah,' said Peg. 'Another one of your conspiracy theorists. You collect them, like some people collect stamps.'

'It's such a crazy theory it might be true.'

'Why do you think he might want to talk to you, after all these years?' She was sullen again, and suspicious.

'Well, he'd be retired, like me,' I said. 'Maybe he wants to go fishing. Reminisce on old times.'

It was a Brisbane phone number. We spoke briefly. Carpenter certainly didn't want to go fishing.

An hour and a half later, I was walking with him through the Brisbane Botanic Gardens at Mount Coot-tha.

'How'd you track me down?' I asked him.

We strolled slowly, with our hands behind our backs, just two retired gentlemen enjoying the gardenias.

'How'd I track you down? For a private citizen living out a quiet retirement, you certainly make a large public target. Last year. The Fairweather escapade. You couldn't have made yourself more conspicuous if you'd stripped off and ridden an elephant through the Queen Street Mall.'

'The press. They made a big deal out of it, that's all.'

'Now you're causing all sorts of waves behind the scenes, let me tell you. Serious waves. I felt obligated to warn you.' He looked around furtively, like there might be electronic surveillance equipment in the herb garden, a sniper behind the bamboo.

He was, I knew from past experience, secretly enjoying all this cloak and dagger stuff.

'What are you talking about?'

'There's a lot of noise about you and the government's water infrastructure, which is being put in place as we speak.'

'Water infrastructure? I was researching my family's ancestry in a little booth in the library, for crying out loud. And what would you know about government business these days anyway? How long you been retired? Ten years?'

He flicked his nose with his forefinger.

'Either you're allergic to pollen or you know more than you're letting on,' I said. Carpenter didn't smile. Public servants whose whole lives have been the past, present and future of water infrastructure don't seem to have a huge sense of humour.

'Let me just say that you are being discussed in the highest of circles.'

The highest of circles? Who was he kidding?

'Would you care to illuminate me on the circles? And the talk?'

We had entered a mini-rainforest, and Carpenter became more jittery in the humid shadows. We re-emerged at the far side of the gardens. There were, down behind some gums, huge mountains of mulch. They looked, from this distance, as big as the pyramids in Egypt.

'Listen,' he said. 'I might be retired, but there is a little group of us who meet regularly, once a month, to discuss water-related matters.'

'Fascinating,' I said. 'Not your own waters, I assume, but the public sort.'

'This is deadly serious.'

'I apologise.'

'We are – and I'm sure this will surprise you – called upon now and again as "consultants" to council and government projects regarding water. And even you would know that water, at this very moment in time, is a major issue in the

community, and to governments. This is the worst drought
in a century. We are under the most severe water restrictions in this city's history. There is a very real concern we
will be the first city in the twenty-first century to run out of
water, unless the infrastructure is up and running in time.'

'Or it rains.'

'Or it rains like it's never rained before.'

I was sweating, and thirsty, now that we'd left the
shaded area of the gardens and walked under the ferocious
midday sun.

'Well, I may be the first retired detective in the Mount
Coot-tha gardens to run out of water in the twenty-first
century,' I said, punching him lightly on the arm. There
was no cheering Mr Carpenter.

'I can see I've wasted my time.'

'I'm sorry. Go on. No more jokes.'

'This thing you've got yourself caught up in. Out at
Wivenhoe. I can't tell you what to do, but I can make a
recommendation. That's what I was good at all my life.'

'And what is your recommendation?'

'I would suggest that if you want to see your grandchildren out of nappies, go back home and forget all about it.'

'You're not the first to make that recommendation in
recent times.'

'I know men like you,' Carpenter went on. 'If someone
warns you off something, you'll go at it even harder.'

'Now you're getting warm.'

'And I assume there is nothing anyone could say to
dissuade you once you've made up your mind to solve a
puzzle.'

'Now you're even warmer. Puzzles are for children,
Carpenter. I'm more interested in matters of life and death.
That's the greatest puzzle of all, for grown-ups.'

I was sweating like a plump hog waiting for the knives of Christmas. Yet Carpenter, in his neat, white short-sleeved shirt, didn't appear to have raised a single bead of the stuff.

'What if that matter of death happened to be your own?' he said finally, stopping and leaning in to smell a rose bush.

We ended up, to my surprise, in the Bonsai House. Could Carpenter have possibly known about the little bonsai I'd received in the library that day? The miniature fig tree that kicked off this bizarre adventure? Exactly how much did this diminutive public servant know?

We were the only two in the house. I could hear water trickling. It was momentarily soothing.

'If my warnings aren't enough to dissuade you, then there's someone I'd like you to meet. Someone from our little water circle.'

'Brisbane sure has a lot of powerful, secret circles.'

'If you want to learn about this city's water infrastructure, its life source, then he's the only man to talk to.'

'I didn't say I wanted to learn about that.'

'Oh, you do,' said Carpenter, effecting what could have been at the least the vague beginnings of an all-knowing smile. 'You most certainly do.'

I admired a number of healthy bonsais, then remembered, with a start, seeing my tiny fig on the kitchen windowsill back home that morning while I was on the phone to Carpenter. Several leaves had fallen from its branches and turned yellow. The soil was dry and crumbling. My bonsai was dying.

If I was a superstitious sort of fellow, I might have seen that as an omen.

10

SOMETIMES LIFE SEEMS to conspire to play quirky practical jokes on certain people. I happen to be one of those people.

A few days after meeting Carpenter in the Brisbane Botanic Gardens I was back again at Wivenhoe Dam for a top-secret meeting with an eighty-three-year-old man who went by the name of Walt Whitman.

Walt Whitman, as it turned out, was to be my informant on all things water-related, and was able to explain why my life was in danger because I'd accidentally crossed the path of a bonsai and a picture of an ancient corpse in the State Library of Queensland. Walt Whitman would fill me in on why the innocent meanderings of an ex-cop and budding family historian could suddenly cause rumblings at the highest levels of government.

Carpenter had called me from a payphone the night before and simply muttered the name and location – Walt Whitman; Captain Logan's Camp. Then he'd hung up.

Was this a public service-style joke? That this strange case of death and drought should involve an informant named after the famous American poet, hobo and author of the world classic *Leaves of Grass* – Walt Whitman, author of a poem called 'The Waters', that began 'The world below the brine'. Was this their tacky and obvious and profoundly unfunny code? Or one of those cosmic jokes that had begun to attach themselves to me like summer flies on the back of a crisp white tennis shirt? Or both?

Ho, ho, Carpenter, I said to myself as I drove into the camping grounds named after the area's most infamous celebrity, the good Captain Logan himself, which lay on the banks of the Wivenhoe.

It was another hot day and the Peugeot had not taken kindly to the conditions and the airless Brisbane Valley Highway out of Ipswich. The car was hissing as I cruised down past empty tent sites and dormant barbecue pits and parked within sight of the dam water.

'Cool down,' I said to the Peugeot and made my way to the picnic tables and benches under a stand of gums, over-looking the dam. I shared the shade with several kangaroos and wallabies.

Within minutes I heard a car approaching, and turned to see a rich maroon ZB Custom Ford Fairlane winding its way towards me. As it got closer, I could see it still bore the original raised crest hood ornament. It would have had a Selectair ventilation system inside and bench seats. I knew this car inside out. My father had owned one.

I vaguely recalled Ford's advertising at the time, announc-ing that the ZB was the car 'most people move up to', and as the Fairlane squeaked to a halt next to the Peugeot, I was filled with nostalgia for my father and the smell of the car when he'd first brought it home, and the maiden voyage I took with him that night, a young copper still living with his parents (though Peg was on the horizon), cruising the streets of South Sydney and Surry Hills and out to Bondi and back.

The driver's door creaked open loudly and several of

the smaller wallabies rose and bolted. An old man emerged and then fastidiously locked the vehicle. It had to be Walt Whitman.

I thought of how he had locked the car and realised that this possession, now almost forty years old, must have been the pinnacle of his achievement as a professional working man. This must have been the symbol of his success as a middle-aged public servant, and from there perhaps he had hit a plateau until retirement.

He shuffled over to the picnic bench.

'You're the idiot who's been causing all the troubles?'

'Nice to meet you, Mr Whitman.'

'We had a place for idiots like you in my day. A small room in George Street with no windows. You'd count paper clips till you learned to shut your trap.'

'And nice to meet you too.'

'What was that?'

'Nothing.'

Walt Whitman had reached an age where the entire architecture of human courtesy and decency had collapsed. At his age, on the shoreline of death, so to speak, why be polite?

'Carpenter suggested ...'

But he wasn't listening to me. He was gazing across the water of the dam, or what was left of it.

'I worked on the Somerset Dam,' he said, 'before and after the war. I knew it'd never be enough for Brisbane and I told them so. Bloody war blew out the construction time. We'd ordered the gates and steelworks from England in the late thirties, and the rearmament program put that on hold. The evil of Hitler, you see, even reached up the Brisbane River. We thought Somerset would see the city through to the eighties, but Brisbane boomed after forty-five. The city got real thirsty. So we had to start looking around again.'

'Wivenhoe,' I said.

'Wivenhoe. It'd been on the drawing board as early as 1902. Not many people know that. They wanted something here for flood mitigation after the great 1883 deluge. But the wheels of government. They move slow.'

I wasn't sure where Walt Whitman's history lesson was leading. But he certainly knew his water.

'In the late sixties, old Bjelke gave it the green light, so we had to start reclaiming land. You got to give people time when you take their land. Twenty years or so, to get used to the idea, to get prepared. Twenty or so years, that's half a working lifetime. That's what we did here. But one person didn't want to leave. We had strife from the start. You'd think he'd found gold and didn't want anyone else to know about it. Then we had a young surveyor from the university out here in the mid-seventies, doing a doctorate or something. Found him with a bullet wound to the chest. Died in hospital. It was covered up, of course. The papers were told it was a roo-hunting accident. Poor kid. We never could prove who did it, but I bet my bottom dollar it was that pest Collison.'

'Collison?'

'The old guy who didn't want to give up his land. He did, in the end. He was hauled off by the cops, and his farm went under.'

'What happened to him?'

'Never found out.'

'There was another shooting out here recently, you know.'

'Course I bloody well know. You think I'm an idiot? That was no suicide. That fellow was no farmer either. He was a caretaker, for the government, trying to get by as best he could.'

'Don't you find it coincidental? The young surveyor

you just told me about, and the so-called farmer? Both shot dead?'

'You been touched by the sun or something? Nothing is coincidental. Not when it involves the most precious resource on earth. When it starts to run out — water — you can forget about diamonds and gold and oil. People'll be tearing each other's hearts out for water.'

As we looked out on the dam, I could just see three men tearing about on jet skis. I didn't know you were allowed to jet ski on Wivenhoe. But there they were, throwing up plumes and larking about.

'Idiots,' was all Walt Whitman said.

When he'd gone, I sat in the gathering dusk and thought long and hard about the old man's history lesson. Just when I thought I'd made connections in the case — if indeed it was a case, for it had clues and evidence so disparate and across generations that any self-respecting law enforcer wouldn't go near it — the whole thing fell apart in my head.

But the name — Collison. It bothered me. It scratched against the furthest recesses of my memory. Where had I heard that name? Collison.

Blast. I needed to get hold of Walt Whitman again. I needed to bounce Collison off him, but by now his old Fairlane would be barrelling towards Brisbane.

I stood to leave then, and on impulse walked to the edge of the water. It was a decent walk, trust me. The dried-out plates of mud cracked under my loafers all the way to the miserable, tepid shoreline of the shrunken lake. I could hear a motor in the distance. It got louder and louder. In a flash one of the jet-ski men emerged from the gloom, slowed not far from me, stood up in the saddle, then turned in a wide arc and disappeared.

On its tail was a clearly legible sticker.

SAVE NOOSA.

11

WHEN I WAS first promoted to detective in the sixties, one of my superiors handed me a copy of Dale Carnegie's enduring classic, *How to Win Friends and Influence People.* 'Memorise it,' my boss told me. 'It might save your life one day.'

I couldn't see how the persuasive techniques of Carnegie, a former Missouri farm boy who cut his teeth selling bacon and lard, could help me on the mean streets of Kings Cross, but I gather the boss's intention was for me to learn how to talk my way out of tough scrapes, if need be.

Funnily, I used one of Carnegie's techniques almost half a century later on the linen-clad multi-millionaire history-obsessed nut job who tried to freeze me to death in a storage freezer just outside Noosa. I utilised one of Dale's methods on how to win people over to your way of thinking. Namely, and to paraphrase, Dramatise Your Ideas.

I found my Noosa friend on one of his early-morning beach walks, and with the help of a small handgun I had in my possession, I dramatised my idea of getting him to tell me what the hell was going on by placing the muzzle beneath his chin in the charming woodlands at the bottom of Hastings Street.

He appreciated this dramatisation quite readily, and promptly urinated in his knee-length designer shorts.

'It wasn't my idea,' he said in a childlike voice.

'What?'

'The freezer.'

I think he'd started to cry, but I wasn't sure if he was gurgling or if it was a nearby bush turkey sitting proudly on its monstrous nest in the dappled shade of the forest.

'Is it true this used to be a caravan park, this delightful glade?' I asked him.

'I ... I think so.'

'Before your time, I guess. Then again, you wouldn't be seen dead in a caravan, would you? Though, strangely, I have seen many dead people in caravan parks. Caravan parks are places of inordinate violence. There was a particularly gruesome homicide in Windsor ...'

'Please don't hurt me.'

'Dale Carnegie recommended several ways to persuade people to like you,' I said, staring at the nails on my trigger hand and picking at them with my free hand. 'One of those ways was to encourage other people to talk about themselves. Let me put it politely. I am now encouraging you to talk about yourself.'

'I have money.'

'I know that, my friend. I just want you to tell me some stories. Historica, for example. Your business card, found on a dead man's fridge.'

'I told you. It's a hobby. An interest in history. A small group of us.'

'Like knitting. Or bridge.'

'Sort of.'

I pushed the gun hard into that soft, flabby, self-indulged turkey neck of his. 'Another Carnegie gem is to arouse in people an urgent want. I WANT you to start talking. Are you feeling it too?'

'I don't want to *diiiiiiiiie*,' he sobbed.

Even the turkey raised its head and looked quizzical.

'For crying out loud.'

I marched him deeper into the woods. I could see the river through the trees. I sat his quivering body down and stood above him.

'Let's start again. The business card.'

The muzzle was now a foot in front of his face. It's amazing the effect it can have, seeing the little unblinking eye at the end of a gun barrel.

'I'm a Queenslander through and through. I love Queensland,' he said.

'Save it for your Queensland Day honours speech.'

'I'm passionate about its history. It's that — the history — that made us what we are today.'

'And what is that?' I kept in check my rising patriotism for New South Wales, despite being a relatively new Queensland citizen. I was a Blue through and through, but in my dotage, who knows? I might be persuaded to turn Maroon. As Dale advised, don't criticise, condemn or complain.

'Proud. Optimistic. Never say die.' He glanced at me quickly when he said 'die', and did not linger on the word. 'This state is booming. It's the envy of the rest of the country. It's finally becoming what we all knew it could be — economic powerhouse, cultural dynamo, the promised land. Our history made it that. And it's our job, at Historica, to keep that history in check.'

'How the hell do you keep history in check?'

'We make sure it's preserved. Laid out and etched in stone. These history wars that have been raging for the past few years. Were Aboriginals massacred, were they not? Can history become the instrument of government power and ideology?'

'Are you asking me these questions, or being rhetorical?'

'Changing history can be extremely damaging — to an economy, a society, to individual people. That's my hobby. To keep history out of the present and where it belongs — in the past.'

I shook the gun in his face.

'You've told me exactly nothing I needed to hear. The dead farmer. Explain.'

The millionaire lowered his head and seemed to stare at his now soiled Italian loafers. They were probably worth more than my annual pension.

'He had come across something — a body — that just might have disrupted the history I was telling you about.'

'I think I know that body. We had a few hours together in an icebox. What sort of body could possibly derail a state's history?'

'Honestly, I don't know who it is. Was. I just got a call and was told to pick it up.'

'Out near Wivenhoe. Decomposed. Vest and buttons. Big round window blown into the forehead.'

'That's right.'

'Who called you?'

'I can't tell you.'

'Can't or won't? Not very Queensland of you. I thought in the new Queensland there was no such word as "can't".'

'Historica has been going for more than a century. It has deep roots. Most of the members don't even know who the other members are. When you get told to do something, from someone in the Index, you do it.'

'The Index?'

'The upper tier. The inner chamber. Whatever you want to call it.'

'History. Index. How cute. You get told by a stranger to murder a complete stranger and you don't even question it?'

'Of course I *dooooooo.*' He was back to wailing again. 'We went out there to the property. The man wasn't cooperative. That was that. We left a card, in case he changed his mind. We had our sources. We knew he was sitting on something the Index was interested in. Late one night when the guy wasn't there, we removed the old corpse. A little while later the guy turns up dead. It had nothing to do with us, honestly.'

'Maybe the Index is feeding you a load of codswallop.'

'I don't know what that is.'

'Look it up in a book,' I said. I was getting annoyed with him. 'So where's the old corpse now?'

'It vanished, I swear to God.'

'This is a very dexterous corpse.'

'It was in the freezer, then it was gone.'

'I don't believe you. In fact, I'm finding your retelling of events historically inaccurate. Who's Collison?'

'I've never heard of a Collison.'

'That geezer in the John Oxley Library, the Johnny Cash look-alike. Who's he?'

'Who?'

'Come *onnnn,*' I said. 'Ringo Starr. Black bob. Likes a full-breasted jacket.'

'I don't know.'

'You're telling me you've been a history aficionado since you were a kid; you're in some secret society called Historica, which has an inner-sanctum called the Index; you've at one point had a human relic stashed in one of your restaurant freezers; and you don't know who one of the primary patrons of the John Oxley Library – only Queensland's most important historical receptacle – is? You're pulling my bookmark here.'

It was then I pressed the gun hard against his forehead. So hard I could see the skin indent.

Tears sprang down his fake-tanned cheeks.

You can imagine my surprise two days later when I opened the local newspaper back home on the Gold Coast and read a story about the body of a Noosa millionaire who'd been found half-buried in sand at the end of that fabled beach. Drowning, they said, though a curious circular contusion had been discovered in the centre of his very dead forehead.

The Index, it seemed, had deep and violent roots indeed.

But it wasn't half as surprising as his ultimate answer to my question about the identity of our man in black at the library. It continues to rattle about in my brain.

Who is it? I had asked.

And I thought he was being physically sick when he finally said. 'Logan. I only know him as Logan.'

12

WHILE WALT WHITMAN was inside the John Oxley Library on a special mission for me, I waddled across to the Gallery of Modern Art and spent some time with Andy Warhol.

What's not to like about Andy? I was hip to Andy in the sixties when I, in fact, saw myself as hip. (Though I was far, far from hip.) I thought he was a big New York advertising executive who worked for Campbell's Soup. What did I know, putting away jugs of VB at the South Sydney leagues club on a Friday and Saturday night? Perusing the GoMA exhibition I understood, as a retired old geezer now, that Andy the artist had become sort of quaint. His work, once so modern, had also aged along with the rest of us, and become of a period. Yet Andy never seemed to age. I guess he would have liked that.

While Whitman – who had become a friend of the John Oxley archivists, having spent many years pecking away at their collection in his quest for all references to the city's water history – set about handwriting copies of certain pages of Captain Logan's journal for me, I drowned myself in the Warhol exhibition.

Leaving the gallery, I wondered what sort of art Andy might have made if he'd lived in Brisbane, and not New York. What might he have done with tins of Golden Circle pineapple? (Far more interesting than Campbell's soup cans.) Or the granite melon of Sir Joh Bjelke-Petersen? Instead of Marilyn Monroe or Elizabeth Taylor, might we have seen a huge, rouge-lipped print of Abigail or Sonia McMahon? I shuddered at the lost possibilities of Andy.

I waited and waited for Walt Whitman. I strolled all the way to the South Bank beach and the pools where the children thrashed about like a sardine shoal, and back to Tognini's, where I enjoyed a coffee and a blueberry friand. I was beginning to think Walt Whitman had been diverted by his own research, that he'd found a previously unseen quote from Logan about the Brisbane River.

Eventually, as I was about to return to the gallery to take a closer look at Warhol's death pictures, old Walt finally shuffled past the café with his little cracked leather briefcase over his shoulder.

'Whitman,' I called. 'WHITMAN.'

He dropped down into the chair at my table.

'You got it?'

'Of course I got it, you idiot,' he said in his usual charming manner.

'Why did you take so long?'

'You want it or don't you? How long do you think it takes for these hands to copy out a lot of words like that? Take a look?' He held up an arthritic right hand as gnarled as a dead tree.

'You want a cup of coffee?'

'What the hell do you think a cup of coffee will do to my ticker? Have you got any idea? I've got to get going.'

'Just hold your horses, old timer,' I said. 'Tell me what they were like. The journal pages.'

'I've wasted enough of my precious time already. You want more of it? You got to pay.'

'What are you, some Los Angeles therapist that charges by the hour?'

'What?'

'Forget it.' I tossed him a twenty-dollar note. 'So?'

'What do you think they were like? Old. Yellowed. Insect damage.'

'Legible?'

'Course they were bloody legible. What do you think I've been doing for the past two hours? Whittling?'

I tried to picture what Andy Warhol might have made of the warty, creased and scaly head of Walt Whitman, then shook my head and tried to break out of this bizarre train of thought. I knew at least what I was thinking. I'd like to see Walt in Andy's electric-chair picture.

'Here,' he said, dropping a sheaf of papers on the table. 'I'm off.'

I ordered another coffee, settled back and read Walt Whitman's transcript. I had to give it to him. He really did have beautiful penmanship, completely at odds with his ugly physical self. I could almost see him as a Queensland schoolboy, the playground tar outside his classroom boiling in the heat of a summer day as he sweated over his lovely copperplate.

And I also had to admire him for his research abilities. Walt Whitman stuck to his brief and cut to the chase.

The excerpts covered a couple of years leading up to Logan's death in 1830. I wanted to skip straight to the final journal entries of his short, miserable life, but delayed my gratification.

Three years before his murder, he had led an expedition into the Fassifern Valley and determined that there was 'no preparation requisite for the ploughshare'.

On 9 June 1827, he wrote: 'shot two beautiful parrots,

not hitherto found in the Colony'. How deliciously
fitting of Logan, to tear down beauty when he saw it. Or
was I just thinking with a twenty-first-century sensibil-
ity? 'Approached Mount Dumaresq towards evening; the
country now exceeded, in beauty and fertility, anything I
had before seen'. There were references to him shooting
emu and kangaroo, and how the shoes of his long-suffering
expedition party had worn through.

I was no literary scholar, but Logan's writings seemed
to change in tone and pace through the excerpts. On
one hand they were formal and dull, and on the other he
reflected his personal thoughts and emotions. If I'd had to
hazard a guess, I'd have said he wrote the official explorer's
journal at the end of the day, and the more emotional
material after some rum at night by the fire, or in the early
morning after a night of nightmares and paranoia. Tyrants
of whatever description, I assumed, must have more
troubled sleeps than the rest of us.

For example, on 2 September 1829 he recorded:
'Collison has begun questioning orders; was forced to
reprimand him for impertinence towards Mrs Logan. Have
withheld favours accorded him on account of his changed
disposition, and a short measure of lashes. He accepted
punishment without complaint. His attitude aggrieves me.'

He would be aggrieved even further a few months later,
on finding Collison wandering the settlement drunk and
half-naked. When confronted, the two pushed and shoved
before a gang of convicts and the 'show' became a source of
humiliation for Logan.

'For as long as I have occupied this uniform I have never
experienced such affrontry ... I personally took the leather
to Collison and had him in irons for Christmas ... it has
been suggested he be removed from my service and join the

animals in the mill work, but despite all, I have an unexplained affection for him.'

Was this Logan's fatal error? The smallest crevice of humanity that led to his downfall?

Now I came to the final diary entries of Logan.

During much of October 1830, as he trudged about the future Wivenhoe Dam region, his explorer's entries were fantastically dull. Then it all changed. The hunter had become the prey.

'Unsure of Collison,' he wrote. 'Since Christmas last he has uttered hardly a dozen sentences, yet continues about his work as if I don't exist … carries my scars with silence … I have observed him staring at me with what could only be ill-intent.'

Then the final two days. History told us Logan wandered alone after he left the party in search of the lost horse from a previous expedition. The journal entries, however, told something else: 'Collison refusing to take orders but still he follows … on his face he expresses the malice of a common convict … raised the crop to him to no avail.'

He then described their final breakfast. 'Roasted chestnuts in the fire and hailed him but no response … he has become a madman, crouched on the far bank of the creek, staring at his master … he remains armed … fail to recall the number of shots Collison discharged at the natives yesterday evening … fail to recall …'

And that was the last earthly journal entry of Captain Patrick Logan. I was shaking as I folded Walt Whitman's notes.

It had been a strange and confusing few weeks. All I'd wanted was to research my family tree and discover that elusive bushranger in its straggly branches. Yet I'd found myself digging out the roots of a far more dangerous and immovable tree – that of history – and bodies had fallen around me, and still I was groping in the dark.

What had happened between Collison and Logan? The supposedly intractable books kept telling us Logan had been bludgeoned to death with a waddy. But had he?

I smelled a rat. Several, in fact. And that was when I reached the inevitable and familiar trigger point of any frustrating investigation. It's a dangerous tactic, but sometimes it's the only one you have left.

I marched up to the John Oxley Library and demanded of the gentle, elderly lady behind the front desk that I speak to the man in black. Ringo. The shadow over this entire mystifying case.

'You must be mistaken,' she said. 'There is nobody of that description here, nor has there ever been. And if you don't leave quietly, I will have to call security.'

I sat in the Peugeot in the library car park, confused and disappointed. I kept hearing Peg in my head – Let it go, let it go.

So I let it go, reached for the ignition key, and that's when I got belted across the back of the head with a waddy.

13

So here I am. Probably the first prisoner of the Old Windmill on Wickham Terrace since the nineteenth century. Though that would not be revealed to me immediately. At first, I didn't know where I was. One minute I'd been sitting in the old Peugeot in the library car park, the next – oblivion.

When I came to, I was trussed up like a Christmas turkey with an eyeless hood over my sore and sorry head. I instinctively reverted to my training, tried to smell beyond the cloth that sucked in and out against my nostrils like a blacksmith's bellows, and found nothing identifiable. Or did I? Wherever I was smelled very old, and beyond that? Was that the scent of rusted copper?

As for my life flashing before my eyes, it had come not as a pleasurable epic film in a cinema, suffused with the wonderful aroma of buttered popcorn, but as a scratchy sequence of old Kodak slides juggled out of sequence. Suddenly, there was my dad in his new Fairlane, both of them beaming and gleaming outside my childhood home. There was me on my graduation day from the police academy. There was Peg standing atop a set of stairs by the door of a TAA aircraft. There was my mother in her Sunday hat.

Then a padlock was sprung, a door was opened and shut, and heavy footsteps approached.

The hood was reefed off and I faced the disconcerting visage of a man who himself had his head hooded.

'Well, that's weird,' I said.

My captor pulled up a wooden chair and slowly sat down opposite me. I could hear traffic outside. Pale light fell through a distant window. My new best friend in the Abu Ghraib hat was wearing overalls, work boots and what appeared to be gardening gloves.

'You're a nuisance,' he said. He sounded like Chips Rafferty, if Chips had been raised in Windsor Castle in Old Blighty.

'You're not the first to tell me that,' I said.

'I'm sure I'm not.'

'What the hell do you think you're doing, clouting innocent old pensioners over the head?' It was all I could think of saying. Getting on the offensive. Dale Carnegie would not have approved.

'You have become what my grandmother would have described as a nosey parker,' he said.

'And as my grandmother would have said, your grandmother didn't know diddly-squat.'

'It's time you joined the animals in the mill work,' he said in his lovely baritone voice, 'despite any unexplained affections I might have towards you.'

The phrase jarred in my brain. I had read it just hours (or was it days?) before in the transcripts of Logan's journal. 'So you're familiar with Captain Logan, then?' I asked.

'Indeed,' he said, folding his arms. 'And where better to quote him than in this, his cathedral.'

'His cathedral?'

'Oh yes, you don't know where you are. Let's keep it that way for the moment.'

'And who might you be?'

'That's not important, for the time being.'

'What sort of lunatic wanders about in the height of summer wearing a boiler suit, a hood and a pair of gardening gloves?' I was trying to tease him into action, to make something happen. He was either going to kill me or he wasn't. I'm the sort of person that doesn't like to be kept guessing. He remained silent.

'No talkies? Okay. I'll do it for both of us. Let me take a wild guess at this. You're some sort of madman, still living at home with your mother – a motel, perhaps, on the outskirts of town? – and who has a grudge against Wivenhoe simpletons and Noosa millionaires. When you were a schoolboy here in Brisbane you identified with the colonial tyrant Patrick Logan. Throughout your teenage years his life and work spoke to you, and gradually you embodied his cruel and sadistic person. You tortured cats and birds, and incinerated ants with a magnifying glass. Now, in between killing people, you like to go out to the Brisbane Valley and dress up in old penal colony outfits and play war games with your beautifully restored muskets. Am I warm?'

'Not even close.'

'Maybe I've met you before. In the John Oxley Library. Black bob. Beatles fan. Spent most of your life defending *The White Album* over *Sergeant Pepper*. Maybe you're not Captain Patrick Logan at all, but Sergeant Pepper.'

'Give me *The White Album* any day. But wrong again.'

'Then what's your name? Come on. Give me a hint.'

'My real name? Or the name I go by?'

'How about the real one?'

'Collison.'

I was left with my mouth half open. I couldn't quite believe what I'd heard.

'Would you mind repeating that?'

'Sure. Collison.'

'Do you happen to know a very short man, patron of the John Oxley Library, by the name of Logan?'

'Sure I do.'

I had to take stock and think. 'You would obviously know that in the history of Queensland, Logan's personal servant was one Private Collison, or so my research tells me, and there has been conjecture, courtesy of Logan's journals and apocryphal anecdote, that Logan was in fact murdered by Collison. This is no coincidence, is it?'

'No, it's not.'

'Please,' I said. 'Before you kill me, or torture me with your thoughts on Beatles albums, could you tell me what in the world has been going on?'

'I don't see why not.' He shuffled in the chair. It barked on the floor and echoed. 'As we both know, a government caretaker out near Esk recently came across a semi-mummified corpse on the edge of Lake Wivenhoe. The water levels have dropped. The drought. This is not news to anyone in Brisbane. He in turn believed he had made some sort of important historical find, and made several phone calls to young, time-poor, uninterested public servants and gatekeepers, who palmed him off to the John Oxley Library. With me so far?'

'Yes.'

'That's when you came in. The caretaker brought the picture of the body to the library, got his instructions wrong, and, voila, there you were in that little red room overlooking the river. Wrong place at the wrong time. It didn't matter. Word was already out about the corpse. Historica. Are you familiar with them?'

'Oh yes.'

'The head of the Index is our friend Mr Logan. And yes, he is directly related to Captain Patrick Logan. It has been his role, as part of that long family line, to protect his forefather's reputation as a frontiersman, a martyr of the Australian colonial experience.'

'Then the caretaker found the real body of Captain Logan,' I said. I wanted to hold up a revelatory index finger, but I couldn't, manacled tight as I was.

'After all those years, who would have thought? The official history was a lie. Logan had to be upheld as a shining example of colonisation. Murdered by an Indigenous tribe. Not delivered to God by a sensitive young private who had for years carried the guilt and shame of this man's cruelty, and even more so been the recipient of it. On behalf of the penal colony of Brisbane, Collison snapped, and exacted retribution. How would Logan have looked then, murdered by an underling and no longer the heroic explorer, after which cities and rivers have been named? So the body of a convict was honoured in his place, and nobody was the wiser.'

'And you, sir, are a descendant of Private Collison?'

'Proudly so,' he said. 'You see, it was in our best interests, too, to keep the family secret. We may have changed our name more than a century ago to protect our interests, but we're a very wealthy and influential Brisbane family, my friend, and a murderer in the cupboard would simply not do.'

'Let alone a contemporary Collison going about murdering people.'

'History is a very powerful thing,' he said from under the hood, and Brisbane is full of very powerful secrets.'

'And Mr Logan, from the library?'

'A cruel little man. Wouldn't it be deliciously ironic if he had suffered the identical fate as his long-lost relative after all this time? A blood relative of Logan, murdered by a blood relative of Collison. Two identical murders, mirroring each other, almost two centuries apart. Isn't that interesting?'

'And the corpse of Logan himself? The original Logan? The real Logan?'

'He made a wonderful fire. And the chestnuts I roasted over the flames were delicious.'

'You're insane, Collison.'

'But my dear fellow, that's not my name. I've never heard of this Collison you talk of.'

I said: 'Two lines of a family tree collide. The apple ...'

'... doesn't fall far from the tree,' he said.

Of course he let me go. He muttered something about history not being history unless it had its witnesses. I walked out of the Old Windmill and was blinded by the afternoon light. And Collison was gone.

Later, on the Gold Coast, Peg bathed the back of my head and wrists. I didn't have the energy to explain the wounds, and she didn't ask. How could I tell her that many years ago, a man had murdered his superior in the scrub outside Brisbane, and the descendant of the murderer had destroyed the corpse to keep the secret and protect the family name? Which suited a descendant of the victim, who also didn't want his noble relative to lose his place in history?

'History,' I muttered to myself. 'A minefield.'

When Peg was done patching me up, she said: 'I've got a surprise for you.'

'Please. No more surprises.' I was finding Queensland simply too full of surprises.

She walked me onto the back deck and pointed to the bonsai in the centre of the table. It was my tiny fig. The soil was black and moist, the roots healthy and several baby shoots were appearing on the limbs.

History. It was never dead, fixed, chiselled into stone. It was like the bonsai. A little attention, a bit of close scrutiny and it could flare to life again.

'The family tree,' I muttered.

'What?' Peg asked.

'Nothing.'

THREE

MURDER ON THE VINE

1

I WOULD NEVER have had the misfortune of meeting the reprobates from the Marx Brothers Kombi Auto Shoppe if I hadn't had the dream. And I would never have had the dream of the Kombinationskraftwagen if I hadn't watched that darned Kevin Costner film, *Field of Dreams*, for the ninety-third time. And I might not have watched the Costner film if I hadn't been seduced by all that seventies 'peace not war' palaver, and the battered Kombi that Costner crosses the country in looking for the meaning of life, and James Earl Jones to boot. I don't think I'd have even been watching *Field of Dreams*, either, if I hadn't been invited back to the inner-city Brisbane apartment of my old friend, the bon vivant and restaurant critic Westchester Zim, to share a few bottles of some of his secret 'finds' – hush-hush.

We drank a lot of wine, and when I drink a lot of wine I get melancholy, and when I get melancholy I watch *Field of Dreams*. Enough said. Might I have been seduced by any of this if I wasn't a sensitive soul with a nostalgic bent for the seventies, having *lived* it, and felt, in these troubled times, that what the world needed was a bit more love and a lot less war? I didn't know my entry into the Kombi world would lead to very little love, and a whole lot of war.

You see, I had a dream. A dream where all vehicles were created equal. No, I said that for effect. For levity. For any pitiful little chortle that would take me away from the nightmare of my acquaintance with the Marx Brothers Kombi Auto Shoppe. You would think I could get through a single year without putting my life in danger, but no. Round the inside of the fishbowl I go, not recognising the same miserable sprig of weed, the lifeless, helmet-wearing deep-sea diver.

This time it wasn't my fault. I could blame Zim, but he's dead. I could point the finger at the unexpected demise of my beloved Peugeot 504, which accidentally caught fire in the car park of the Main Beach Surf Club late one afternoon as I was enjoying a dip at dusk. Oh, it caused all sorts of panic. The next morning the local rag claimed that Al Qaeda had come to the coast! Suicide bomber at the beach! But, alas, a post-mortem of the Peugeot's charred remains revealed just a rupture in the fuel tank on a hot day. A veritable confluence of unfortunate circumstances, which saw her blow like a cheap Chinese firecracker. I have to say, it was pretty impressive. Even from the shallows, where I was wallowing, oblivious, the car park's neighbouring casuarinas went up with an impressive *whoof*.

So I was car-less. And it was then that I felt a nostalgic pull for all things simpler and purer. Sure, I'd loved the Peugeot. But I'd always yearned for a Kombi van. And thus the dream of a Kombinationskraftwagen. Not a split-screen, or a Splittie, as they're so eye-wateringly known. No, nothing pre-seventies, but a classic Bay Window model. I would buy the ultimate freedom box. I would have one restored, fitted out as a camper, and I would take my son, Jack, away from his fraught, TV-dominated, computer-game-ravaged pixel-poxy future. I would remind

him of the forests and the oceans, and we would sit about
a campfire on weekends away and bond, as they say these
days, and have real discussions, and we would fish and swim
and take in lungfuls of fresh, eucalyptus-scented air on our
bushwalks, and with any luck he would remember these
moments, and possibly take them into his own fatherhood,
and hand the baton over to his children. (And being happily
predisposed to me, courtesy of all those Kombi trips, lodge
his dribbling, incontinent, befuddled old father in a better
class of nursing home.)

So where did I find the Kombi of my dreams? On
the blasted computer, of course. And I made a phone
call. 'Could I see the Kombi you have advertised on the
internet?'

'Sure,' said Rufus T. Firefly, owner and proprietor of
the Marx Brothers Kombi Auto Shoppe. 'I'll need a two-
thousand-dollar holding fee.'

You see? Can you already hear the jingle-jangle of coins
in his malodorous voice? Can you detect, too, the whiff of
a sucker coming?

I declined to hand over the fee and temporarily abandoned the idea. But the dream scratched away. So a month
later I decided to drive down to Duck Soup Beach, home of
the Shoppe, and see the freedom box for myself. And that's
when I stepped into the rabbit hole.

You would think I might have shown more sense, hmm?
I had, after all, worked for a part of my career in the vice
squad. I had cracked heads that contained such complicated
and intricate devilry that even these young contemporary
computer hackers couldn't find a way in. I had reduced
some of my era's meanest men to tears. (One actually
slumped to the floor of the interrogation room, assumed a
foetal position, and wailed for his mammy. I sang him an

Al Jolson song, which only made him wail even louder.) I
was once a great believer in the Eight-Point Philosophy of
Persuasion. That'd be the eight bony points revealed when
you close both fists.

But no. I was too fuzzy with the call of the wide-open
road. Too blinded by the Kombi, a machine the equiva-
lent of the good old-fashioned Australian swag. A bed on
wheels. A hotel on four Dunlops. Peace. Love. Groovy,
man. I was blinded by rainbows and Lucy, in the sky, with
her ruddy diamonds.

I'd done my research. Since retiring to the Gold Coast,
Peg had insisted I take on some 'projects'. This is what
happens when you retire. You do 'projects', which is code
for something to keep decaying, pre-senile minds occupied,
but which don't actually contribute anything to society or
impinge on it in any way. 'Get a project,' my doctor had
said. Jack telephoned: 'What project you got going?' I had a
yarn one day to the postman, astride his puttering Kawasaki.
'You doing any projects?' he shouted through his helmet
visor. I sensed a conspiracy.

So I took on the Kombi project. I immersed myself in
the vehicle's fascinating history. I read everything I could on
that canny Dutch businessman, Ben Pon, who'd visited the
German VW factories in Minden shortly after the Second
World War. He loved Volkswagens, Mr Pon, and planned to
become the Netherlands' importer. (How dear Westchester
Zim would have enjoyed Pon. How proudly they would
have compared each other's three-letter surnames.) It was in
the factory, taken over by the British, that Pon first noticed
the little Plattenwagen zipping about the floor on that
April day in 1947. The Plattenwagen was a small, toy-like
transport vehicle made exclusively to move parts about the
factory. But in it – and this is genius – Pon saw the future.

He scribbled down in his notebook a drawing of a van that looked like a loaf of bread on wheels. And there it was. The VW transporter. Able to carry about everything from a brass band to a gaggle of handcuffed war criminals.

So Pon is widely considered the big daddy of the Kombi. He was also daddy to Ben Pon Junior, a famous sports-car racer, who competed for the Netherlands in clay-pigeon shooting at the 1972 Olympics in Munich. Pon Junior now owns a winery in Carmel, California. (This, too, would have pleased dear Zim no end.)

All this scholarship was on my mind when I first stepped onto the oil-spattered driveway of the Marx Brothers Kombi Auto Shoppe at Duck Soup Beach. I'd caught the bus that day and en route had checked out the surf. (You see how adolescent my thinking had become, within the orbit of a Kombi?) Then I took the short stroll to the workshop in an industrial estate behind a row of hoop pines.

I was admiring the shells of several dozen Kombis littered about the Shoppe and wondering about Pon and how he couldn't have known that the little bread box he sketched would lead to all this industry and dream-weaving on the other side of the world more than sixty years later, when I saw him for the first time – Rufus T. Firefly. He was wearing the uniform of Gold Coast tradesmen – Bermuda shorts, soiled runners without socks, a surf T-shirt and enormous tattoos. I've met some tough cases in my time, but Firefly sent a shiver down my spine. As did one tattoo on the back of his left calf, which later became the centrepiece of several of my nightmares. It was a picture of a Kombi submerged in water, with a woman trapped in the cabin, apparently drowning. Her floating aura of hair looked spooky beneath Firefly's own wiry leg hairs.

'Yeah?' sneered Firefly. He had the eloquence of a

caveman at the very dawn of human speech, when grunt gave way to words.

'I'm here about the Kombi,' I said.

He merely flicked his head. I followed him into the workshop, its dark corners sporadically illuminated by explosions of spark from a welder's gun.

If I'd known this lowlife had had a hand in my good mate Westchester Zim's death just a fortnight earlier, I would have popped him right there in his office chair, sitting all smug and evil below a calendar of a naked woman doing strange things on the pop-top roof of an innocent Kombinationskraftwagen. But I didn't. I couldn't have dreamt of the connection at that stage. Like an ageing baby deer in an old Hollywood animation, I had stumbled into a forest of fantastic depravity and wrongdoing. Its evil would reach deep into the soil like an ancient grapevine, and enter the dark corners of the police, the judiciary and government itself. I was busy wondering whether I was of too ripe a vintage to learn how to surf, or wear a tie-dyed T-shirt without looking daft.

And had you told me what was in store for my scarred and bloated frame, I might have avoided the great art of vehicle restoration and picked up a little Toyota straight off the showroom floor.

'Have I gotta deal for you,' Firefly said, setting fire to a small cheroot with a lighter fashioned in the shape of a woman with large, flashing breasts. That time-honoured phrase, that almost genetic cliché of the second-hand car salesman, should have set off every bulb on my switchboard. But it didn't. I was in what the best psychoanalysts might refer to as a 'Kombi trance'.

Then the fun began.

2

LET'S GO BACK a few weeks, so I can tell you what my dear friend Westchester Zim was like – when he was alive.

Zimmy, as he was fondly known, was one of Queensland's first, and finest, restaurant critics. He was first because when he started reviewing in Brisbane in the sixties, he only had about three restaurants over which he could cast his fearsome eye and skewer with his devastating turn of phrase. That's not a terribly big and bountiful carousel to go around on.

He told me, confidentially, that to fill his newspaper column space in those days he simply reviewed the dinner parties he was invited to, and invented a name and address for the 'restaurant'. His newspaper received hundreds of complaints from readers trying unsuccessfully to find, for example, 'Le Petit Poulet', or 'Slappers and Flappers New York Ribs'. Once, after reviewing his tennis partner Mary Kostas's souvlaki, giving the entirely fictitious 'Dimitri's Moustache' a big thumbs-down, he was approached in Queen Street by a burly gentleman sporting a Mediterranean handlebar moustache big enough for a children's bicycle. 'You Zim?' the brute said. 'Me Dimitri.' And he socked poor Westchester in the face.

Zim's little ruse was soon uncovered, and he made his way to Sydney in the early seventies, where there were enough restaurants to preclude him from actually inventing them. That's where I met Zimmy, in a tacky South Korean chophouse in Chinatown one evening. When I say I met him there, I should be more precise. We were in fact conducting a fairly routine drug raid, and Zim was soon lined up against the wall with the other startled customers. Our guns were drawn. 'I'm not a suspect!' Zim shouted, his hands trembling. 'I'm a restaurant reviewer!' (Oh, how many times have I quoted that luscious line back at him?) It was lucky we were there. Zim had given the chophouse half a star only the year before, and just as we quietly entered, our hands on our holsters, the restaurant manager had shrieked, raced across the room and tried to throttle a startled Zim. It was deliciously chaotic. The lobsters in their tanks had a front-row seat. In my official report later that night, I wrote that we'd conducted a successful raid, and additionally had prevented a murder.

That's how Zim and I had got to know each other, and he would often give me insider knowledge on the best places to eat across town. 'Zimmy,' I'd say to him on the phone, 'I feel like something Turkish, and it's the wife's birthday.' And, sure enough, we'd arrive at his recommendation and be made a fuss of. Even Zim muttered in Turkish still sounds like Zim.

He was ahead of his time, Westchester. He was, he said, born to review restaurants. It's the way his head worked. It was how he saw the world. He reviewed everything as he experienced it – a bus ride to work ('The driver was firm but courteous, the transport itself clean and without frills'), watching men mowing in the Botanic Gardens ('The grass was left unattractive near the harbour rocks, thus ruining the overall aesthetics'), even having a bath ('Once again, I found the Sydney water harsh and not conducive to a good lather, but altogether splendid compared to the ammonic headiness of Brisbane water'). He'd been a fussy eater as a child, and had quite literally put his mother in an asylum for six months when he was a toddler. He'd stayed with his aunt during her convalescence. 'A chance,' he said many times, 'to expand my developing palate.' I cannot blame Zim here. I once ate at his mother's house near the end of her life, and her boiled brisket made me dry retch.

He could, as you might have already guessed, be a little off-putting with his verbose manner. Strangely, the way he spoke – full of pomp and wind – was the opposite to his printed prose. His reviews were sharp and crisp, without an ounce of fat. I, and most certainly the restaurant owners, will never forget his classic review of a Tibetan eatery called The Sound of One Hand Clapping. The entire review was just six words: 'The sound of no hands clapping.'

Zimmy was perhaps a decade older than me, and I was not surprised that he finally left Sydney and returned to his hometown of Brisbane to semi-retire. What he found, after a thirty-year absence, was a culinary transformation. Brisbane was no longer a place where the year's gastronomic highlight was the arrival of the frozen dim sim. He was like an old horse that had returned to a magical orchard, and in his excitement he went back to full-time reviewing, becoming, in the process, something of a celebrity around town. Zim and the age of the celebrity chef–reviewer collided. He was a man to be feared. He could close a restaurant overnight, such was his power.

You would think, with all that professional eating, that Zim would be a man of formidable proportions. But he was the opposite. Zim had hollow legs, as his mother had always told him. It was a phrase, in fact, that he had usurped as the title for his perennially incomplete autobiography. He was sensationally thin, and too tall for his weight. Clothes dangled off the wire of him. His hair, too, though thick and white, defied the teeth of a comb and grew into a sort of edifice of spun sugar. Zim had the top knot all his life. His enemies called him Pigeon.

When I, too, retired to the Gold Coast, he invited me up for the odd meal, and if I drank too much, which I always did with Zim, we'd return to his inner-city apartment overlooking the river, its walls heavy with art, and he'd read to me passages from his favourite restaurant critics from around the world. He loved the internet, did Zim, because he could raid newspaper and magazine websites for great food writing.

In this last year of his life, he'd been fanatical about the British critic A. A. Gill, even memorising the Londoner's best passages. With the muddy brown Brisbane River oozing past behind him, he'd recite them to me like some amateur Shakespearean actor.

"'I sat down, touched the stickiness of a table that had been wiped with a dirty cloth, and knew instantly that you should never eat the same thing twice,'" pronounced Zim, quoting Gill. He continued: "'Like history, food repeats itself – once is comedy, twice is vomit. The ribs and that barbecue flavour – such a cosmopolitan, grown-up Hollywood version of home-grown brown sauce – tasted as if they'd been boiled in an ashtray ... This is bad from a bad place where the bad people live. This is a glutinously awful pig-swamp bad, out all on its own in the badlands. This is, to put it simply, just so you don't forget, terribly bad food.'"

At this Zim would have to sit down to compose himself.
'He's brilliant, this Gill,' he'd say. 'So daring. So *fresh*. I wish
I had his courage. And his country's more lenient defama-
tion laws. Here, get a load of this: '"Next, my milk–fed
lamb was three squiggly, munchkin bits of nascent sheep.
You rarely get this in England, and I can't think why – the
place is lousy with the sodden, limping, maggoty things,
with farmers always complaining that they can't give them
away at car–boot sales. The Easter milk–fed lamb has a
serious premium. A drunk man with a stocking on his head
has to grab the teeny-weeny, gambolling, gamine-eyed,
plaintively bleating baby from its mother's nipple, then
shoot it in the face with a nail gun while mumsy runs in
circles. I can't imagine why you can't get it at Tesco ... it is
utterly delicious and worth every soft, sentimental bleat."'

'Now that's good,' I said.

'Now that's brilliant,' he replied.

I miss Zim. They said he'd had a heart attack at some
new and trendy restaurant/vineyard in the Gold Coast
hinterland. Dropped stone dead while taking a stroll
through the trellises and vines.

Only later would I find out he'd been murdered.

At his funeral, I read out his favourite A. A. Gill passage:
'"I started with a complimentary shot glass of insemination-
temperature cauliflower soup, with a cold cream cappuc-
cino top and a grey, slimy nose-blow of truffle oil as a
garnish. You can sip it like espresso, the waiter said helpfully. Liquidised cauliflower tastes like fat boy's farts.
Effluent cauliflower with added truffle oil tastes like corpse
bloat. I didn't ask for it, I didn't want it and I don't care to
be quizzed about why I didn't enjoy it."'

This was, of course, an allusion to death itself. Everyone
laughed. Except the expensively dressed man with blond,

gelled hair in the back pew. Our eyes locked for a moment. I jotted a mental note. I thought later – how might Zim have reviewed him?

'Potentially fatal to a good palate.' How right he would have been.

3

A DAY AFTER Westchester Zim's funeral, I was shocked to receive a call from his solicitor, asking – no, *begging* – me, to take charge of his affairs.

'You are the only one I can talk to about this,' he said. 'There is nobody else.'

Nobody else? Zim might have had his enemies in the foodie circles of Australia, but he had loyal friends and devotees as well. Didn't he? I always pictured him out on the town each night, supping at the finest eateries with the most important people of the day, shooting bons mots across the silverware, being confided in with grave or titil-lating secrets. A good meal, he always said, opens the most private of doors. But a great meal invites you inside. (Or something like that.)

'What do you mean there's no one else?' I said to the solicitor. 'We only met about once a month.'

'Please,' the solicitor said. 'There is no next of kin. It's very sad. You'd be doing him a great favour. Or the memory of him.'

So I ended up as executor of poor Zim's estate, and one maudlin, stormy Friday I travelled to Brisbane to sort through his apartment.

As a former homicide detective, I can tell you something. The dwellings of the recently dead can be forbidding places. I have poked through squalid bedsits where lonely, forgotten pensioners have passed away; rifled through the bedroom drawers of missing persons; upturned the houses of drug dealers and fraudsters. But nothing gives you a chill like wandering amongst the furniture and belongings of a murder victim. Knowing they'll never be coming back. Knowing they've left the place as some sort of unforeseen museum to themselves, their last moments frozen in time and space.

Yes, I knew in my bones, as soon as I opened the door to his apartment, and quietly closed it behind me, that I was inspecting the landscape of a murder victim.

Zim's was a very comfortable apartment. The open lounge and dining area faced a series of sliding glass doors that led onto a balcony. It had a beautiful southern view of the city that took in the Kangaroo Point cliffs, the Botanic Gardens, Parliament House and the river's dramatic about-face at the tip of the gardens. The leafy promontory appeared, from this elevation, like the prow of a magnificent ship, its decks crowded with fig trees and tropical plants and mangroves.

I sat for some minutes on a squatter's chair on the balcony, admiring the vista. In the distance, black clouds gathered and roiled, and threw twigs of lightning at Logan and beyond. Birds wheeled and shrieked above the gardens and little tethered boats bobbed at its perimeter. The storm was heading this way.

Back inside the apartment, my radar was sensitive to more than just a dead man's possessions and how they might be dispersed. More than debts that had to be resolved. That's the thing about death. It can leave a multitude of

loose ends, long and short, all of which have to be tied off
before we're truly assigned to oblivion. For when those
threads disappear, you only exist in the memories of others.
And when the memories go ...

Zim had taste, I'll give him that. He had an entire wall
of Cézanne reproductions – all the famous fruit paintings. What did Cézanne say? 'I'll astonish Paris with an
apple.' Not bad. Zim's restaurant reviews, you felt, always
built towards his encounter with the dessert. Entrees and
mains were the scaffolding that you climbed to get to the
sweet platform.

'It was my mother's fault,' he once confided in me over
a crème brûlée. 'She was a terrible cook, but she always
brought in magnificent desserts. She had what you called, in
the old days, a sweet tooth. I confess I was a trifle spoiled in
the dessert department. Trifle. You see, I cannot even say
the word without making reference to the dessert.'

I wandered into the kitchen. Over time I have learned
that there's nothing sadder than a bachelor's kitchen.
With Zim, it was a bit different. He had no cookbooks
on display, no dishes drying on a rack, no glass containers
of rice or pasta on show, because Zim never ate at home.
I mean never. He took his breakfast coffee at a favoured
café down on Albert Street, and ventured out for both
lunch and dinner. If he felt peckish late at night, he merely
phoned down to the restaurant housed on the ground
floor of his apartment building, which had a sort of 'room
service' arrangement with certain occupants. Zim was one
such occupant.

So his kitchen was immaculate, and not just because of
lack of use. Under the sink I found an enormous variety
of rags and sponges, cleaning utensils and liquid abrasives.
He cared for it like the altar in a church.

His bedroom was similarly immaculate. A standard queen-sized bed and lamps. Built-in cupboards. Another print of a baked fowl and vegetables above the bed head. The gathering winds thumped against the sliding doors off the bedroom. The curtains were closed, but I could see the camera flash of lightning at their frills.

He had one book by his bedside – a 1949 edition of Jean Anthelme Brillat-Savarin's *The Physiology of Taste*. He had mentioned Brillat-Savarin to me on many occasions. Too often, when Zim got deeper and deeper into his philosophies on food and cooking, and quoted obscure texts and gourmands at me, I switched off. But I remembered Brillat-Savarin, because he sounded like a very funny man.

'You would know of him, of course,' Zim had said one evening over some delicious Cantonese dishes in a restaurant on Margaret Street, just metres from his apartment.

'Why would I know of him?' I said, fumbling with my chopsticks. 'The meals of my working-class childhood were a procession of bread and dripping. Mutton. Peas and spuds. Then I became a policeman. The closest I got to gourmet in those years was when a pie came in its own tin-foil plate and not just a paper bag. Are you getting the picture, Zim?'

'He was the man who coined the phrase "Tell me what you eat, and I will tell you what you are." Heard of that?'

'Of course I've heard of that.'

'Well, that's a start.'

'What am I, Zim?'

'You? On Brillat-Savarin's scale? A barbarian, barely out of the cave.'

'Always a pleasure dining with you, Zim.'

'And me? What am I from your observation?'

'You? You're the man who's going to pay the bill tonight, that's who.'

We finished our mains and Zim spent an age considering the desserts. He never felt it necessary to ask me what I
might like. He ordered for both of us.

'You know, Brillat-Savarin also had another famous
quote,' he said. '"A dessert without cheese is like a beautiful
woman with one eye."'

How peculiar it was to learn that Zim, when his heart
had exploded amongst the vineyards on the Gold Coast,
had fallen face first into the flowering vines, and had had
an eye cleanly removed by a piece of errant wire hidden
amongst the leaves. A police mate told me confidentially
that the eyeball had given the young female constable who
was first on the scene a terrible fright. God can pull some
horrible practical jokes when He/She so chooses.

The storm was over the city now. The wind didn't just
howl, it moaned about Zim's apartment building, and I
could hear a thudding through the air-conditioning vents.

I sat on the edge of Zim's perfect bed, and opened *The
Physiology of Taste* at one of the pages he'd bookmarked. He
had underlined a quote in a chapter about the pleasures of
eating, and the table. 'At the first course everyone eats and
pays no attention to conversation; all ranks and grades are
forgotten together in the great manufacture of life. When,
however, hunger begins to be satisfied, reflection begins,
and conversation commences. The person who, hitherto,
had been a mere consumer, becomes an amiable guest, in
proportion as the master of all things provides him with the
means of gratification.'

Poor Zim. I should have paid more attention to you.

A mighty crack of thunder shook the building, the lights
flickered, and as I wandered out into the lounge room, I
noticed the front door wide open.

'What the ...' I said.

Then I heard a high-pitched scream and something – a baby gorilla? A small, hyperactive child? – was on my back. I swung around, he swivelled on my neck, and I whacked him flush in the face with the hardcover Brillat-Savarin.

It fell to bits in a spectacular flurry of pages and dust motes and long-dead weevils, and fluttered over my unconscious child assassin. The first thing I thought was that I must get Zim a replacement copy. But dead men don't need books.

The second was, could I persuade my wife Peg that knocking out children wearing fake moustaches counted as a retirement 'project'?

4

I'D SEEN SOME funny things during my time in law enforcement, but I never expected, in my retirement, to be extracting with tweezers the carcass of a Second World War vintage bug from the weeping eye of a janitor named Joe Santorini in the apartment of a dead friend.

Joe thought I was a burglar. I didn't know who he was. Perhaps a circus performer, or an old-looking child on a permanent diet of red cordial. When he had attached himself to my back, he'd given me a fright, and copped a face full of the writings of Brillat-Savarin.

When everything had calmed down, and soon after little Joe came to, he began clawing at his eye. He was crying profusely, whimpering like a small boy.

'Sorry about that,' I said. I genuinely felt for him. He was wearing his little janitor's outfit – slate-grey shorts and a matching shirt, with the word JANITOR embroidered above the pocket. The creases in his pants and on his sleeves were so fine and sharp you could have cut a slice of Gâteau Savarin with them. If it hadn't been for the JANITOR giveaway, he could have been a lad on his first day at school.

'You doan understand,' he said. 'I gotta blocked tear duck condition. Now there something in my eye. My *eyeeeeeee.*'

It turned out I had pulverised into his face an ancient insect from the book. I got most of the bug out. He didn't seem happy.

'What the hell you doin' here anyway?' said Joe. His eye continued to pour a single salty stream down his cheek.

'Zim's solicitor sent me, to take care of his estate.'

'He dead,' said Joe, lowering his face, the permanent river of tear somehow fitting.

'Yes, he dead,' I said. Joe sniffed. We had half a minute's silence for Zim. 'Now. Can I ask you the same question? What the hell are *you* doing here? A blocked sink?'

'Is Mr Zim's wine,' he said. 'I come for the key.'

'Key?'

'To his wine. Downstairs. It has to be moved away. I sneak him a storage cage downstairs for his wine, see? Sometimes he give Joe a bottle. A present. "Here, Joe, this for you," he sometimes say. Now the room, someone want to use. So I have to move the wine. But Mr Zim, he lock the cage. I need the key.'

'Boy,' I said. 'You city slickers move fast around here when someone drops off the perch.'

'Hey, space, she the premium in the inner-city nowadays, mate.' He pronounced it *marrrrt*, like the word had suffered a flat tyre.

Zim had admirable organisational skills. We both went into his office and opened his filing cabinets. There, in a small freezer bag, in a folder marked WINE − KEYS, we found the wine keys. I liked Zim's logical mind. In the cabinet, I would later discover, were the secret table notes he took on every meal in every restaurant he'd ever reviewed in his career. Zim and I were some of the few men left in the world who used five- by three-inch index cards. He scribbled his notes on these, holding them in his lap as he ate and pondered each course. Every card was numbered and dated. And he kept them, I presume, for litigation purposes. Or a future book. They were his diary, and many were covered in the small food splashes and droplets of the meal under review at that moment.

'You wanna see the wine of Mr Zim?' Joe said, wiping the tears from his cheek. We went to the basement.

I followed Joe to a storage cage behind the lift well. There were several other cages on either side of it, open and exposed to the underground car park, stuffed with people's junk beyond the wire. But Zim's was the only one that had been lined with flimsy sheets of plywood. He had wanted his privacy. Or wanted his wine to have some privacy. Expensive wine can have a strange effect on people. They've been known to kill for a good vintage. Or perhaps he thought the temptation might be too great for thirsty teenage hoons. (On reflection, would today's teenage hoons even know what wine was? 'Oi,' I can hear them say. 'This stuff's two years old – it's *orrrf*. It's *gaaayyy!*)

Joe fiddled with the lock and we entered the cage. He pulled a light cord and a single bulb came on. Before us were hundreds of bottles stacked neatly on wooden racks.

'Mr Zim, he no alcoholic, just so you know,' said Joe, lowering his gaze 'He a good man.'

I scanned the racks and a cluster of bottles caught my eye. Faced with a wall of blank black wine bottle tops, both cork and screw-on, these stood out. On the top of the cap each had the stamped symbol of VW, the car manufacturers. I pulled a VW bottle from the rack.

Now I'm no wine buff. Peg once tried to get me involved in a fine-wine tasting club on the Gold Coast. She thought it could be one of my retirement 'projects'. I went to the first meeting. It involved some plonker (I know it's a bad pun, but it's the only way I could ever think of him) swishing about various wines in large glasses and rinsing his teeth with the wine before spewing it into what became a very messy and stomach-flipping bucket of warm human discharge. He was, he said, looking for bouquets, delineating vintage, seeking what notes lay behind the wine and travelling – via his palate – through the vines and down into the soil. One's tongue, he said, could be trained as a sort of living archaeologist. What tosh. I raised my hand and said that if one's tongue was to dig deep into the soils of a hillside in Stanthorpe or a slope in the Hunter Valley, shouldn't we train it to be a geologist? He did not talk to me for the rest of the class.

Nevertheless, I swigged and spat, and tried to excavate soil sub-stratas for tannin and saddle-sweat and hints of gravel. But it wasn't for me. I had of course embarrassed Peg. I had, she later told me repeatedly, become *boorish* in my old age.

'I tried to introduce you to a civilised "project" and what do you do? You spit it back in my face.'

'I spat it in the bucket.'

'I thought you might make some new friends,' she said, sulkily. I didn't tell her that I liked people who actually *drank* the wine, not flushed it about their mouths like a haywire lavatory cistern.

But the VW bottles in Zim's cellar – they interested me. On the label was a lovely pale watercolour of your standard grape vines, but parked on a ridge in the distance, small as a lady beetle, was a pale red Bay Window Kombi van. The wine came from a vineyard in the Gold Coast hinterland.

I had seen this bottle before. On the night we'd come back to Zim's place after our last ever monthly meal in Brisbane, and we'd knocked the tops off a few bottles of some of his 'secret gems', discovered over the years on tours of wineries and in various restaurants, then watched *Field of Dreams* together, both of us melancholy and weeping deep down inside with the memories of our fathers, he had shown me one of these Kombi bottles. He had produced it, excitedly, because there was a Kombi being driven by Kevin Costner in the movie, and he popped on his spectacles and pointed to the little red Kombi on the ridge in the wine label.

'Is it wine or motor oil, Zim?' I asked.

'It has been recommended to me by a very, very fine nose,' said Zim.

'I beg your pardon?'

'A man with an impeccable palate. A peerless nose for bouquet. A man born to be a winemaker, or at the very least a sommelier. It's his little investment, in the hills behind the Gold Coast. It has been a well-kept secret in local wine circles. But soon everybody will know about it. It's the best wine ever made in Queensland.'

'So it was made last month, instead of last week?'

'Trust me. They will shower it with medals.'

'This nose of yours, what does he do for a real crust?'

'He's a very powerful developer—'

But I didn't let Zim finish, because the movie was just getting to the part where James Earl Jones gets invited into the cornfield to see 'the other side', and I loved it when he went with the ghostly baseball players to find out what it was like in heaven.

'Imagine it, Zim. Heaven,' I said.

'Yesssss,' said Zim. 'I should like to go there, just like James Earl Jones.'

Not long after that final get-together I like to think he did. Not a cornfield for Zim, but a vineyard. I also hoped

Zim ate well in heaven, drank wonderful vintages that he'd only ever read about in books, and perhaps even met his hero, the pioneering gourmand Jean Anthelme Brillat-Savarin, and exchanged notes on the meaning of wine in life, and good cheeses and the best desserts in history.

It wasn't until I sat in the filthy office of Rufus T. Firefly, proprietor of the Marx Brothers Auto Shoppe, that I saw a bottle of that Kombi wine once again, on an otherwise bare shelf behind his office desk, standing in between what appeared to be a knuckleduster and a small pile of naked lady cigarette lighters.

And if I squinted hard, I could see the tiny red Kombi parked on the ridge, a clot on my future.

5

YOU MAY NOT have noticed, but at the moment there's a lot of money to be made in nostalgia. Why? I'm no sociologist, but I have a theory. The world has lost its regard for the past. We don't treasure it. We don't warm our feet by it. We don't treat it with respect. Today there is no past.

Poppycock, you say. (Now *that's* a word from the past.) But at the risk of sounding like a winsome old geezer repeating the generational adage that the past was always rosier, that its water was sweeter, and its values strong and true, I'm going to lay it down for you. The fact is the current generation has no affection for the past, has no understanding of it, because they don't know what it is. How can you blame them? Their lives are predicated on an exact moment in present time. Life to them is what they see on a computer screen – itself an illusion, for what is a computer screen and that which appears on it but a pixellated, illuminated nothingness? What is the World Wide Web but a connecting tissue of lights and sounds, a 'thing' that has no feet in the actual world except for the cord that connects it to an electrical socket? Tell me what happens when the power goes off, then the computer battery dies? *Poof.* All gone. The show's over.

The youngsters have their mobile phones, too. Oh, do they have their phones. All these words and images streaking from tower to tower across the world, finding their targets, all creating an unending and dreary 'present', the great language of Shakespeare abbreviated to the point of incomprehension, the slander and slang, the blips and beeps of a whole slab of youthful humanity with no thoughts beyond the moments of their connectivity. Once upon a time we got excited by a letter turning up in the postbox. Once, we collected *stamps*. How quaint it all seems now. Today, kids get hundreds of letters a day on their phones. When life speeds up, some very human joys are lost forever.

Moan on, old man, I hear you say. But to eliminate the past. Well, there are enough clichés on that endeavour that don't need to be repeated by me. Yet I can't help but feel we have left behind some of the crucial essences of what it is to be human – to communicate via speech and ear, to look at the world with our own eyes, to anticipate, to genuinely feel. For some of us, nostalgia is a path back to that state. A return to being sentient.

Thus my yearning for a Kombi. And thus my uncomfortable meeting with Mr Firefly at the Marx Brothers Kombi Auto Shoppe. I loathed him on sight, as I've said. I knew from years of experience he was a bad man, permanently disconnected from human decency. I resented that I had to go through his repulsive self to get to my dream. I had no doubt, too, that this place of business was a good, old-fashioned chop shop, and not the edible kind but the recycled-vehicle variety. Cars were being stolen and reborn here. Parts taken off legitimate vehicles and screwed onto illegitimate ones. It was an unending puzzle of truth and lies. Places like this, and people like Firefly, if that was his real name, leached off people's dreams. Sucked the marrow out of their ambitions. He was nothing but a bottom feeder, and a waste of good oxygen. Outside of prison, the community paid for having grubs like this in its presence. Inside prison, they paid as well. There was always a levy for men like Firefly.

There was only one way to deal with him. You had to let him at least sense you might be prepared to get down on his scabrous level of humanity.

'That bus you looking at, she's ten grand cash, money up front and you drive away,' he said.

'I haven't even seen it yet.'

'Got a lot of people interested. Gonna be gone in a flash. Take it or leave it.'

'I would have thought the purchaser could at least get the vehicle checked over by professionals, the motor, the—'

'Take it or leave it. You're wastin' my time.'

In the bright neon of his office I could see some badly hand-drawn, do-it-yourself prison tattoos on his forearms.

'How long you been in the Kombi game?'

'None of your freakin' business. What are ya, a cop?' His face hardened, which was saying something, as it was already cold and granite-like and pitted with the ghost of some teenage acne before it changed.

'Don't be rude, Rufus. I'm just trying to establish your antecedents.'

'What'd you call me?'

'Your mother and father must have had some sense of humour, calling you Rufus T. Firefly, eh? Couple of wags,' I said. 'To me you suggest a baboon.'

'What's that sposed to mean?'

'It's from the movie. The Marx Brothers movie.'

'The who?'

'The Marx Brothers. The name of your business.'

'I don't know who they are, if that's what you're asking. I'm just the manager here.'

'Is your name Rufus T. Firefly?'

'What's it to you? You want the van or not?'

It sometimes takes a decent degree of investigation to work out whether someone is a frontman for a business or dodgy operation, but I didn't need to dig too deep with Firefly. He was illiterate and an idiot to boot. He was as much a part of the Marx Brothers Kombi Auto Shoppe as a hood ornament on a Splittie. (Memo to non-Kombi people – they don't have hoods. Got me?)

'You're a real tough guy, Rufus.'

'You're not kiddin'.' He cracked his knuckles. I had not met a dumber man since my long-time hairdresser in western Sydney. Sylvio had a good heart, but his cranium was so empty he could have rented it out. (He'd unexpectedly come out with things like: 'I got my wisdom teeth out last week. Cost me a bomb, but the *amnesia* guy who put me under was the most expensive. Woah wah, he charged through the nose. I should have knocked meself out, would've been cheaper. Me. I shoulda trained to be one of those amnesia guys. Never have to work again.' Thanks Sylvio.)

'You like wine, Rufus?'

'Wha?'

'That bottle of plonk there. On your shelf. Nice drop?'

'I'm a beer man.'

'Of course you are.'

I stood and walked around the desk, took the wine off the shelf and fondled the bottle.

'Nice,' I said.

'Fifty bucks, if you buy the Kombi now.'

'My, my, Rufus, you're an entrepreneur as well, eh?'

Sure enough, it was the exact brand of wine I had been shown while watching *Field of Dreams* with Zim, and had seen in his basement cellar. I made a mental note of the name of the winery. Ertrinken Estate. Gold Coast hinterland. I put it back on the shelf, next to the knuckleduster that appeared, to the naked eye, to have blood and strands of hair gruesomely attached to it.

'You a knucklehead, Rufus?' I asked.

'Wha?'

I put my hands in my trouser pockets, elaborately enough to lift my Hawaiian shirt and show him my neat Beretta tucked into my belt. 'Show me the van.'

I have to say, it was a beauty. A dull cream, and fitted out with rotting chipboard cupboards and a dicky fold-down bed. The second I stepped into it and inhaled its mouldy aroma, I was twenty again, staring out through a broad, curved windscreen at pristine beaches and ancient forests and a magnificent future full of song, women and, coincidentally enough, wine. Inside that van, all the ills and evils of the world disappeared. Until Rufus's scratchy, beer and smoke-ravaged voice dragged me back to the present.

'So?'

'So what?'

'Don't waste any more of me time. You want it?'

Of course, I bought it. I was about to lay down the cash there and then. I could see a nirvana beyond this wretched industrial estate and the seething hatred that came off Firefly like the heat off severely sunburned skin.

I checked my watch. Right on time, my old mate Bluey Stone, former expert mechanic, pulled up in his restored Mustang as prearranged, walked straight to the back of the van and lifted the motor hatch for inspection.

'What is this?' said a surprised Firefly. 'The frickin' Wild Bunch for pensioners?'

Bluey wore very thick spectacles. I mean, forget the glass bottoms of a Coke bottle. Bluey's were Hubble telescopes in a horn-rimmed frame. When he looked at you, the impression was not of a man severely visually impaired, but of a lunatic freshly escaped from the asylum. Bluey glanced up at Rufus, still without saying a word, and I could see the prison tough in Firefly momentarily recoil. There is one thing as powerful as a gun, and that's madness.

'What do you think, Dr Stone?'

And after a few tweaks and taps, Bluey silently nodded.

'Thank you, Rufus,' I said, producing a roll of cash. 'We're done here.'

I should have driven straight home in my bus and met the wrath of Peg head-on. It would be a storm I could not avoid. I had raided the retirement fund for a silly old man's dream. There were a few consequences I could foresee. I'd either be divorced very soon, which was fine because at least I now had somewhere to sleep when she kicked me out of the house. Or she'd kill me and I'd be buried in my Kombi. Which was fine, too. Have you noticed how expensive a good coffin can be nowadays?

But I didn't drive home. I had some wine to taste, up at the Ertrinken Estate vineyard in the hills.

6

WHEN MY DECEASED friend Westchester Zim heard that I was to attend a wine appreciation course with Peg, he laughed with such throaty vigour that I thought he might have suffered a stroke at the end of the telephone line.

'Zim, are you okay?' I asked, genuinely concerned.

'Fine, fine,' he finally spluttered.

'I'm pleased you find me amusing.'

'I'm sorry. It's just, it's ...'

'What? Out with it, Zim.'

'... like bringing together tomato sauce and duck confit.'

'Zim, I do believe you are a bone fide snob.'

To make amends and appear encouraging, he sent me a chapter of medical educator Dr Philip E. Muskett's book, *The Art of Living in Australia* from 1893. The chapter – 'On Australian Wine' – I found fantastically dull, but there were a few gems embedded in its dry prose. He was very enthusiastic about starting a national wine industry, was Dr Muskett. I sensed he liked more than the occasional tipple. 'Apart from its beneficial influence on the national health,' Muskett wrote with more bounce than usual, 'it would cover the land with smiling vineyards ... it would absorb thousands from the fever and fret of city wear and tear into the more natural life of the country'.

Good old Dr Muskett. He had to have been one of the pioneer sea-changers of Australia. (How crowded could our feverish and fretful cities have possibly been in the 1890s? Have another drink, Dr Muskett.) But what a lovely turn of phrase – *smiling* vineyards.

When I turned into the Ertrinken Estate in the hills behind the Gold Coast, I immediately felt the opposite. In fact, it was worse than that. The entrance gate was something out of an early gothic horror movie, all mossy stones and rusted metal arches. (Fake, of course, right down to the moss. This was the Gold Coast after all.) I swear there was a vulture fashioned into the ironwork, though it could have been a poorly rendered eagle. And believe you me (I've always favoured that odd phrase, uttered habitually by my grandfather Herb), *believe you me*, it seemed sunny on the road through the hinterland (perhaps I was experiencing that inner-dawn of driving my new/old Kombi bus), but instantly dark once I crossed the vineyard's threshold. Then there was the long driveway bordered with tall and eerie pines, straight out of some dank fairytale in which innocent children in lemon-starched white smocks wander into the maw of a European forest. It was a set from *Edward Scissorhands*. It would not have surprised me in the least if a wolf standing on its hind legs and dressed as Grandma in puffy pantaloon pyjamas had greeted me inside.

It may be encroaching dementia, but shadows loom large as you get older, and for comfort I patted the Beretta on the passenger's seat of the Kombi as I puttered over the crunching gravel.

I locked the vehicle, straightened my Hawaiian shirt and made for the open cellar door. If only Zim could have seen me now. (Was he watching me, halfway through some fifty-course degustation up in heaven? Smirking? Possibly coughing on a shaving of truffle with the comedy of it all?) I was acting on pure instinct. It had always served me well. I still had a hunch that my friend had not suffered a fateful heart attack that day in these very vineyards, but that his demise had been brought on, and swiftly, by persons as yet unknown. And by a method yet to be determined.

Why kill Zim? Surely a bad restaurant review couldn't lead to the sanction of a professional hit. Or could it? I had seen people murdered for less. But it was hard to imagine a human life being taken for criticism of a roasted tomato or an undercooked lamb shank. Then again, Zim could be cutting, much like his beloved A. A. Gill. 'The calamari,' Zim once memorably wrote, 'would have brought smiles of recognition to legions of Malayan rubber plantation workers, or factory hands at the headquarters of Dunlop Volley tennis shoes. It had the same texture, and age, of something that might have shod the feet of Ken Rosewall during his Wimbledon singles disappointments.'

Perhaps Zim had stumbled across something, as a journalist, and not just a food critic, that someone didn't want known to the general public. He was acquainted with an enormous number of people in high places, and a lot of them told him things at the end of a good meal that they would never have uttered otherwise. Some combinations of wine and food can open fissures in the human heart, let alone the brain. These people trusted Zim. But what if something found its way onto one of those little pocket index cards of his? And what if someone wanted to destroy that card, and Zim along with it?

'Can I help you?'

A man had appeared at the cellar door, startling me. He

had extraordinary hair. If you could call it hair. He was short, so I had a brilliant view of his cranium. He had follicles that sprouted in tufts aligned in perfect equidistance from his forehead to his crown. A hair transplant, but a fantastically bad one. It was almost as though a miniature vineyard had been planted upon his scalp. A vineyard in the dead of a permanent winter.

His teeth were yellowed and crooked, as if all his savings had been absorbed by the vineyard, and he had nothing left for his dental work. I did not want to get near him, just as one might keep a safe distance from a poisonous plant.

'Wine,' I said stupidly.

'You've come to the right place.' He spotted the Kombi on the drive. The grin broadened. 'Wo kommen sie? Deutchland?'

'Could you repeat that?'

'You come from Germany?'

'I come from Erskineville.'

'Sorry,' he said, shaking his head. 'I don't know Erskineville.'

'No need to apologise. I'm looking for your Kombi wine. Heard great things about it.'

'Kombi wine?'

'Yes. Your white wine with the red Kombi on the label. Little VW symbol on the top.'

His grin disappeared. So this was not to be one of Dr Muskett's smiling vineyards.

'I am lost. So sorry. The little ...'

'A friend of mine put me on to it. Name of Zim. Westchester Zim.'

'Zim?'

'Little red Kombi. On a ridge. On the label. Nein?'

'No,' he said firmly now. 'You must have the wrong place.'

'This is the Ertrinken Estate?'

'Ertrinken. Correct.'

'Tell me, what does it mean, Ertrinken?'

'Ertrinken. It means the drowning. To drown, you know?'

'Happy stuff.'

'How do you say? To drown one's sorrows.'

'Very amusing.'

He seemed annoyed by this banter, the man with the vineyard on his head. The skin between the tufts had turned pale pink.

'Why don't you take a seat inside, and I'll ask the cellarman about this Kombi wine, hmm? Please. Wait here.'

He disappeared into the gloom of the cellar and I began to feel agitated. When my host did not return after ten minutes, I ambled about the grounds. The air was moist and fresh, the soil a rich red, the vineyard restaurant perched on the edge of a ridge. It commanded a magnificent view of the Gold Coast, the high-rises needle-like and chalky from this distance. To the right of the winery buildings was a wall of rainforest and at its base a small entranceway. Again, it was something out of a sinister fairytale, but aren't we irresistibly lured to such doorways, to the portal that separates civilisation from terror? From what we know and what we don't? Don't we love to have the stuffing scared out of us? It's only a story, right?

I cautiously crept closer to the entranceway and there found a tiny hand-painted sign. To the Pools.

I looked back and saw no sign of life at the cellar door, so in I walked, into the gloom. It took a while for my eyes to adjust, and I blindly bumbled along the track. I heard things scurrying in the ground foliage, and a distant whipbird.

The track gradually descended for a hundred metres

then lifted and fell again. The forest seemed to darken. My heart pounded. I heard a crash behind me and pulled out the Beretta, swinging it around wildly. It was the type of darkness you might see figures in. Or might imagine you've seen. The fear was still the same. Fear always is.

'Idiot,' I said to myself, and walked on. I kept the Beretta out.

Five minutes later I began to hear running water, then, unexpectedly, the track led into a huge open amphitheatre, and at its base was a series of deep pools cut into stone. It was eerie. Almost unnatural. A perfect narrow waterfall flushed into the pools. The water was loud here, close to deafening, as it bounced back off the tall stands of rainforest. I half expected to see a semi-naked woman washing her hair with a new brand of apple-scented shampoo under the cascades.

I went to the edge of one of the smaller pools and looked down. It was a very dark. It was deep. It appeared infinite. Foam flecked the surface. I could see my frothy wobbling reflection.

That's when I heard a gunshot. I swung around, let off two bullets myself and fell backwards into the pool as crazed and startled birds exploded from the trees.

7

THE LEECH IS a fascinating creature. Did you know the gnatbobdellida variety has three jaws, and may have more than one set of eyes? It possesses very handy suckers and its multi-toothed jaws chomp away like miniature chainsaws, before sucking your blood and greasing the meal with an anticoagulant. The fact that it's also a hermaphrodite makes it the perfect solo unit. It's got it all.

I had never seen a leech in my life, being an inner-city Sydney type of boy. Even my Boy Scout clubhouse was a disused factory shed on an oily concrete apron in Alexandria. No grass or forests there, unless you counted the weeds in the concrete cracks. (Which, in fact, I think I did, to earn my Bushcraft badge.)

No, leeches and I were strangers to each other, until that afternoon when I was pulled out of the rainforest adjoining the Ertrinken Estate winery in the Gold Coast hinterland, in pursuit of the killer of my old friend Westchester Zim. I must have hit my head on the edge of the rock pool, because when I awoke I was reclining on a long settee in a walnut-walled office at the winery, with the creepy man with a vineyard planted on his head poring over me with a pair of tweezers. He had beside him an open glass containing eleven leeches he had extracted from my person. He had another twelve to go. At least. I didn't want to think where else these ghoulies had burrowed beneath my clothing.

'They like you,' he said, pulling another from my arm, inadvertently poking his tongue out of the corner of his mouth with the concentration. 'They think you taste good, hmm?'

I couldn't stop looking at his broken, yellowed teeth. The transplanted tufts were a pleasing Monet landscape compared to the canines. I glanced at the glass. The leeches were squirming about in there, wet and gleaming with my blood.

'Wouldn't have a drink on you, would you?' I asked, thinking this a passable gag in a winery, and under the circumstances, but my creepy friend continued with his grisly work.

'What happened, Sherlock?' I said.

'I am Hans,' he said.

'Many Hans make light work.'

'Please, stop talking. You banged your head. You talking funny.'

'What happened?'

'You fell in the pool. We get you out. You covered in leeches. We get them off.'

'You're a one-stop shop, Hans.'

'I don't know what that means.'

'For a surgeon, you got steady Hans.'

'I don't know what that means.'

'Forget it.'

He dropped several more leeches into the glass before I noticed a man sitting quietly by the window. He was dressed in an immaculate navy suit, polished shoes, a crisp white shirt and burgundy tie. I couldn't see his face because the light diffusing through the fine curtains, but his slicked-back hair seemed to glow in a way that only heavily gelled naturally blond hair can. Perhaps I had mistaken him for a reading lamp. What was it with people's hair in this place? Still, I had seen this pate before.

'And who are you?' I boomed across the room. 'Nurse Ratched?'

He remained silent and motionless. I hate that. I hate all that 'silence is power' malarky. As you might have guessed, I prefer a verbal exchange. The more I stared at him, the more his glowing dome seemed like Nurse Ratched's immaculate white cap in *One Flew Over the Cuckoo's Nest*. Come to think of it, if I'd watched *One Flew Over the Cuckoo's Nest* – another in my top ten films of all time – with Zim instead of that blasted *Field of Dreams*, I might not be covered in leeches, Zim could still be alive, and the Kombi dream could have been postponed for another year or two.

'Sorry?' I said to the dark stranger by the window. 'I didn't catch that. Perhaps you're Chief Bromden. Deaf and dumb.'

'You got a wise mouth, mate,' the suit finally said. He too pronounced it *marrrrt*, flat as a pancake, just like Joe the janitor. How come nobody could say 'mate' properly any more?

'It speaks!'

'Is the bump on the head, Herr Fleek, I'm sure,' said my leech hunter.

'Hair Fleek?' I said, incredulous. And when I'm incredulous, my voice cracks and goes up like a teenage boy in maturational transition with a solo whisker on his chin.

'Flick,' the suit said. 'Johann Flick. Friends call me Joe. You can call me Johann.' Another Joe. Perhaps I'd been wrong all along. I was actually an extra in *Groundhog Day*.

'And you can call me Nancy,' I said. 'Hey, hey, Dr Zhivago, that one hurt.'

'Sorry,' said the hair transplant.

'So, Fleek,' I said. 'I came in here for a bottle of plonk, fell into a rock pool and got lathered with man-eating beasties. Why are you here, overseeing my recovery?'

'I own this winery.'

'Ohhhh, I see. You're worried about an insurance claim from me.'

'Not at all,' he said. 'I happened to be in the restaurant today for lunch when I heard some yobbo had let off a gun at the pools and nearly fractured his skull. This winery has an impeccable reputation worldwide. I'm not about to see it soiled by some demented grub disconnected with my enterprise.'

'I've been called a lot of things, Fleek ...'

'What's your business here?'

'Wine, Fleek. The VW vintage. I'm a Kombi nut.'

'How long have you been a Kombi nut, as you call it?'

I checked my watch. 'About three hours.'

Still I could not see his face, though he lit a cigarette and the smoke eased about his upper torso. The light through the window captured its paisley swirls.

'The VW wine, as you call it. It was discontinued. It is no more. So sorry.'

'Oh, what a shame. Maybe I could nab a bottle on eBay.'

'It was promotional. A handful of cases. May I ask how you came to learn of it? You're a wine expert too, are you?'

'A dead friend of mine gave it a favourable review. Man called Zim. First-rate palate. He recommended it. Admired the body, so to speak.'

'Then he was a man of impeccable taste.'

'You never heard of him? He passed away, right here, down amongst your impeccable vines.'

'Can't say I have heard of him, no.'

'A man drops dead in your vineyard and you didn't hear about it? Tsk tsk, Herr Fleek.'

'I'm a busy man. What was it — a heart attack? People die every day. Do you hear about every one of them?'

'Busy doing what?'

'I'm sorry — you illegally discharge a firearm on my property, cause a major disturbance to my business and, worst of all, you interrupt my lunch. Are you in any position to ask me questions?' His voice had changed. I had heard this type of voice before. It had the timbre of a man with a very substantial temper, as deep as a rainforest rock pool.

'One more to go,' said my doctor with the hideous teeth, as he triumphantly dropped the final leech into the glass. They looked as though they were attacking each other, those leeches, fighting for the pint of blood, or so it seemed, they had sucked from me.

'I want to see where he died,' I said. 'Zim.'

The blond-haired man stood, smashed out his cigarette in a large glass ashtray and walked to the door. As he left he said, without turning to face me, 'Children should never play with firearms. They could meet with a nasty accident.'

I sat up in the settee and observed my arms and legs. The hair transplant had brought the glass of leeches up to his face and was watching them with a little too much excitement for my liking.

'Herr Doctor,' I said. 'Can I go?'

'Nobody's keeping you,' he said, relishing the writhing annelids.

I hobbled out to the vestibule, then down the stairs to

the driveway. The Kombi was parked exactly where I'd left it, but the driver's door was unlocked. I didn't wait to warm the motor and gave her a little rev on the way out, kicking up some gravel.

As soon as I hit the tarred bitumen outside the creepy gates of Ertrinken Estate, the sun burst through a phalanx of clouds. The world was a sunny vineyard again.

I opened the glove box, retrieved my mobile and listened to a message. It was from an old contact in forensics in Brisbane. 'Your mate Westchester's results are in. Poisoned. Very sophisticated. Thought you'd like to know.'

I knew I had to get back to Zim's apartment as soon as I could. I also knew, halfway down the range, that I was being followed. By a black split-screen Kombi, as big as a hearse.

With dread, I slapped my belt and pictured my beautiful Beretta sinking to the centre of the earth in that infinite rainforest pool, picking up legions of leeches as it disappeared forever.

I remembered that in *Groundhog Day* the lead character tries, time and again, to kill himself, but wakes every morning to a new and interminable day. I was beginning to know how he felt.

8

I'M NOT A big motor-racing fan. It just doesn't do it for me, all the noise and fumes and lap after tedious lap. As a television spectacle it is incomprehensible to my feeble mind. I'd rather watch a film on the grazing habits of Tibetan yaks. Did you know they have bigger hearts and lungs than your garden variety bovine? All the better for munching at high altitude.

Oh, I could go on about yaks. But motor racing. I had it in mind that afternoon I left the Gold Coast vineyard and made a beeline for Westchester Zim's apartment because I was hurtling down the range in my Kombi being followed by a black split-screen Kombi that could only have been driven by villains, but very dumb villains. Why would smart villains announce their villainry in a villainous black car? Also, the moment we hit the Pacific Highway to Brisbane, I got involved in the third car chase of my life.

The first was at the Sydney Easter Show when I was eight and my brother, Stanley, was five. We were riding the dodgem cars. I won't bore you with the details, but suffice to say a chase ensued and poor Stanley ended up with a fractured skull and a lifelong fear of motorised vehicular transport. He will still not ride with me in a car − any car.

The second happened when I was a cop in Sydney and was in a high-speed pursuit with a Leyland P76 Coupe. It ended up head-butting a streetlight. Its bonnet flew off and landed on the windshield of my police vehicle. My car collided with another streetlight. The coupe driver and I were both rushed to hospital in the same ambulance.

Now I was in another, and if you know unmodified Kombis, you'll know that this particular chase resembled my ding-dong dodgem battle with little Stanley, though possibly at a lower level of velocity.

At the high point of the chase, just as we were passing the Logan Hyperdome, we must have hit the clipping sonic speed of just under 80 km an hour, full throttle. Considering it was a 100 km zone, it's a miracle we weren't both pulled over by the highway patrol for going too *slowly*. Nevertheless, the chase was on, and we clicked and clacked all the way to the city like two snails racing for a freshly detected puddle of beer. (Snails, if you didn't know, are very much like a large proportion of the Australian male population. They adore beer, throw it down, get promptly drunk and invariably drown in it. Not a bad way to go.)

As we hit the cross-city tunnel roadworks to the south of the CBD, I still had my persistent tail, but she was coughing a bit of smoke. With some crafty manoeuvring I knew I could hold out for a full engine blow. But Splittie drivers are persistent – they carry an air of superiority over us common Bay Window Kombi owners, and though she belched out a fair bit of blue stuff, I couldn't lose her.

The villains got so close to my tail at one point that I realised they were driving not just any old Splittie, but a multi-windowed Samba, which was top-notch, arguably the Queen of Kombis. But as I slipped up the Margaret Street exit, this final turn was the Samba's undoing. She erupted

in a pyre of delicious smoke and came to an uncere-
monious halt, and I slipped into the anonymity of the city.

I still had the key to Zim's apartment, but out of courtesy
I rang the janitor's bell. He did not appear. By the time I
got to Zim's door, I knew I was too late. The door was
half-open and inside it looked as though a herd of yaks had
passed through en route to some choice grazing on Mount
Coot-tha.

Everything had been upturned and routed. Zim's
pristine kitchen had been soiled, possibly for the first time.
His framed Cézanne's on the wall were cock-eyed. On
the kitchen bench I found several bottles of wine that had
been opened and drained. They'd raided Zim's fridge and
savoured a particular sticky that might have accounted for
their monthly wages, if indeed henchmen were on salary.
They knew not what they had drunk.

I went straight to Zim's office and found it similarly
trashed. The drawers to his index-card filing cabinet were all
open, but incredibly none of the cards had been disturbed.
This made sense. In my experience, when lug-headed
moronic petty criminals whose reading experiences stopped
with *The Little Engine That Could* are faced with any sort of
laborious paperwork or sheer weight of wordage – and trust
me, Zim had neatly filed many thousands of those pocket-
sized cards – a small wire in their heads almost instantly
disconnects from the brain's mainframe and they move on
to something else. (A very similar process to when I witness
motor racing.) I could be thankful for small mercies.

For the remainder of the afternoon, before I reported the
burglary to police, I sat down with a glass of the only wine
left in the house – a Stanthorpe Merlot that put lead in my
weary pencil – and made a few phone calls.

My newfound friend Mr Johann Flick was, it turned

out, no stranger to the local police authorities, nor was he entirely unknown to the Crime and Misconduct Commission. He was, as one source told me, on his way to becoming 'the biggest and most ruthless developer in south-east Queensland', and if an aerial map of Brisbane city's newest developments was ever drawn up, Flick's portfolio would include neat parcels of fevered construction at either end of the city's anticipated north–south tunnel. Herr Flick, I also learned, had a strong interest in the city's water grid, specifically the Southern Regional Water Pipeline. Flick was scrambling for any patch of dirt that the pipeline abutted or passed through. He was also influential in the emerging satellite cities of Ipswich and the Sunshine Coast.

For no reason, I immediately thought of a very old phrase – 'and He turned water into wine'.

I rang the janitor. No answer. I went down to the basement. Zim's wine cage door was open, but the bottles remained neatly stacked. All except for half a dozen bottles with VW stamped on the lid. They were missing.

Back in the apartment, Peg called on my mobile.

'Yes, dear,' I said.

'You'll be home for dinner?'

'I'll be a little late tonight, dear.'

'What have you been doing with yourself all day?'

This is the moment when men who have been doing something they shouldn't have been doing involuntarily swallow. I had been doing a lot of swallowing lately. How could I tell her I had, in the space of a single day, bought a Kombi, entered the gates of hell, knocked myself unconscious in a rainforest, lost half my body volume of blood to a gang of ravenous leeches, had a dodgem-car pursuit up the Pacific Highway and consumed an entire bottle of absolutely dreadful Stanthorpe wine? As Captain Blackadder said, 'This is the stickiest situation since Sticky the stick insect got stuck on a sticky bun.' Or words to that effect.

'I've been doing a project, dear,' I said.

'You have?'

'I have been further educating myself in the great art of the vintner. I have—'

'What have you *really* been up to?'

'Why do you say that? Dear?'

'Because you only ever call me 'dear' when—'

'Hello? Hello?' I interrupted. 'Sorry, you're breaking up ... dear.'

I felt melancholy in that apartment. For the first time since Westchester Zim's death, the true impact of his passing hit me. It's always terrible to lose a friend, but at my age? I would miss the old bon vivant. His humour and unexpected witticisms. He once said, 'I find "rack of lamb" offensive. To the lamb. It is also known as a "Crown roast", which is much more regal and respectful to these animal children who died for our pleasure. So why don't we use that? We don't call rump steak "backside of cow", do we?' Where on earth will I get lines like that any more?

Out of respect for Zim, I cleaned his apartment. Yes, I did. I tidied everything, straightened the pictures, even mopped the tiles in the kitchen. I plumped the couch cushions and aligned the strangely old-fashioned anti-macassars. Then I rinsed the wine bottles, including the Stanthorpe red, put them in a bag and took it out to the garbage chute.

I opened it, and I found the very dead corpse of janitor Joe Santorini, stuffed in head-first, his polished work boots stuck skyward, revealing – poor little Joe – that he only wore a size seven.

9

I WAITED OUTSIDE Herr Johann Flick's office with a briefcase at my feet. It was the late Westchester Zim's case, one I remembered from the first time I met him, decades earlier, in Sydney. He took it everywhere. He lived out of it, had his life in it. He once told me that if he ever had to walk out on his life, he could survive if he had the case. It was nicked and battered and scarred, like old Zim. I felt I owed it to him. To have a part of him with me when I wreaked almighty justice on those who had so rudely killed him.

The developer's foyer was expansive and expensive and made entirely of glass and steel. I could see virtually all aspects of Brisbane from my knotty, embroidered waiting couch. I was sitting on an elaborately rendered black eagle. Very Germanic. After my encounter with the leeches, sitting on a tapestry eagle head was strangely discomforting.

I wore a fresh Hawaiian shirt, relatively clean shorts and my perennial boatie loafers, decorated with so many fish guts and spilled wine and oil and canal water and samples of assorted TV dinners that had missed my belly and gone floor-bound that it was no longer possible to distinguish which stain was which. They had become, at least in my opinion, a fetching pea-soup green. Inside all this clean glass, I felt everything about me was magnified, like a germ sample under a laboratory slide.

Too bad. Clothes do not maketh the man, my father always said. And mint jelly doth not make the roast, said Westchester Zim.

The office assistant, a pretty young woman who had a little too much of the Eva Braun about her, answered the phone, crinkled up her nose at me, and said, 'Mr Flick will see you now.'

'Sehr gut,' said I, and shuffled with the hoary old brief-case into Flick's inner sanctum.

Flick sat behind his desk at the far end of the room. It was a long way from the door. I could have used a golf cart to get there. I resented his intimidating office ergonomics. I had to pass one of those glass-cased models of what looked like a housing estate to get to him. It was a little green valley with very neat, red-roofed houses abutting a network of roads and cul-de-sacs. The fake bitumen with miniature plastic cars of all the colours of the rainbow swirled about artistically. There was the perfect community in the stale air of the cabinet. For no logical reason I immediately thought of Julie Andrews pirouetting about on an Austrian hillside bearded with buttercups in *The Sound of Music.* I try to think of Julie Andrews as little as possible. I suddenly felt squeamish.

Flick sat smoking at his desk. He did not stand to greet me. He did not offer me a chair.

'Take a seat,' I said to myself. 'Don't mind if I do.'

Flick exhaled a long column of smoke.

'Where did you learn them?' he said.

'What's that?'

'Your manners.'

'Swiss finishing school.'

'What do you want?'

It was a comfortable chair. I would have liked one for the rumpus room back home.

'Does this come with a pouffe?' I asked, squeezing the padded arms of the chair.

'What do you want?'

'Did you know "pouffe" is French? The word. Nineteenth century. It refers to something "puffed out". I learned it from my good friend Westchester Zim.'

'Good for you.'

'Ever meet Westchester?'

'As I've told you, I'm afraid not.'

'You would have liked him. He could pick a Castelnaudary cassoulet from one made in the Toulouse tradition simply by sniffing the steam coming off the dish.'

Flick scrunched his nose at me much in the way of Eva Braun outside his heavy oak office door. I was either really on the nose to this crowd, or they liked snorting a bit of Charlie in between business meetings. Or both.

'That's a pretty little town in the box over there.'

'That's the future. Master-planned cities. That's our next project, near Ipswich.'

'What's it called? Flickville?'

'Serenity Downs.'

'Nice. Sounds like a great place to sleep. I'm getting drowsy already.'

'You've got one minute.'

I lifted the briefcase onto my lap and tapped the battered leather. I could see in the distance, through a broad pane of glass, the second span of the Gateway Bridge coming together. The finished Portside Wharf. Cranes here. New motorways there. Boy, this town was really on the move. And when towns like Brisbane started moving, the sharks could smell blood in the water.

'Been doing a bit of research, Flicky old boy. Knowledge is power, and all that guff. Know what I mean? Amazing what you can find out these days with modern technology, like that internet thingy. Fascinating what you can dig up if you have a hunch about somebody. Like I have a hunch about you. You see, I had a dream. A dream of a car that would take me away from our complicated world to a purer place. Get my drift?'

'I have no idea what you're talking about.'

'A Kombi, Flick. Slept in her last night, actually, down by the Botanic Gardens. Haven't slept that good in years. Better than your little Snooze-away Downs here. Anyway, I had plenty of time to think, there in the back of the van. And the most extraordinary dots started joining together. As if by magic. A few phone calls later, Flicky my lad, and I was starting to see a richer picture. An evil picture. A picture of an unscrupulous developer who arrived out of nowhere and started buying up half of a booming little tropical city. A man who, once upon a time, in a European forest far, far away, did some pretty naughty things, then changed his name. No, not just his name, but his entire life. Indeed, his actual *face*. It's almost a German version of *My Fair Lady*, the way this fellow, this grub from the streets of Bremen, this Paul Smith, or should I say, Herr Paul *Schmidt*, had such a chameleonic ascent. How he went from cashier in a sex shop to low-level drug dealing to creatively laundering international drug funds into legitimate projects on behalf of the big boys.'

Flick murdered his cigarette. He snorted the last drag out his nose, sat back, folded his arms and stared at me.

'But that wasn't enough for Paul from Bremen,' I went on. 'Once he was reborn he had a "big idea". The old light bulb above the head. The *glühbirne* atop *der kopf*. Pauly had a vision. Not an entirely original one, I'll admit. But what if Pauly from Bremen greased the right palms, feathered the correct nests, targeted the right pouffes to plump up, and got insider knowledge of a booming city's future plans, and what if lucky Pauly just happened to own property that not only doubled, tripled, but increased in value tenfold when grand infrastructure projects just happened to synchronise with his investments. Can you believe that Pauly Smith, they'd all say? A *genius.* Then, what if he replicated that uncanny talent across the country? Well, Pauly would be a very sought-after man, wouldn't he? And he'd also be very rich.'

Flick coughed. He smiled. He lit another cigarette. 'Your one minute is up.'

'I'm not finished,' I said. Through the smoke, I could see a giant eagle finely etched into the glass behind his desk. 'Our Pauly, though, should have remembered his roots in bland Bremen with its brass pig statue downtown. Did you ever rub its nose for luck when you were a little thief living on the streets? Bet you did. You see, Paul, cities on the make don't lose their small-town endearments. You should have done your research. Brisbane is a place that has *known* corruption. Has lived it. It's in the soil. It's also a place, despite its explosive growth and grand vision, which has gossip and tittle-tattle as its bedrock. People here still talk over the back fence. That's what I like about it. And that was your big mistake. Did you honestly think you could bribe your way through government without anybody noticing? Cosmopolitanism in one town, Paul, can be seen as ignorance and idiocy in another. Not everything translates. If the premier uses the wrong cutlery in a fine dining restaurant here, it's news the next day. Am I getting through to you, *Paul*? Small inside the big. A place and its people still connected to the earth.

'You thought the little boutique winery on the side, the gestures to some cultural depth, could blind people to your common heritage? And your little Kombi chop shop? The scumbags you hang out with there? Still a common thief, hey, Paul? You don't understand much about Kombi people either, I'm afraid. They're bonded. Blood brothers and sisters. They talk, find things out, share, for the common good. The way it used to be – looking out for each other. I know some things about you that even *you* don't know, my friend. All reported to me by Kombi spies. You thought you'd come to a place like this and bluff your way through? This is *Brisbane*, man. Once a grub, always a grub. And in a town like this, there are three primary ways that secrets move around. In the bedroom. Over the back fence. And over a meal. Has mankind ever been any different? But someone found you out, didn't they?'

'Is that a question?'

'The last time I checked my primary school grammar book, yes, it was.'

'Why don't I have you shown out.' He pressed a buzzer on his desk. Can you believe that? The villain with a red emergency button on his desk? This guy had seen too many movies.

Doors behind me opened.

'You like technology, Paul? Computers? Laptops? Digital voice recorders?'

'Get him out!' Herr Flick/Schmidt shouted to some approaching goons. I didn't need to turn around to see their shiny European suits and passé ponytails. When had I stumbled on to the set of *Die Hard*?

'Sometimes,' I said, gripping Zim's briefcase before being reefed out of the chair, 'just a pencil and a little square of paper can do all the damage. The might of the pen, Paul. *The might of the pen.'*

In a struggle with the German henchmen from central casting, I accidentally managed to knock over the model of Snoozeville, and shattered glass and little fragments of roofs and trees and shopping malls and train stations spilled across the shiny office floor. They got under our feet, these broken pieces of domestic bliss, and down we all went, giving me enough time to pull out my cheap pawnshop .38. Before I knew it the darned thing had gone off by itself, exploding a huge window that looked out over the hills of Mount Coot-tha.

And as the gorillas threw me, still clutching Zim's bag, out of the building from the twenty-first floor, the brief-case latch opened and hundreds of my late friend's lovingly inscribed index cards fluttered about me. It was a throw of confetti from Zim himself. And, I thought, the last thing I would see in my life.

10

WHEN MY BROKEN left leg had finally healed, Peg and I decided we'd make that trip to Tasmania after all. So we packed up the Kombi, waved goodbye to the family, pulled out of our driveway to much fanfare from the neighbours and turned right onto the Pacific Highway.

'How's this?' I said to Peg, barely containing my exhilaration. This was what it was all about. The freedom of the open road. The limitless possibilities. The great human desire for locomotion. I was as giddy as a schoolboy.

'How long will it take to get there?' Peg said, filing her nails. We'd been driving for four minutes.

She could not deflate me. I had almost died at the hands of Herr Johann Flick. It's not every day you go abseiling from a Brisbane high-rise, without a parachute, kite, bungee rope or cocktail umbrella, and live to tell the tale.

Of course, I'd made the papers again. Thus our hurried trip to the Apple Isle. I had become an embarrassment to Peg. It was something I hadn't counted on being for another twenty years, as a permanently dribbling, nappy-wearing, chair-bound, ga-ga old fruit who thought that 'the war' was still raging. The Vietnam War, that is.

So to Tasmania we went, where my recent escapades would hopefully be unknown.

Still, they had lauded me as the luckiest man alive. Proclaimed that God was on my side. That my number wasn't up. They lavished every pun and cliché in the book on me. And why not? It may well have been a higher power who decided a window cleaner's platform would be there to greet me, one storey down, when I was thrown from that building; that I would land on the window cleaner himself – a man of portly dimensions; and that his equipment, including a platform net strong enough to stop a runaway Kombi, would be in perfect working order. The platform and the net, that is. Not the window cleaner himself, who was taken to hospital with several broken ribs, a cracked pelvis and a mashed nose courtesy of my old .38, which hit him so cleanly I could hear the bone break like a snapped quail leg the second the two made contact. I agreed – free of charge, and in lieu of a lawsuit – to be used in a new advertisement for the window-cleaning scaffolding, and be photographed in a red rubber super-hero mask. Miracle Man! they called me. This, too, may have added to Peg's mortification.

Nevertheless, I was alive. Flick, of course, got nicked. For my attempted murder. Then for killing Westchester Zim and Joe Santorini. Corruption charges would follow, so whichever way you looked at it, plain old Paul Smith from Bremen would be spending the rest of his life in jail.

The moment Flick went down, the entire house of cards noisily collapsed. The ripple effect was impressive. Several senior government ministers resigned, citing a 'need to spend more time with my family'. I've always liked this excuse. Staff attrition at the local council was suddenly enormous. An entire department associated with infrastructure property acquisitions just disappeared. They left steaming coffee mugs at their desks. Half-eaten doughnuts. 'Flickgate', as it became known, ran deep and wide, and fumigated whole swathes of Brisbane's professional workforce. At the same time, the world economy collapsed, the state's water grid ceased construction, plans for dams disappeared and master-planned cities stayed tightly in their miniature airless cases. I know Flick wasn't responsible for this landslide, but I like to think his demise loosened the rocks a little.

In my days as a rouseabout cop, I was known for certain eccentricities. I never saw it that way. I now see myself as a pioneer of psychological detective work. If you bear this in mind, I want to tell you precisely what I did when I was released from hospital. There was one piece of the puzzle missing, and I needed to get inside it, to work it out as a method actor may inhabit a character. I needed to do it for Zim.

So I returned to the Ertrinken Estate winery in the Gold Coast hinterland. It had, of course, stopped functioning the moment the cuffs were slapped on Flick. It was abandoned. Within minutes of the news reaching this scenic ridge over-looking the glitter strip, the cellar door was quite literally left swinging in the breeze. Half-washed dishes were abandoned in the sink in the restaurant kitchen. A profiterole, with a scalloped bite mark in it (clearly from someone with *terrible* teeth), was left to go stale on a plate. Time stood still at the place where one had drowned one's sorrows.

I had had plenty of time to work out the nuts and bolts of Zim's death as I recuperated in hospital. And I had thousands of his minutely inscribed index cards to pore over. (I had not taken the genuine incriminating ones with me the day I visited Herr Flick in his office. What do you think I am, daft?)

But it wasn't until I sat in the chair he'd sat in, inside that empty winery restaurant, that I could truly see what happened. As I said, I had to go the hard yards for Zim, out of respect, out of courtesy.

You see, Zim had been here twice for the purpose of reviewing Ertrinken's restaurant. That's how darned diligent he was, how particular. And how fair. On the first test run, two weeks before his death, he had, according to his notes, experienced what he described as 'quite possibly the worst meal of my professional career'. I won't go into the details he had jotted in his crablike handwriting on the cards, but let's just say the detection of various cockroach antennae and thorny leg parts in his water glass kicked off the whole disaster, which included a steak with actual ice particles at its centre, and a guinea fowl that he suspected was a chicken in disguise.

As for the wine, he had sipped on a glass of the winery's own dry white, and found it to be re-fermented. He actually wrote, 'Nips horribly at the tongue.' He sent the bottle back and ordered another. The same. He went for a third – the old three strikes you're out rule. They were ruled out.

The spy game is not confined to governments and big business. The wine and food world is heaving with double agents. When Zim left that night after an argument over not paying for the three bottles of appalling white wine, they knew who he was by the time he'd driven under the rusty metal arch out the front and headed for home. A system of deception and fraud surrounding Zim had been activated by the time he'd pulled into his basement car park in Brisbane that very evening.

Two days after his first Ertrinken visit, he was coincidentally given a complimentary bottle of the VW wine by a Flick associate – a dodgy new sommelier in one of Zim's favourite restaurants in Eagle Street. Zim studied the label. Could it possibly be from the same vineyard as the one that had turned his stomach and offended his palate just forty-eight hours earlier? Three days after that, at an official state-government function on the Parliament House lawn, a backbencher who was on a judging committee with Zim for the annual fine food awards told him about an incredible 'secret stash' he had of the finest white wine ever made in Queensland. Would he care to come back to his office for a taste? Would he like half a dozen bottles for his private cellar? It was, of course, the VW wine. Zim was dizzy with the serendipity of it all. (The wine, tests would later prove, not only contained lethal poisons, but had never been produced in Queensland. It was in fact an award-winning French sauvignon blanc that had been decanted into the VW bottles. Zim may have been onto this. But with wine that good, who cares what it's wrapped in? Human pleasure can be a blinding, and dangerous, thing.)

So when Zim returned to the winery restaurant for lunch a fortnight later, the manager and staff had a carefully orchestrated plan that came 'from the top', namely Johann Flick. Zim walked into an elaborate trap.

As I sat there by the window, in Zim's chair overlooking the coast, I felt teary. My dear friend. I wished I could have warned him. How could we have known he would indeed be killed to prevent a bad review? Had it ever happened, anywhere, in the history of gastronomy?

When Zim came into the restaurant on the day of his death, he was fêted like a head of state, given the best table in the house (which was, incredibly, full), and found himself seated amongst other diners of a very high calibre (if you're into societal hierarchy), including several government figures, a once-famous movie star and even a celebrity chef from Great Britain. Now you don't think Zim saw through all this? A man of his worldliness and culture? Sure he did. But the meal was perfect. (Had it been shipped in from elsewhere, and disguised, or concocted by an imported hand? We will never know.) And the wine was superlative, particularly the Kombi drop, with which Zim was now so familiar.

Sometime during the lunch, however, his government friend on the food and wine judging panel had sidled up to the table and uttered some quiet words to Zim. And that's when Zim wandered out to the flagstone balcony with the million-dollar view, wrote down a few notes on one of his little index cards, then strolled over to inspect the vines that ran in trellises down the front of the red-soiled ridge. Flick had hoped to get Zim – and prevent the bad review – in the quietness of Zim's own Brisbane apartment with the poisoned VW wines that, through government contacts, had made their way into the reviewer's hands. But Zim wasn't of such low breed as Flick. He didn't guzzle the wine straight away. It was something Flick, despite his physical transformation, could never understand. Of course Zim had cellared the wine. Of course he had postponed the satisfaction for the perfect moment. Had waited for the right meal to complement the wine.

Frustrated, and not sure what Zim knew, Flick had to supervise the killing himself. At the winery restaurant. A heart attack. Right there in front of the lunchtime crowd. Flick knew a thing or two about human nature, I'll give him that. When Zim went down, the diners didn't rush to his aid or run about screaming and waving their arms in the air. They did what most people do. They kept on eating, and felt both sorry and embarrassed for the old guy out in the vines. They thought briefly about their own mortality, in between dessert and the cheese plate. And that was that. It would have been bad manners to watch as his body was removed on a stretcher. Zim's VW wine had been poisoned with something that promoted the illusion of sudden death by heart attack. But those few words on the index card – they were worse than a bad review. And they had survived, and I had retrieved them. Zim. He was a true journalist to the end.

What nobody knew was that when Zim encountered a bad restaurant experience, he gave the establishment the professional courtesy of returning for a second time to test the first experience. Maybe they'd had an off day. He'd been there once before, you see, and filed away his first set of notes. And he'd returned to those exact notes, after his extended tipple in the backbencher's room at Parliament House, and jotted down some explosive gossip about a German developer called Flick. And there they stayed, in the file drawer.

'Do you enjoying reviewing restaurants, Zim, even after all these years?' I had once asked him. And he said resolutely, 'It's the job to die for.'

The Kombi made it to the Tweed border before the crank shaft seized and she died on us. Peg hadn't even finished filing her nails.

As I kneeled down at the back of the van, peering into the engine cavity and pretending I knew what I was looking for, my wife, standing behind me, let out a little exhortation of surprise.

'Have you been dyeing your hair?' she asked, shocked.

Ahhh, I thought. Isn't it nice to be noticed, albeit belatedly?

FOUR

MURDER, SHE TWEETED

1

IT IS SAID that when grown men are about to meet their maker, they cry out for one of two things – God, or their Mammy.

I have discussed this with my long-suffering wife, Peg – being the post-modern, non-sexist, egalitarian metrosexual that I am. I would probably holler for a doctor. If my doctor happened to be my Mammy, even better. Who would *women* shout for at their time of death? Their saviour? Their father? 'Their hairdresser,' said Peg. I had a feeling she wasn't taking me seriously.

But I was taking me *very* seriously. I had been thinking about death a lot. I mean a lot. When you ponder the grim reaper during the drinks break of a cracker 20/20 cricket match, you know what's in the forefront of your mind. And when you have a dream in which a figure who looks remarkably similar to Ricky Ponting, in a black hooded cloak wielding a scythe, is chasing you through a misty wood at midnight, you know it's playing on your subconscious. (That would have to be better than Merv Hughes with a scythe, my analyst reasoned. Thank you, I said to her, but can you save the sport-themed gags for a time that's not on my coin?) And when you awaken bolt upright and lathered in sweat from the aforementioned dream, holding your index finger in the air and shouting 'Out!', you know you need professional help.

It was Peg's idea, the analyst. Peg's theory was that my retirement had become some sort of subconscious frustration that I could only salve by creating the drama of my previous working life, and that this in turn may go back even further — to a possible undiagnosed post-traumatic disorder relating to the violence inherent in my career as a police officer and the vast quantities of human carnage I had taken on board over the decades. Either that, or I had an undiagnosed tumour short-circuiting my brainbox.

That's how I met My Analyst, as I called her, who had a small consultation room between a plastic surgeon and an ice cream shoppe at Main Beach.

During this time of my personal angst, my beloved Peg was considerate. During my cricket death dreams she assigned me to the fold-out bed in the guest room. Fair enough. She said if I started calling for a third umpire I'd be in the garage.

'What is it with you and death at this time of year?' Peg said. 'You're supposed to be happy, full of yuletide warmth, a cuddly Christmas feeling. This is a time for family, not thoughts of death.'

'And when is your mother arriving again?'

For that little gem I was sent to the garage anyway.

But hey, I have every reason to be skittish. Is it any wonder why, in my sixties, I'm thinking about eternity a little more than usual after all I've been through in the past few years? What is it about Queensland? I came up here to enjoy what my colleagues and friends called my 'autumnal period', and I've been shot at more in the past three years than in the entire thirty-seven I spent in the New South

Wales police force. And *that's* taking into account the era in which I served, especially around Kings Cross and Surry Hills, when bullets rained like, well, rain. They were tough times, kiddo. You needed a shotgun and a hardhat just to cross the road from the station to buy a cream bun from Madame Petrovsky's continental bakery on Macleay Street. (Madame Petrovsky, on the other hand, needed no weapons — not with that steely single black whisker squiggling out of a mole on her chin, and a gaze hard enough to slice clean through a block of *borodinsky* rye.)

But Queensland in the new millennium? Peace and quiet? Forget it. I should have been enjoying some quality time on my banana lounge, watching with fascination the colour change in my feet, year by year, as my circulation plummeted. I should have been left alone in my dotage to find new sprigs of hair in unexpected bodily crevices, remember nothing about the day before yet recall with excruciating clarity the wet carcasses of bunnies swinging on the rabbit-oh's cart when I was a wee lad in South Sydney, and to discover, all of a sudden, that the only things that really matter at the end of life are food and the exact locations of public lavatories. This was no autumn, brothers and sisters. This was permanent summer, global-warming style.

What did Queensland have against me? Is it because I'm from New South Wales? And before you get started, don't worry. I know the history. I've read all about Separation in 1859 and how the resentment of New South Wales was formally introduced to the Queensland genetic make-up on that day in December a century and a half ago when statehood was formalised from a balcony in Adelaide Street.

I know there's blood in the soil in Brisbane. The lash across the convicts' backs. The hanging of two innocent Indigenous men from the Old Windmill on Wickham

Terrace. The murders. The barbarity. The suffering. And *then* there's State of Origin. So don't get pernickety with me.

But there's something about the folk up here that likes a stoush.

Recently, Peg and I were in Brisbane town for a show and stayed overnight in a hotel. (From our window we could see the night lights of the Gabba, and I had to request a change of room. Reminders of cricket, death and all that. Peg said nothing during this, my *delicate* stage, but her eyebrows did move up and down curiously.)

Anyway, early the next morning I decided to take some exercise. I happily strode the walkways alongside the river. The birds were a'tweeting. The river a'wending. The light was a glorious dawn orange. I was slap-bang in the middle of a darned Constable landscape (the only artist I knew from that period, or virtually any period, because it had been a trick question on one of our cadet police examinations, constables needing to know Constable, a joke that had circulated forever in police circles, ha ha) when, in a flash, an elderly helmeted cyclist with yellow teeth was gnashing and spitting an inch from my face.

'Why don't you $5#@@! watch where you're %8$#@! going you &^$#@!'

'And good morning to you, sir,' I said.

'You're walking in the *^$3(#@! bike lane you half-witted *^7%$##@`~+?/ moron!'

'Do you always cuss in clusters of symbols and asterisks at this time of day?' I asked him politely. 'Get on your bike, dropkick, before I do the job your orthodontist should have done years ago.'

He continued to rant and rave at high decibels, to the point where everything was jiggling obscenely in his baggy lycra kit. He was like an old hot-air balloon losing its flame. I won't go into his straggly wicker. For some reason his outfit was covered in sponsor logos and various tidbits of advertising. He'd either stolen the gear, or someone was paying an enormous amount of money for this spotty old geezer to haul his bony backside up and down the Brisbane River at a little over walking pace, his knees clicking, his ancient sweat splashing the path, and his methane output making him a serious climate liability. He had to be stopped for the sake of the environment alone.

In the end, I snapped back, which wasn't very Christian of me, but I had to put an end to the flow of spittle. It was flipping my stomach.

'Listen, *Lance*,' I said, 'I'm terribly sorry if I accidentally interrupted your interior fantasy monologue of doing that final stretch of the Tour de France down the Champs Elysées before thousands of your adoring fans despite rattling like a pharmacopeia, but you're in *Brisbane*, and there is *no one cheering you on*, and your arse in those pants looks like *a broken umbrella*, and you need to get back to your job as *parking meter coin counter at the council* before I *kick you up your velodromes* and send you and your frackin' tricycle to hospital!'

He stopped then, offended. A reasonable response.

'I *don't work* for the council! I'm *retired*. I'm a multi!' he spluttered.

A multi? A *multi*? Did he really just say that?

'Yes,' I said in a language familiar to him, 'a multi-#@!&★^`~!!!' And I walked off.

Hair triggers, I told Peg over breakfast. They have hair triggers in Queensland. She said 'Hmmm' between mouthfuls of fresh pawpaw.

But how else can you explain the fact that just a week

later when I was back in Brisbane on a strange religious pilgrimage, suggested to me by My Analyst, I found myself in yet *another* pickle. But no ordinary pickle. Oh dear me, no. This pickle would make my other recent skirmishes with psychopathic antique dealers, murderous billionaire developers, the rabid relatives of long-dead Brisbane historical figures, Kombi-loving career criminals and the killers of benign and learned restaurant critics look like a small dish of soggy cocktail onions.

This pickle would see me drawn into a festering and fatal mystery involving church and state, a time capsule full to the brim with religious relics, and the ancient secrets of a swamp slap-bang in the middle of the Brisbane CBD. It would take me underneath the metropolis and into catacombs that you never knew existed in the Queensland capital. It would result in me being knocked out by a horse on the City Hall stage in front of the giant organ pipes. Stripped naked. And it would bring me into close proximity with an angel of death who twittered like the most beautiful nightingale, yet was as deadly as anyone or anything I've ever met in my meagre time on earth. Even if she did wear Chanel No. 5.

It would also bring me precisely to where I am now: trussed – courtesy of some elaborate and impressive handiwork, I have to admit – to the inside of the primary bell in the clock tower of the Brisbane City Hall.

I'm sure the view up here during the day is very nice. But it's dark now, in fact getting close to midnight. Has anyone below noticed that the dear old bell has not tolled the hour, or quarter, or half, for the last three hours? No, why would they? It's New Year's Eve. I can hear the little squalls of their laughter and hooting and happiness down in King George Square.

You see, Peg? Do you see now why I was obsessed with the grim reaper? Lord knows I warned you, Peg. But who listens to an old former cop with his feet the colour of marbled Sicilian sausage, his memory shot, his portly frame oft shot at, and his foolish trusting heart in the goodness of the human race broken more times than white plates at a Greek wedding?

I can, too, see my wristwatch from this uncomfortable trussed position. In exactly twenty-seven minutes my tweetering songbird will reactivate the clock, and the enormous clapper will strike my head against the waist of the brass bell. And it's goodnight nurse for me.

Down below, they will cheer in the New Year to the familiar sound of a much-loved donger, albeit in a slightly wet A-flat.

2

I'LL TELL YOU one thing. Proximity to death certainly clears the head. And nasal passages for that matter. I found, strapped and dangling inside the City Hall bell, that my sense of smell became extremely sharp. I could pick a lamb kebab being scoffed in Queen Street a few hundred metres away. Some jasmine, probably way over in the Roma Street Parkland. And I caught a whiff of cigar smoke somewhere down below me in the clock tower. My killer, my little tweety bird, was having her last suck on a Monte Christo before the New Year.

There, ninety metres above King George Square and its monster Christmas Tree and star, with my melon just minutes away from being dashed by a clock hammer against a 4.25 tonne bell (ding-dong, you're dead), I thought of what Peg might put on my tombstone. He Was Never Immediately Recognised, but His Face Rang a Bell? Not even Peg would stoop that low. (Would she?)

How did this all begin?

It ain't no Hollywood murder drama, I can tell you that. Life – or should I say death – doesn't work that way. There are two main ingredients in the murder biscuit, son, a wise old homicide-squad detective once told me. Greed and sex. What about killing for pleasure? Revenge? Pure hatred? A pesky mother-in-law? A moment of madness? Too complicated, son. You're thinking *gordon blur* (I think he meant *cordon bleu*) when you should be thinking *Arrowroot biscuit*, my boy.

The things you learn in the police force.

No, this started in church. Well, let me be specific. This started in a confessional booth in a nondescript house of worship in Gold Coast suburbia. This started with me going down on my spectacularly cartilage-challenged knees in a dull white cube of plywood and pine with a purple plastic faceted door handle in 35-degree heat in late November.

'Bless me, Father, for I have sinned . . .' And that, I have to say, lit the fuse.

What was I doing there? What was a grizzled agnostic with dicky knees and half a university degree in nothing much doing in a holy sweatbox in Marilyn Monroe Drive on the Glitter Strip?

My Analyst. I blamed My Analyst.

'Do you believe in God?' she had asked me the week before.

'Do you know, I wish I had thought of and patented that question,' I said, wriggling my socked toes on her studded leather couch, trying to get some colour back in my pinkies, which I knew were now whities, courtesy of the ageing process, or, to be accurate, grey-yellowish-violetish-custardish protrusions with nails the colour, quality and curvature of a hoary mythical dragon's talons. (You now know why I don't remove my socks very often.) 'I wish I had a dollar for every time you'd asked that question in your professional career,' I went on. 'That would have to be the most repeated question in human linguistic history, apart from "How are you?", "Can you pass the gravy?" and "Where's the remote control?"'

'This is avoidance,' she said. 'You are avoiding the question.'

I hadn't heard her. I was, in fact, asking myself, 'Where *is* the remote control?' I'd hoped to catch a little live test cricket on the television before my session, and hadn't been able to find the darned thing. I cursed the cleaners. Not only did they take it as part of their brief to rearrange the furniture and alter the geography of the refrigerator during each visit, but they also took the odd swig from the bottles on my drinks trolley. Oh yes, I was onto them. I marked the bottles, and I used an age-old trick suggested to me by an old friend in Fiji, who'd had similar problems with *his* cleaners. You turn the bottle *upside down*, then mark the level. They never twig, these hordes of house-cleaning lushes. I ordered Peg to sack them. She sent me back out to the camp stretcher in the garage.

'Yes?' my analyst persisted.

'Yes, what?'

'You're avoiding the question. About God.'

'What do I know about God? If Einstein couldn't figure it out, then what do you expect from me?'

'More avoidance. Let me take a wild guess. You had a repressive religious upbringing – you had heaven, hell, good and bad, black and white, you had guilt and subservience, then you went into the police force, into the wider world, saw that life wasn't so straightforward, read a bit of Jung, toyed with a little Marx and Trotsky, rebelled against the faith of your parents, wore a beret, smoked French cigarettes and decided that was enough to rid you of your theological childhood baggage.'

'Noooo!' I said, a little too dramatically.

'You didn't do that?'

'I *never* wore my beret in public!' I resented being so

transparent. I sulked for a short while. I wanted a therapist who couldn't read me, went off on wild and amusing
tangents about my inner life, gave me laughable remedies
and sent me on my way. I wanted to feel superior. It was
one of the reasons I was in therapy in the first place.

Wasn't it the late, great Puerto Rican actor Raúl Juliá who
asked, why spend a hundred bucks on therapy when you
could smoke a good cigar for twenty-five, and if your psychological problem came back, so what? Go smoke another
cigar. Then again, hadn't Raúl died of stomach cancer? I
didn't want to get into that carcinogenic conundrum. But
I would *not* be accused of wearing a beret in public.

'See you next week,' said My Analyst, glancing up at
her clock.

But it preyed on me, the question of God. I mulled
it over. It grew bothersome. It was an itch that needed a
back scratcher.

I got home and double-checked the levels in the whisky
and gin bottles and found the remote where the cleaners
had hidden it, wedged down beside the couch cushions
where I sat every night, and decided to go to confession for
the first time in half a century, just to see if there was any life
in the old dog yet.

'Bless me Father, for I have sinned,' I said in the confessional box in Marilyn Monroe Drive, deep in a suburb
that neither Peg nor my friends and associates would
ever visit. I had to nut out this question of faith with
complete anonymity.

'It is,' I went on, 'it is ...'

'Yes, my son.'

'It is ...'

'Yes, my son.'

'It is ...'

'A long time since your last confession?'

'Yes, Father.'

'So what are your sins?'

Now that's not a question you hear every day. And it's not a question any right-minded padre would be asking *me*, what with fifty years of credits in the sin department. Did this guy really know what he was getting into? It was like someone offering to help take your rubbish to the tip, then seeing a thousand dump trucks, filled to the gunnels with vile detritus, parked out the front of the house. With their motors idling. With crows pecking at the filth.

'Er ...' was all I could say.

'Long time away, comrade?' the priest asked.

And at that very second I knew it was him. Father Dillon O'Shee. Prison chaplain. Long Bay. Sydney. Seventies. When I was working in 21 Division, the notorious vice squad, I'd crack heads and he'd bless them. We had a harmonious working relationship.

'Father Dill?' I asked.

Later, we went out for beer at a nearby tavern in James Dean Boulevard (what *was it* about street names on the Gold Coast?) and he filled me in on his clerical career. He was due any month for retirement.

'You look good,' he said.

'I look like a dog's breakfast.'

'Life's treated you well.'

'I have feet the colour of Italian sausage.'

We slotted straight back into our old affection for each other, and as he drank his schooner I noted a little pinch of concern in his eyes.

'Time for you to confess, Dill.'

'What are you talking about?'

'Out with it, Dill.'

'Ah, comrade, it's nothing ...'

And after a few more beers – he could never hold his booze, Father Dill – he told me about how he'd gone from chaplain at Long Bay to Brisbane's Boggo Road, then, when that place had shut its doors, to a little parish in South Brisbane, where he thought he'd see out his career, until just a few months ago, when he was abruptly ordered to Marilyn Monroe Drive. That's when he told me about the little rusted tin box that had been brought to him by a concerned Christian who feared for its safety. That's when he told me about Alan Beechnut, and the funeral of his mother, Mirabelle Beechnut.

It was the first time I'd heard of the Beechnuts. And I couldn't know that dear, kind, gentle Father Dill would be brutally murdered and lowered into the earth at his own funeral just a week later. That I would be standing by the grave. That I would look up and catch the malevolent, psychotic grin of Alan Beechnut. That I would, in the not-too-distant future, lock ferocious horns with this nut, on a beach.

Life works in mysterious ways. I wish I'd patented *that* little cluster of words too.

3

'How did he die?'

I was sitting in a small office at the Roma Street police headquarters, learning the fate of poor Father Dill. A little birdie in homicide had given me a tip-off and I'd headed directly to Brisbane in the old Kombi.

I'd had plenty of time to contemplate my dear friend's untimely death. I was due in the city at nine that morning, but limped into Roma Street close to ten-thirty.

Brisbane traffic. I thought Sydney was bad. In just the few years I'd lived in south-east Queensland, its roads had gone haywire. Why? Where had everyone come from? Brisbane was the new Sydney, with one small twist. Brisbane people weren't used to this sort of congestive mayhem. They didn't know how to merge lanes at peak hour, because they'd never had to before. They weren't *au fait* with the 'thank you' wave. They waved, more often than not, with their middle finger. They leaned on the horn and tailgated and cut in and out and screamed and spat and wailed and punched the air and brandished screwdrivers. And that was just the women drivers.

If this city was a person, it was suffering serious, almost hospital-worthy indigestion. Brisbane, the ten-minute town where everything was just ten minutes away? Whoever kept saying that was blowing hot exhaust out of that place where the sun don't shine.

But the tunnels were coming. The Clem7. Australia's longest tunnel, being burrowed through that unique granite known as Brisbane Tuff. Talk about tuff. Brisbane traffic was tuff. It made driving across Sydney look like a trip in the kiddies' train at a shopping plaza.

I'd unwittingly dashed into a space in the conga line of cars passing through Mount Gravatt, and the dopey teenager I'd inconvenienced had followed me all the way into the city and as I parked had pulled up beside me, given me the two-handed centre finger, then curled his right hand into a fist, slapped his left hand against his right forearm, raising the said fist, and screamed a very short sentence at me. The first word rhymed with 'truck', and the second was 'orf'. Then he sped away in a puff of carbon monoxide. Nice way to start the day.

Anyway, I had learned, speaking with my police contact at Roma Street, that during that morning's drive I had unwittingly passed the site where Father Dill's body, or bits of it, had been found.

'Gibbon Street shaft, the Gabba,' he said.

'What's that, the name of a gang or something?'

'Gibbon Street shaft. The giant vent. For the Clem7 tunnel. They found him in there. In six pieces. We have no idea how he got in there. Or why he was dumped there. Drained of blood. No prints. It's a strange one.'

'Six pieces of him?'

'Head, arms, legs, all severed from the torso. Neatly stacked. I've never seen anything like it.'

'Chainsaw?'

'No. We don't know what was used.'

'How can you not know? This is the homicide squad isn't it? Haven't you seen it all?'

'The cuts weren't clean. Whatever the killer used, it was blunt. And I mean blunt.'

'Good Lord,' I said. Not only was Father Dill's manner of death shocking, but so was the creeping infiltration of religious references in my day-to-day speech.

It had started after my belated confession in Marilyn Monroe Drive. That night, after a few beers with poor Father Dill, I'd gone home and asked Peg where the television remote was. The cleaners had been. But the ensuing debate didn't unfold as it usually did. I said to Peg. 'Thou shalt ask those cleaners where the ruddy thing is and why they keep moving it.' And she said, after a short pause. 'Did you just say "thou shalt"?' And I said. 'Are you daft? Who in their right mind would use the words "thou shalt"?' And she said, 'You did. You just said "thou shalt".' I thought using the word 'ruddy' was more peculiar. (Could that have been our ex-prime minister's nickname at school? Did they shout 'Rudd-y, Rudd-y' at him through the pineapple fields?)

Anyway, I went and sulked on my camp stretcher in the garage.

'We've seen similar cuts to the body,' my police contact said, 'on train suicides. The train wheels.'

'So he was thrown under a train?'

'That's the thing,' he said. 'There was no bruising, no cuts and abrasions, anywhere else on the body. And what train could dexterously carve off a man's legs, arms and head in a single motion? Physically impossible.' He scratched his head.

'Good Lord,' I repeated, scratching my own head.

I gave my friend some background details on Father Dill.

He didn't really need them. But I needed to talk. I needed to vent, and that was not a pun on Gibbon Street.

What I didn't tell him was the discussion Dill and I had had in the tavern on James Dean Boulevard. About the mysterious tin box that had been entrusted to Dill. The confession he had taken, his last in Brisbane before being shafted (again, no pun intended) to the Gold Coast, which had chilled him to the bone.

'What was it about?' I'd asked Dill.

'I'm sorry, comrade. I can't reveal that.'

'Who was it?'

'That's sacred, brother.'

'For Christ's sake, Dill,' I'd said. 'How serious is it?'

'It's life and death, comrade,' he'd said, tears welling in his eyes as he lifted his beer. 'As serious as it gets.'

Who had sought Dill for absolution? Who had slipped into the confessional and said something that made this saintly priest fear for his life? It didn't take blind Freddy to conclude that the sinner would be worth questioning in light of Father Dill's blunt and bloodless dismemberment.

A few days after the tavern, I had telephoned him and his voice was thin down the line. The last thing he said to me was, and I'm paraphrasing: 'Hezekiah stopped the upper watercourse of Gihon and brought it down to the city of David. And Hezekiah prospered in all his works. There's fire in the tunnels this time, comrade. Fire in the tunnels.'

Four days later someone turned him into a three-dimensional human jigsaw in the dark shafts of Brisbane. Who could he have met in the holy booth? Was he giving me a clue? The identity of his future killer?

Finally he'd whispered: 'Mary. Blessed Mary.'

'Dill?'

'O beloved Mary. Sweet Mary. Give me strength.'

'Dill?'

And the phone had gone dead.

I rang again. No answer. So I took a quick swing by the chapel on Marilyn Monroe Drive and knocked at the back door.

'Father Dillon?' The office smelled of pine needles and incense and the colour purple. Yes, purple. For me the church, since I was a kid, had smelled of purple.

I'd crept inside and found nothing. Then I'd opened the doors to the confessional. For no reason. It was how I always used to work as a detective. I'd snoop in places for no reason. I'd poke through kitty-litter trays, check refrigerator cheese boxes, prod away at sofa cushions. Colleagues would ask, what are you doing that for, Detective? No reason, I'd say. The reasoning of my non-reasoning had solved four murders during my spell in homicide. There was nothing in the good Father's booth. Then, just as I was about to close the sinner's door, I'd seen a little triangle of yellow in the shadows beneath the kneeling stool.

I'd bent down low on my creaky knees, and retrieved the object.

It was a small ticket. An old ticket. On one side was a numbered grid with B.C.C. Dept. of Transport printed across the top in small letters. On the other was a very crude picture of a kangaroo and the words 'Hop Into! Trittons'.

What the hell was this? And had the clerk who put the exclamation mark after 'Into' been given the heave-ho for poor grammar all those years ago? Was he drunk? Sloppy stuff.

I'd pocketed the ticket, and had it in my wallet when I visited my contact at the Roma Street headquarters. I didn't share it with him either.

And I was flicking it with my thumbnail in the pocket of

my old shiny suit trousers days later at Father Dill's funeral.
That's when I caught Alan Beechnut's gaze. That's when
the hairs on my neck bristled. And that's when I decided to
pay Mr Beechnut a quiet visit.

·4

THE PROBLEM WITH short, eccentric men with strange fetishes is that they have a taste for bringing about the end of the world.

As my favourite television celebrity of all time, Professor Julius Sumner Miller, always said: 'Why is it so?'

I'll tell you why, Julius — and you don't have to know how to suck an egg into a milk bottle to get the gist of this. *Unpredictability.* Short megalomaniacs can be unpredictable, a quality that is the bane of a copper's life.

Julius had it. Unpredictability. Not an Armageddon-esque unpredictability, though I'm sure his influence led to more childhood chemistry-set explosions than at any other time in history. The reason Julius's unpredictability worked was that he knew his audience was a bunch of scientific halfwits. *Everything* he did was unpredictable to the dopey, cow-like masses who oohed and ahhed at Julius's magic. I include myself in the herd.

I remember his 'Millergrams', which were published in the daily newspaper, with the answer provided the next day. How tall a mirror do you need to see all of you? he asked. How can you measure out half a cup of hard, solid butter without melting it? Boy, Julius could be infuriating. Yet he was compulsive viewing, responsible for shaping an entire generation of eggheads. And getting that *actual* egg into the milk bottle. Watch it. *Watch it!* There it goes. Why is it so? Such an existential question, and one I used often, to the annoyance of my colleagues, when I arrived at a murder scene. Why is it so?

The trouble with Alan Beechnut was that you knew, on sight, that he was the kind of man who would call out for his Mammy on his deathbed. In fact, you knew he was the kind of man who had spent his entire life *living* with his Mammy. And he had. Until she expired, and poor little Beechnut had to stay home alone.

That's where I found him one Saturday afternoon when I decided to pay a visit to his house in Scarborough, a pretty little bayside point north of Redcliffe, outside Brisbane. It had taken me almost three hours to get there, this time on the Gateway. A tomato truck had lost its load and the motorway had ground to a halt somewhere near Underwood. Brisbane traffic, again. I am not a fan of tomatoes. To be honest, I have a tomato phobia. It was something I had yet to discuss with My Analyst. I thought we'd get my religious conundrums out of the way before we moved on to fruit and vegetables. I was even less of a tomato fan that day. I'd got seeds on my mudflaps.

Beechnut's place was a little fibro fishing shack two streets back from the bay. I didn't like the feel of it one bit. It was the type of house – the windows all tightly shut, the grass long, the paint peeling off – I had seen before. These sorts of places had dead bodies in them, mummified corpses lying on beds while weeds towered over the yard, and free local newspapers rotting on the front path. Places like this had secrets.

It was hot. I could smell briny water. I felt nauseous.

But not half as bilious as I became when I knocked and Beechnut opened the door.

What hit me was a wall of smell that told me a lot about Alan Beechnut. It was the odour of unwashed human beings in warm conditions that had accumulated over many years. It was the throat-constricting perfume of an old lady and her middle-aged boy existing quietly in a small house with no ventilation. Now it was just the boy, but the smell had a lot of dear, departed Mammy still in it. Oh dear me, yes. It was so foul, a hair in my nose coiled tight.

'Can I help you?' Beechnut asked me.

'Cut the Little Lord Fauntleroy crap, Beechnut. We need to talk.' I had cupped my hand over my nose and mouth.

He was about five feet tall and sported a comb-over. At least, I guess it was a comb-over. In fact, his hair had probably not seen a comb since little Alan was potty-trained, which may have been last year by the smell of the house. And while it had been a long time since I'd had anything to do with babies, I think the man was still suffering from cradle cap. He also had two pieces of blood-stained toilet paper stuck to his face. Looked like he shaved with a chisel blade. His ears were spectacularly protuberant and not unlike small, fleshy seashells. I could imagine his classmates swinging off them in his schooldays. He wore a red and black checked flannelette shirt buttoned to the neck and at the wrists, though it was close to thirty-five degrees. He had narrow shoulders and baggy grey trousers. He wore – of course – navy-blue socks and plastic sandals. Alan Beechnut looked like a little old man, though he couldn't have been more than fifty. At a hunch, he would have been an old-looking baby. Older than his Mammy and Pappy when he was born. Prune-faced and hunchbacked. I doubted there were many baby photos of little Alan framed throughout the house.

The disturbing thing about Alan — apart from the fact that his eyes seemed to be looking in two different directions, he was rank, had cradle cap and enough plaque on his teeth to make, well, a plaque to poor dental hygiene — was the malevolence he carried about his eyes and mouth.

He had the look of a boy who'd just set fire to the local church and was wetting his Y-fronts waiting for the fire truck to arrive. *Wee-wah, wee-wah!* And his eyelashes were very dark and very thick, as if they'd been drawn on with a child's crayon. Both top and bottom lashes were of equal length. I had met men whose eyes were totally framed by thick eyelashes. They were invariably arsonists, or scam artists, or animal torturers, or had a future in cross-dressing. Or they were murderers.

'Come in,' he said in a flat voice.

I was dry retching. I could see, beyond him and into the house, towering piles of old, yellowing newspapers and bags of garbage and, I think, a rat gambolling on the linoleum bench in the dim kitchen.

'Let's take a walk, Beechnut,' I said, and grabbed him by the flannelette arm. It was wet with old, cold sweat.

'You got a warrant?'

'Cork it, Alan. I got two fists the size of Christmas hams. That do?'

'You're hurting me.'

'Be a good boy, Alan.'

I let go of his arm and he reluctantly followed. He had the sullen look of a lad whose favourite choo-choo train had just been broken.

We went down to the water. I sat at one end of a park bench and ordered him to seat his rump at the other end. Even through the fishy stench of the bay I could smell him and his house and his dead mother.

'Friend of Father Dillon's, were you, Beechnut?'

'I don't have to say nothing.'

'You seemed a pretty happy chappy for a bloke at another man's funeral.'

'I could call the cops.'

'And I could pin those ears of yours back permanently, without surgery. You get my drift?'

'You a cop? You talk like some TV cop or something.' He stared out at the water. His left toe was jiggling away inside his sandal. The toe gave him away. People trying to hide something should never wear sandals.

'I'm the man who can put your egg inside a milk bottle, Alan.'

'What?'

'Nothing. So tell me, how's your Mammy?'

At this, his body stiffened and those eyes came alive. Not just alive – they burned with a heat you could roast a marshmallow over.

'You loved your Mammy, didn't you, Alan? Yesss. Poor little Alan. Tell me. Did Father Dillon do a nice job at the funeral?'

Beechnut just stared at me. And I saw, as I had at Dill's funeral, that crooked corner of his mouth. If I had to continue in this religious frame of mind, the only emotion that could produce such a hateful, malevolent, murderous face was pure, organic wrath.

'Don't talk about my mother,' said Beechnut, finally.

'No? Why not?'

'Don't talk about my mother.' His voice had changed. It now had the guttural whine of a toy losing its battery power and had a deeper timbre. It went to the heart of the Beechnut.

'I'm just curious, Alan. Why you chose Father Dillon to

perform the service, all the way down in South Brisbane, when I'm sure you've got perfectly adequate priests and churches and caskets and ground to bury people in, or rose bushes to scatter ashes under, here in delightful Scarborough.'

His toe stopped. He got up and started walking back to his fibro cesspit.

'Alan!' I shouted after him playfully. 'Pweese come back, Alan!'

He strode off, hunched and purposeful. But I wasn't done with Beechnut yet.

It took hours, but my surveillance paid off. At dusk he pedalled down the side of the house and into the street on a Malvern Star that should have been in a glass museum cabinet.

I waited until he reached the end of the street and turned out of sight. I waited another few minutes.

Then I entered the house of death. Why do I do these things? *Why is it so?*

5

I TIPTOED THROUGH the back door of Maison Beechnut, hit
the Maglite torch button, and instantly recognised the depth
and quality of screwball I was dealing with.

Oh, My Analyst would have loved this little Scarborough
seaside shack. There was at least a decade's worth of work
for her in the maze of Beechnut's psychoses. There was also
at least a decade's work here for my bum-lush cleaners. A
quick bench wipe, a run over with the mop and a swig of
Bombay Sapphire this was not.

Alan Beechnut was not next to godliness, let's put it
that way.

Luckily I had found some of my emergency leftover face
masks from the swine-flu scare tucked away in the Kombi. I
snapped one on in Beechnut's foul kitchen, yet the house's
pungent gruel of dead air still managed to creep through the
sieve and thicken my tongue.

'You dirty little boy, Beechnut,' I mumbled through the
mask. The torch beam picked up a great V-shaped fan of fat
on the wall behind the ancient stove. It went up the wall
and extended a short way across the ceiling. There was fifty
years of grease here, a grand slick of it the colour of nicotine.
I burped through the mask. There were sauce bottles on a

shelf that had stopped being made when Menzies was prime minister. There were tins and boxes of powdered mustard and jelly that collectors would have bid for on eBay. Just a fragment of the filthy linoleum floor would have excited scientists in any self-respecting disease research unit. I was not amazed that Alan Beechnut lived here. I was amazed he was still *alive* in this filth.

I passed the bathroom. I didn't even want to look in there. I imagined the drains filled with human hair plugs. I burped again.

I inched my way down a short hall, squeezing past huge stacks of bundled newspapers, then entered what should have been a lounge or dining room. And there it was — the epicentre of Alan Beechnut.

In my time as a police officer I saw many strange things, let me tell you. You get access to private dwellings and you're going to witness some weird stuff. You wouldn't believe the half of what I stumbled upon. Altars. Grottos. Indoor temples. Hundreds of candles around a single photograph or object. Porcelain-cat collections, jam-lid collections, collections dedicated to Elvis, stones, suggestively shaped vegetables, forgotten pop stars, even a dust collection. The strangest was a penthouse suite in Double Bay that venerated a particular breed of merino ... Well, I won't go into that here.

But I had never, until Beechnut, come across a shrine to public transport.

I whistled through the mask. Public transport en masse would have been odd enough. But, no. Beechnut's worship was focused. He was, it seemed, in love with the Brisbane tram.

A third of the room was filled with the sawn-off, snub-nosed front end of a real Brisbane tram — a little three-window cabin with a single headlight. I imagined Beechnut sometimes donned a small, stiff white cap and ding-dinged his way down the Queen Street of his imagination. He had shelves and shelves filled with little handmade tram models. On his wall were framed tram-route maps and, curiously, an old advertisement for Vincent's headache powder.

In a tall bookcase he had neatly placed dozens and dozens of thin, red-coloured notebooks. I pulled one out from the middle shelf, opened it and strafed the contents with my torchlight. There were dates in a left-hand column and notes in tight, cramped handwriting, the letters teeming on the page like sugar ants. The notations were tedious, strangely abbreviated diary entries for tram rides taken in the city of Brisbane dating back to the mid-sixties. I checked the top-shelf notebooks. These were in different handwriting and went back to the late thirties. Perhaps his father's missives. On the bottom shelf the last notebook ended on 13 April 1969.

One book was different from all the others. It was a facsimile of a ledger simply titled *Fatal Book 1897*. You're a wack job, Beechnut, I said to myself.

On another shelf were neatly filed green notebooks. These were crammed cover to cover with the handwritten minutes of the Scarborough Tram Society. Each meeting was run by the president of the society, A. Beechnut. Each resolution was seconded by A. Beechnut. The minutes were recorded by A. Beechnut. Guest lectures were delivered by special guest and world tram authority, A. Beechnut. I had a sickening feeling the Scarborough Tram Society had a membership of one.

Beside this bookshelf on the wall was a black and white photograph of a street scene. It showed a small crowd with one man holding up a hand-drawn sign – 'Scrap the Jones Administration, Not the Trams'. And in front of this man was a small boy with very large, shell-like ears waving to the camera. The picture was dated 13.4.69.

Jones. *Jones?* Clem Jones? Could it be the same Clem the Clem7 tunnel was named after? The tunnel in whose vent my dear friend Father Dill was found in six pieces?

I stood over Beechnut's large desk and riffled through stacks of paper. Here were more tram-route maps. But halfway through the pile were detailed drawings and maps of the Clem7 tunnel. There were complicated engineering drafts, cross-section diagrams, geological surveys. And underneath them were documents relating to the Brisbane City Hall – maps, old architectural plans, plumbing and electrical data, drawings of foundations, doorways, ladders, stairwells, hatches. There was a business card stapled to some of the paperwork. It belonged to a council engineer, a Mr Barrie Barry. I issued a double burp into the swine-flu mask, an accidental homage to the twin-named council worker.

Beneath the desk, next to several cans of red paving paint, I found a small cairn of books that were the property of the Redcliffe City Library. They were all about one person. Mary MacKillop, the primary candidate to become Australia's first saint.

I stood in the centre of the room, turned off the torch and had a quiet think.

I recalled a conversation I had had with my police friend at Roma Street about the murder of Father Dill.

'How did his body get into the Gibbon Street shaft?' I had asked.

'We don't know,' the officer said.

'Is it freely accessible? To the public?'

'No.'

'You'd need special access?'

'Correct.'

'When will the tunnel be finished?'

'First half of 2010.'

'Could it have been a tunnel worker? With access to the shaft?' I went on, thinking out loud.

'It could have been.'

'What was Dill doing in that part of Brisbane anyway, when he lived on the coast?'

'He's either been murdered somewhere on the Gold Coast and his body cut up and transported to South Brisbane, or he's made his way to Brisbane – perhaps he was lured – and murdered somewhere in the city and his body dumped at the vent. He didn't have a car.'

'But why the vent? South Brisbane?'

'The body was stacked, not dumped. It was a sign. A symbol of something, the way the body was presented for discovery. The tunnel, or the area, meant something to the killer. He or she is telling us something.'

'He or she is telling us he or she is out of his or her frackin' mind,' I said.

In Beechnut's dark living room I tried to establish a case narrative. Dillon's old parish was South Brisbane. He'd been dumped and ushered out after years of service there. And he ends up an anatomical display. Back in South Brisbane. O beloved Mary. Sweet Mary. Give me strength, Father Dill had said to me.

'Come on, Dill, throw us a miracle here. A bit of divine intervention,' I said quietly to myself, my olfactories longing for some fresh air inside the swine mask.

I turned the torch back on and started to make my way out.

The torchlight caught on a tiny picture frame at the end

of the room. I clambered around an old slatted tram seat and had a closer look. In the centre of the cheap frame was a small yellow rectangle.

I whistled through my mask. I pulled out the little cardboard ticket I'd found in Dill's confessional, and held it up beside the one under glass.

'Thanks, comrade,' I said.

Then the back door creaked open.

6

It was nice to see my Jack again. He was sitting quietly in the chair beside my hospital bed when I regained consciousness.

'Hello, son,' I said.

'Hello, Dad.'

'Fancy seeing you here,' I said.

'And fancy seeing you here,' he said.

'Where am I?' I asked.

'Hospital, Dad,' he said.

'Been here long, have I?' I asked.

'Day and a half, Dad,' he said.

'Oh, that's nice,' I said. 'Any idea why I'm here, son?'

'Yes, Dad,' he said. 'You were found naked and unconscious in the back of your Kombi down at Redcliffe.'

'Is that so?' I asked.

'Yes, Dad.'

'Naked, you say?'

'I'm afraid so.'

I ran my hand through my hair and felt yet another half-grapefruit on the back of my head. I ached from tip to toe. It started to come back to me. Trains. No, trams. Smell. A bad smell. Rats. A picture. No, a little rectangular ticket.

Alwin Beernut? Alvin Barebutt? Yes! Alan Beechnut! The rogue, the swine, the dirty little street-scrapper.

'Been well, son?'

'Yes, Dad.'

'What you doing there, son?' My boy was hunched over his mobile phone, tapping away with both thumbs.

'Tweeting, Dad.'

'That's nice,' I said. I could hear the gadget clicking. 'Tweeting. What is that? Some sort of young people's code for something?'

'It's social networking, Dad. Twitter. You send tweets to your friends and they send tweets back.'

'Nothing to do with birds?'

'No, Dad.'

For a moment I was back in the room at Beechnut's filth palace in Scarborough. I'd heard the back door creak open. I'd frozen. I'd thought of hiding in the sawn-off tram chassis. Then again, he might want to play driver and toot-toots, and there was no way the two of us would have fitted in there. I'd thought I might dash out the front door, but I didn't know where it was in that jumbled shrine to public transport. I'd clicked off the torch and waited. I'd blind him with the Maglite and push through the kitchen and out. I'd zap him and flee. He had turned on the kitchen light and I could see his long shadow spilling into the tram room. He'd walked slowly across the linoleum. The shadow had grown. Then he was in the doorway.

'Social nitpicking, you say,' I said to my son.

'Social networking.'

'What is that, son?'

'Yes, Dad. It's keeping in touch with friends via the internet on a computer, or your mobile phone. You send text messages, post pictures, web links, that sort of thing.'

'Why don't you just ring them up if you want to talk to them, son?'

'This way, Dad, you can keep in touch with a lot of people simultaneously.'

'That's very social,' I said.

'Yes, Dad.'

'Are you bleeting now?'

'Tweeting.'

'Oh.'

'Yes, I am,' Jack said. 'I'm telling everyone that I'm a sitting here in a chair beside your hospital bed.'

'Oh. That's nice. And your friends would find that interesting, son?'

'I think so, yes.'

'Read it to me.'

'"Sitting in a chair beside my father's hospital bed."'

'That's it?'

'Yes.'

'Short and tweet,' I said. He didn't laugh.

'With each tweet, Dad, you can use a maximum of 140 characters.'

'Only 140?'

'Yes, Dad.'

'Who says?'

'That's the rules.'

'What can you say with 140 characters? That doesn't sound like a lot, son.'

'That's the way it is.'

'What are you writing now?'

'"Explaining tweeting to my sick father."'

I'd had the torch ready to blast Beechnut. He'd stopped in the doorway. Perhaps he could smell me. Perhaps he'd detected something different in the soupy bouquet of

excrement and urine and dead rodents and filthy dishes and
rotting food that was his life, like a hint of soap or deodor-
ant on a human being who actually thought washing and
cleanliness were a part of everyday civilisation.

I'd hit the torch button.

'Thank you, nurse,' I said. A nice nurse had wheeled in
my lunch. I sat up. I lifted the steel tray cover. Roast lamb,
peas, mashed potato and some boiled carrot. I belched.
Rather loudly. My head pounded.

'What are you writing now, son?'

'"My father is having disgusting hospital roast dinner for
lunch."'

'You wrote that?'

'Yes, Dad.'

I nudged the peas with my fork.

'What are you writing now?'

'"Lunch smells like dog sick."'

'Your friends would find that interesting?'

'Yes, because I'm tweeting it.'

'So because you tweet it they will find it interesting.
I see. What now?'

'"My father issues foul belch."'

I was growing suspicious of Jack and his tweeting. Just
140 characters. I noticed that he hadn't stopped tweeting
since I'd woken from my stupefaction. He hadn't looked
me in the eye. He hadn't looked at me at all. And his
responses to my questions were snappy, clipped, truncated.
He was answering me in 140 characters or less. And all the
while his thumbs were hammering away at a furious pace.

I still didn't understand what this twittering business
was all about. Lunch? Belches? How could that be of any
interest whatsoever to a sensible, sentient, halfway intelligent
person? Had the world gone mad? You just blithered away

to each other on a computer or phone screen? Whatever happened to meeting people face to face? Chatting over a coffee or a wine? Enjoying the pleasure of another person's company? How could they call it social networking? Antisocial networking would be more appropriate.

I looked to the hospital door, and again recalled Beechnut's place. For it wasn't Alan, the president of the Scarborough Tram Society, who'd taken the full brunt of my torch beam. It was one of the most beautiful, curvaceous, well-proportioned – dare I say *generously* proportioned in this politically correct age – women I had ever seen in my life. Small. Brunette. A Veronica Lake-inspired fall to her hair. Sheer black cocktail dress. High heels. She made you suck in your breath for a fraction of a second. And she smelled, for the brief time I was conscious in her presence, of a combination of Chanel No. 5 and a very expensive cigar.

She'd smiled. Then her martial arts kick to my head had sent me all a'twitter. And into oblivion.

'Ha!' Jack roared.

'What is it, son?'

'One of my followers just sent through a tweet. Pretty cool, whatever it means.'

'What does it say?'

'"Tell your father – Murder, she tweeted."'

7

DURING THOSE RESTFUL days in hospital, as my bruised melon returned to its normal size and the stiletto puncture wound to my neck healed nicely, I resorted to my age-old method of detective work. I wrote each pertinent fact on a small five- by three-inch index card and placed each one in front of me on my little tray table like a solitaire player.

What did I have?

I had rekindled my friendship with Father Dill after a chance encounter at his chapel in Marilyn Monroe Drive. He seemed disturbed about a recent event, something to do with an old tin box given to him for safekeeping. Within days Dill was dead, sliced up and stacked like grain-fed wagyu beef intended for an organic-butcher shop window. But not anywhere near Marilyn Monroe Drive. The dismembered cairn of my dear friend had been located in a tunnel vent in Gibbon Street, South Brisbane – a street that had once fallen into the orbit of Dill's former parish, before he was abruptly relocated around the time of the metal-box discovery.

Dill had told me about a peculiar family called the Beechnuts, Mammy Beechnut having recently passed away, and at Dill's funeral I'd caught sight of that reprobate Alan

Beechnut. I had interrogated the cross-eyed public transport fanatic and turned up little, though an inspection of
his Scarborough house, the smell of which would have
made the eyes of vultures and hyenas water, had exposed
his peculiar fetish. I'd discovered what might have been a
clue to Dill's murder in the old framed tram ticket. Then
a long-haired siren had stepped into the picture, and sent
me to hospital with one swift kick of her beautifully shod
foot. To add to the humiliation she – or was it Beechnut,
the putrescent little pervert – had stripped me starkers and
left me in my Kombi.

I had not seen Peg enter the room, so enmeshed was I in
the twists and turns of this peculiar mystery.

'Hello, darling,' she finally said.

She sat in the chair my twittery son Jack had occupied a
couple of days earlier.

'When will this end?' she asked.

'I hope to be around for a few years yet, Peg,' I snorted.
'No rush is there?'

'Not your life, you goose. This … this … *mayhem*.'

'Hardly mayhem, dear.'

'Naked and unconscious. In the Kombi. At Redcliffe.
And at *your* age?'

'Yes,' I double-snorted. 'Should have gotten those
curtains fitted in the old bus after all, eh? Funny, the oddities
life throws at you.'

'So this is an annual thing of yours now, is it? These
oddities, as you call them.'

Dogs can scent a coming storm. My storm scent was
twitching. Luckily, Peg always telegraphed her building
rage with her left eyebrow, which lifted up and down
with gathering frequency. I won't say some parts of my
anatomy beneath the lemon-smelling hospital sheet didn't

shrivel at the sight, but at least the agitated brow gave me some warning.

'Now, darling—'

'Don't darling me. I had expected to see out my years with a husband who aged gracefully. With someone I could share some time with. Not an old cop with a death wish. You can't let it go, can you?'

I had no answer to that. We were silent in the room for ten minutes before the eyebrow lowered and she got up. She dropped a heavy bag on my swivel tray.

'The books you asked for,' she said, and left.

Peg was right, of course. It got me thinking. Ever since I'd come to Queensland, people around me had got killed. Last year it was the raconteur Westchester Zim. A week ago, Father Dill. I was a deity of death. A death lord of the underworld. I looked down at my spherical waist-line holding up the hospital sheet. Yes, I was the original Under Belly.

Then the nurse brought me a custard tart and I got back to business.

I took the books out of the bag, and there she was — Mary MacKillop. Blessed Mary, as Father Dill had cryptically said.

I read the story of her life with awe. What an extra-ordinary woman. Born in Fitzroy, Melbourne, in 1842 to Scottish immigrants, she'd dedicated her life to educating poor children with the Sisters of St Joseph of the Sacred Heart, constantly on the move in Australia and Europe, full of courage and hope.

My son had been on the internet, and inside one of the books I found a print-out of a feature story from the *Brisbane Courier* published in February 1883. It was written by Julian Thomas, a pen name for John Stanley James, a journalist who had pioneered fly-on-the-wall newspaper writing in

Australia. He also wrote under the name 'The Vagabond'. In the feature my son had discovered – titled 'An Australian Order' – Thomas had done an in-depth first-hand account of the Sisters of St Joseph of the Sacred Heart, and had actually interviewed MacKillop, the woman most likely to become Australia's first saint, in South Australia.

'We are welcomed by "Mother Mary",' he wrote, 'the superioress and founder of the order.' She had given him a tour of the order's 'refuge for fallen women'.

'It is far better that we should take these children, and bring them up properly, than that their mothers should neglect them to be reared in misery and vice,' she'd reportedly said. Thomas told MacKillop that it appeared to be a great struggle to keep the Sisters of St Joseph running, to which she'd replied: 'But if we gave this up, what would become of the poor creatures?'

MacKillop had regularly faced difficulties with both the church and state bureaucracies of the day. She was excommunicated for supposed insubordination, but this was later reversed.

And, incredibly, she'd attempted to spread her good work in Brisbane, arriving in this rough colonial town in late 1869, just a decade after Separation.

'In the northern colony I heard a great deal of the good they [the Sisters of St Joseph] had done, but for some cause or other they incurred the displeasure of the late Bishop Quinn,' wrote Thomas. 'A controversy as to his authority ensued. I remember a dear friend of mine, a Catholic priest, once saying to me, "We have to obey our Bishop, but we needn't love him."'

So Mary suffered grief in early Brisbane. Why didn't that surprise me? I thought of that Catholic priest over at South Brisbane having his own ideological stoush with the bishop not long ago. And his church was St Mary's, too, wasn't it? The more things change …

Still, I was fascinated with Mary. She was beatified in 1995 by Pope John Paul II, and one miracle had been attributed to her. But she needed two for canonisation, a second 'intercession through prayer'.

Just last winter she'd been made patron of the Brisbane Catholic archdiocese.

I put down the paperwork and closed my eyes. Saints. Miracles. A little tin box. The crucified Father Dill. For someone who'd decided to simply dip his toe back in the religion of his past, I was suddenly all at sea in faith. Maybe Peg was right. Maybe it was time I let it all go and looked to the future.

When I opened my eyes Jack was back in the chair beside the bed. He had just appeared. Miraculously.

'Hello, Dad.'

'Nice to see you, son. Still twitching?'

'Tweeting, Dad.'

'Ah yes.'

'Got another few from your friend.'

'My friend?'

'The murder tweeter.'

'Ah yes. What do they say, son?'

'"Ding-dong, you're dead."'

'That's a bit harsh, don't you think?'

'And, "For whom the bell tolls."'

'Good movie. Gary Cooper. Ingrid Bergman.'

'Whatever,' Jack said.

'Come to think of it, didn't Bergman play a nun in *The Bells of St Mary's*?'

'Dunno, Dad.'

Then he left.

I made a quick call on my room phone. I rang the imaginatively named council engineer Barrie Barry. I was put on hold.

While I was waiting for Barrie Barry, I flicked through one of my MacKillop books and something caught my eye. A phrase. Don't know why. For no reason.

I crooked the phone between my ear and left shoulder and held the book open. I read a paragraph about Blessed Mary and her time in Brisbane. I read of the hardship. The sacrifice.

Then I dropped the phone and it bounced clean off the bed.

Mary MacKillop, future saint, had for a short time lived in South Brisbane.

In Gibbon Street.

8

WHILE I WAS waiting for Barrie Barry in King George Square, I wondered where everybody was. The square was empty, except for King George on his horse and the two lions guarding City Hall. I could see people over at Roma Street, and others in the Queen Street Mall, but *bubkis*, diddly, *nada*, in the square.

Then I wondered why, as I crossed Adelaide Street earlier, it was close to thirty degrees in Greater Brisbane, and yet sitting in the newly renovated square, denuded of trees and fountains, it appeared twice that. On top of it all, I couldn't see a darned thing through the glare that bounced off the new square's giant pad of concrete or tiling or crushed glass or whatever it was. The clock tower was all ghostly and shimmering. If anyone ever wanted to orchestrate a world-record attempt at cooking eggs, this would be the place. It was a frying pan. The King George Skillet. I felt like an ant under a naughty boy's microscope, and he had a face like Beechnut.

I'd arrived early for our meeting. I'd wandered the halls of City Hall. I'd never been inside. Impressive. Lots of deco curves. Veined marble. Stately columns. Hard to believe the place was sinking into the earth.

I struck up a conversation with an old boy in the Museum of Brisbane.

'Terribly sad, terribly sad,' he said of the crumbling icon. 'I enlisted here as a young man. Double-you, double-you two. Down in the Red Cross rooms. Terribly sad. Terribly sad.'

He kept repeating things. It gave his conversation a powerful bedrock, which is more than I could say for the terribly sad City Hall.

'How come she's going under?' I asked.

'Built on a swamp. A swamp. Was a swamp from day one and no matter what you put over the top of a swamp, she stays a swamp.'

'That so?'

'Oh yes. Oh yes. A swamp's a swamp.'

'Then why did they build it here?'

'Because the council owned the land. Owned the land.'

'Simple as that?'

'Argh, yes. Yes.'

I saw a slender figure approach me through the heat haze. It was Barrie Barry. Strange. I was having a day of repetitions.

'You're Barry? Barrie?'

He nodded, flicked his head, and walked straight past me towards Ann Street. I followed. We didn't speak until we'd taken up a seat on the grass in the Roma Street Parkland. Barrie Barry was twitching and checking over his shoulder, a veritable bundle of tics and tweaks. He had a bald pate that was very shiny. Too long in King George Square and he'd be in an emergency neurology unit. I had a very silly urge to ask him if his middle name was Barrey.

'How did you find me?' Barrie whispered.

'Well, Barry − or is it Barrie? I came upon you via a rather circuitous route involving a tram fanatic with stupendous halitosis and the death of a very good friend, a man of the cloth. I have a hunch you met him too.'

'Father Dillon.'

'Father Dillon.'

'And Beechnut,' Barrie Barrey Barry said.

'I'm afraid so.'

'He came to me, Beechnut, interested in the restoration work at the City Hall. He said he was from some transport group.'

'The Scarborough Tram Society,' I nodded.

'Yes. He seemed ... well ... we have, at council, the occasional difficulties with public-transport fanatics. They can become ... difficult. Any road change, bus route alteration, even modifications to ticketing systems, even the tickets themselves − they have an opinion.'

'Each to his own, I suppose,' I said flippantly.

'Well, we can't afford to be cavalier, I'm afraid. Things can get ... beyond our control. We have to be extremely diplomatic. Every change creates a reaction to some degree. Confidentially, take the tunnel projects. We've had fires. Burning effigies of the mayor down below. Wiring cut. Someone doesn't want the tunnels in Brisbane. Someone wants the tram back. How do these things happen, with security and twenty-four-hour work shifts? It's beyond me. Then again, so is dedicating one's life to a tram.'

'You suspect Beechnut?'

'He is on our list.'

'Then there's Father Dillon.'

'You were close?' the councilman asked. He was checking me out, testing my authenticity. I told him stories he'd probably never heard about Dill. I told him I had acci-dentally met him, after many lost years, in the confessional booth. I told him I had been on the brink of re-examining my faith when all this happened. Barrie Barry had tears in his eyes.

'Father Dillon was a good man,' he said. 'He was my parish priest for years. I was over at Gibbon Street one day when a tunnel worker who I knew from church took me aside and gave me the tin box. I didn't know what it was. I didn't know what to do.'

Then Barrie Barry started to cry. Not loudly. Just small, short, stabbing sobs into the hands he'd rested his face in. I patted him softly on the back.

He recovered himself.

'They'd found it in the early stages of digging the ventilation shaft. Surprisingly well preserved. The worker told me to keep it safe. That it contained something powerful enough to enable the tunnel naysayers to call a halt to the project, or at least delay it for a substantial period of time.'

'What was inside?'

He didn't hear me. He was off and away with his monologue — an unpunctuated, sincere confession, which he had to get out in one hit.

'I panicked,' continued Barrie Barry. 'I didn't know what to do. I brought it to Father Dillon. He hid it. He told me where he'd put it. But word was getting around. That something had been retrieved from the soil at Gibbon Street. Something big enough and *profound* enough to halt the tunnels. It would gain the attention of the entire country. Maybe the world. Then, when Father Dill was ... was murdered ... I went and got the box. I knew where he'd put it. I knew it was important. I knew what I had to do. I couldn't let it get into the wrong hands. It was a question of *faith* ... O God.'

He broke down again.

We were attracting some attention in the gardens

with all his sobbing. I had the distinct feeling we were being watched.

He calmed down again, and went on. 'I figured if I could secure it safely until the tunnels were finished, then we could reveal it to the world. It would be too late for them to use the box for their own selfish reasons. I have been threatened. I am afraid for my life. I am just a humble council engineer —'

I grabbed his shoulder before he could cry once more.

'Barrie. *Barry.* I need you to listen to me very carefully or I can't help you. *What* is in the box, and *where* is it?'

I heard the City Hall clock dong away in the near-distance. It was midday. Between the twelve dongs Barrie Barry told me about the miracle of Gibbon Street. He told me where he'd stashed the box. He told me if I met him at his office later that evening he would take me to it and show me the contents. He walked back alone to the skillet.

My mobile rang. It was Jack.

'Hello, son.'

'Hello, Dad.'

'What's new?'

'I need you to get on to Twitter, Dad.'

'Why is that, son?'

'Because your friend is driving me nuts with the cryptic quotes.'

'For whom the bell tolls? What's the latest?'

'"Nice spot on the grass with your little bald friend."'

'No, no, son. What's the latest twitch?'

'Tweet, Dad. And that was it.'

'What?'

'"Nice spot on the grass with your little bald friend." Then, "As the clock strikes midday, let the madness begin." Then, "Bye bye, Barrie Barry Barrey Barry Barrie Barrey." Dad? Dad? You there, Dad?'

9

THANK GOODNESS FOR Tex Gallon. Tex Gallon gave me comfort. Tex Gallon gave me shelter. Tex Gallon also knocked me out with his horse.

To know Tex Gallon was to love him. No, he was not some whisky-soaked country and western hack who played out his life in remote Australian RSL halls singing songs about other whisky-soaked hacks who cried into their bourbon in remote RSL halls pining the loss of a woman, a dog, a horse, a ute, whatever. No, Tex Gallon was the city hall reporter for *The Courier-Mail* and I'd met him a year ago at the funeral of my old friend Westchester Zim. And yes, Texaco Gallon was his real name. His father, a one-time oil rigger in the States, had named him after an oil can.

Tex lived in Brisbane, but he had a property on the Queensland–New South Wales border, and some time ago he'd invited me there for some R and R and a chinwag about journalism and police. Really, he just needed someone to give him a hand cutting back the noxious weeds on his little ponderosa. It was just me and Tex in the bush. For three days, and in something of an alcohol-related stupor, we told stories around an open fire, and played games with sharp hunting knives, and lassoed cattle (at least I think they were cattle, groggy as I was) and plaited his horse Bingo's mane. Surprisingly for a big man, Tex could fashion a very delicate plait. He rarely went anywhere without Bingo. Sometimes he stabled Bingo in his house in inner-city Brisbane. Tex wasn't married, and he didn't mind the smell of horse manure, the two necessary qualities a cowboy has to have if he's stabling a horse in his city pad.

On the afternoon Jack phoned me to say I was being spied on in the Roma Street Parkland by a person or persons unknown, I didn't know what to do. I rushed towards King George Square, noticed the statue of King George V astride his horse, and thought of Bingo. I went straight into City Hall and asked an attendant for the press room. As I walked down a long, dark corridor I could hear honky-tonk music. It had to be Tex. And sure enough, there he was squeezed inside the impossibly small closet of a room, leaning back in his chair, his briar and teal-coloured Buckaroo boots up on the desk.

'Hey, pardner!' he hollered. Sometimes, it has to be said, Tex slipped into stereotype. 'You look like you just found a rattlesnake in your rhododendrons. What's up?'

I spent the afternoon with Tex, who had nothing better to do. Council wasn't sitting.

I told him I was very concerned for the welfare of my friend Barrie Barry.

'Say that again?' he said.

'Barrie Barry.'

'You pulling my cowpoke?'

'No, I'm not.'

'Council engineer, you say?'

'Yes.'

'I'll make some calls. First, I want to show you something.'

Tex gave me a guided tour of City Hall. He pointed out the water-damaged walls. We went up to the former library and he gave me a lengthy dissertation on its cracked concrete beams. Then he took me downstairs, through a low doorway and down another set of wooden stairs into a small, gloomy room. He lifted a little hatch set into the floor.

'Take a look,' he said, pointing down.

'Is that water?' I said.

'Yes, siree,' he replied.

It was a metre or so deep. Black as ink. No wonder the place was going down. Thousands of tonnes of copper, glass and sandstone were sitting on a sponge.

'One last thing,' Tex said. He took me through a maze of corridors to a storage-room door. He swung the door wide open.

'Bingo!' I said.

There she stood — Tex's horse — polishing off a large bale of sweet hay. The room reeked of the digested product of the hay, which had dropped out of Bingo's rear end.

'She's going to be a star,' said Tex, patting her flank. 'She's in a friend's daughter's school Christmas pageant tonight in the main auditorium.'

'Don't you have donkeys in Christmas pageants?' I asked.

'You know how much it costs to hire a donkey in Brisbane these days?'

No, I didn't. But Tex did. He knew those sorts of things. Still, I was pleased Bingo was making her debut.

Later, back in the press room, I ran a few things by Tex.

'Ever heard of a lunatic called Alan Beechnut?' I asked.

'Scarborough Tram Society,' he said immediately. 'He sends me two dozen emails a week. One was fifteen thousand words long. A treatise on the Brisbane tram. Not long ago he sat outside the mayor's office eight hours a day, five days a week, for a fortnight, dressed as an old-fashioned tram conductor. A silent protest. I couldn't write about it. Too pathetic. Editor's sick of Beechnut too. He gets more emails than me. No tunnels! Ban the car! Bring back the trams! Editor didn't even run the picture of Beechnut *dressed up as a tram* in the city a few years ago. Police arrested him in the Mall. Didn't know where to cuff him, all tucked up inside that cardboard tram of his. Mayor's worried, too. He's had his car tyres slashed. Threatening letters. Then there's the sabotage in the tunnels. And the red lines.'

'What red lines?'

'Started about eight months ago. This nutball started painting red lines down the centre of a few roads in Paddington and Toowong. Then more appeared in other suburbs. People were waking up to find a bright red line down their street. This kept happening in the dark of night, see? Nobody knew what to make of it. They had a few vague sightings but that was it. But now they've worked out what the fruitcake is doing.'

'What is the fruitcake doing?'

'Painting the entire old Brisbane trams route map on the roads.'

'That's not just peculiar. That's insane.'

'Could be Beechnut. Who knows?'

'Smells like Beechnut,' I said, knowing a bit about that.

It was getting late. I'd successfully hidden myself from my enemy, had had no more details about tweeting from my son, and was due to meet Barrie Barry out the front of City Hall at eight that evening. So to kill some time I waited with Tex and Bingo backstage at the Christmas concert. It was heart-warming to see the little children dressed as Mary and Jesus and the Three Wise Men. Made me feel

Christmassy all of a sudden. Then the children poured onto the stage, and finally Tex and Bingo. Tex was dressed as Santa, and Bingo was wearing some antlers.

'Break a leg, Tex!' I said. Which is exactly what he did about a minute later. For while I was peering from backstage at the wondrous spectacle, I was suddenly enveloped in an invisible cloud of very expensive perfume, and before I could turn around, the cold steel of a handgun muzzle was pressed against the back of my neck.

'Ding-dong,' a sultry voice whispered.

And I said the first thing that popped into my mind was: 'Avon calling?'

'Ding-dong,' the voice repeated, 'you're dead.'

With astonishing agility, I sprang onto the stage from a standing start. The children howled and screamed with joy, thinking I was some demented surprise element to the show. I stepped to the right, then the left, trying to dodge a bullet that never came. I was bamboozled by the lights, the squealing of small children, a Wise Man I had sent flying in my panic. I slipped. And that's when my forehead connected with Bingo's bony knee. When I hit the knee, Bingo apparently reared up (I would only find this out later, as I was unconscious, again, before I hit the stage floorboards) and tossed Tex for six, fracturing his ankle. The pageant had become a horror show. I was out onstage. Tex was howling, grabbing his leg above his left Buckaroo boot. Bingo was limping casually amongst the traumatised Jesus, Mary, Joseph and Wise Men. And my killer was somewhere backstage probably having a good laugh.

When I woke up I was lying on the floor in the Red Cross room of City Hall, a bandage on my head. Sitting in a chair beside me was Barrie Barry.

'That was some performance,' he said.

'How's Tex?'

'You mean Santa? Santa's gone to hospital.'

'How's Bingo?'

'You mean the horse? She wandered out into King George Square, couldn't find any grass, and came back in. We've got her temporarily housed in the press room.'

I sat up with difficulty.

Barrie Barry checked his phone and smiled.

'What is it? I could do with a laugh,' I said.

'You're famous. They're tweeting you.'

'What? Who?'

'The kids in the audience. The staff here. They're tweeting all their friends. You'll be a viral smash hit by tomorrow.'

'I see,' I said. I didn't know what 'viral smash hit' meant, but it sounded nasty. And the 's', when I said 'see', came out strangely. I'd chipped a tooth. The 's' came out suspiciously like a little birdie's tweet. 'To be honest, Barrie, tomorrow can't come soon enough.'

It came soon enough for Barrie Barry. In just over a week I would face eternity, strapped inside the bell in the clock tower. But tomorrow, *tomorrow*, they would find my little bald council engineer friend naked, his body painted completely red, dead atop the unfinished Go Between Bridge. Go figure.

'First, I need to show you something,' Barrie Barry said, helping me to my feet.

And that's when I went back down into the bowels of City Hall, and found God. Oh, and the first stop on my short tram ride to hell.

10

LASHED INSIDE THE giant bell in Brisbane's City Hall clock tower, the timepiece about to be redecorated with my brains, I could smell that cigar smoke getting stronger and stronger.

Yes, I was about to meet my killer. The last person I would see as the old year folded into the new. The last person I would see, full stop.

As the Monte Christo grew more pungent, I thought of Peg and Jack wondering where I was (or not); the laundry tub back home full of party ice and cheap champagne, a few friends, the air a'twitter with fresh starts, with New Year resolutions.

I had a few. I vowed to trust our house cleaners, even if they did constantly lose my remote control and hoover my booze. I vowed not to get knocked unconscious and turn up naked in the back of the Kombi ever again. I vowed to steer clear of public-transport fanatics with shell-shaped ears. I vowed to investigate this Twitter thing now that my own teeth twittered and tweeted, and to send inoffensive messages to my Twitter friends such as, 'Just had a piece of lemon meringue. Numnumnum.' I vowed to be a better husband. And to be nicer to God.

Then my femme fatale was standing below the bell, looking up at me.

'Happy New Year,' she said, dragging casually on her cigar. The tip glowed a menacing red. Her greeting came out 'Appy Nu Yee-har.'

'Well, well, well, if it isn't Monte Christo,' I said. 'We have met before, haven't we, Mont?'

'We 'ave?' she said in her strange, Euro-trash accent. She was wearing a black cocktail dress, high heels and diamonds twinkled on her ears. 'Am not sure eef we 'ave. Your face, zough, eet rings a bell.'

'Now that's a knee-slapper. You'd get along very well with my wife. Hey, why don't you let me down so we can have a decent chinwag and sort this out.' I was losing circulation to my feet. Half an hour ago they'd been tingling. Now I couldn't feel them at all. Her elaborate rope work would have won her a badge in the Scouts.

I couldn't see her face properly from my elevated position. But she looked tiny. Embarrassingly so, having had my physical measure on each of our encounters, though I guess she wasn't responsible for my forehead connecting with Bingo's knotty knee.

'Don't theenk so,' she said. 'Not until I have ze box. No box, no deal.'

'What is this, a game show?'

'Is no game,' she said. 'Give me ze box.'

'Then you get me away from big clock donger?' I said, adopting her truncated Eastern European patter.

'Box first, zen maybe no donger for you.'

Could I have ever imagined being stuck in a life-threatening situation in a dark clock tower with a pocket-sized assassin saying 'Maybe no donger for you' when I first moved to Queensland to retire? I won't answer that.

'You know Beechnut?'

'What nut you talk of?'

'Alan Beechnut?'

'Allah who nut?'

'You decked me in his house.'

'Ohhhh,' she giggled. 'Smelly man. I just following you. I not know smelly man.'

'Why you want box?'

'No business of yours.'

'You kill me for box and it no business of mine? Ding-dong, you are joking. Tell me why you want box first.'

I was getting tired of speaking like a Romanian potato grubber. And I was getting tired of hanging around. Literally.

I had seen the holy box, of course. Oh yes. That poor shmuck Barrie Barry had taken me down into the deep, dark foundations of City Hall, a place he knew like the back of his hand, and removed it from an old brick cavity, where he'd stashed it. The box was pitted with rust. But its contents were remarkably well preserved – a small diary, a sheaf of letters, a set of wooden rosary beads and the porcelain statue of a small bluebird, all wrapped in a sheet of soft leather. I sat beside that moist, damp, dank subterranean foundation wall beneath Brisbane and read the diary entries and letters by torchlight. What I saw convinced me – oh he of little faith – that Mary MacKillop would become the first Australian saint. South Brisbane. 1870. Not far from Gibbon Street. A boy kicked in the head by a carthorse. And Mother Mary kneeling beside his still warm corpse. I won't go any further. You'll read about it in the future. But this was dynamite. This was of major theological and historical importance.

If the insane Beechnut had gotten his grubby mitts on the box, it might have halted the Clem7 tunnel and given his insane Millennium Tram Master Plan some more traction. But Father Dill and Barrie Barry were right. These relics could not be used for political purposes. Certainly not by some unhinged Scarborough missing link who only changed his Y-fronts once a week.

Why, then, was a slick, jet-setting Euro clubber and curvaceous assassin after a small, rusted tin box in Brisbane?

'You kill Dill?' I asked. It was time to get to the point.

'Who Dill?'

'The priest. My friend. Cut into tiny bits?'

'Oh yeah. That's what happen when you don't hand over box.'

'Why did you have to cut him up so ... so roughly? Without dignity or mercy?'

'I test myself. Keep sharp. Sometimes I use just what's at hand.'

'What was at hand?'

'Piece of sheet metal.'

Poor Dill, I thought.

'Please, *please* explain to me why you want this box so badly. I've seen the contents. I know what's in there. It was under the ground for almost 150 years. Why now?'

She puffed away on the cigar. It was getting shorter. So was my time to wriggle out of this pickle.

'Zere is group, around long time, who don't vant to see more saints. Naming of saints very political. Naming of saints offend lots of countries. Naming of saints upset governments and peoples. I paid to stop saints. I paid to destroy evidence. You get?'

I was agog. I no get. Whose sensibilities could the Blessed Mother offend? More than a century after her death? In Australia? At the bottom of the world?

I politely asked my assassin.

'So many saints. Too many for my bosses to pick and

choose, you understand? My bosses go after *all* saints. I hired. Is just job.'

'To get to the evidence first?'

'Now you understand.'

'And kill anyone who gets in your way.'

'Sure. Is nothing personal against this Meery. She good lady. Is only job for me. I like. I travel. Get paid lot of Euro. Is good. I do lot of southern-hemisphere saints. I working my way up. Top guys do China, important places. Very political, saints. You understand? Now where box?'

'Why don't you just ding-dong the Pope?'

'Zere vill be another Pope.'

'And there'll always be saints,' I said proudly.

She tapped a long nail on her wristwatch. 'Time run out. Nearly time for ding-dong. No box, I turn clock back on. Peoples in Breesbane waiting for New Year clock, yes? For ding-dong.'

'Why don't you just use bang-bang and get it over with?' I asked.

And at that precise moment I could have sworn that I heard a horse whinny echo up the clock tower. And I could have sworn I heard a deep, guttural, Texan-style *yahoo* that would have scared the britches off Tonto. And I could have sworn I heard the lift in the tower shaft stop and the old concertina cage doors open.

Seems Vampira the saint killer had heard it all too, because she let off a single shot from a tiny handgun. The muzzle flashed. The bullet ricocheted. I closed my eyes, waiting for a hit. I heard a bell sound a delicate *ting*, like someone tapping a champagne flute with a knife handle. Then, before I'd opened my eyes again, I heard an almighty crack, then a thud. I opened my eyes, and there below me was my lady killer, sprawled out and unconscious. Beside her was a chunk of sandstone the size of a large bread bap. It had cracked off part of the tower above her head. This beautiful, crumbling, deteriorating iconic landmark of the city of Brisbane had saved my life.

Tex Gallon appeared, unsteady on his feet with the plaster encasing his broken ankle. 'Holy cactus, pardner! What you doin' up there?'

I had to wait ten minutes for the blood to finally re-enter my feet. Then I had a New Year drink with Texaco Gallon and Bingo in the crowded press room while the cops took my little European killer friend away. (Tex would be arrested for DUI while riding Bingo home to Red Hill, I would discover the next day.)

I hopped into the Kombi, drove over several fresh lines of red paint around Edward Street. I was caught in some drag-racing-induced traffic jam at Yatala. I didn't arrive on the Gold Coast until dawn. As the sun came up over the Pacific, and threw a veil of blush over the coast, I felt cleansed. Almost forgiven of my sins. It gave me added comfort to think of the precious little tin box I had stashed under the Kombi seat, and all the good it would bring to the world when I finally placed it in the right hands.

Peg was asleep. I hauled my sore and sorry self out to the back patio and eased into my faithful old banana lounge. I opened a warm beer I'd retrieved from the laundry tub full of melted ice water, and popped a small party hat on my head.

'Happy New Year,' I said to myself.

I fell asleep and, as Peg was to tell me later, my cracked tooth happily tweeted and twittered like a nightingale.

FIVE

THE GOOD MURDER GUIDE

1

IN ALL MY long years as a homicide detective, there were few sadder murder scenes than the homes of middle-aged bachelors.

I'm not trying to be cute. I saw it all. Anything to do with children was tragic, your greatest nightmare – and believe me some of those cases still stalk the dark corners of my substantial skull.

And there was the usual gamut of horror – the revenge slaughterhouses, the messy suicides, the blood-drenched domestics, the gob-smacking intestine-draped altars of psychotic religious messengers. I studied death by gun, knife, vehicle, drug, fire, poison, wrench, paper spike, sword and, once, an expensive Mont Blanc rollerball pen.

When it comes to murder, I've been everywhere, man.

Perhaps it's an ageing guy thing with the bachelors. The pitiful bachelors. Not tragic. Just sad. The older I became, the more I understood, and the more they got to me. Theirs – before death set them free, of course – were the parallel futures of all men. One misstep, a card not played right, and woeful bachelor country awaited all of us.

Some of these men were – to use a polite, old-fashioned newspaper euphemism – *confirmed* bachelors. Not, as they say, that there's anything wrong with that. I found, in my ceaseless snooping about the dwellings of the dead, that *confirmed* bachelors by and large kept a well-ordered house, and were beyond reproach when it came to tidiness, cleanliness, and their taste in, for example, obscure thirties West Midlands pottery.

No, the men I am recalling now, from the comfort of retirement and my sagging banana lounge on the Gold Coast, are those men who have savoured all the glories of family life, and for one reason or another have been cut adrift and cast onto the craggy, lonely shoals of late bachelorhood. The scant wardrobes with their profusion of ill-shaped wire hangers. The negligible toiletries in the bathroom. The bare refrigerators, uncleaned and stained with the sepia leakage of food long gone. The one, worn armchair in front of the television set.

I speak with authority. And while you may question this after several of my recent, and sadly well-publicised, adventures since putting up my feet on life's pouffe here on the Glitter Strip, I can offer proof. Proof, you might say, from the pouffe.

It is a little known fact that my dear wife Peg and I once separated for exactly twenty-seven days in the early years of our marriage. It was before Jack, and even he, bless him, remains unaware of this little moth-nibbled hole in his parents' marital fabric.

But I am going to tell you all about it now because, having recently stood in the blood-spattered Surfers Paradise unit of a Mr Hubert Dunkle Junior, 53, it's important to give you context.

What does this regrettable, but minor moment, in the domestic life of a tired, knee-weak, big-bellied former Sydney copper have to do with the late Hubert Dunkle Junior? All will be revealed.

Good detectives have their mentors. As a young man hoeing the mean streets of Surry Hills, Darlinghurst and Kings Cross in Sydney, mine was a man we affectionately referred to as Old Bug Eyes, or Obe for short.

Obe was a great detective. His passion for detail unrivalled. We never worked out whether his monstrous black-rimmed spectacles and his almost daily orbital deterioration were the by-product of this innate passion for minutiae, or the source of it. He had huge eyes, did Obe, which the spectacles magnified to an even more frightening level. We're talking grasshopper in a magnifying glass here.

Obe also had a large head, perhaps the largest head in the entire New South Wales police force, which was saying something back in the sixties. A quick glance at police academy photographs from that era might lead you to assume that head size was a requirement of induction. Big heads were very popular in the constabulary in the sixties, just like the Besser blocks they resembled.

Obe's frame was slight. From a distance he looked like a pencil with a plum stuck on the top, if that plum had eyes, and if that plum's eyes were swollen. His strength was deceptive. I once saw him deck, with a single punch, a Macleay Street nightclub bouncer called Girder. Girder was built not like your proverbial brick lavatory, but like a string of them, a cluster of them, enough of them to comfortably service the annual Christmas party of heavy-drinking allied nightclub bouncers with metal, brick or wood-related nicknames. And their families.

There was a lot of lead in Obe's pencil.

Despite these juxtapositions, Obe had his acolytes, of which I was one. He prided himself on using his brain – accommodated amply in that box head – over brawn. Which put him in stark contrast with another more glamorous section of the force, led by the legendary hard-man detective Ray Kelly and, to a lesser extent, Freddy Krahe. Kelly was a superstar in the fifties and sixties — a smart, hardworking, fancy-suit-wearing killer cop who spoke with his gun. Kelly's gun had a very loud mouth. Krahe's wasn't a shrinking violet either.

Obe was the antithesis of these hard men. But his brain could fell a criminal as effectively as a bullet.

As a greenhorn, I fancied I could take a bit of Kelly and a bit of Obe, and fashion myself as some new type of detective. The smart–tough guy. I figured this would make me very popular with all cliques in the force. I would be admired by men and women alike. I could solve complicated murders with the powers of my perception by lunch, clock a notorious gunman with the butt of my revolver before knock-off, and be whispered about in the city's finest clubs and restaurants in the evening. I would join that elite class of officer who had a university degree under his belt, what with my passion for psychology. All in a day's work.

The trouble with all this image-fashioning was that it took time. I was, in reality, running around whacking bad guys in the greasy laneways of the inner-city, racing to the lab and peering into microscopes, brushing up on forensic techniques, taking statements from drug-addled rats and ladies of the night, typing reports with swollen fingers (see 'whacking bad guys'), checking toe tags and watching my back. I thought I was on the make, and to be made in the New South Wales police required considerable effort.

I was, too, newly married to my beloved Peg.

She quietly accepted a raincheck on our honeymoon. And she tolerated the long, lonely nights without me, half-sleeping with an ear out for the sound of the front-door latch.

But it was the suicide of Obe, in a toilet cubicle at the station, which sent her out of my life for twenty-seven interminable days, changed our marriage and halted my stellar trajectory in the police force.

She was fond of Obe, you see. She admired his big square brain. But she also knew that it was he, of the massive spectacles and magnified eyes, with his work ethic and passion for the truth, who kept her husband away from his wife.

When I heard the gunshot in the cubicle at police headquarters that day, and literally ran into my sidekick Greave, ordering him to secure the entire washroom, then kicked open the unlocked door of the receptacle and found Obe's body, still warm, still issuing blood, curled awkwardly around the bowl, it was, Peg told me much later, as though I had crashed in on a version of a future, broken self.

She took it bad, did Peg. We both did. Overnight, she finally understood what she may have married into.

She went to the Blue Mountains to stay with her mother. I remained in our little house. I was given a week's leave. And in that week I hurt the brain in my big fat head trawling through the past few weeks, then months, looking for any signs from Obe that he was about to end his own life. I ran a fine toothcomb across everything I could remember, looking for that singular piece of evidence, for that dog hair of truth, that would help explain Obe's death. In that house, sitting in the dark, I was also revising my own life.

Obe's family had a private funeral. No grand police exit. No thin blue line, epaulettes and trumpets. I was invited. I went alone, in civilian clothes.

We buried Obe that day in the cemetery by the sea.

I had been to many funerals – as guest, anonymous mourner, policeman, undercover agent – and after a while they all began to resemble one another.

But at Obe's, around the grave by the sea, I never forgot the sight of his twelve-year-old son, standing there in his crisp white short-sleeved shirt and narrow tie, his baggy grey school shorts, and his long socks and school shoes. His head was large and square like his daddy's, his face white, his eyes two unblinking black currants. He stood to attention, his hands by his sides, his fists clenched.

I can see that face now. It carried a look not of great grief, or of bottomless sorrow, but a sort of shock at events that his young mind, no matter how large, had yet to catch up with. This moment would hit him, later, with colossal force. But at that instance beside the grave and the lowered coffin of his father, he was merely a piece of blotting paper, absorbing the ink of tragedy. Only down the track would he see a pattern, and recognise it as they greatest loss of his life.

A steady breeze coming up over the slabs and headstones from the ocean played with a small twig of hair at the back of that big head, and it was this, the playfulness of the hair, wriggling about, that told you he was just a boy.

I never forgot him.

And I never forgot his father, Obe, or, as his gravestone correctly attested – Hubert Dunkle Senior.

At my age, nothing surprises me any more.

So when, all these decades later, the phone rang and a detective mate told me about the presumed murder of Obe's little boy, now a lonely middle-aged bachelor living in a Gold Coast unit with too many wire hangers, a stained refrigerator, a worn armchair and blood thrown across the cream walls, I barely raised an eyebrow.

'You sitting down?' my mate told me, calling on his mobile from the scene.

'Is that a joke?' I said, wriggling in my sagging banana lounge, *still* sore from my embarrassing encounter with an Eastern European assassin in the old Brisbane City Hall building a full year before. 'What you got?'

'How well did you know Obe's son, Junior?'

'The last time I saw Junior was when a new sheet of Seven Seas Stamps got me all excited. Come on. What you got?'

'You're not going to believe this.'

'Flummox me.'

'We found, in the unit, an old New South Wales police diary from 1972. It's got your name all over it.'

'Waddya mean, it's got my name all over it?'

'I mean it's got your name all over it. It's *your* diary.'

'*What?*'

'Junior's highlighted one entry. 21 July. "Obe dead. Single gunshot wound to head. 6.47 pm. Second cubicle. Basement. Not possible." You know what that's about?'

'Yeah.'

'See you in twenty minutes?'

'Yeah.'

I didn't move for what seemed like an eternity after that call. For the first time in thirty-eight years, the copper smell of Obe's blood in that tiny stall came back and hit me in the back of the throat.

I just stared towards the water of the canal out back, unblinking, like a boy at a funeral.

2

Funny thing, memory.

I recall reading somewhere that everything we ever see and hear is retained by the brain. That it's filed away like old library cards or film negatives, or these gigabyte things they have today, and sits in the dark waiting for us to remember it and draw it back out into the light.

I don't believe this. Sounds a bit too fancy-pants to me.

But I'll never forget my dear old father's last words, on his deathbed. He faced the end with great courage. A moment before he died, he called me closer and whispered: 'Less sugar next time, Dad. Remember the war.'

I knew exactly what this meant. He was living at home in Surry Hills with his parents at the start of the Second World War. Everyone was edgy. Windows were blacked out. Australia waited to be attacked.

Then, in the early hours of a crisp spring morning, the street came under fire. Was it a machine gun? A fighter plane? Shells lobbed in from the harbour off an enemy warship?

No, it was Grandpa's stash of home-brewed beer going off in the back shed. It was the day the blitz came to a narrow street in the inner-city, albeit under a fusillade of sugar, yeast and tin caps.

That's what my father remembered with clarity, the moment before he left this world.

Why did he retrieve that particular card from his life file? And how, sitting in the car outside the Surfers Paradise apartment building of the late Hubert Dunkle Junior, did I know that I had seen this place before? Not in situ. And not the exact building that now occupied the address – a gleaming twenty-one-storey superstructure, hardly five years old. But the street, and the gnarled old pandanus trees up and down the footpath, and the saggy fibro beach shack to the left of the modern apartment building, its walls moulded, the points of its spiky, rusted television aerial decorated by some drunken wags with empty beer stubbies?

Where have I seen you? I asked myself in the car. How do I know you?

My detective mate was waiting in the posh foyer, beside a little trickling fountain.

He flicked his head for me to follow, and once we were in the lift he pressed the button for the nineteenth floor.

The lift carriage was mirrored on three sides. Big, fat, red, scarred coppers' mugs stretching back to the dawn of time. We were not one of the world's more attractive professions.

'You retired how long ago?' he asked me.

'About four years,' I said.

'From Sydney, right?'

'Yeah.'

'Thought you'd come up here, catch a bit of sun?'

'You got it.'

'Throw in a lazy line?'

'Spot on.'

'And that was you last year, right? Nearly got your head blown off at City Hall?'

'I'm the man.'

'And the year before? Got thrown out of a high-rise office building in Brisbane?'

'That's me.'

'Now you're linked to a murder scene by a forty-year-old diary?'

'Apparently so.'

'You got a funny way of retiring.'

'Side-splitting, innit?' I said.

The elevator door opened. 'Second on your left,' the detective said.

I was fumbling for my sunglasses on that short walk to Hubert Dunkle Junior's apartment. What was it with these new Gold Coast buildings? It was as sunny inside them as out, all glass and blinding white surfaces and brushed metal.

One of the nineteenth-floor residents, a painfully thin old lady in crisp leopard-spotted knickerbockers, a head scarf and sunglasses the size of saucers you might fill with milk for your kitty-cat, scurried past towards the lifts, busy as an over-tanned hen, all cluck and clack on the tiled floor. In the glare she had almost completely dissolved, a blur of wrinkled alligator skin and gold. She left trailing behind her the faint aroma of burned hair.

I stepped into Junior's abode and the moment I crossed the threshold I got that old, tingling feeling that detectives never lose. The thrill. The exhilaration of a fresh crime; struggling against the pity of it all. The rush of seeing, and then *really* seeing. The perversely enjoyable effort of decoding the perverse human brain. Stepping through the immediate dimension. The ordinary suddenly extraordinary. The commonplace a priceless treasure. You gotta be there.

I didn't even notice the uniform copper standing guard just inside the door.

'Who you?' he grunted.

'Who me?' I said, brushing past him. 'Screw you.' I could be terribly adolescent at times.

'Oi,' he said, in the way that so many males on the Gold Coast aged between ten and forty said 'Oi.'

I ignored him.

I stood at the entrance to the lounge room and took in the scene. My mate quietly joined me.

'Waddya reckon?' he said, hands on hips.

I lamented the days of old Obe, and the power of silence in detective work. Nothing today seemed to happen without ceaseless noise, chatter, music, aimless discussion, moronic pleasantries and twaddle. I despised twaddle. I was twaddle's number one public enemy.

I sighed like a set of old leather bellows. No one could go for a walk these days without listening to something on headphones. Or talking on the phone. Or texting. Or tweeting. Good lord, don't talk to me about tweeting after last year's fiasco. It wasn't that nobody stopped to think any more. People's lives were so full of static, and movement and distraction, they had no *time* to think. And thinking is like exercise. Do it, or lose it.

'Could you, as my Great-Aunt Petunia used to say, close your cakehole for a moment?' I asked my detective friend.

'Oi,' the copper by the door snorted.

He was a regular porcine doorbell.

'And could you get Porky over there to vacate the sty for a few minutes?' I asked.

My haughtiness was out of line. I was long retired, had no official role in the investigation and hadn't even been invited as a casual observer. My opinions meant nothing.

But this was Obe's boy, Junior. And it was my old police

diary sitting slap-bang in the middle of his blood-spattered bachelor pad.

Splattered was an understatement. Someone had decided to completely redecorate Junior's walls. There were great tendrils of crimson spray criss-crossing both lounge-room walls, blood spots across the ceiling, the plasma television, the spectacularly bad oil painting of pelicans at feeding time. There were pools of the stuff on the carpet, continents of it on the pastel cloth-covered couches and a great wheel of it across the open granite kitchen bench. Some flecks had even made it to the fridge at the back of the kitchen, and onto Junior's handwritten shopping list magnetised to the door. A perfect pinpoint of blood had alighted between 'cabbage' and 'bread'.

I stood there for a long time, and another feeling passed through my weary frame. Something wasn't right. There was blood here, but I couldn't *feel* death. I don't know how to explain it. You can add up the facts, Obe used to say, but they don't always equal the truth.

I went into the kitchen and opened the fridge.

I heard a distant 'Oi' again from beyond the front door.

I poked my head into Junior's impossibly neat bedroom, stepped in, looked through his closets. The whole place felt unlived in. I joined the other detectives in Junior's study. It had a pleasant view of the beach. I scanned the bookshelves.

Finally, I stood in front of his desk and stared down at my open police diary from the wonderful and tragic year of 1972. It was mine all right, and had aged as I had. It was weathered, discoloured and creaky at the spine.

21 July, 6.47 pm.

I looked up suddenly and the glare hurt my eyes. That's when I remembered when I'd been here before.

3

IT WAS AFTER nine in the evening when the coppers pulled
up stumps at poor Junior's bachelor pad. My detective mate
called me immediately and I dropped back to the scene for
some quiet contemplation.

'Keep your grubby mitts off everything,' he told me as
he left, 'or it's my job. And lock up on your way out.'

'You're a good man,' I said to him. 'I'll have you stuffed
and mounted for this.'

'Whatever,' he said.

It was a different apartment at night. All soft and moody.
The lights of the Surfers metropolis twinkled through the
glass. Glass everywhere you looked. It was a monument to
transparency. It *was* the Gold Coast. So much glass, for a
place with so many secrets.

Of course, I had come back to the flat for the police
diary. Naturally I planned to take it. I had to. It was mine,
and it had something to do with Junior's death.

Or did it?

Against all protocol, I had kept a few of my diaries from
my years as a detective in Sydney, and secreted them into
retirement. Who would miss them?

If caught with this worthless police property, I would

claim they were important to me for a potential future auto-biography. I can hear my imaginary interrogator groan at the thought – what, another cop-on-the-inside-big-belly-under-the-belly book about the bloody seventies, full of flares and bad hair and officers that all looked and sounded like Bill Hunter?

But there was another very good reason the diaries were under my wing, and it was all because of Obe. One of the first things he taught me was how to write a police diary.

'I know how to write,' I said, upstart of a young thing that I was.

'Not like this,' Obe said.

Every diary, he told me, had to contain brief daily summaries of police duties, no matter how mundane, right? But in every police force there is a parallel narrative going on. The things you see but don't see. The conversations you hear but can't repeat. The friendships you notice, the connections you see forming, even the very language police use with each other. A threat can be an invitation. A kindly phrase a threat. An innocuous query a test.

So Obe taught me, with an ingenious code of his own devising, how to embed a truthful observation of police life beneath the record of phone calls made and paperwork completed and interviews typed. For a period before and after Obe's death, my diaries were halls of mirrors.

At the time, they could have meant the difference between life and death. Mine, that is. Decades later, I took them. Better safe than sorry.

And there was a name in one of those diaries, too, that had come back to me just a few hours earlier. The name of a young woman who had lived at the precise address as Hubert Dunkle Junior, albeit forty years earlier.

She was Susan Haag, and she had once resided in an

orange-brick block of flats called the Ace Royale apartments, which had stood where Junior's swish high-rise now
towered. At police headquarters in Sydney around 1971 I
had seen photographs of the street, and the flats, and inside
Susan's specific flat, and then inside Susan's bedroom. And I
had seen photographs of Susan's naked body on her bed, and
a bottle of Scotch and empty pill bottles on her bedside table.

Susan Haag's death was, you see, a very big deal for a
time in Sydney. Various combinations of detectives flew
back and forth from the Gold Coast, investigating her
suicide. Dozens of witnesses were questioned. An inquest
was held. She was deemed to have taken her own life.

But that's not how I remembered it. And it's not what
I wrote, in code, in my 1972 diary.

Funny thing, memory, I thought as I sat back in
Junior's accommodating desk chair, and contemplated
the coincidence.

A young woman, supposedly a prostitute, had died at this
address almost forty years ago. I had made a few notes about
it from what I'd heard and seen in Sydney. Now, as an
older man and standing at the border of that strange country
where you wear giant diapers and eat runny food and sit all
day in your pyjamas amongst strangers trying to remember
what the devil your name is, I was back in the same spot,
trying to work out who would kill my mentor's son.

Did Susan Haag have anything to do with Junior? He
would have been eleven years old when she popped those
pills in her mouth and chug-a-lugged half a bottle of Scotch
on her way to eternity.

What if nothing had anything to do with anything, and
I already had half a foot in the Land of Ga Ga?

'Talk to me, Obe,' I said into the dark study, and the
chair beneath me issued a long, mournful creak.

'I'm going to call the police,' a dry voice said.

'Obe? Is that a joke?' I asked of nobody.

'No, it's not a joke. I'm going to call the *police*.'

I swivelled around in the chair, and there was the human alligator handbag, the neighbour, Madame Mutton, who I'd seen in the corridor earlier in the day.

'Pipe down,' I said. 'I *am* the police.'

'You don't look like the police.'

'And you don't look like Sophia Loren.'

'Are you always this rude?'

'Always. Even when I'm asleep.'

'You might want to get up off your backside then and find that lovely boy.'

'Junior?'

'He was a good boy.'

Junior had been fifty-three, so for this super-tanned Dolly Varden to call him a 'boy' just showed you how old *she* was.

'How long you know him?' I asked.

'He'd only been here six weeks. Real neighbourly, he was. Not like the rest of them in here. All fillum people in here. In and out. Naked parties in the spa. The drugs and all.'

'Did you say fillum?'

'Fillum. The cinema. I can't keep track. But Mr Dunkle was a real gentleman.'

I caught her looking over my shoulder at a photograph in a frame on the desk. It was a shot of Senior and Junior, in happier days. Days when both of them were alive.

Obe was dressed in his uniform. And little Junior was attired in his own specially made policeman's outfit. It must have been taken just months before Obe died. Junior had that little twig of hair in the picture, too.

In the picture Obe's eyes were, of course, huge behind the spectacles. They were kind eyes. Sharp as razors, but kind. There was love there too, with little Junior by his side. These were not the eyes of a man about to blow his brains out.

But I didn't share any of that with Dolly.

'He have any visitors lately?'

'He kept to himself from what I could see.'

'No lady friends? Gents?'

'He cooked me dinner twice. Lovely it was. Made the pasta himself. Not many young men these days who bother to make their own pasta.'

'Or make their own beds,' I said, nodding.

I got up to leave. The swivel chair seemed to issue a groan of relief as I rose to my feet. I slipped the diary into the large pockets of my cargo pants. Little Dolly seemed to have fallen into a quiet reverie. She had made in Junior a new friend here in the gulag of her apartment building, and he had just as quickly been snatched from her. Poor Dolly.

'Time to lock up,' I said, turning her brittle shoulders around, nudging her to the door. She still smelled of burned hair. Something glittered between the furrows of her old neck.

She stood and waited in the hallway while I locked up.

'You take care, then,' I said.

'Would you like to have dinner with me?' she asked quietly, her voice a fragile breath of breeze in the lonely corridor. I had forgotten about all the bachelorettes out there in the world.

'Maybe some other time,' I said.

I thought of sad Dolly for about three seconds as the lift descended. I had greater riddles to solve in this crazy universe of ours.

I had to get to my storage cage in Nerang out the back of the Coast to see if anyone had helped themselves to my once-secret, now very public, police diary archive, down amongst the silverfishes.

4

THIS IS HOW well my wife Peg knows me, how familiar she is with my louche habits, general all-round grubbiness, forgetfulness and, quite clearly, my dreary predictability. I was an ever-expanding continent that she had traced and mapped many, many times, and there was no nook and cranny of me she hadn't, sometimes disgustingly, come across.

I sat in the car outside the Ali Baba Self Storage facilities in an industrial estate in Nerang and phoned her on my mobile.

She answered after one ring.

'Just promise me you won't get shot, bound, gagged, thrown from a window or tossed from a boat tonight.'

'I could be ringing to see if you need milk and bread.'

'You have never phoned to ask if I need milk or bread.'

'I could be in hospital having suffered a heart attack.'

'You have not suffered a heart attack and you are nowhere near a hospital. You are investigating a murder, someone called Carbunkle. I saw you on the news.'

'It's Dunkle. Junior. You saw me on the news?'

'I saw your belly on the news.'

'My belly?'

'They showed some police standing outside an apartment building and your belly was poking into the frame.'

'You recognised me by my belly?'

'Just keep out of trouble.'

Good woman, Peg. The belly was a worry, though. I had spent much of my early career immersed in the under-belly of life. Now I was all belly and no under.

I gathered my thoughts in that dark street. I could see the faint outline of Ali Baba's cheesy grin on the unilluminated sign outside the storage facility. He too had a spherical belly. I didn't understand why a storage facility, meant to keep your chattels safe in this dangerous world, would name itself after a legendary thief. Never mind. Nothing made much sense to me in the twenty-first century.

I took the old diary from my pocket. I could feel its dry cover and spine in my dry old hands.

Someone, be it Junior or his assassin, had shown tremen-dous interest in this prehistoric volume. It mentioned Obe's death, but just in passing. Nothing dramatic.

What was it that had driven someone to break into cage 143 at Ali Baba's, rifle through some battered book cartons, remove the volume, study it, and place it at the scene of a murder?

It took me back, the diary – just holding it in the cabin of the car late at night. It returned me to my fake walnut desk at Sydney police headquarters, a magic carpet I thought would deliver me all the way to the rank of commissioner. Then Obe died, and everything changed.

I continued to turn up at that tatty desk. But from that day onward, I felt untethered, vulnerable.

I never shared my theory about Obe's death with anybody. I was young. Wet behind the ears. I still didn't know who to trust – besides Obe – in the great labyrinthine machine that is any police force. While I was watching all of them, they were watching me. Was this young detective one of us? Would he have our back? Would he keep his mouth shut when he had to? Avert his eyes when necessary?

On some nights Obe and I used to catch a quick meal in a noodle house down in Chinatown. It was there, over green tea and duck pancakes, that he took me under his wing and gave me a few survival tips.

'Forget about eyes in the back of your head, kid,' he'd say, tucking a shallot back into his folded pancake. 'Grow some on the sides as well.'

He was a family man. He was well respected. He had collared a murderer by successfully proving that the seeds found on the accused's trousers came from only one plant, at a certain time of year, which just happened to be minding its business and growing heartily not far from the body of the victim.

That prosecution had earned him kudos, and a reputation for being what kids today might call a nerd. And nerds were dangerous in a police force. They usually had smarts. And smarts were unpredictable.

Obe knew where the bodies were buried. Knew who was crooked and who was straight. Who was connected to whom. He understood the lingo. The little tests of character other officers threw at me, the newbie. He had the radar of a bat. Nothing, and I mean nothing, avoided his attention.

So I was schooled up when he allegedly killed himself. And I had a theory, too. Hubert Dunkle Senior would never take his own life. Hubert Dunkle Senior was murdered, in a police lavatory, in the heart of a major police complex, in a place reserved for the most private human business of police officers. Hubert Dunkle Senior was slain by another police officer.

I knew who the killer was, too. I was a damn detective, wasn't I? It took me years of close listening, and a few lucky breaks when a piece of the puzzle here and another there fell into my lap. But in the end I knew who killed Obe and why. And just knowing that gave my daily life as a New South Wales police officer a certain degree of tension.

A lot, actually. A hell of a lot.

So I did what Obe trained me to do. I watched my back. I did everything by the book. I never breathed a word to anyone and I never took a misstep. If I did, I knew I'd join Obe on the dishonourable list of depressed officers who couldn't cut it, who couldn't make it, who took the coward's way out.

I progressed through the ranks. I never had definitive proof of who murdered Obe. You rarely get that *inside* the police machine. For all its energies, its sole focus is towards the big, bad world *outside*. But sometimes your gut tells you something and you know it's right. Good gut instinct maketh a good copper.

I kept an eye on my suspect throughout my career. I watched him rise, saw the pictures of him with the commissioner, and him as deputy. He was the model officer.

I went to his retirement party. Stood at the back of the room at Dick's Hotel in Balmain and watched them shower him with praise. I slipped out before I had to shake his hand.

When he too died, an old man on a sweet pension, I wished him luck in hell.

And now I went to the locked entrance of the storage facility and let myself in. I took the huge lift to the first floor.

I found cage 143 and checked the padlock and bolt with my pocket torch. It was pristine. Unscathed.

Removing the padlock, I entered the cage.

I hadn't been here in a year. I didn't like storage cages. They were the unkempt corner of the cage renter's mind; that little part of ourselves we try hard to ignore. It was dusty in there. A sheet was still draped over a rusting fan on a stand. Old garden tools were stacked in the corner. The book boxes were at the far end.

I stood and looked at the boxes. If my police diary for 1972 was missing from the small number I'd souvenired and stacked in one of those boxes, then someone had been in here and lifted it. If the diary was still there, then the one in my pocket was a fake. It certainly didn't look like a fake.

But who in their right mind would counterfeit such a thing? And for what purpose?

I rubbed my hands together. 'Okay, 1972,' I said to myself. 'Here we come.'

Then someone said 'Oi' behind me, and it echoed through Ali Baba's, and as I turned the cold metal scoop of a shovel caught me flush in the face.

5

When I came to in the police holding cell, having been walloped with a garden spade and had my nose substantially rearranged, I had a hazy vision of a John Travolta-like figure circa *Saturday Night Fever* standing beyond the bars.

The apparition was tall, wearing flared trousers, and a nylon and largely unbuttoned duckbill-collared shirt revealing enough chest hair to make winter blankets for an entire village in Uzbekistan.

'Stayin' alive, stayin' alive,' I said to the ghost.

I had a large white bandaged affixed to the centre of my face. I thought I could feel my nose hairs tickling my left ear.

'You got bail,' Travolta said, 'but the boys in blue want a little word before you go.'

'It must be the night fever,' I garbled.

'Coffee? We need to talk first.'

'How deep is your love? Got any aspirin, by the way?'

My discotheque angel was no vision. He was Johnny K. Tapas, the Gold Coast's pre-eminent celebrity lawyer. If you were suing plastic surgeons, seeking damages after scoffing a dodgy oyster in a glamorous Broadbeach restaurant, or defending yourself in a murder case that involved, for example, a yacht full of cocaine, a diamond-encrusted handgun, a transsexual cabaret performer called Lady Bump and a small and impossibly spoiled pet Shih Tzu named Moopie, then Johnny K. Tapas was your man.

'Big night under the mirror ball?' I asked him after I'd drained a mug of instant.

'I suggest you avoid mirrors for a while,' Tapas said.

'What's the charge? Breaking and entering my own storage facility?'

'Impeding a murder investigation. Tampering with a crime scene.'

'Bit low rent for you, Tapas. What's in it for you?'

'A former client has requested I take very good care of you.'

'That so?' I said. 'Why would Ivan the Terrible, Russian computer fraudster and playboy, or Donger, dubiously moustachioed captain of the Bandoleros motorcycle gang, give a fig about me?'

'Wrong clients.'

'Cut the twaddle, Tapas. Who is it?'

'Confidential. Condition of my services.'

'That so?'

'That's so.'

'You're a terrible tease, Tapas.'

Later, in the interview room, with the fragrant Tapas by my side, the coppers apologised for turning me into a Picasso portrait with the spade to the face.

They explained that they knew I'd been in Junior's apartment the night before and had followed me to the Ali Baba storage facility on suspicion of having removed an exhibit from the scene. I was then observed transporting the exhibit to a storage cage in the aforementioned facility, and the officer had attempted to prevent me secreting the aforementioned evidence. They said the aforementioned officer, noting my antecedents as a former police officer and, in more recent times, my involvement in well-publicised incidents that involved various levels of violence, took the necessary measures to ensure the aforementioned evidence was not secreted and that I was delivered into custody.

'Why don't you take your aforementioned allegations and shove them up your oft-mentioned aft region,' I said.

'My client is still suffering from his injuries and I request that comment not be used against him in any future proceedings,' Tapas interjected.

They said I would be released on bail and that a court order to be lodged later in the morning would prevent me from coming within a 100-metre radius of the murder scene and communicating with any officers involved in the aforementioned murder investigation.

'Oi,' I said. 'Whatever.'

Tapas merely checked his manicured fingernails. 'Wait outside,' he said to me.

Later, in his air-conditioned, imported black Maybach, the cabin gaggingly rich with Tapas's sticky, icky, sweet aftershave, he asked me why I had such an intense interest in the death of Hubert Dunkle Junior.

'Long story, Tapas. It would require an attention span to digest it.' I was staring at the little mirror ball dangling from his rear-vision mirror.

'Try me.' We had stopped at a set of red lights.

'I can hear your meter running, Tapas, and I'm not buying. It's history.'

'Then you won't need this,' he said. He reached into the back seat and retrieved a large brown envelope. He dropped it in my lap.

It was a full photocopy of my 1972 diary. From when I'd

gone nigh-nigh courtesy of a garden spade to slipping into
the whoofy Maybach, someone had copied the old diary,
bundled it up and slipped it into the hands of the coast's
most fashion-challenged legal mind.

'You cheeky dog, Tapas, how did you get it?'

'Johnny K. Tapas got history, too, my friend,' he said.
'Old friends. Old favours.'

Old Spice more like it, I wanted to say.

'I owe you,' I said, holding the diary copy.

'Maybe,' he said.

At home, Peg ignored me. Which was good, because it
gave me a chance to properly examine my old handiwork.

I had arrived at the supposition that the discovery of
my diary at the murder scene was no accident. It had been
planted there to lure me. But why had I been reeled in?
And by whom?

I repaired to my study, sadly neglected since my Russian-
assassin fiasco last year, and flicked on my trusty and reliable
super-bright desk lamp. I made myself comfy, brought out
my jumbo-sized magnifying glass, and started on page 1,
1 January 1972.

I had an almost out-of-body experience going through
those old entries. It was a flickering slideshow of my past,
and long forgotten scenes and people's faces and snatches
of conversation whirled about me in that quiet room
that afternoon.

Trust me, I am not a melancholy man. But it's a strange
thing, to meet your younger self once again. He is the
stranger that lives within you, and if you don't like him,
there's very little you can do about it.

I remained open-minded about the young stranger
of me.

Around the month of March in the diary, I noticed

something peculiar. Between two sentences in an innocuous entry – something about a break and enter – was the world's smallest number. It was tiny. The footprint of an ant. Written in pencil. But it was definitely a number. The number seven.

A week later in the diary I found another, a three. By the time I got to 21 July – the date of Obe's death – I had discovered nine different numbers.

I wrote them in sequence. I had a hunch. I went back to the entries between January and April. Sure enough, my miniature calligrapher had secreted a zero in a note on an informant I was cultivating.

I sat back and stared at the numerical sequence. It didn't take Einstein to work it out.

It was a telephone number. In Brisbane.

I got on the phone, and after three rings someone picked up at the other end.

'Well, well, well,' a male voice said. 'About time.'

6

I WAS DUE to meet my mystery diary calligrapher at Samuel Griffith's grave on the top of the hill that presided over Brisbane's Toowong Cemetery.

Just what I needed. An informant with a dramatic sense of occasion.

This guy had thus far entangled me in a murder investigation by breaking into my storage cage at Nerang, pillaged my private papers, indirectly given me a broken nose, left a microscopic phone number secreted within my old police diary and now wanted to rendezvous at the grave of a Queensland pillar of justice.

The last thing I needed, with a shattered proboscis, was a meeting with some dipstick who'd seen too many Humphrey Bogart movies.

Still, with Peg not speaking to me and the Dunkle murder gnawing away at my aching brain, I headed to Brisbane in my old Kombi. And yes, I still have her, despite my near-fatal run-in with the villains from the Marx Brothers Kombi Auto Shoppe a couple of years back, and a few minor mechanical niggles such as snapped accelerator cables, oil leaks, failed brakes and – oh yes – the motor blowing up and requiring a total recondition. But what's new in the world of the Kombinationskraftwagen?

Before my little assignation in the land of the dead, however, I needed to pay a visit to Queensland's state archives, south of the CBD.

I had been thinking about a woman, you see. A lot. I had been thinking about the young, blonde Susan Haag who had taken her own life in a small bedroom in the Ace Royale apartments on the Gold Coast in 1971. Why, nearly four decades later, had Junior died in a modern apartment in the air space above the old Ace Royale? Was there a connection?

I had been vaguely familiar with the Haag case as a young detective. I'd been close to the late Obe Dunkle, who'd also apparently suicided. And I'd last met Junior at his daddy's graveside. There were dots here, and I needed to join them.

It was time to call in some favours. This time, I tapped my son on the shoulder. In between his incessant tweeting he had actually found the time to establish a relationship with a lovely girl, who I'll simply call X.

X was an attractive, bookish young lady who had seen something in my boy and, I'll be honest, performed the impossible. She'd got him into reading books.

To see my son with a book is like going big-game hunting in East Africa and stumbling across a hippopotamus who's making martinis with a silver shaker at sunset. And that is an exercise in only slight improbability.

So X had earned my unswerving admiration. She had expressed to me an interest in criminal cases, and in particular the monolithic Fitzgerald Inquiry, which had been the best show in Brisbane town for two years in the late eighties.

There was one minor problem. Whenever we met, she looked at me with that ever-so-slight, yet unmistakable revulsion that a young girlfriend or boyfriend registers when looking at the parents of partners, and thinking, my God, is that what I'm getting into in forty years' time?

This is completely understandable, and I empathised with dear X. I often looked at myself in the same way.

Nevertheless, on this morning I arrived at the slightly shed-like state archives and met her for a coffee, and she slipped me copies of some vital documents concerning the life and death of the late Susan Haag. All had non-publication court orders on them, prohibiting their public perusal for between sixty-five and one hundred years.

I couldn't wait that long to get to the bottom of my suspicions about Senior and Junior.

I had about five hours before my appointment at Samuel Griffiths' grave, so I immediately drove to New Farm Park with my cache from X, parked, picked up a takeaway coffee from the snack wagon near the kids' swings, returned to the van, pulled back the Kombi's sliding door and in a cool breeze off the river settled into some serious reading.

'Talk to me, Susan,' I said, opening the X files, blowing the steam off my latte.

I immediately wondered if X, possible future daughter-in-law, had browsed any of the material. She probably had, little bookish minx. And she was probably surprised at what she read.

Susan Haag packed a lot into her twenty-one years. She'd had an unfortunate start to life. A bum of a father who'd scratched a living as a barman, trinket dealer and tannery workhorse before he discovered that getting his wife on the game and existing off the proceeds of her late-night work suited him to a tee. Susan's mother had in fact become very successful at a very old profession and by 1967, when she'd died of a drug overdose, had shown her teenage daughter an irresistible, perhaps unavoidable, career. She had also passed on to her daughter something invaluable – account books that noted every cent of protection money she had paid to police both in New South Wales and Queensland, where her empire flourished.

Susan took over her mother's business. She secreted the damning account books. But she kept on with her mother's profitable system of kickbacks to cops. Just as before with her mother, nobody bothered Ms Haag. The cash fell into the right hands. The money flowed, unimpeded.

Then a new licensing branch officer, desperate for promotion, decided to charge Ms Haag with various offences. He could not be swayed. He was threatened, intimidated, shot at, and still he waved the flag for proper policing.

The charges, subsequently, quietly slipped into and through the justice system, irrespective of the mayhem they caused outside on the streets.

And that's when Ms Haag made her fatal error. She would, in the name of her mother, spite the many dozens of officers, senior and junior, who had enjoyed the family's largesse over many years. She would speak to the newspapers and allude to the account books.

Sometimes events gather a life of their own, and this is precisely what happened to Ms Haag and her public allegations. She had lit a fuse in New South Wales. Cops were diving left, right and centre. It went all the way to the top, to the commissioner's desk, then jumped species and grew more heads in state parliament. A fuse was also lit in Queensland, a thousand kilometres north, but Ms Haag, in her youth, ignored the volatility of the northerners. They were laid-back cow cockies. They were small fry.

Which is why she accepted their invitation to fly north and disappear into the arms of their protection. They would look after her. Her mother was a Queenslander by birth, and they had an obligation to protect their own.

She went north, all right. They put her in a safe house. And six days later she was dead. Pills and booze. No suicide note.

And X, bless her cotton socks, had done my work for me.

Inside the file were papers relating to a string of other prostitute suicides dating back to 1955. All had died from pills and booze in south-east Queensland. All, presumably, had been paying off cops for protection; some in New South Wales as well.

In all the investigations, according to the police reports that X had dug up for me, two names kept appearing. One from Queensland. One from New South Wales. Throughout the dossier X had helpfully highlighted both names with a bright yellow marker.

Was I surprised to find that the New South Wales gentleman who had looked into the deaths of several of these women, including Ms Haag and her mother, over a period of more than twenty years, was none other than the officer I knew, in my gut, had killed my dear old friend Hubert Dunkle Senior on that grey day in the washroom of police headquarters? Was I shocked to discover, via these old documents, that a sinister thread which stretched across at least two generations of cops and crims had found its way to me here in the cabin of my Kombi nearly forty years later? And that it had drawn to the surface of my memory a myth I had first heard as a young detective − a myth of a book, a handwritten book on how to commit the perfect murder, that was so preposterous and so well known in the ranks that it may well have been true?

Well, yes. Enough for me to have left my coffee to go cold.

But I had a meeting to attend. At a gravestone.

7

So while we're being honest with each other, I'll come clean about something. I'm a taphophiliac.

A *wha*, I hear you say? I'm not a strict, letter-of-the-law taphophiliac. But there is a hint of taphophiliasm about me.

As the Greeks once said, *tapho* is grave, and *phileo* is to love. There. Now you know. I love cemeteries.

Pray, judge not. This, as far as I can tell, is not a morbid thing within me. I just like them. Full stop. They're ordered. Often well organised. Quiet. Peaceful. They have trees and wildlife and occasionally fresh flowers. And they make great reading. All those words, chiselled in stone. The endless yarns. The cryptic messages. The joy. The tragedy. Cemeteries are the great books of human existence.

While you as a kid were thumbing through *National Geographic* and mounting your stamps and playing with your new Mister Potato Head toy, I was skipping across the gravestones at the Rookwood Cemetery and Necropolis. Oh, a day at Rookwood for me was up there with the Easter Show.

So it was that I found Toowong a big thrill that afternoon. It was close to the city. Had good geography – hills and valleys. It was chock-a-block with history. And it had excellent mobile-phone coverage.

As I waited in the van on a dirt road not far from Samuel Griffith's last resting place, I got a call from my detective mate down on the Gold Coast.

'Firstly,' he said, 'if you could stay away from me for about the next fifty years I'd be really grateful.'

'You're not the first person to say that,' I told him.

'Secondly, there's all sorts of stuff going down here that I'm not sure I understand.'

'Such as?'

'I overheard a couple of hard heads in here saying you were a nuisance.'

'That so?'

'A big nuisance.'

'Did they actually use the word "nuisance"?'

'Not quite.'

'I didn't think so.'

'Anyway, they've thrown a wall around the Dunkle case. Closed shop. All superfluous bodies have been told to go away.'

'That'd be us.'

'That'd be me. And word has it the Dunkle matter has gone to the big boss in Brisbane.'

'That'd be the commissioner.'

'That'd be him.'

I'd heard all this before. I had a call coming through.

'Call you back,' I said.

'Please don't,' he said, and hung up.

I could smell pine needles outside the cabin of the Kombi. There was a gentle whoosh of breeze through the trees. I felt like a nap.

I took the other call.

'Fire away,' I said into the phone, 'but not literally.'

'Tapas here.'

'Ah, Mr Tapas. I hear your name and it makes me feel peckish. Why do you think that is?'

'Congratulations,' Tapas said. 'You are the five millionth person to make that joke.'

I'd heard this numerical gag before.

'Get on with it, Disco Boy.'

'The police want to bring more serious charges against you over the Dunkle diary business.'

'What are they proposing? Manslaughter? That Dunkle Junior read my diary and I bored him to death?'

'They've got a witness.'

'To what?'

'Says she saw you hanging around the high-rise three weeks before the murder. Says she was in Junior's apartment one night for dinner and Junior brought out an old photograph album and, bingo, there you were.'

Dolly Varden, the leathery stickybeak from down the hall.

'Did you just say "bingo"? Who says "bingo" in the twenty-first century, Tapas, except people actually playing bingo?'

'I'm telling you what I heard.'

'You're telling me diddly, and you're telling me squat,' I said. 'Get off the line, Tapas. The line's probably Tapas'ed.'

'Pardon?'

'Do you get it? The phone line. It's probably Tapas'ed.'

'Congratulations. You're the six millionth person to make *that* joke.'

'Anyway, all will be revealed in about ten minutes. I'm here in Brisbane to meet your special client. The one who employed you as my lawyer.'

He was silent for a moment. I could still smell his Old Spice down the line.

'You're mistaken,' Tapas said quietly.

'Afraid not, Johnny old boy. You're behind on this one, and you've been lagging all the way.'

'You're wrong, because I just saw our special client five minutes ago. Here on the Gold Coast.'

'You did?'

It was then I saw the car in my rear-vision mirror, creeping past the graves.

'Gotta go,' I said.

I stepped out of the Kombi, walked the short distance to Samuel's broken gravestone, and waited. I scoped the surrounding laneways. The trees. The headstones that might provide me with some cover.

I had no weapon.

The car stopped behind the Kombi, and the driver waited. He kept his motor running for a full minute, then cut it.

'If there's any justice in this world,' I whispered to Samuel out of the corner of my mouth, 'you won't let me die here. Be a good boy, Sammy.'

A tall young man stepped out of the car. He was wearing a suit and tie. He looked around, adjusted his belt, then his tie, and walked towards me.

Gravel crunched beneath his highly polished black shoes.

'Samuel Pepys, I presume,' I said to him.

He was clean-cut and did not seem to have the face of a murderer. Then again, killers came in all shapes and sizes these days.

'You've gotta come with me,' he said. He had a firm stare. But I had stared down the best of them. He looked strangely familiar. It was something about the eyes.

'Have we met before?'

'Let's go.'

'I don't gotta go nowhere,' I said. 'Waddya want from me?'

'Just come with me.'

'You draw me into a murder investigation by stealing my property, get my face flattened by a garden implement, hide a phone number in a thirty-eight-year-old diary, and now you want to abduct me. Would it be rude to ask what's going on?'

And at that precise moment I heard a short, sharp crack that my DNA told me instantly was a gunshot, and saw in the corner of my eye a bullet ricochet off Sir Samuel's ninety-year-old marble monument. I was pretty sure it was the first time in our history that a chief justice of the High Court of Australia had been shot at.

'Get down!' the suited stranger said.

He didn't need to tell me.

Together, we duck-waddled behind the shelter of plaques erected in the memory of pastoralists and public servants and little-old-lady church organists from yesteryear, as bullets whistled around us.

I heard a dull, metallic thud, and knew the Kombi had been hit. I had no idea how I was going to explain this to my long-suffering mechanic.

Then all of a sudden I was in the stranger's sedan and we were hurtling through Toowong cemetery towards Birdwood Terrace.

'Do you think,' I said, breathing heavily, 'that it might be a good time to call the police?'

'Waddya mean,' my driver said, feverishly checking the rear-vision mirror, the car screaming and squealing towards the city. 'I *am* the police.'

8

As OUR SILVER sedan sped towards the city, taking a circuitous route through the back streets, I remained quiet,
waiting for more shots from our cemetery attackers.
But nobody seemed to have followed us. My driver and
abductor stayed cool and collected.

'Put this on,' he said. He took a blindfold out of the
centre console.

'You always carry these around, do you?'

'Just put it on.'

'I'm an eyes-wide-open sort of guy.'

He quietly pulled a handgun from the pocket in the
driver's door, swivelled it and presented its solid butt.

'And I'm a shut-your-mouth and do-what-you're-told
sort of guy.'

I put the blindfold on.

Despite my darkened world, I could tell he was turning
right over the new Go Between Bridge.

'Hope you've registered online for the toll,' I said.
'Because if you haven't registered online ...'

An hour later, a day later – it could have been a year – I
woke up on a couch in a strange hotel room with a large
bump on my right temple. My driver was obviously not one

for meaningless conversation. So be it. Let him get a Go Between fine. I'd warned him.

At least someone – while I'd been in oblivion – had dressed the temple wound, and applied a fresh dressing to my mashed bugle. It was refreshing to know violent people who paid care and attention to medical niceties.

My headache was terrible, but I wasn't sure if it stemmed from the handgun butt or the fantastically bad art on the hotel room walls.

At the far end of the room I saw a tall man standing beside a sliding glass door, and beyond it the slow-moving Wheel of Brisbane on the river's edge at South Bank. The man had his arms crossed.

'The great wheel,' he said. I assumed he was talking to me as I was the only other person in the room. 'Sixty metres high. Forty-two climate-controlled capsules. Thirteen minutes for a full rotation.'

'Wheely?' I said. 'The wheel of life. The wheel thing.' Pain always brought out the humour in me.

He was dressed in grey slacks and a perfectly ironed white short-sleeved shirt. His hair was steel-grey.

'I needed to speak with you,' he said.

'And here I am. There are more civilised ways to arrange a meeting, you know. Like knocking on my front door, or picking up the phone. Fracturing my skull seems a bit, how would you say, heavy-handed.'

'I'm sorry about that.' He still watched the wheel with the fascination of a child.

It was then I noticed a little sprig of hair at the back of his head. That's when he turned towards me. After more than forty years, I recognised him instantly.

'Hubert Dunkle Junior,' I said.

He had large eyes, and the wrinkles that splayed from

their corners gave him a kindly demeanour. It could have been Obe standing before me.

'Nice to see you again,' he said. His arms were still crossed. He resembled a gentle English literature professor.

'Likewise, Junior,' I said. 'Been a long time since we buried your daddy.'

'Indeed.'

'So that wasn't your blood at that abattoir of a flat in Surfers.'

'It had once belonged to a Bangalow pig.'

'Tell me, Junior. Why set up a fake murder scene for yourself, steal one of my diaries, draw me in, get me roughed up, get me shot at, and abduct me after more than four decades? I'm just curious, is all.'

He walked over and sat in a chair opposite me. He rested his elbows on his knees.

'I'm sorry about your nose,' he said. 'I couldn't have seen that coming. As for the blow to your temple, I'll apologise for that too. My son can get a little overexcited.'

'Your *son*?'

'That's right. Detective. Sydney HQ.'

'A detective, just like his grandpa.'

'In the blood, I suppose. So to speak.'

I was back in a hall of mirrors.

'Junior, as we used to say in the trade, why don't we start at the beginning?'

He smiled. And we were back at Obe's grave together, two mourners, in the cemetery by the sea.

'My father was a good man,' he said quietly.

'Yes, he was.'

'His death was inexplicable to me. From the day I learned he had killed himself I made a vow that I would discover the truth about his death. My father would not, and did not, take his own life in a toilet cubicle in Sydney police headquarters in 1972.'

'I could have told you that over the phone forty years ago.'

'I began my own investigation,' Junior went on. 'I would be as scrupulous as my father. When I left school I decided I would join the police force as a way of working my inquiry from the inside. I would be a double agent. Pull files. Listen and observe. It was an adolescent notion. Besides, I didn't meet their requirements.'

'Eyesight?'

'Eyesight. I'm worse than my father ever was. But I stayed sharp, made some contacts, went to police reunions, befriended the children of serving officers. I was, to a degree, embedded enough to pick up the scent and run with it.'

'Why didn't you come to me? I had theories of my own.'

'My father trusted you,' Junior said. 'But that didn't mean I had to.'

'You're a chip off the old man's block.'

'I spent years checking you out. And the others. I established the identity of every single human being who was in that building the hour before and after my father's death. In that group was my father's killer. I drew up a wall-sized diagram. I had every name, every credential and function of each person in the building. Then I methodically worked that group from the outside in. Checked every background. Every link to my father. I collated more than a hundred thousand pages of files. Many thousands of photographs and documents. I worked my way towards that singular cubicle in which my father had lost his life. If I eliminated everybody by the time I metaphorically got downstairs and into that washroom between a quarter to seven and seven that evening, I'd have just a couple of suspects left, and one of them would have to be the killer. You, of course, were in that select group.'

'Because I found his body.'

'Correct. And as it turned out, it took me until four weeks ago on the Gold Coast – four decades after I'd started – to find my father's killer.'

'Your son, the detective. He helped you from the inside?'

'Just for the last few years. It's the only reason he joined the police. And he will resign when our job is done.'

'The single-minded Dunkles.'

'That's us.'

'I always figured it was Deputy Commissioner Meekin.'

'Sorry. You were wrong.'

'You say your job is done?'

'Almost.'

'Then why bring me in? Why the staged murder scene at the exact location of Susan Haag's death? Who was trying to kill us in Toowong cemetery?'

'I'm not sure you're ready for what I've found.'

'Junior, after all this, nothing will surprise me.'

'My father had a great affection for you. He was grooming you as his successor. But in his fastidiousness he came across something that cost him his life. In honour of his memory, and your friendship, I couldn't let the same thing happen to you. I brought you in to *save* your life.'

'What? That was forty years ago – a generation.'

'I'm afraid not,' he said. 'There is something you don't understand.'

'Now is as good a time as any, Junior.'

'I suppose it is.'

He left the room and returned with a large shopping bag. From it he retrieved a huge old ledger with a green frayed cover and marbled paper ends. He lowered it onto the coffee table in front of the couch, then quietly resumed his position in front of the sliding doors. He watched the great wheel turn and turn.

I looked at him for a long time. Then I opened the cover.

Written in archaic lettering, the floral flourishes clearly rendered with a black fountain pen, was the title.

The Good Murder Guide.

9

OF COURSE I'D heard of the book – *The Good Murder Guide* – even when I was a fresher in the police academy. It was mythical. It was what a few wags called The Dead Scrolls. Forget the sea.

It was, as rumour had it, an old text that originated in Sydney in the twenties in the bad old days of razor gangs and street slayings, when prostitution got organised and police graft equally so. The book, as legend had it, was started by a few hard-head detectives who wanted to keep track of those early corrupt monies, and who was connected to whom, and who was protecting which lady of the night, and who had guns, who didn't, who owed favours, who collected on bad debts. It was a fledgling blueprint of the Sydney underworld.

As the book grew, though, it organically developed a parallel, and infinitely more dangerous, narrative. While it maintained a primitive spreadsheet on the bad crooks, it also yielded a map of the bad cops.

The men who knew of, featured in or helped to create and maintain *The Good Murder Guide* were, I was to learn from Junior, a very tight group of police officers. The mere existence of the ledger was either a life-insurance policy or a potential death sentence for these men. The ledger, then, gave birth to the first real embedded cabal of corrupt officers in the New South Wales force.

And the myth grew. The word amongst the criminal elite was that the guide was a secret dossier on all their activities, their monetary transactions, the assaults and murders they'd committed and got off by chance or through bribing police.

When the cops raised their protection fees, the hikes could hardly be protested. Behind everything and everyone was the guide.

Junior explained all this to me in the hotel room with a view of the Wheel of Brisbane. It was obvious, I know, but in the hours it took for Junior to lay out forty years of his brilliant detective work on the death of his father, I'd glance at that wheel and couldn't help but think that it was, indeed, a metaphor for life, and Junior's investigations, and the many thousands of rotations that he had patiently endured as he moved closer and closer to his father's killer.

'So as the years went by,' I asked him, 'what happened to the guide?'

'It kept going. It has never stopped.'

'But what happened to that original group of policemen? The first authors of the guide? How many were there? Six, seven?'

'Five.'

'What happened when they left the force? Or died?'

Junior paused and looked away. Did he have tears in his big round eyes?

'Fathers have sons,' he said quietly.

At that moment, his own son emerged from a bedroom in boxer shorts and a singlet. He wore a holster and he checked the balcony.

'We change hotels at five this afternoon,' he reminded his father, then went back to the bedroom.

'Let me get this straight,' I said, rubbing my eyes. 'Those old coppers from the twenties kept this book going until they eventually retired, and in turn they had sons who joined the force and took over custodianship of the guide.'

'Correct.'

'A family affair.'

'Precisely.'

'The guide has never seen the light of day outside those families.'

'The sons of two of those original custodians, as you put it, decided to start a new life in Queensland in the early fifties. As expected, they joined the force up here. Thus began a new facet of the guide. They started a guide, then, just for Queensland. Two sets, in Brisbane and Sydney.'

'If I didn't know your father, I'd say you were making this up,' I said.

'Another son of one of the originals, upon retirement in Sydney in the late seventies, moved up here for the weather. He left behind a boy in the Sydney force who contributed to maintain the guide, and now has a grandson in the Queensland force. He too could be considered one of the generational co-authors.'

'Three generations of corruption.'

'And murder,' said Junior.

The guide sat fat and heavy in front of me. I had noticed on the spine a large IV.

'Volume four?' I asked Junior.

He nodded.

'Where are the others?'

'No idea.'

'Where did you get this?'

He didn't answer.

I played at the frayed edges of the heavy cover. I hadn't

opened it. I wasn't sure I wanted to. Even touching it gave me a bad feeling. The litany of instructions Obe had given me in the noodle house in Chinatown all those years ago came back to me. All the whispers I'd trained myself not to hear. The things I deliberately chose not to see. This book was a trove of everything I had avoided. I had never been party to *The Good Murder Guide*, and it was probably why I was still alive.

'Is Susan Haag in one of the volumes?'

Junior nodded.

'They killed her, back in seventy-one?'

He nodded again.

'She was threatening to go to the press,' said Junior. 'By accident she'd laid eyes on the guide in one of the coppers' flats. She was shifted up here for her own protection, so she thought. But the book, you see, had long tentacles. And suddenly she was dead of an overdose.'

'You faked your death there, at the same address on the Gold Coast, as a message. To the whole guide fraternity.'

'Call it a dark gesture of humour. A bloody warning. That after ninety years of fun and games, the jig was up.'

'Only your old man would use a word like "jig".'

'I am my father's son,' he said.

It took me a long time to ask my next question. I sat back and stared at the book. I had grown uncomfortable just being in the same room with it.

'Tell me,' I said. 'Am I in it?'

Junior looked at me straight in the eyes and after a moment's hesitation he nodded.

'A recent entry?'

'Yes,' he said eventually.

'Marked for death?'

Junior said nothing. He had answered the question.

'So you brought me in,' I said quietly, 'to protect me.'

'I needed to bring you in, firstly, to verify something about the day Dad died. I couldn't risk a call or a visit. I could have undone a lifetime of work. This was the grand finale I'd played over in my mind, one way or the other, since the day we buried my father. That's why I planted the phone number in your diary. I thought it'd be simple. You reclaim your old diary. The men investigating my murder see you as a nuisance and move you on. You'd find the phone number and we'd meet. But they were more suspicious and paranoid than I thought. It's infinitely worse, here in Queensland, than in New South Wales. The paranoia. Clearly someone did a little reading, back in volume three of the guide that covered 1969, and they discovered who you were, and how close you were to the epicentre of my father's murder.'

'What did you need to verify with me?'

'Your partner. In the downstairs bureau, with my father.'

'Greaves.'

'Greaves,' Junior said. Now his eyes were the coldest and darkest I'd seen them.

Greaves. The blockheaded journeyman I sat next to in that dreary office. A barely competent detective. Drinker. Smoker. Philanderer. I couldn't wait to see the back of him and the stink of his Craven As. Greaves. He was gone a month or so after Obe's death. Disappeared into the great police maw. I only saw him one more time. At the farewell function for Deputy Commissioner Meekin, who I was convinced had killed Obe.

'You asked him to secure the washroom straight after my father was shot,' Junior said firmly.

'Yes.'

'You heard the shot, and you ran straight for the toilet

doors which were precisely 7.7 metres from your desk in the office just across the hall.'

'Yes.'

'*Where did you run into Greaves before you found my father's body?*'

The room spun around. My head felt like exploding. I grabbed it with both hands.

And when the tear-gas cartridge smashed through the sliding glass doors of the room and disgorged its pitiful load, and the room door exploded in shards of cheap timber, it couldn't have better reflected my inner turmoil.

10

THEY WERE ONLY after one thing, of course, and they took it.

After a SWAT team the size of the Bolivian army raided our hotel room, and I slipped off the couch in shock and – would you believe it? – smashed my *other* temple against the corner of the coffee table, and when the tear gas had disappeared, *The Good Murder Guide*, volume four, had predictably vanished.

They played tough guys with me and Junior and his son, zip-locked our wrists, made a show of checking through every cupboard and drawer of the hotel room, then apologised. There had been a terrible mistake, they said. They'd had a tip-off about some drug dealers. Sorry for the inconvenience. Then they were gone. And so was the book.

Junior's son bandaged my freshly damaged temple. Now I had taped bandages on both temples, and the flattened bugle. I looked like an old koala.

'We'd better go now,' Junior's son said.

'I'd like a lie down,' I said. I was tired of all this cops-and-robbers stuff. And I was dreading explaining to Peg my new cranial decorations.

'Their first objective was to secure the guide,' he said. 'Who knows what they have planned for phase two.'

'There's a phase two?' I said. There were tears in my voice.

'Best to be prepared and assume that there is.'

'I agree,' Junior said.

The goddam Dunkles and their unceasing meticulous nature.

'I need a Scotch,' I said.

Within the hour we were in another hotel room, over by the old Botanic Gardens. I would have gone home, but there was one part of the story I needed to know. This whole adventure had been like a forty-year-long movie. How could I walk out before the ending?

'Here,' Junior said, handing me a Johnny Walker on ice.

'Bless you, my son,' I said.

'You want to know about Greaves.'

'You read my mind.'

He, too, poured himself a drink. It looked odd in his hand. He was not a drinker, and people who didn't drink held their booze in a different way to those of us who did. Delicately. Cautiously. Like a sweaty stick of gelignite that just might detonate. He took a small sip.

'Six months before my father was killed, he was having a drink at the London Hotel in Balmain with a small-time petty thief,' Junior said. 'Like any decent detective he maintained his contacts on the ground, as you know.'

'Who was it?'

'Willie Hamm.'

'The Hammer. I remember him.'

'Anyway, Hamm had a few too many schooners and the next thing you know he's gabbling on about a burglary he'd done a few weeks before in nearby Rozelle. Said he'd lifted a bunch of stuff, including an old book full of dates and names and mugshots and money columns.'

'The guide?'

'He'd unwittingly broken into the home of Inspector Norman Greaves, father of young detective Don Greaves, your desk buddy at headquarters.'

'A troubling example of poor judgement. Sounds like Hamm.'

'Word got out that Big Daddy Greaves' place had been hit, and it finally reached Hamm, and he quietly and anonymously returned the goods. A week after his booze-up in the London Hotel with my father, Hammer was dead.'

'That was six months before Obe's murder, you say?' I reached back into my memory, beyond my two swollen temples. 'That's about when Don Greaves came to work for us.'

It was getting dark outside. I could see, beyond the window, a little clutch of yachts moored alongside the long, dark avenue of Hoop pines in the gardens. Bats stitched across the sky.

'That's when my father started investigating the existence of the guide. The Greaveses, of course, were one of the five families that had controlled it since the twenties.'

'I didn't have a clue what was going on, did I?'

'You were young,' Junior said. 'And my father was only just starting to fit the pieces of the puzzle together when he was shot dead that day.'

'Greaves,' I said, shaking my head.

'You have to remember, the guide, by the late sixties, was now quite substantive, and the men it implicated in crime and corruption were now in the highest ranks of the force.'

'But why did they keep on with it?' I said. 'Why didn't they just abandon it, destroy it, get on with life without it?'

Junior took another sip of Scotch, and revealed a modest smile.

'Simple,' he said. 'Good, old-fashioned power. The mere existence of the book, and its long and deep pedigree, gave those five families incredible caché. More importantly, it generated fear. And that fear grew with each generation. To this day, its exposure could bring down police forces in two states.'

'So you found Greaves.'

'He was the last man standing in the wake of four decades of research,' Junior said. 'It was Greaves. He killed my father to protect his own father, to maintain the security of the guide. You had never considered your desk buddy as a suspect because to you he was a nothing – an incompetent, a man who, to you, barely existed.'

I lowered my head. I knew he was right.

'I found him in a private room in a nursing home at the back of Coolangatta,' Junior went on. 'He had become what you already knew as a young man – a man who barely existed.'

'He's not that old, is he?' I asked.

'Emphysema,' he said.

'The Craven As,' I said, nodding at the floor.

'He was sitting in a chair by the bed,' Junior went on. 'He was rigged up to breathing apparatus. There was a book on the floor beside him.'

'Volume four of the guide.'

'Greaves' own son had brought it in the day before. We took surveillance pictures. Why? Maybe to let a dying old man reminisce, to lose himself in better days. I sat opposite him in that room and waited for him to wake up. I studied that face and foul open mouth for maybe twenty minutes. This useless waste of space had taken my daddy from me. I could have killed him with my bare hands.'

Junior looked away. Again he was on the brink of tears.

'But you didn't,' I said.

'He opened his eyes and looked at me, puzzled. The tough man; the killer. Here he was, reliant on a machine for air, not strong enough to lift a handkerchief to his nose or wipe his own backside. Time levels all.'

'What did you do?'

'I stood up and went over to him and put my face a few inches from his and said the words I had waited to say all my life — "You are under arrest for the murder of Hubert Dunkle Senior."'

Junior had a cold, hard look on his face that I had not seen before. It was intimidating. Frightening. He had lead in his pencil, like his old man.

'He started breathing erratically,' Junior said. 'I took the guide and left. He was dead that night. Stroke.'

'The end.'

'Not quite,' said Junior. He drained the Scotch, and shivered at its impact.

The next morning I was back on the Gold Coast in my banana lounge overlooking the canal. Peg had last seen me on the banana lounge, and I hoped she'd assume I'd been there all along. But how to account for the three fluffy bandages encasing my pitiful mug?

She came through the sliding door and dropped the local newspaper on my large belly, then went back inside.

The front page, and six pages inside, were dedicated to the exposure of a nearly century-old corruption scandal involving hundreds of policemen, some as senior as deputy commissioner.

There was a picture of my old mentor Obe, and my one-time drop-kick partner Greaves, and poor young Susan Haag, and face after face of blockheaded police officers stemming back to the twenties.

ACKNOWLEDGEMENTS

IN MID-2006 IT was my greatest good fortune to field what I thought initially was a rhetorical question from David Fagan, the Queensland Editorial Director of News Queensland.

Why, he asked, don't newspapers publish fictional serials anymore, à la Dickens?

At that moment, and against all odds, *The Toe Tag Quintet* was born, and while not claiming there is a scintilla of Dickensian qualities in the novellas, writing an annual summer crime caper for *The Courier-Mail* in Brisbane has been one of the more enjoyable adventures in my journalistic career.

So, thank you, David, for launching an odyssey that I don't think any other Australian newspaper, or editor, would have had the courage to take on, let alone sustain over the years.

I would also like to pay tribute to the editor of *The Courier-Mail*, Michael Crutcher, for his unstinting support of the arts and his willingness to always take a punt on something a little outside the proverbial square.

Thank you to my many talented friends and colleagues in journalism for your support and kindness, including: Des

There were politicians calling for a royal commission. There were photographs of records being seized. And a spoof cartoon of *The Good Murder Guide*, with star ratings for crimes and misdemeanours.

Junior had, as always, done his job with enviable thoroughness.

Peg brought me out a coffee.

'You look like a koala,' she said.

I grabbed her wrist, and smiled, and wanted to never let her go.

THE END

Houghton, Hedley Thomas, Grant Jones, Brett Thomas, Alex Mitchell, Judith White, Susan Johnson, Mike Colman, Leisa Scott, Amanda Watt, Matthew Fynes-Clinton, Trent Dalton, Frances Whiting, Alison Walsh, Phil Stafford, Genevieve Faulkner, David Kelly, Bruce McMahon, John Shakespeare, Robert Shakespeare, Russell Shakespeare, Anne-Maree Lyons, Michael McKenna, Christine Middap, Graham Clark, Julianne Schultz, Frank Moorhouse and Paul Weston. An additional salute to Krissy Kneen, Dr Benjamin Law, Dr Stuart Glover, Claire Booth, Alex Adsett, Elizabeth Reynolds and Fiona Stager of Avid Reader bookshop, West End, Brisbane.

For their patience and sense of fun, I owe a great deal to my publishers, Random House Australia, in particular the wonderfully even-keeled Meredith Curnow and my invaluable editor, Catherine Hill.

Of course, all roads ultimately lead back to my precious family: my wonderful wife, Katie Kate; my beautiful son and fellow writer, Finnigan; and my gorgeous and indefatigable daughter, Bridie Rose.